MW01110006

WOLF WARRIORS III

WINTER WOLVES

THE NATIONAL WOLFWATCHER COALITION ANTHOLOGY

EDITED BY

JONATHAN W. THURSTON

A THURSTON HOWL PUBLICATIONS BOOK

No part of this work may be reproduced or transmitted in any form or by any means, electronic or mechanical, including photocopying and recording, or by any information storage or retrieval system without the proper written permission of the copyright owner unless such copying is expressly permitted by federal copyright law. Thurston Howl Publications is not authorized to grant permission for further uses of copyrighted selections in this book without the permission of their owners. Permission must be obtained by the individual copyright owners as identified herein. Address requests for permission to make copies of material here to the email address jonathan.thurstonhowlpub@gmail.com.

ISBN 978-1-945247-06-4

WOLF WARRIORS III: WINTER WOLVES

Copyright © 2016 by Jonathan W. Thurston

First Edition, 2016. All rights reserved.

A Thurston Howl Publications Book
Published by Thurston Howl Publications
thurstonhowlpublications.com
Knoxville, TN

jonathan.thurstonhowlpub@gmail.com

Cover image by Khaosdog

Edited by Jonathan W. Thurston.

Printed in the United States of America
10 9 8 7 6 5 4 3 2 1

ACKNOWLEDGMENTS

"Spirit of Winter" by T. Thomas Abernathy. Copyright © 2016 by T. Thomas Abernathy.

"A Christmas Story" by Chris Albert. Copyright © 2016 by Chris Albert. (Look! No hands!)

"Yuletide Carols" by Shannon Barnsley. Copyright © 2016 by Shannon Barnsley.

"Secrets of Northern Spirits" by Autumn Beverly. Copyright © 2016 by Autumn Beverly.

"Hephaestus is a Brand of Fire" by Hannah Christopher. Copyright © 2016 by Hannah Christopher.

"Beauty" and "Snowfall" by Alex Clarke. Copyright © 2016 by Alex Clarke.

"Contemplations" by Cottaterra. Copyright © 2016 by Cottaterra.

"Always the Wind" by Maxwell Coviello. Copyright © 2016 by Maxwell Coviello.

"Life River" by Dylan DiPrima. Copyright © 2016 by Dylan DiPrima.

"Matriarchal Complications" by Varzen Dralmort. Copyright © 2016 by Varzen Dralmort.

"White Lullaby" by Alice Dryden. Copyright © 2016 by Alice Dryden.

"Night Keeper" by Chelsea Dub. Copyright © 2016 by Chelsea Dub.

"The Last Dire Wolf" by Kerry Duncan. Copyright © 2016 by Kerry Duncan.

"Fairytale Wonderland" by Samantha Dutton. Copyright © 2016 by Samantha Dutton.

"Winter White" by A. M. Duvall. Copyright © 2016 by A. M. Duvall.

"The Piercing Eyes" by Gulten Dye. Copyright © 2016 by Gulten Dye.

"A Hero Liberated," "Winter's Peace," and "Winter's Storm" by Christian Esche. Copyright © 2016 by Christian Esche.

"Cages," "Heraldry Dance," "Paradise," "Renegade," "The Voice," and "Winter Song" by Amy Fontaine. Copyright © 2016 by Amy Fontaine.

"Howling Good Christmas" by Lou Gagliardi. Copyright © 2016 by Lou Gagliardi.

"The Summer Stag and the Winter Wolves" by Renee Carter Hall. Copyright © 2016 by Renee Carter Hall.

"the eyes of winter" by Juley Harvey. Copyright © 2016 by Juley Harvey.

"The Winter Wolves of Spring" by Jessica Haynes. Copyright © 2016 by J. Noelle.

"The Wolf and the Figs" by Graham Houghton. Copyright © 2016 by Graham Houghton.

"Charming Gaze" and "Holiday Howl" by Wolfy Howell. Copyright © 2016 by Wolfy Howell.

"The Winter Wolf" and accompanying art piece by Kristen Hubschmid. Copyright © 2016 by Kristen Hubschmid.

"Winter Count" by William Huggins. Copyright © 2016 by William Huggins.

"Brothers in Flux" by Bill Kieffer. Copyright © 2016 by Bill Kieffer.

"First Taste of Winter" by Patricia Lehtola. Copyright © 2016 by Patricia Lehtola.

"American Dream" by Jane Lee McCracken. Copyright © 2016 by Jane McCracken.

"The Wolf's Song" by Justin Monroe. Copyright © 2016 by Justin Monroe.

"My Pack" by Matt Newman. Copyright © 2016 by Matt Newman.

"Ragnårök: Gray-Furred Sons of Midgård, White'Winged Sisters, and Wolf'Kin Come a'Viking" by BanWynn Oakshadow. Copyright © 2016 by BanWynn Oakshadow.

"Snow Stories" by Frances Pauli. Copyright © 2016 by Frances Pauli.

"Am I the Bad Guy?" by David Popovich. Copyright © 2016 by David Popovich.

"A Christmas Story for Pups" by Hemal Rana. Copyright © 2016 by Hemal Rana.

"Out of the Circle" by Adam Robertson. Copyright © 2016 by Adam Robertson.

"El sueño del bosque" and "Forest Dream" by Laura Cristina Sánchez Sáenz. Copyright © 2016 by Laura Cristina Sánchez Sáenz.

"The Night Pack" by Ryft Sarri. Copyright © 2016 by Ryft Sarri.

"Snow Time" by Dawn Sharman. Copyright © 2016 by Dawn Sharman.

"Atka's Villanelle," "Guardian Spirit," and "Zephyr" by Dana Sonnenschein. Copyright © 2016 by Dana Sonnenschein.

"Shift to Spring" by Televassi. Copyright © 2016 by Televassi.

"Solongo" by Allison Thai. Copyright © 2016 by Allison Thai.

"Wintry Dreams" by Angel L. Thurston. Copyright © 2016 by Angel L. Thurston.

"Echoes" by Sean Weaver. Copyright © 2016 by Sean Weaver.

"Final Breath" by T. F. Webb. Copyright © 2016 by T. F. Webb.

"Winter's Dance" by Forest Wells. Copyright © 2016 by Forest Wells.

"First Contact: From the Files of Department 118" by Layson Williams. Copyright © 2016 by Layson Williams.

To my grandmother, who finally gets her holiday book.

To the family of friends who have supported me this year:
Dustin, Kelsey, Ken, Hype, Taka, Sherayah, Temerita, and Tabs.

Finally, to the people spending their holidays alone this year: stay strong.
Find warmth in these stories to protect you from the cold out there.

CONTENTS

Introduction   1

T. Thomas Abernathy
Spirit of Winter   3

Chris Albert
A Christmas Story   4

Shannon Barnsley
Yuletide Carols   9

Autumn Beverly
Secrets of Northern Spirits   23

Hannah Christopher
Hephaestus is a Brand of Fire   24

Alex Clarke
Beauty   29
Snowfall   30

Cottaterra
Contemplations   31

Maxwell Coviello
Always the Wind   32

Dylan DiPrima
Life River   56

Varzen Dralmort
Matriarchal Complications   57

Alice Dryden
White Lullaby   74

Chelsea Dub
Night Keeper   75

Kerry Duncan
The Last Dire Wolf   77

Samantha Dutton
Fairytale Wonderland   79

A. M. Duvall
Winter White   80

Gulten Dye
The Piercing Eyes   81

Christian Esche
A Hero Liberated   83
Winter's Peace   85
Winter's Storm   86

Amy Fontaine
Cages   87
Heraldry Dance   90
Paradise   91
Renegade   94
The Voice   96
Winter Song   100

Lou Gagliardi
Howling Good Christmas   101

Renee Carter Hall
The Summer Stag and the Winter Wolves   103

Juley Harvey
the eyes of winter   105

Graham Houghton
The Wolf and the Figs   109

Wolfy Howell
Charming Gaze   112
Holiday Howl   113

Kristen Hubschmid
The Winter Wolf   114

William Huggins
Winter Count   130

Bill Kieffer
Brothers in Flux   140

Patricia Lehtola
First Taste of Winter   145

Jane Lee McCracken
American Dream   146

Justin Monroe
The Wolf's Song   148

Matt Newman
My Pack   149

J. Noelle
The Winter Wolves of Spring   158

BanWynn Oakshadow
Ragnårök: Gray-Furred Sons of Midgård, White'Winged Sisters,
and Wolf-Kin Come a'Viking   177

Frances Pauli
Snow Stories   184

David Popovich
Am I the Bad Guy?   185

Hemal Rana
A Christmas Story for Pups   187

Adam Robertson
Out of the Circle   189

Laura Cristina Sánchez Sáenz
El sueño del bosque   208
Forest Dream   210

Ryft Sarri
The Night Pack   211

Dawn Sharman
Snow Time   228

Dana Sonnenschein
Atka's Villanelle   229
Guardian Spirit   230
Zephyr   231

Televassi
Shift to Spring   232

Allison Thai
Solongo   233

Angel L. Thurston
Wintry Dreams   243

Sean Weaver
Echoes   244

T. F. Webb
Final Breath   245

Forest Wells
Winter's Dance   246

Layson Williams
First Contact: From the Files of Department 118   248

List of Wolf Veterans   272

INTRODUCTION

Wolves walk a fine line, between angels and demons, between dreams and reality, somewhere between the world of light and the world of shadows. There are those who would kill them for their strength and those who would tame them for their beauty. Even scientists today dispute how dangerous wolves truly are. One of the only things we can accurately say about all wolves is that they have been a part of our history, literature, and culture since recorded time. Inherent in this dualism, this walking alongside humans even as they dodge our spears, bullets, and traps, wolves are fighters: they are warriors that stand dignified against a raging war of corrupt politics and hatred rooted solely in myths.

For authors like Jack London and Ernest Thompson Seton, the wolves' midnight howls were enough voices to prompt them to action, to preserve the forest warriors. However, in today's society, the wolf's voice has become mute. Gunshots ring across the fields, and their echoes linger, howls unheard. Through this silence, people have arisen to help give wolves their voices back. Some of these people have contributed to this very anthology, but make note that even these contributors mark only a small percentage of the warriors that speak for wolves. Warriors that are wolves and warriors that speak for wolves work together, creating one enormous pack, the titular Wolf Warriors.

In 2014, I discussed with the National Wolfwatcher Coalition's Southeast Regional Director Janet Hoben the possibility of creating a charity anthology for the NWC, allowing people to submit art, poetry, essays, and short stories. I had not expected it would actually receive over two hundred submissions and eventually become an Amazon best-selling anthology for over a month. For that collection, we were honored to receive contributions from the best-selling and award-winning authors David Clement-Davies and Catherynne Valente.

Then, last year, we published *Wolf Warriors II* to showcase even more wonderful wolf advocates, with a larger range of poetry and a formal howl to those who have been with us as contributors over the years.

This year, we decided to try something different: we gave the series a theme, Winter Wolves. This volume contains creative works set in the depths of winter, the morning of Christmas, the night of Yule celebrations, and near the comforts of warm fires. To make this volume even more special, however, we have released both the standard volume plus a deluxe edition, featuring different cover art, colored illustration, and some extra art from the previous volumes at the back of the book.

I already left a dedication at the beginning of the book, but I want to thank a few for the production of this book. Thank you eternally to the lovely lupine lady Candice Copeland, my secretary and liaison with the NWC, for all of the hard work and dedication she put into the scores of advertisements and communications I asked her to endure. A salute to the National Wolfwatcher Coalition for continuing to educate. A salute to the many contributors of this anthology. And, of course, a final salute to you the reader.

As you begin this book, I ask that you have happy holidays, wherever you are. Whether it is with a full and perhaps rambunctious family or by yourself dreaming of a white Christmas, find warmth in these stories. Hear these tales, and, maybe, over the din of the wind howling outside your window, you might hear the sounds of jingle bells and wolves howling.

Jonathan W. Thurston
Editor

T. THOMAS ABERNATHY
SPIRIT OF WINTER

Spirit of Winter. Digital art.

CHRIS ALBERT
A CHRISTMAS STORY

Chris Albert is a veterinarian, farmer, wife, grandmother, mother, and wolf and wildlife advocate. She believes that stories are the most potent way to help others appreciate wolves and be their advocates.

10-year-old Manuel and 19-year-old George had been in many places, many ugly places, since their family left Central America as refugees. Manuel was thriving, doing well in school, and had many friends. George was not doing as well. He was quick to anger, and had barely scraped by in school. He did not keep any job he tried, and seemed destined to be an angry young man. Everyone was worried about George.

Papi had been a sheep farmer in Central America and loved farming. After many trials, the family had settled and had begun to make a living once again farming sheep in North Carolina.

The farm was beautiful, with red dirt and a cheerful creek, grassy hills, old trees, and wildlife all around. The sheep were thriving, but farming was always fraught with challenges. The challenge that the neighbors were grumbling about most lately was the wolves.

Red wolves had lived in this part of the country long ago, and the government was trying to bring them back. There were maybe 80, released in the Alligator National Wildlife Refuge just miles from farms. Wolves don't understand boundaries, and some had started to expand into the farm country.

"The only good wolf is a dead wolf" threatened some farmers. Manuel and George didn't like those words. They had heard those words said about them.

Manuel and George thought the red wolves were beautiful. They had seen videos of captive red wolves and learned about their families. The wolves formed strong bonds. Mother and father raised their children, and the family stayed together until a grown youngster was ready to head out on its own. They felt a kinship with these wolves. They didn't want them harmed.

George was quiet—you never really knew what he was thinking. Manuel worried. The loss of a sheep could be a blow to the newly thriving family. He wanted the wolves to do well, but he wanted his family to do well, too.

One day in early December, red wolves killed six sheep on a neighbor's farm. The local farmers were frightened and angry. They were going to get permission to shoot the pack. Manuel was upset, but what could one little boy do? They didn't know it yet, but Manuel would have a wonderful idea, and George would see it through.

December was family time in Manuel's home, filled with many traditions. One of the favorites was the night the family gathered in the living room and read the Christmas story. They passed around a beautiful family book that had survived all their travels.

It was Manuel's turn. He read, "And there were in the same country shepherds abiding in the field, keeping watch over their flock by night…"

Suddenly, he was so startled, he faltered. The answer was *right there*, in the Bible. Manuel's father often told him that there would be answers in the Bible, but he had never found a solution to a modern problem in the ancient text.

Manuel knew enough not to interrupt the rhythm of the reading. He coughed and continued… "And lo, the angel of the Lord came upon them, and the glory of the lord shone round about them: and they were sore afraid. And the angel said unto them, Fear not: for behold, I bring you good tidings of great joy which shall be to all people."

After everyone had had a turn reading, and the story was over, Manuel's father looked at him.

"In the middle of the Christmas story, you looked very excited, son, but you continued reading. I am proud of you. But I am also eager to hear what is on your mind."

"Papi, you've told me before that the Bible holds many answers, even though it is very old. I've never really found an answer, but tonight I did."

"Go on," his father smiled.

"Papi, in the Christmas story, it says the shepherds were *watching* their sheep at night. We never *watch* our sheep at night. If we could watch them they would be safe, and we wouldn't have to kill the red wolves."

Manuel hung his head. It suddenly seemed like a dumb idea. Who, after all, would watch them? He had to go to school, and Mama and Papi were far too busy during the day to stay up all night.

Just then, George spoke up.

"I will watch the sheep at night," he said quietly, before anyone could tell Manuel that the idea was impractical.

The family was stunned silent. George had never seemed interested before. He had never volunteered for anything before.

Papi looked thoughtful. "I think the Christmas story in our beloved Bible has shown us a way, and we should follow the path that we have been shown, just like following a Christmas star!"

That very night, George bunched the sheep and kept watch over them. The red wolves were close and howled, but they did not approach. The sheep were safe. The wolves stayed safe; the whole family was glad.

Two days later, Papi bought George a horse. It was an old plodding gelding, his useful days long gone. But George immediately took to him, brushing him, whispering in his ear. The horse had been neglected for a while, and he also seemed to cheer up at having a friend and a job.

Papi smiled at Manuel when they were doing farm chores. "What a wonderful idea you had, to watch the sheep. It is already a Christmas miracle. George has not been able to open his heart and love anybody or anything. Now, he loves the horse."

With a horse, George could ride the perimeter of the neighbors' fields also, and still keep an eye on his family's sheep. The grateful neighbors paid George a small fee.

Once again, the family was thrilled and grateful. Here was a job George could do. He loved the farms at night, his spirit was soothed by the horse, and the sheep and even the wolves that sang.

Four nights later, a wolf took a sheep from a neighbor several miles away. The farmers once again took up the cry to shoot the wolf pack. The family looked grim. George's work could protect the nearby farms, but not the ones miles from them. The wolves would be killed, and the family didn't want that.

For the first time ever, George dug in. "Can you show me how to work the computer?" he asked Manuel. Then, he spent hours looking up solutions.

"Papi, there are dogs," he announced the next morning. "Big, fierce dogs who live with the sheep and protect them. People use them where they have to live with wolves."

"But dogs left unattended frequently kill sheep," Papi responded.

"Not these kinds of dogs," George insisted, "let me show you." And George, George who had refused to have anything to do with computers before, walked over and sat down like he had been doing this all along. He showed Papi the Anatolian Shepherds that walked the perimeter of the fences, he showed him the Great Pyrenees that stayed right with the sheep, and many more breeds.

Meanwhile, time was nearly up for the wolves. Farmers were angry. Fish and Wildlife was on the verge of granting a permit to wipe out the pack.

Papi prayed. "Somehow, these wolves have saved my older son," he said. "They have given him a purpose, and his first friend the horse, and the will to learn. I am grateful that our farm is doing well, but please...help us help the wolves."

Christmas miracles were not over yet! Manuel, who was quicker navigating the computer, retraced the links George had found. Buried in information about dogs, he found a group of people who *supplied* these dogs to farmers, so they wouldn't need to kill wolves.

Manuel excitedly gathered George and Papi. George made the call, and there was a grateful woman on the other end of the phone:

"We've been looking for a contact in your area!" she sounded so excited, "But everyone wanted to just kill the wolves. The kill order is likely to be given soon. But *we have dogs*, dogs enough for 10 farms, for a start, can you help us get them to the right people?"

Sunday before Christmas, in church, Papi asked to speak.

"We have had a Christmas miracle in our home," he began. "I think it can be your miracle, too, but I'll need your help to fulfill it."

Everyone was listening, rapt with attention.

He began with the part of the Christmas story that had given Manuel the first idea. "...and there were in the same country shepherds abiding in the field, keeping watch over their flock by night..."

People looked confused—they all knew this story—it wasn't a miracle, so Papi continued. "My son, Manuel, pointed out that the answer was in the Bible all along...we have forgotten to *watch* the flocks"

People looked interested.

"As some of you know," he went on, "my son George has offered to watch our flocks. We got him a horse so he could do this better, and he can now watch the neighbors' flocks also. We have had no losses to the red wolves since he started."

"Now, I know that's just fine for us and the immediate neighbors, but what about those of you that live further away? I don't think anyone else has a family member that can stay up all night and watch sheep."

"It turns out, there are others who can help us watch: they are dogs. Special kinds of dogs called livestock guardian dogs. And there are people who are ready and willing to give ten families dogs. "

Then, Papi turned serious. "Many of you know it has been hard for George, and his mother and I were very, very worried about him. This…project…has been a miracle for us. Our oldest son has found a purpose and a calling."

"I have always thought God had a sense of humor. We prayed for our son, and he sent us….wolves." Papi smiled. "But then God showed us the way, through the Christmas story, my sons found that the Bible has lessons that apply today."

"I would ask you not to kill the wolves," he said quietly. "Let us try these dogs. Let us *watch* our flocks at night, just like the Christmas story says, with the help of my son and these dogs."

And so the dogs arrived, just in time for Christmas. With a few wrinkles, they settled in, and miraculously there were *no* more livestock kills.

Christmas day, Papi woke up, grateful for everything that had happened.

"Thank you, God," he prayed silently, "for sending us wolves."

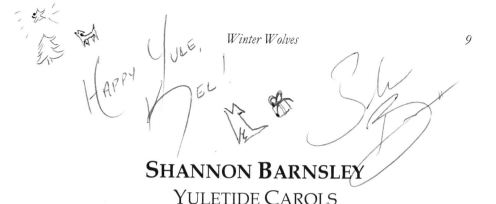

SHANNON BARNSLEY
YULETIDE CAROLS

Shannon Barnsley is a writer, poet, and folklore devotee from New Hampshire, currently living in Brooklyn. She holds a degree in Creative Writing / Mythology & Religion from Hampshire College. Her first book, Beneath Blair Mountain, *was published by 1888 in Fall 2015. Much of Shannon's fiction is inspired by her childhood in rural New England, whether it was picking wild blueberries behind her house, roasting marshmallows in the damp woods with other UU kids, or camping under the stars with the other girls in her Goddess Guides group. "Yuletide Carols" is both a love letter and a thank you note to the unique Unitarian Universalist and pagan communities of Northern New England that helped shape her, her love of nature, and her writing.*

It was Midwinter, or nearly so. Just a few more hours now. Already, the teachers at Deerfield Elementary had given up. Miss Weaver had instructed the children to cut paper snowflakes (which in reality meant two students cut paper snowflakes while the rest ran wild as the trolls in McKenna's favorite Jan Brett book).

In years past, the teachers had instructed the children to perfect their letters to Santa or make popsicle stick reindeer. There were still about a hundred tiny red puff balls in the art supply cabinet to prove it. However, those traditions had fallen by the wayside when two Jewish families and a Hindu one had moved to the district and enrolled their children in the small town school.

McKenna had had to laugh at the school's sudden realization that other religions existed. There had been non-Christian children at Deerfield Elementary for years; they'd just never bothered to notice, assuming a girl with a name like McKenna Randolph and a playground taunt of "Freckles" had to be some flavor of Protestant or other.

After being chided for balancing each hand on a desk and swinging her legs back and forth between the rows, McKenna's friend, Emma, was press-ganged into passing back the pictures the class had drawn earlier that week. Her strawberry blonde braids bounced as she skipped down the row between desks. Four desks down, she passed back McKenna's drawing.

"Cool reindeer," Emma said. "You did the legs really good."

"Thanks." McKenna beamed with pride. She'd been perfecting horse legs all year, copying them off the covers of her older sister's fantasy novels.

"You're missing Rudolph," Emma noted.

"Oh. No. These reindeer are older than Rudolph."

"Cool," Emma said, moving on to pass back Jayden H.'s drawing of Iron Man fighting one of the giant robot things from Pacific Rim.

Miss Weaver instructed Jaiden F. and Callie for the third time that the paper cutter was off limits and to stop pretending to decapitate each other while shouting, "Winter vacation is coming!" After that, Miss Weaver conceded and allowed the "wildlings" of her fourth grade class to go get their coats and bags.

McKenna tucked her reindeer drawing into her backpack, trying not to tear or bend it.

"Is Chanukah over?" she asked her friend, Avery.

"No, there's two more nights." Avery fiddled with her mittens at the desk next to McKenna's. "I already got what I wanted, though. It's a giant, purple stuffed narwhal. His name is Professor Purplepuff."

"I'm so jealous," Emma lamented, scurrying over to the two. "I have to wait four whole more days. I have an app that can track Santa, though. It's pretty cool."

"Santa isn't real!" Callie shouted from across the room.

"Neither are your boobs, Callie!" Jayden H. called back as he stuffed his Captain America lunchbox into his bag.

Miss Weaver's look of abject horror melted into relief as the school bell rang and Jayden H. bolted from the room before she could give him detention.

"Happy Holidays, class," Miss Weaver managed before collapsing into her wheely desk chair. "See you next year."

A great raucous chatter rose in the green- and white-tiled halls of Deerfield Elementary as the children tasted sweet, sweet freedom and the promise of Santa's imminent arrival (and that of the boob fairy, if Callie's Christmas wish came true). The merry cacophony followed them out the door and all the way down to the buses. McKenna bid Emma a Merry Christmas and Avery a Happy Chanukah as the two eagerly boarded the bus with promises of a sledding day sometime soon.

"Merry Christmas, Freckles!" Jayden H. called from the open window on the bus.

"Merry Christmas, Shorty," McKenna called back.

McKenna pulled her parka hood up and watched the yellow bus pull away. She'd always been a walker. Her cousin's school in the city wouldn't even let kids walk home anymore, not without a parent. McKenna didn't know what she'd do without the fifteen minutes a day to decompress and breathe in the fresh—albeit cold at this time of year—air. However, today she would not be walking alone.

McKenna turned to see her big sister, Dakota, sitting on the crumbling stone wall in front of the school. The high school had been released precisely twenty-five minutes ago and all after-school programs had been cancelled today.

"Hey, McKenna." Dakota got to her feet, hoisting an obscenely heavy backpack onto one shoulder. "You excited about tonight?"

"Absolutely!" McKenna exclaimed. "I hope I see the wolf again."

"You didn't ever see a wolf," Dakota said. "It was probably a stray dog. Or a fox."

"I did too see it!" McKenna insisted. "On our Sunday School group Halloween camp-out. Kaitlyn saw it too!"

"Just like Kaitlyn saw a ghost in her grandmother's house?" Dakota raised a blonde eyebrow that didn't match her aquamarine hair.

"You've never slept over at Kaitlyn's grandmother's house," McKenna said. "Otherwise you'd know it was haunted."

The two argued about wolves, ghosts, and whether or not Dakota had a boyfriend until they reached the weather-stripped wooden door of their house. McKenna picked at the chipping green paint as Dakota rummaged for her keys.

Once inside the aging yet welcoming farmhouse, McKenna and Dakota got busy decorating reindeer-, snowflake-, and star-shaped spice cookies. Between the two of them, they ate about as much frosting as wound up on the cookies themselves. Then, Dakota disappeared to text her not-boyfriend. McKenna broke out her hand-me-down art kit and started trying to draw a wolf.

"That's pretty good." Dakota loomed over McKenna's shoulder, having finally forgone her phone's sweet nothings. "The charcoal gives it some nice shading."

"Thanks." McKenna busied herself herding her art supplies back into the kit labeled 'Dakota' in a childish scrawl. "Emma's the best artist in class, though."

"So? Doesn't make it any less good," said Dakota. "Anyway, Mom called. She and Dad are meeting us at the church, so I'm driving. Get your coat on. I'll grab the cookies."

McKenna practically flew to the mudroom to retrieve her coat, hat, and mittens.

"My snow boots are still wet from the walk home," McKenna called.

"I thought I told you to put them by the woodstove?" Dakota called back from the hall as she pulled a Norwegian pattern sweater dress on over a thermal.

"I forgot!" McKenna poked her head around the doorway.

"Then wear your wellies," Dakota said.

"You've been watching too much Doctor Who," McKenna told her. "They're called rain boots."

Dakota swept her aquamarine hair into a side plait, her fingers moving as deftly as a spider spinning a web. "Uncultured American."

McKenna stuck her tongue out, slipped on her red rain boots, and raced to the car.

The road to the church was one of those winding New England roads that had never realized roads were supposed to be both straight and level, or at least one of the two. It wove up and down the hill, following the river to and fro. When Dakota was little she used to call it "Rollercoaster Road." It was years before McKenna realized that wasn't its real name. One time when Aunt Karen was visiting, she had tried using a GPS and it freaked out, thinking the road didn't exist and they were driving in the river.

The river was frozen now, and Dakota took the turns slowly, not too keen on how close the road was to the water. McKenna stared out the window as they passed the run-down general store, houses with picturesque Christmas decorations, a ramshackle cottage that looked as though one heavy sigh would send it tumbling into the river, historic homes with candles in the window, derelict gas stations, and medical offices in aging brick buildings or old manors with sprawling front porches.

McKenna absorbed it all passively, but all she really saw was the wolf. She and Kaitlyn had seen its eyes, two glowing crescents by the old well out in the woods beyond the church. They'd watched it dart away when Kaitlyn screamed. It had only been a blur of motion, but they'd seen it. It was real.

The white building loomed in the distance, a rainbow flag next to the sign waving in the slight northerly gust. It was already dark, but a light by the sign illuminated the words "Deerfield Unitarian Universalist Church." Beneath that were the dates and times for the Yule and Christmas Eve services, along with the last drop-off dates for the food, cold weather clothing, and toy drives.

Snow crunched as they pulled into the long driveway, fenced in by forest. McKenna always loved the menagerie of bumper stickers and vanity plates that could be found here. She grabbed the cookies and followed Dakota inside.

The church was the kind of older building that couldn't decide if it wanted to be open and airy or narrow and economical. McKenna was already flushed with warmth and hurried to take off her coat, hanging it on the long coat rack in the hall. The smell of old building and old books accosted her, along with a heavy-set, ruana-clad woman who permanently smelled of sage.

All around them was a flurry of people. Women with long gray tresses who aged unabashed, young parents struggling to stamp snow boots and free their mummy-like children from scarves, a small girl with shiny blonde hair flitting about in a cape, a little Asian girl with Christmas-tree-light earrings and a grandmother-knit reindeer sweater, a bearded man with a guitar, moms of every age in tasteful dresses and cardigans or garden-worn overalls, hippie burnouts in tie-dye t-shirts, and all manner of characters both unique and unassuming.

Some were in jeans and t-shirts, some in work clothes, some in layers of skirts and shawls with bangles and rings jingling with each gesture. McKenna silently noted that there were few places you could see a plethora of both tattoos and penny loafers. A little girl in a bright red holiday dress and a mass of curls ran to join the caped waif of a girl and the one with the fantastically loud earrings. The three practically danced down the hall and into the sanctuary.

A teenage girl in a felted purple witch hat and an older woman in the kind of holiday sweater worn by elementary school teachers ushered McKenna aside. They unburdened her of the tupperware of cookies at the table set up in the little foyer off to the side of the hallway. Already, a medley of cookies, brownies, and chips had gathered.

McKenna raced off to the sanctuary, taking a green paper program and a little white candle with a paper drip-guard from a basket-laden man in an elegant, wine-dark Santa hat. She waited for Dakota and then scanned the rows for their parents. Upon spotting them, she dashed through the pews and plopped down on the wooden seat. She kicked her legs in anticipation, eager for the ceremony to begin.

The great circular room was alight. The lights on the high ceiling shone on the hardwood floor. Candles burned all around. Behind the podium at the front hung three banners, one with the UU chalice, one with an evergreen tree over a setting (rising?) solstice sun, and another with a normal tree quilted in four sections so that the tree simultaneously existed in all four seasons.

A motley of jean and cloak clad figures started things off. The man with the guitar played a song and the elements were invoked. The story of Yule was told, followed by a round of "The Earth, the Air, the Fire, the Water."

The importance of winter for pre-modern people was stressed, along with the reverence for fire and deer. Both meant food. Both meant life. The deer gives his life so that we might live. So that we may survive the winter and the darkness.

The woman in the ruana explained that darkness is not something to be feared. It's a part of life and the turn of the wheel. To everything a season, even death. But no darkness lasts forever.

McKenna could barely contain her excitement. The ceiling lights dimmed and then turned off. Only the candles remained. Far off, she could hear a thin warble of music from a pipe. McKenna had never figured out what the song the piper played was called, but something about it woke some primal part of her, locked away during the rest of the year.

Hooded figures holding antler staves followed a hooded piper into the sanctuary and spread out in both directions. They began to dance as the piper played, snuffing out candle after candle as they passed. On every final note of the round, the stag dancers nearest each other would clack their antler staves together in the growing dark.

Soon, only a smattering of little flames lit the large room. Faces were harder to see, but somehow McKenna felt closer to everyone. The music and the stag dancers wove in and out. Pipe. Flit. Clack. Pipe. Flit. Clack. The candles went out one by one until there was only darkness. A great black blanket of it that fell over the room.

It was Midwinter, Yule, the longest night of the year. And the room, full of pagans and non-pagans alike, embraced the dark night together, their hearts beating in one chorus even if not in unison.

McKenna loved Yule best, not just because of the stag dancers and the shrinking sea of candles, but because everyone came out for Yule. At the other pagan holidays put on at the church only a dozen or so would show, all of them pagan or considering being pagan. However, at Yule, they filled the sanctuary with near half the congregation.

Everyone came, pagan, Christian, Jewish, Buddhist, Atheist, agnostic, multi-faith families, and everything else under the sun (or the moon now, McKenna supposed). People with crosses and Stars of David around their necks mingled with those who bore pentagrams, triple moons, hammers, troll crosses, and all manner of other symbols.

There was something about Yule that transcended sect or creed. No wonder there were so many winter holidays, McKenna thought. The dark part of the year was a reality no matter what gods you had. The changing seasons, the sun setting earlier and earlier, the dying crops, axial tilt, the growing cold. These were realities, even if they varied considerably by region.

Staving off cold and hunger was a timeless human experience. And why not throw a party to get through it, to keep some small candle of hope alive in the bleak dead of winter? To feast together on the harvest and the hunt, the stag and the grains having both died so others could live.

McKenna had once tried to explain Yule to her friends, thinking they would get it because so many people of other faiths at her church did. She had wound up stumbling over her words, trying to explain and failing. Avery had kept asking why there was a Christmas tree if it wasn't Christmas and getting very upset about it for reasons McKenna hadn't understood. Emma, meanwhile, had gotten stuck on the darkness and death bit and thought it sounded terribly scary.

But scary things can be meaningful and beautiful and a part of the natural world. They can be necessary. They can even be worth celebrating. The way McKenna saw it, we could hide under the covers from the dark or we could hold hands and sing our way through it.

We could face it together until it wasn't really scary at all. Just something that was, that had always been, and that always would be. Our lives would be much less rich if all the scary things that quickened hearts and tugged at our most basic fears were gone. What else would children scare each other with on Halloween or while roasting marshmallows around a fire?

The high-pitched music faded and the clacks went silent as the stag dancers made their way out of the sanctuary and off into some far corner of the church. A single candle appeared somewhere, and the folks running the event reminded everyone to tip the unlit candle into their neighbor's lit candle and not the other way around. Row by row, the candles were lit, one to the other, until the whole room was alight with a hundred tiny candles.

The woman in the ruana spoke about the rebirth of the sun and the promise of spring even as the plants sleep under the snows. All those who were able were welcomed to follow the stag dancers out of the church and into the woods for the solstice walk. McKenna nearly leapt out of her seat.

"Mom, Dad, are you coming?" McKenna asked.

Mom shook her head. "We'll stay here with Steve."

She gestured to the man with the guitar, who tuned his instrument slightly as he prepared to entertain the elderly, the very young, and those averse to walking or the cold. McKenna saw that the waif in the cape would not be deterred by either, despite her little legs.

"Go with Dakota," said Dad.

Dakota and McKenna, still holding their candles, filed out of the sanctuary, along with a dozen or so of the outdoorsier folks. Their candles lit the now dark hallway of the church. Up ahead by the foyer were the other candles of the stag dancers.

They began their procession anew out the sliding glass doors of the foyer and into the courtyard. McKenna watched the shadows of the couches, the piano, and the snack table dance through the foyer. Outside the air was sharp, but it wasn't cold enough that they'd need their full coats. Dakota was fine in her sweater dress and McKenna was still all warm inside from the candles and the piper's song dancing through her blood.

The piper struck up his tune again as they headed out past the swing-set and the memorial garden and straight into the woods. They passed the firepit and the old well McKenna and Kaitlyn had been exploring when they first came upon the wolf.

The trees were close together and very tall. Pine and barren oak and maple now. Dead leaves crunched underfoot wherever the snow had not clung. At some point one of the stag dancers slowed down and broke off from the others. Dakota quickened her pace. She took his hand.

The candles wound their way through the forest, bringing back the light to this world of darkness and winter. The piper stopped playing and the group took up another round of "The Earth, the Air, the Fire, the Water" followed by "Mother of Darkness/Mother of Light." Before the second round of the latter, Dakota and the stag dancer had vanished altogether.

McKenna heard a sound in the woods. Most likely a deer, but her imagination got the better of her. She wanted to see the wolf.

She slowed down until she brought up the rear and then veered off the path, her red rain boots crunching into virgin snow as she did. She followed the sound further and further off the trail until she came across a terrified deer.

McKenna's breath hung in the air, and the deer bolted. But not from her. When McKenna turned to reorient herself, she was met with a pair of golden eyes. In the light of the candle, she could make out the shape of what definitely was not a stray dog or a fox or even a coyote.

His paws were too big to start. He was tall, with a low-hanging tail swished through with bits of brown, cream, and heather gray. The fur on his body was mostly gray but with touches of white and a darker storm-gray, as though someone had taken a charcoal to him just as McKenna had to her wolf drawing. He was winter-lean but with the regal bearing and majestic chest ruff of a woodland lord.

What had she been thinking? She was smarter than this. Why had she gone looking for a wild animal all alone with no one to know to look for her? She could no longer hear the sounds of the group shuffling along in their winter procession. Their Yule songs were far off and barely audible now.

But the wolf didn't move. He just stared, transfixed by the light. McKenna stood just as still. She knew what to do if a bear attacked. Get as big as possible and make as much noise as possible and hope the bear goes away. It would probably work on a wolf.

She knew the fire might scare a wolf too. But she didn't want to scare this wolf. She'd already cost him his Christmas dinner.

The wolf's ears pricked. A branch snapped somewhere. He turned his head to the source of the sound.

"McKenna!" She heard Dakota's voice somewhere in the wood. "McKenna? McKenna! McKenna, where are you? McKenna!"

"I'm here," McKenna said, not too loudly lest she scare off the wolf.

"McKenna!" Dakota and her own candle appeared through the black of the wood. She grabbed McKenna by the arm. "What were you thinking wandering off from the gr—" Her eyes fell on the wolf. "Holy crap!" She pulled McKenna behind her and brandished her candle wildly to scare off the wolf.

He looked alarmed and shifted his stance lower, his legs ready to flee or lunge.

"Stop, Dakota!" McKenna said in a hush. "He isn't hurting anyone!"

Somewhere in the distance came the faint sound of another wolf. Another voice joined in from equally far away. The wolf before them cocked his head, his ears twitching in the direction of his fellows.

Deciding Dakota and McKenna weren't an immediate threat, the wolf lifted his snout to the air. A long, throaty warble escaped him. It was an eerie sound that pricked at the back of McKenna's neck the same way the stag dancer song did. It was something ancient, still encoded into her DNA despite her modern life and minimal tests of survival.

Dakota's hand was so tight on McKenna's arm that it was starting to hurt. McKenna pulled her arm away and cupped her free hand around her mouth. She tilted back her head and tried her best wolf howl.

"Are you crazy?" Dakota hissed.

"Dakota, they're singing," McKenna told her. "They're singing away the long night. Just like us." She howled again.

Dakota looked from the wolf to McKenna. The wolf looked back at both of them and raised his voice with McKenna's and the two other wolves' somewhere even deeper into the wood.

Hot wax escaped the confines of the paper guard on McKenna's candle and dripped onto her fingers. She ignored it. She was singing with a wolf on Yule. Not even Kaitlyn would believe this.

Slowly, very slowly, Dakota raised her own hand and her voice. The two sisters and the wolf all stood there howling, their voices not quite in unison but raised together, calling out to the two other wolves they couldn't see but knew were there. Five voices filled the night for a few fleeting moments that held lifetimes between them.

Everything else fell away. The only things that felt real were the forest and the wolfsong and their hearts beating against their chests. McKenna felt her cheeks burn against the cold.

Suddenly, the wolf started and dashed back into the brush and the trees and the shadows beyond their candles. The other two went silent.

They heard voices somewhere. Song.

"The group!" Dakota exclaimed. She grabbed McKenna's free hand. "Come on. They must be on their way back. Not a word of this, okay? If Mom finds out I left you to go make-out with Shane in the woods she's gonna kill me. Throw a wolf on that and I'll be grounded until I'm a crone."

"I told you he was your boyfriend," McKenna teased.

"Oh, shut up."

"Dakota?" McKenna asked. "Odin's wolf is named Freki, right?"

"Yeah, I think so," Dakota panted in dragon whispers, her uneven breath hanging in the grave-cold air as she reeled from the encounter.

"I'm going to name him Freki too," McKenna declared. "It's a good wolf name."

Dakota mussed McKenna's hair in some combination of a noogie and a hug. "Freki and Freckles."

McKenna made a face but didn't protest her sister's noogie-hug.

The two latched onto the group of Yuletide wassailers on their way back to the church. An unmanned basket awaited their extinguished candles by the door of the sanctuary. Everyone else was already forming two circles—one for men and one for women, with those who chose not to identify or who didn't like the idea of holding strangers' hands forming a free dance in the middle. McKenna and Dakota were swept up in a chain of women as the woman in the ruana took Dakota's hand and the girl with the Christmas light earrings took McKenna's in one and the caped waif's in another.

The two circles danced in opposite directions, one singing "Hoof and Horn" as the other sang "We All Come from the Goddess." Some voices were quiet, some belted the song, some were gifted, some were so off-key McKenna wondered if they even knew what the songs were supposed to sound like.

McKenna was nearly dragged at one point as the chain of hand-holding was strained by some quickened pace up ahead and then was nearly in a mosh pit at other points when the chain lagged. Eventually, both chains fell apart. Someone played a hide drum with an antler for a handle and everyone danced, though few as joyously as the caped waif and a white-haired old woman bellydancing with abandon. Once everyone was red in the face and out of breath, the man with the guitar and the woman in the ruana asked everyone to release the energy back into the earth.

A few closing words later, everyone spilled out into the foyer, where a motley of cheeses, ciders, and fruit and veggie plates had joined the cookies and chips. McKenna wolfed down four kinds of cookies, three kinds of cheese, a handful of grapes, a strawberry, and two mini-cupcakes before chasing it down with a red plastic cup of cider. Folks trickled out the door as others mingled and some settled in by the couches for a bardic circle. The curly-haired girl in the holiday dress attempted to play the piano next to a trim, salt- and pepper-haired woman in head-to-toe beige business casual wear. Dakota found Shane, now free of his stag regalia and back in normal teenage boy garb.

All too soon, Mr. and Mrs. Randolph were telling McKenna and Dakota it was time to go. It was pitch-black out, but the candles in the windows and the lights on the lawn lit their way home. Old Christmas carols warbled through static on the radio.

A few blocks from home, they passed another white church with a sign out front imploring people to remember the real reason for the season. McKenna smiled to herself. She knew the reason for the season. The wolf in the forest knew the reason, perhaps better than anyone.

A light snow was falling by the time they got home. Light flooded the dark house as they came in, empty tupperware box in tow. McKenna looked around their cozy living room with its scuffed hardwood floor, old rugs, overflowing bookshelves, and presents piled around the tree. She hoped the wolf was safe at home in his den with the others.

Dad made cocoa and McKenna read Christmas Trolls covertly, worried she might be too old for a picture book. Mom read some old book with a library binding as she nibbled a surviving cookie. Dakota alternated between texting Shane and hanging up their stockings.

Soon after, Dad went to bed, and Dakota scurried off to her room. McKenna followed after to find her on her bed painting her toenails red and green while listening to "The Holly and the Ivy." McKenna joined her, painting her own toenails red, orange, and yellow, so she could bring the fire with her wherever she went. The two spoke in the language of whispers and giggles only sisters know until their mom came in.

"McKenna, what's this doing in your coat pocket?" Mom asked, holding out the little white candle with a crumpled paper guard. "You were supposed to leave it in the basket for next year."

"I wanted it for my memory box," McKenna said, sheepishly putting away the red nail polish.

"That's what the program's for."

"But tonight—" McKenna faltered, unable to explain without telling.

"McKenna, you aren't still afraid of trolls eating you on Yule, are you?" Mom asked. "Because I told your father not to read you those Icelandic fairy tales. You don't need a nightlight or a candle to protect you."

McKenna shook her head. "No. No. I'm not afraid of trolls. I like trolls. They're just as scared of us as we are of them. Besides, we have heat and electricity. We don't need fire to get through the long night anymore. That's just symbolic."

Mom nodded, impressed. "Alright, well, lights out in five, girls."

"So, if you're not afraid of the dark, what are you doing hiding out in my room?" Dakota asked, undoing her braid. Her aquamarine hair sprang into loose curls from being plaited all evening.

"The wolf gets it," said McKenna, picking at Dakota's old t-shirt quilt.

"Oh?"

McKenna leaned her head on Dakota's shoulder, buzzing with excitement about Yule, about the presents in the other room, about the mittens Mom knit them every year, about the popovers and bacon Dad and Dakota made every Christmas morning, about their grandparents visiting on Christmas Day, about Dakota inviting Shane over for New Year's Eve, about the wolves in the churchwood that Kaitlyn would never believe and Emma and Avery would never, ever believe (though Jayden H. might).

"Pack."

When Mom came back in five minutes to enforce lights out McKenna was already fast asleep. Mom bent to pick her up and carry her off to her bed.

"It's okay, Mom," Dakota said, putting away a worn Tamora Pierce paperback. "She can stay."

"Okay," said Mom, turning off the lights. "Good night, sweetheart. Happy Yule."

"Happy Yule," Dakota whispered in the dark.

AUTUMN BEVERLY
SECRETS OF NORTHERN SPIRITS

Autumn Beverly is a pet/wildlife/fantasy artist. Her art is inspired by her passion for all animals and a desire to spread awareness, knowledge, and share beauty about them through her images. To do so accurately, Autumn enjoys studying up on biology, ecology, and ethology and even lore, with a specific interest in canids, particularly wolves. In her spare time, she plays video games, blogs, makes animal-themed symbolic jewelry, and most of all plays with and cares for her six animal companions, and her fiancé too!

Secrets of Northern Spirits. Colored pencil and Bristol board.

HANNAH CHRISTOPHER
HEPHAESTUS IS A BRAND OF FIRE

Hannah Christopher lives in northern Ohio with a part-time job at a college library. She has worked as an editor on the college's literary journal Penmarks, *in addition to having a short story published through the journal, and is a member of the English Honors Society. Her hobbies range from cactus care to cross-county texting, finding paths in the woods for people who lost them to hours lying in bed. She is working on a degree in English and Creative Writing.*

The snow was gray like cinders, and it filled the streets like cinders filling the chimney flue of an old man's lungs, with little black creases only often enough for him to tell that the stretch of flat land now expanding before him had at one point been a brick road. He grew up on a brick road. He remembered car rides home from school, with his backpack buckled in to the seat next to him, and his mother telling him not to look out the window. He remembered this so vividly, he could almost feel the terror in her voice tickling the hairs in his ears. But it wasn't her breath that stirred him now: it was the wolf's. He wished he didn't have to die with this wolf. He thought he deserved more dignity than that. But he'd seen enough death to know that it had equal and unfair ways of dealing with everyone in its own due time, and all he could do now with his lot was dream of sleep, taking him away.

The wolf's ribs shuddered under his like a broken set of bellows. A warm spot leaked through his shirt and touched the goose-pimples marching their slow soldier-steps over his chest. A small sigh escaped the creature's parted jaws.

Footsteps crunched soft into the top layer of the snow only yards away, but he couldn't move to look. Couldn't be bothered. Also, his neck hurt, and he wasn't sure if they'd broken it. He figured: they were coming back to finish the job. Now he'd die with this wolf pressed into the ice underneath him. He'd die, and future wanderers wouldn't be able to pick apart his bones from the wolf's, their blood forever mingled in the grass (if only there was any). The footsteps stopped at his head and waited. A shadow passed over the snow, fingers gripped the matted back of his bloodied head, pulling his eyes up to level. Two narrow black eyes inquired an unasked question out of his features. It was a woman, but only just. A dark array of furs and fabrics muffled her neck and ears, a green jacket hid any curves she'd kept. A silky fringe of bangs poked from her hood, slick and black against the curve of her broad forehead.

"What is your name?" she asked.

"I don't have one."

"Of course you don't. No one ever has a name anymore." Her eyes flicked from his face to the red ribs of the wolf underneath him. "Did you do this? Did you hurt this animal?"

He didn't answer. She nodded.

"Can you walk?" she asked.

"I'm not sure."

"You better try. It will be a few moments longer."

She helped him find his feet again with a firm but brief embrace, sticking him up in the snow like a discarded walking stick. The sticky gray slush rooted him to the ground.

This woman, she knelt by the wolf and combed through its darkened mane, examined her fingers when they came away warm and bloody. She gently eased the animal into her arms and onto a sled fashioned from wooden pallets and rope. In all his curiosity, he forgot to test his legs. She turned and motioned him forward. His first few steps were small; he thought of police and that trick they'd play when they thought someone was drunk. Before all this, when the world was better, a police cruiser pulled him over and asked for identification. The blood welling up from the cuts in his mouth also reminded him of this encounter, and its aftermath.

He followed the woman off the shoulder of the road, through a few abandoned yards, even a small stretch of woods. A playscape like a bloated fishnet lurched into the remains of a sandbox enclosure. A swing hung by a single tendril from its frame.

She stopped in front of a tall fence and propped open the gate.

"After you," she said, nodding. He stepped around the wolf on the sled, through the gate. The wolf raised its long head at him, nostrils flaring, but otherwise was unresponsive, and watchful.

The fence enclosed a gas station, or what used to be a gas station. There was an overhang and some pumps and a building with lots of windows for the advertisements to get through, but the advertisements were long gone, and also the hoses for all the pumps, and the gas had probably been siphoned down to the last molecule. The woman took the lead again. She went to the building and opened the front door with a key she took from her jacket. Again, she held it open for him. He entered without signal this time.

He knew this store: it was called Stop-N-Buy. He used to purchase *Popular Science* magazines at this store back when he was a boy. He thought of the last one he bought before they stopped selling them, the one about Little Guns That Can Kill Tanks. He'd bought it for 20 cents, not even a quarter. Nowadays, something like that ran the cost of a life. But there were no more *Popular Science* magazines covering the shelves of this store anymore anyway, only skulls and furs. He thought, this is odd. People usually left those to the side of the road as warnings, or trophies. And that this woman must be a witch of some kind, using these trophies for voodoo. They covered the walls up and down, left to right, and he could feel the eyeless sockets of the skulls staring at him from all angles.

The witch woman said, "You must be hungry. I have some soup. I can warm it up, and we can all eat."

"Even the dog?"

She raised one eyebrow. "Yes, even the dog."

A rust-hardened oil lamp threw soft shadows underneath the shelves and painted reflections on the windows like still-life portraits; "The Irony of Man" in watercolors, or some other title to that degree. She'd lit the lamp with a flint and a bottle of Hephaestus-brand oil, in one of those neat glass bottles that recently were so hard to come by. He used to collect them from holes in his backyard. He used to line them up on his windowsill and watch them catch the light and throw it across his brown carpet in little squares and fractals.

The witch scuttled behind the counter and returned with a red cotton bag. She overturned it on the floor between the man and the wolf, took a bottle of unlabeled salve and a roll of gauze from the pile, and turned to the wolf. It was a big gray wolf, with those yellow eyes like he remembered from the magazines. On second thought, she took a needle and thread also. The wolf peeled back its upper lip to flaunt its teeth at her.

"I am helping you," she said, and the wolf closed its mouth, but kept a wary eye on her hands. A gurgle rolled in the back of its throat.

The man asked, "Why'd you bring me here? What are you doing?"

"Too many living things die nowadays."

"That doesn't answer my question."

She sighed. "I am trying to be kind to you. Do you understand? I am trying to be kind."

"Why would you risk your life for that dog?" he asked, and the question came out strained, as if the words alone manifested the jealousy in him he hadn't before realized existed.

She said, "And why would I not? Answer that for me first. Even you fell upon him during the beating, to protect him, and you ask me why I do what I do?"

"I didn't do that."

"You did," she said. "I saw you, and you did."

She sewed a long black line into the wolf's abdomen, though the wound couldn't have been more than artificial. There wasn't that much blood on his shirt, just enough to give him a skeevy sensation about the whole ordeal.

The witch put away her red satchel and washed her hands in a tin bucket. She didn't look up from her hands.

"About that soup," he said. She shook her head.

"It can wait until morning," she said. "We've all waited much longer for food and drink, and we can stand to wait that much more."

"It's getting dark."

"You should learn to save your words."

He sat with his back to the wolf; he stared out the gray windows at the grayer thumbprints forming on the glass, and he wondered when the earth would be covered enough to fall asleep for good. And it would stay that way all through the night and deep into the morning. She'd rouse him and the wolf would be gone, she'd make him soup from a can and stand by the wall while he tried not to burn himself on the jagged lip of metal holding in all that divine sustenance.

He looked up. The witch polished her bucks with a rag of tattered shirt sleeves. Her back was to him. "Once," he said, "I wanted to see the world. Now, I'm afraid there's nothing to see anymore, or else I've seen it all."

She didn't look away from her skulls, but her hands made smaller circles; patches of matte creams and mossy greens appearing in the dust.

"And what about this day?" she asked. "Have you not learned anything yet?"

He thought, any kindness shown in these days is a wasted effort, and that he'd really like to see some white snow again. He honestly didn't know the answer to her question.

Outside, the wolf made leaps like needle-punctures in the earth.

ALEX CLARKE
BEAUTY

Having graduated from Endicott College in 2016 with a BFA in visual communications, Alex Clarke is a photographer, videographer, and a wolf activist. With his passionate devotion toward helping wolves and his keen eye for detail, Alex uses his photographic skills when volunteering at a wolf sanctuary to capture photos of their wolves either from a distance or lying right beside them. His main purposes are not only to spread awareness about the positive importance of wolves and why they should exist, but also to show the elegant beauty of them through his work.

Beauty. Photography.

SNOWFALL

Snowfall. Photography.

COTTATERRA
CONTEMPLATIONS

Theresa is a 23-year-old freelance artist from Chicago! She's probably been drawing since she was four or five years old. She wasn't very good but she's gotten so much better with years of practice. Theresa has won multiple art awards in high school and is improving her craft every day. Her Deviantart is terra0tta, and her Tumblr is cottaterra. Feel free to check out what other art she has made!

Contemplations. Digital art.

MAXWELL COVIELLO
ALWAYS THE WIND

Maxwell Coviello is a published fiction writer and journalist with an interest in civil rights, social justice, and video game culture. A native New Englander with New York ancestral ties, he is a graduate of Hampshire College and currently lives in the Washington Heights neighborhood of Manhattan. He has written for several publications, including NEXT: Magazine *and the electronic gaming website,* Pixelitis.

When not writing, Coviello can be found navigating the startup culture of New York City. He serves as the content coordinator for the upcoming multi-media and social app, B•OUT. *His interests include physical fitness, gaming, reading, and travel. Selections of his other written works can be found on* JukePop.

When the others in the caravan weren't looking, he tied an insulated bag around her wrist before stepping away from the young woman, the unwanted, to let her die a frozen death.

Synna stood alone on the crest of the hill as her former people became dark specks on a boundless white stretch. On these plains, visibility was the only abundance. Synna remained, and they walked, armored with insulation, furs, and protection, into a lighter, unfeeling snowfall.

At fifty paces, she felt fear. At one hundred, sorrow. And when at last Synna could not see the remnants of her village, rage took hold.

But anger expended heat, and this was not something she could afford to lose, so she stilled her emotions and surveyed her situation.

First, Synna opened the bag, which smelled of smoke and meat. Inside: jerky, leathery and sweet and no need for heating. Initially, they weren't supposed to send her away with anything. Why waste a resource on the dark-skinned exile? The red-headed youth who had committed this crime of charity was the son of her parent's friends. In those early years, in warmer times, they had cherished her. The boy must have felt some sense of obligation, and so ensured Synna's prolonged survival.

Anger was useless. And what malice should she have against any of the men and women of a divided and desperate village, lost and fighting against the winter unending? When machines failed them and the fuel had all but dried up, there was only the path of the nomad. And when the herd needed to be culled, it was culled.

Behind the frame of her parka, black eyes and brown skin had always made Synna stand out against the white wilderness, even in the warmer times when the village of the valley was gentler. Back then, nestled between two cliffs to keep out the cold, and with grass that had not yet turned gray, windmills made energy for the machines, and the end of fuel had not yet dawned.

Back then, Synna's mother's hands were always dark with soil and the juice of stems. There were few green things to eat, but bellies rarely went empty. Her father, with the lighter skin, was a watchman on the edge of town. He, along with others, kept their ears open for the sound of stranger machinery and the blue lights that had first brought the snows, well before Synna's time, and even before her parents.

Only once did she remember, when she was still quite small and unaware of the struggles of the world, a night when the alarms blared and every door in every organic thatch was sealed and bolted. There were sounds of gunfire and pulses of electricity. She could smell static and her hair had curled upward. Her mother assured her that these pulses would keep the night things at bay, that the electricity stopped them somehow. But even back then, Synna could see through people's faces, and she saw her mother's fear too clearly.

In the present, Synna tried to keep her own fear away just as her father had kept the night things, the clanking, twisted things, out of her village. She looked deeper into the satchel, tempted to try a piece of jerky, and forced hunger down. This meat was sacred. It had to last. But in her exploration of the satchel, she found a sealed box of tinder, and a transparent plastic bag containing flint. She knew how to use both, and for this she gave a silent prayer to the God of her parents. With this, and with all directions at her disposal, she judged the light behind the clouds for the sun and decided on a path based on this.

Though the snow was not the worst it could be, the wind seared her flesh where the parka failed, and lifting up her shirt to her bare face could only do so much. It was never the snow that hurt. It was the wind, always the wind that robbed you of will and worked the body down. And all the while, as Synna crossed that barren field, she could only tell herself, move. *Do not sleep, Move. And keep moving.*

There were other villages out there. In warmer times, there was no way to communicate with them—methods such as these had not been in place for many years. When the old war raged against the night things, a failed effort—those blasts of electricity, she recalled her father mentioning—did away with the old means of messaging. Back then, it was as simple as pressing a button.

Back then, the old woman and her council kept the village running, settling disputes as they came and rationing out resources for all. The fires billowed, and beds were warmer. Back then, the children laughed. When strangers came, rarely, to seek sanctuary in the valley walls, the old woman and her council would assess them and, if proven worthy, given a home and a duty. Strangers became friends. It was, as in the older days, how the village first came to be. And none were judged on malady or past or belief as long as they promised to safekeep the land and their neighbor.

But as with the land, so too did the old woman die, and more ambitious members of her council decided to steer the course of the valley village in other directions. The cold intruded right around the time the old woman fell ill, and whispers rose up among the men that the phenomena were somehow related. The spiritually minded and charismatic believed the colder weather to be the punishment for a wrongdoing. Suspicions ran high. Fingers were pointed. And when the old woman passed, a younger man took advantage of the people's anxieties and made promises and deals. Whereas the old woman preached the tenants of nature, power through variety, the younger man preached the importance of sacrifice. He prognosticated bitter and cold years, and a scarcity of food and water. He made decrees of abandonment. First, the sick were marched out beyond the walls of the village and given over to winter unending. They did not come back. Many in the village were placated, and though there was more food on the table—it only lasted for but awhile.

Crops failed. The oil ran low. And when these things came to pass, the younger man, now ruling without a council, made more decrees. He banished the elderly. And when some protested, he used force to silence them. These were the times of the fires and the fights, when Synna's mother locked her in a basement. Then, her father lost his life, and her mother soon followed. And when all finally remained, there was no valley village left standing.

This was the dawn of the time of the caravan, when mobility gave way to scavenging, and as the caravan headed deeper out into the wilds, more and more of its members were sent away. Synna had been taught by her mother, during the first days of the new rule, that in order to survive, she would have to make herself useful. From her mother, she learned of all the edible plants and how to hunt. Her father taught her all the ways of protection and of the nature of man, its light side and its dark. He also taught her of animals and how to tame them.

But as the first year went into the next, and Synna approached her seventeenth birthday, the others found her existence outweighed her use. And though she had allies at first, the days went on when she would wake up to the disappearance of another companion. Fanaticism ran high, and the younger man, who had won the war and lost everything, now surrounded himself with a council of his own, who looked and acted very much the same as he. He had thought very little of Synna, had paid her no mind at all, did not (for her own sake) even know her parentage. But there was a day when his eyes passed by hers and, be it the expression on her face or some other ineffable quality, he deemed her unfit to exist. He ordered her removal.

And so the girl remained, dark against the canvas of the snows, as she bounded for lower land.

The most important thing in the world would be to get hands on a means of defense. A weapon. A firearm would be a dream, but at this stage a knife would do. Rabbits still existed around the snow-capped forests, and she knew how to skin and clean them. But then, she would need fire, and when everything was a cold wet, procuring this would be difficult.

On the first night, she took shelter under a sunken structure, a road that had once bridged above another road. She had hoped to chance upon an old vehicle, as they made great shelters. But she had heard stories of waylayers hiding among these wrecks and that fear won out against her need for a peaceful sleep. In the end, on that first night, sleep did not come except for brief lapses in consciousness. On that first night, it was the wind that won.

Life began at dawn, and Synna forced her way up a hill to see the first tinges of sunrise. The sky had cleared, but for a miraculous moment, the tiny, black things that traveled in the atmosphere would regroup again, meshing to create more snow clouds.

For that moment though, a golden pink hue lapped up the gray light, and Synna allowed her stomach a small piece of the jerky. Water wasn't scarce in this climate, obviously, but she had to wait until dawn for it to melt. No need for more cold to find its way into her body. She accomplished this via a castoff artifact, an old tin can. With no fire for warming the water, it stung its way down her throat. But she was sated as she watched the sun rise, and nearly choked back the rest of the water when she spotted the curious way the light traveled across the mountains.

Because they weren't mountains at all, as she caught sight of the gleaming on the glass. The structure, a handful of miles away, was something she had only seen in old photographs. It was a city, and though many had fled these communities long ago—as they had fallen with the first snows—there was gossip among travelers that some cities called home to trading posts and major junctions. That is, if they were safe and not infested with the whirring, mechanical things that thrived in and fed the snows.

There was no better option, and so Synna did not hesitate. If she ventured into the territory of the things that came at night, then she would surely die. Maybe. But death would be far more certain if she waited out here in the wildlands.

As the light crept and the shadows across the lands receded, a circular structure or building emerged from the ambiguous gray. A compound of some sort, Synna judged, and was reminded of the pens of livestock back in the village. She took note that many buildings inside this strange structure had plenty coverings for shelter. How had the caravan not known about this? But then again, they were far removed from any known map.

Synna's breath ran smoky in the frigid air, and she could feel her body ache and tense against the dropping temperature. A cold snap, and judging from the unnatural and sudden gathering of the clouds, the telltale swirl of a thousand microscopic machines setting on their duties, Synna knew that she would be dead if she remained out here uncovered. So, she positioned herself just so and slid down the hill, praying the incline wasn't steep enough for an avalanche.

She had never seen these colors before, these crude, cartoonish faces of animals on a sign she read as "Zoo," a funny word that played off her tongue and managed to bestow her with her first smile in days. She brushed past the snow on the faded sign and drew back, if only due to the alien nature of where she stood, as she tried to make sense of these images of strange animals and not so strange animals.

The plaza was circular, and the architecture of no practical use. Stranger still were the rocks and the pikes of wood, all made of plastic. They were facsimiles of natural things, and Synna couldn't wrap her head around the point of it all. But she accepted that this was from the time before winter unending, and supposed it was understandable that none of it made any sense. They did things much differently in the past.

Walking through the open air of the trash-strewn gallery, and deciphering the signage, Synna understood that this was a place where animals had been kept, though not for any discernible practical use.

Light filtered in through the broken windows of the halls, and the shadow of snowfall drifted in pools of light behind glass. Synna walked past a chamber of dead trees and saw bones on the ground. There were many skeletons in many of the enclosed pens. They had all been abandoned, most likely, when the warm world had fallen.

So, it was a surprise to Synna when she heard a sound other than her footfalls and the piercing howl of the wind. At first, she thought she was going crazy from hunger, so she permitted herself another few pieces of the jerky. But her stomach became greedy, and, in a moment of resignation to the inevitable, she allowed herself to consume a whole stick of the meat. When she had finished, she felt neither sated nor better about her situation and did everything in her power to keep from crying. A wet face would spell a painful end in this environment.

But that sound again. A shuffle. A scratch. A groan. Something was alive here, close by. But how was that possible?

She rounded a corner and came to a pen with carcasses that were freshly decomposing. These beasts were large and woolly, almost like sheep, but resembling cattle. There was no telling how long ago these creatures had died because the cold preserved most organic things.

Synna nearly fell backward as one of the shapes lying in the pen suddenly rose, and then fell just as quickly. The thing was still alive. Shocked by the alien nature of it all, Synna backed out of the enclosure and into another hallway, trying to stagger her breath.

And in doing so, the girl locked eyes with a creature at the far end of the hall. It was standing there in a circle of light, snow shadow playing over its red fur. The canine looked emaciated. Small. And Synna couldn't imagine how it had survived this long. Then again, it had managed to free itself somehow, perhaps taking advantage of this crumbling infrastructure.

Synna refused to move, and when she realized she was not looking at a dog—as she had previously thought—she held her breath entirely. It was a wolf. Fur like red river clay, and eyes that were golden like the elusive sun. It was beautiful, but it was still a wolf. And she knew to fear their capabilities, and respect them from afar.

For some reason, however, this wolf did not make Synna afraid. In fact, she sensed it was processing her same exact thoughts: *What is this creature standing before me? What will it do?*

A soft growl came, and Synna forced herself not to step backward or forwards. No sudden movement. There was one idea she had, however, though she knew it would cost her dearly. She moved slow, a slow that felt like a year's worth of movement from her hand to the satchel. She undid it, and only once did the red wolf raise its ears and haunches. Synna withdrew a stick of jerky. Whistling, as if to catch the attention of a village dog, she threw the meat in the air toward the creature.

The wolf threw itself down for an attack, but it did not leap forward. Immediately, it smelled food and, refusing to take its eyes off this strange girl who had entered its territory, drew closer to the meat. It sniffed it twice and then took it into its jaws, greedily chewing down on it.

Synna didn't let this opportunity pass her by. She promptly turned on her heels and walked—knowing it best not to run—toward a building that could provide coverage and safe distance from the wolf. Though in her heart, she knew not to be worried. Aside from a rational response to a foreign creature, the wolf had not acted aggressively with her. She only then remembered hearing, perhaps from a watchman, that wolves were more shy than ferocious. Wildcats posed deadlier threats.

The interior of the building was far removed from the pens of the animals. It functioned, Synna assumed, as a gathering place or knowledge hub of a sort. A case of waterlogged booklets, and a map of the wall, indicated this. It was warmer inside the building, but not by much. And it was dark, which always stirred the imagination. She had no light, no bioluminescent torch, and she would be blind to any presences lurking within the dark.

She knew the night things did not need light to see.

Synna let her eyes adjust and then found her way to a back room. She reached for the door, and it was only then she realized that she had dropped the satchel during her flight from the wolf; the bag's fall muffled by the snowfall. She cursed and restrained herself from kicking the wall. This would do no good. She would have to go back for it later and hope the wolf hadn't eaten all her jerky.

Now, she was without resource, and there was no point in dwelling on the meat she could have used to fill her belly. Still, she pressed on.

Fortune interceded more swiftly than she could have possibly imagined as Synna recognized that she was standing inside a kitchen. So, this had been an eating area after all. Any food leftover from the blackout would have spoiled long ago, but canned goods were still an option. She rifled through a few cabinets and found nothing but dust.

But then, her eyes fell upon a cutlery rack, and a pang of hope rose up in her heart. Sure enough, several knives lined the magnetic strip. She took the largest of the knife, a kitchen knife, off the rack and held it in the air. It was no gun, and certainly no bow and arrow, but it was a means of defense.

The first thing she thought of was the injured creature. Yes, that would have to do. She searched the room for other utilities. No food, but there were salt and pepper still in the shakers. Who could ask for better luxuries than seasoning? She took these too.

No sign of the wolf friend from earlier, but retrieving the satchel was no longer a priority. She approached the enclosure and saw the still-living creature on the ground, taking in shallow, labored breaths. This act would be a mercy.

The sign named the creature: *bison*, and described its natural habitat, which winter had most likely rendered extinct. Synna used the sign as leverage for her footing and hoisted herself over the glass, careful not to land on her feet the wrong way. She could not afford a twisted ankle; even a sprain would be far too costly.

Synna placed her hand on the beast's matted fur, and it tensed up, causing her to retract. But it had no fight left in it. Synna knew it would be harder if she troubled herself about it any longer, so she carried out the motions, reaching below the neck and making the cut, just as she had been shown back in the village. This was not her first slaughter, but it had been a while.

The snow soaked up red, and Synna went about the process of carving off a substantial size of meat. She would come back for the rest later. She would now need a vessel for transport, but that could be dug up with a little ingenuity.

A bloody slab of fat and flesh in her hand, Synna hoped she wouldn't attract competition from the wolf still roaming the premises. She allowed herself a moment to breathe and envisioned the compound as it might have been from the time before. In her mind's eye, she saw translucent ghosts of those who had once wandered around the zoo, and the animals in their enclosures, all creatures ignorant of the cataclysm that would eventually befall their world.

She had meat. Now to find a way to cook it.

Night came quicker than expected, and Synna didn't dare linger out in the open. The zoo had been dotted with barrels, which Synna deemed as receptacles for waste during the zoo's days of operation. She dragged one of these into an enclosure, a house for reptiles decorated in the manner of an exotic forest, "jungle" as one of the helpful signs indicated. She chose this due to the grating at the top of the ceiling—it would be a well-ventilated room for a fire. Or so she hoped.

She doubled back and found the satchel. To her chagrin, the remaining jerky had been removed. Damn. But the wolf was courteous enough to leave the flint and tinder untouched.

Oh well, Synna thought. *No use fretting over the past.* She had better food now anyway.

Scooping out the wet innards, Synna let the barrel dry for an hour. All the while, the hunk of bison meat transformed itself from an unappealing bloody lump, into the promise of the most delicious meal.

More kindling had been collected from the various open air pens, gathered from all of the dead trees and branches. Synna feared the wood would be too wet, even after letting it sit, but her stomach made her impatient, and she tried to light the barrel. Though it was immensely difficult to start it, it wasn't long before she had started a modest fire. The warmth was indescribable, and the feeling was restored to her palms.

A piece of meat was cut and ran through with a stick, and, before long, it was roasted and warm. Synna burnt her tongue on the cooked bison; too eager for the taste. It was worth it. In that bite and release of juices, perhaps a bit too gamey than what she had been accustomed to, her hope was sated as well. She thought of nothing for a time, only chewing, and the warmth of the fire. As far as surviving was concerned, Synna had exceeded her expectations, and she improved her comfort by digging out some of the "fake" moss and netting from the iguana pen to accommodate for bedding.

Then, she looked up, and there he was, the wolf. Her heart sunk, but she steadied herself. The wolf was only a few paces away, yes, but its head was lowered and its ears back.

She knew, in the back of her head, that this was a submissive gesture. The thing wasn't going to attack her; it wanted food. It recognized her as a provider, an alpha. Packless, she was the only creature it could rely on.

She pitied it, but even though there was a whole bison to subsist off of, there was no telling when she would access nourishment again. This was not a time to share needed food with a wild animal.

But though the winds had nearly frozen her to the bone several times before, the fire in the drum had thawed her heart, and she threw the wolf a scrap, which it lapped up—never daring to come closer— and then another piece. Synna cursed herself; this was foolish and dangerous. It saw her as a food provider. What would happen when she had nothing more to provide?

She became full sooner than anticipated and threw the ruddy-furred wolf another slice. It too looked to be satisfied, and in the fire it laid down, much like a village dog, to warm up.

Clearly, it did not fear her. But Synna did not know if she should still fear *it*. In the light, she could see the creature clearer now. It was small, perhaps the runt of its litter, and its fur made it stand out. It was also a male. Due to its complacent nature, it had likely come from within the zoo and not from the world outside. But what had happened to the rest of its pack?

Same as the bison, no doubt, Synna thought. And these were her last thoughts of the night as sleep intruded, unannounced, and took her away.

Dreamlessly, Synna awoke to a softer, dying fire. She had only thought briefly of putting it out the night before, but fires around the perimeter of her village had kept the night things at bay.

The lizard house provided no context for daylight or nighttime, so Synna couldn't guess the time. But she was surprised to see that her wolf companion had sidled up closer to her during sleep. It was still unconscious, but it appeared to be content in its slumber.

Guess that answers the question of whether or not it would eat me, Synna thought. But of course it wouldn't have; on a deeper level, Synna knew this.

There was enough light through the clouds to indicate the presence of day or morning, and Synna felt rested enough to press on. The air had gotten colder, the snow harder, and the winds angrier, which was not a good sign. How long had it been since a blizzard, a real blizzard? There were snows one survived and snows from which no amount of makeshift shelter could spare you.

The zoo kitchen continued to provide for her, this time with an insulated and lightweight box that would be perfect for transporting the rest of the bison meat. She found, in a storage closet, some cord for tying down large objects for transport. She ran a bit of the flexible rope through the loops of the box, and with a little creativity, made it possible to transport it on her back.

Carrion was little concern in the wilds, but Synna worried over leaving a fresh kill out overnight. Fortunately, she found the bison wholly intact and steeled herself to cut off as much usable meat as possible for transport. In the animal, she found other uses: skin and fur that could provide better isolation (after some tanning out of course), and fat for a fire. The bones wouldn't budge without a sharper instrument, so reluctantly Synna decided to leave those be as she carved and sawed and made a bloody mess on herself.

Footfalls alerted her to an approaching animal, and she held the bloody knife out as a first warning. But when she turned, all she found the wolf behind the enclosed glass. Its tail wagged, and it looked to be in high spirits, and she wondered if the beast was more like a dog after all.

"Hungry again?" Synna asked, smiling. She threw her new friend a slab of meat and then went on hoisting herself over the pen. There were old folk's tales of raw meat turning canines feral, but Synna figured she knew enough of the natural world that this was nothing more than superstition.

The city was where she needed to go now, especially before the sky broke, and the city is where she headed. However, as she followed the signs toward the exit, she noticed she was being followed by the enthusiastic, red wolf.

She rolled her eyes. *Great.*

She feared this would happen. But then, she thought, perhaps this circumstance was more auspicious than troublesome. In the wilderness, what better ally than a creature for whom tundra was habitat? And certainly, there was enough meat inside the cooler to sustain both of them for at least a week, if not two.

Synna leaned over the wolf, who responded by reclining on its haunches, looking up at her, wondering why she had stopped them.

"If you're going to come along," she said. "You'll need a name." She narrowed her stare, too mentally fatigued to come up with a better name than the obvious. "Red," she said, and the wolf perked its ears up, which she took for a good sign.

The city appeared no closer than before Synna had entered the zoo, and there was at least a good mile of frozen marshland between. Fortunately, it hadn't gotten any colder, and Synna felt more emboldened now with a companion. The road wasn't so lonely anymore.

Red was content to do as he pleased, sniffing hovels and digging up patches of dirt between the frost. But whenever he got a certain distance away, the wolf would notice the gap and quickly catch up. This amused her, and the last few days were bereft of amusement. She never had a pet of her own—to own an animal that didn't produce food was a luxury back home—but she imagined this was something just as good.

A half hour into their walk, Synna stopped when she noticed Red had halted abruptly. She blinked and stepped forward, only to be growled at.

"What?" She said, dismayed. "What do you want?" There was nothing around, no animals or stimuli, to agitate him.

Then, she noticed the unusual change in the ice, and pressing her toe down on a telltale spot, she found that she was but a foot away from falling into a half-frozen brook. The snow had successfully concealed most of it, blending the little river into the landscape. Synna judged it probably wasn't deep, but getting wet in this weather was a death sentence and an excruciatingly painful way to go.

"Thank you," Synna said, and reached into the cooler on her back to tear off a piece of meat as a reward.

Getting her bearings, Synna saw a broken highway in the distance and decided it would be the clearest way into the town. The only issue was the river, which would require circumnavigation or a bridge. She surveyed the landscape and followed downstream, hoping for a break or a footbridge.

A half hour passed, and the river kept going. Synna gritted teeth, frustrated and afraid. The snow had begun to pick up, and the sky looked mean. If she didn't reach the city before nightfall, shelter needed to be found and quick. Fortunately, though the river had no end in sight, it was starting to thin. Synna let Red take a drink from the cold water and was envious of his fur. They moved on.

A shape in the water, and it resembled another carcass of an exotic animal from back in the zoo. Only, as Synna got a closer look, she noticed it was a machine. An overturned vehicle—but a vehicle from after the blackout. An off-road terrain thing from one of the more technologically advanced communes out west, perhaps. Synna had no idea what it was doing here, but she took note of the deep, twisted gashes in the side of the vehicle. A lump formed in her throat, and she looked over at Red. She didn't want to meet whatever had caused this accident. Saying a prayer, she used the overturned backside of the machine as a bridge to the other side.

Darkness came swiftly, and the snow showed no signs of abetting. Synna took caution and sought out refuge in the highway's overpass, rather than chance trying to take the road into the town. There was no telling who else would be on that road. Out in the wildlands, people did whatever they had to survive, and worse, some did whatever they pleased to whomever they wanted.

But Synna felt more confident with Red at her side, and when they reached a dry spot below the dark, she found the wolf had gotten quite friendly with her, brushing up against her leg, almost as a sign of assurance. She took a risk and scratched him behind the ears and found the wolf, or at least this one anyway, really wasn't so far removed from its dog descendants.

Icicles hung from either edge of the highway overpass, but the interior was free of any dangers from above—that Synna could identify at least. Faded graffiti remained on the wall, esoteric and lost names in giant swoops and harsh swirls. Since their creation, vandalism had become hieroglyphs.

Synna ran her finger along the painted wall, and, somewhere behind her, Red groaned, weary with exhaustion.

Synna sighed. "I know how you feel."

She managed to build a fire pit, and with some woody detritus and paper refuse coated in bison fat, built a modest campfire. Pleased with her capabilities, Synna sat down in the twilight of the flame and studied the concrete wall. In the light, the pictures became mobile. They depicted a shining and advanced city with enormous machinery, but its citizens clashed with an army from the opposite side of the wall. From the fires of war, a swarm of machines clouded the sky. And in the next scene, the city was covered in snow, and only the machines remained.

Synna and Red ate together, and it reminded her of home, back in the village, before the cruel and scavenging caravan. She wondered how she would be received by the next commune when she pledged asylum; this night-skinned girl and the wolf. She knew her quick tongue would save her, it always had.

Before sleep came on, Synna was jolted awake by a noise she could not at first identify. Red was already on his haunches, growling at the edge of the fire, leering into the dark.

She didn't need to ask out loud if something was out there. She knew, but not knowing what it was absolutely frightened her. She begged her heart to slow, and the numb cold was replaced with perspiration. She wondered if she should snuff out the fire, but no, whatever it was out there had clearly seen her, and placing herself in the dark would only put her at a disadvantage.

Shapes moved, and, then, they moved faster. At first, Synna, stupidly and for no reason, was grateful they were just animals. The ragged, wild things sprung into the light. Wild dogs, a roaming pack, hungry and riddled with mange.

Of course, they had probably smelled the meat.

Synna counted five of their rank before Red jumped in first, teeth clamping down throat. Then, the other ones sprang for her. Synna took the snap of a second to reach into the fire pit and withdraw a brand, which she swung in a vicious sweep at the wild animals.

Sparks flung, and the dogs scurried away from the fire. But a larger, bolder one snapped its jaws, too close. Synna swung and slammed the torch into the creature, which whined with pain and retreated.

Red was bigger than them, but he was outnumbered, and Synna watched him clawing on his back as the two dogs overwhelmed him. She knew she was risking injury, but she dove into the fray, her scream echoing off the concrete, as she drove the fire into the battle. That was enough for the dogs. This meal wasn't worth it, and the dark of the night took them back.

Synna, her sweat turning chill, threw the brand back into the pit and collapsed onto her knees, joining Red in his desperate panting.

"Are you okay?"

No wounds that she could see, but he had torn the throat off the dog.

Though it turned her stomach, her first thought was, *Good, more meat.* But she would leave this one for Red; it meant one less helping of bison to give away.

Morning was barely distinguishable from night. Synna had hoped the snow would have lessened. It didn't. The only thing she could do was take the dried-out bison skin and apply it to a layer beneath her parka. It seemed to help.

Though the highway was clear, the horizon was not, and it looked like she and Red would be walking into a solid, featureless void. Every footstep was a trudge, the snow almost up to her knees. Red didn't look like he minded: he was still full and happy.

"We need to find an enclosure," she said to him. "A real one. There's a blizzard coming."

So they pushed on, the only two colors in a sea of endless white.

Several hours of ice and walking, Synna felt like she was about to collapse. Without the bison skin, she would have, and even Red was lethargic.

Shadows towered as they got off the ramp into the city proper, but Synna could not make out the buildings. Not that it mattered. There was nobody here. The city was dead, vacant, everyone fled long ago. It was as she had feared.

The only thing to do now was find an open building and take shelter within.

It couldn't come soon enough. Even with the added layer, Synna felt the cold biting into her hands, and the wind sliced her face with every step forward.

They rounded a corner, and Synna tried to make out the shapes emerging from the white. Of course, all the shapes here were alien, an assortment of metal objects that bore no significance or meaning. But there was *something*—a few somethings by her count—lying in the middle of the buried street. She assumed it was machinery or wreckage, but then she saw the frozen face, the permanent stare.

People. And the maroon snow, blood. These people had been attacked, and it had come quickly. Synna looked side to side and saw disruptions, massive divots in the fresher snowfall. This had been recent. It had probably been a caravan that was assaulted.

And she didn't have to guess what had done it. Blue sparks sputtered from the snow mound, and Synna jumped back. But the thing in the mound was dead—she knew enough of death by now to tell right away. The nomads must have struck at least one successful blow before succumbing to the onslaught.

Half buried, and some of it scattered around its frame, the mechanoid looked like a gelatinous lizard, its skin thousands of translucent cell-like machines. Synna didn't have the proper names to describe it, but she knew enough.

This was one of the night things.

"We're turning around," she said to Red through chattering teeth. But the wolf was already at attention, growling at invisible enemies.

"Come on," Synna yelled, moving away from him to drive home her directive. "We need to go."

But the wolf persisted, and as Synna, angry and exhausted and cold, went to retrieve her companion, she saw the reason for his threats.

A fury of blue electricity, a crackle in the air. A haunting glow returned to the eyes of the mechanoid. It creaked and shook and pushed itself upward, at least eight feet tall.

It hadn't been killed. It had only gone into stasis.

Synna blanched and tried to tell Red to run, but it came out as a jumbled scream. There was no fighting this. She made a split-second decision and abandoned her case of provisions in the snow, pushing herself forward and hoping Red would follow. But in the back of her mind, she knew there was little point—there was no hope in outrunning these things.

Her legs gave out, and Synna fell. She knew better than to lie there—there were rumors that these things saw via heat, and some survivors of the night things had avoided death by concealing themselves in snow or water. She heard the unearthly crackle and hiss, but it was still several feet behind. The thing had been injured, but these things didn't stop.

Synna turned her head and saw Red circling around the mechanoid. He was vicious and regal, and each time the machine threw down its mantis-like claws, sharper than anything, the wolf swiftly avoided it.

And then, in a blink, the wolf jumped and sunk its jaws into one of the machine's fleshy parts, its chest cavity, already exposed from the caravan's blow—a pulse gun probably, if Synna knew her artillery well enough.

"No, Red, don't!" She screamed, but there was no deterring him. He had, after all, provided her with all the defense she'd needed so far. What else could she expect?

But there was nothing she could do to protect *him*, and that killed her.

Wire nervous system and neon blue fluid spouted from the night thing's chest wound, and it bled electricity into the air, melting the snow before it even touched earth.

Was it possible? Could he fell it? Synna knelt in the snow and watched, forgetting to breathe.

The creature stumbled back, and its oculars blinked in and out of its head. It was going. Thank God or whoever, it was dying.

And with one, trembling arm, it threw its hand out and struck Red. One short yelp, and the wolf flew through the air, his landing muffled by the clamor of metal thundering to earth.

Traces of sparks remained. The machine smoked. It was dead, surely dead now, but Synna couldn't move herself to care. She sprang forward, beyond the night thing, beyond the corpses of the fallen, and threw herself at Red's side.

When she pulled her hand back, there was blood. She saw the wound in his side, and it wasn't at all a scratch to simply brush off.

"No. Please. No."

Synna panicked, the first time since abandonment, and even dogs, and frozen rivers, and night things hadn't pushed her to this point yet. She saw Red's eyes, looking ahead, steadfast. But his body shook, and he wined, kept whining.

Synna pulled and ripped a patch of the bison fur out if her sleeve and pressed it to the wound. It was barely a bandage, but she had nothing else to offer.

As if to mock them, the snow fell harder, and the wind raged. Synna had no choice but to move, but she couldn't bring herself more than a few steps before she stopped. She couldn't leave him. She just couldn't. Not after what he had done for her.

She abandoned the vessel and its meat—part of her knew it wouldn't matter much now anyway. But she kept the lid and the cords, fashioning a sled.

Synna buried her face into Red's fur and slid her hands beneath his body. "I'm sorry."

The wolf yelped, in impossible pain, as Synna transferred him to the sled. She knew she would have to move slow, slower than she'd want, to keep him from falling off.

He wasn't the lightest either, and Synna could feel her strength fleeing her by the second, stolen by the wind. Still, she pushed forward. She needed to see what was on the other side of the city. Even if she didn't make it. She needed to know.

It was beyond the point of a blizzard when Synna pulled Red across the last part of the bridge. She couldn't even tell what was below, the snow reducing her vision to near blindness. Maybe nothing existed at all. Maybe this snow would finally do what the other snows hadn't; erase the world entire.

At several points, sleep tempted Synna. *Just two seconds,* it promised her. And she bargained. But each time she found her body give out or her eyes hunger for sleep, she leaned over and placed her hands on Red's neck. Still a pulse. But each time, the distance between heartbeats grew greater.

"Just hold on," Synna said, but she didn't know for what...

At some point, Synna realized they had gone past the bridge. So that was it. Nothing. Just more white. Only more winter. But she kept going. She asked herself, what's the point? But life was the point. It was defiance against all of this, this nothingness. The longer she remained alive, she thought, the more she hurt the cold and the snows, rendering them impotent.

Only when she checked Red's pulse and found none did she allow herself to collapse then and there.

Through the white, her vision blurred, and unconsciousness toyed with her. Her only thought was that her body hadn't enough energy to shed tears for the companion that had saved her, for no reason, other than she had done him one act of kindness.

In the crystalline abyss, she thought she saw blue lights in the distance. Of course, she couldn't trust anything now. She was still conscious enough to recognize this. But there *were* lights. If not the glow of more night things ready to finish winter's job, then perhaps this was just what dying was like. Maybe there was something more after all—Synna supposed that was the only thing she could hope for now. But there *were* lights. And they were coming closer.

A white place. But not the harsh white of snow. No, something was different now. This light was softer, warmer.

So she had been right after all. There was a life beyond.

There were voices, too.

"Hey. Hey. Can you hear me? Miss?"

Emissaries of the next world.

Wet. But not *cold* wet. Warm, soothing. And it smelled good, too, like flowers, with the undercurrent of sweet chemicals. Synna felt water all around her, and though her first instinct was to bolt up in shock, her body just didn't have the energy for it.

A beeping. Electricity. No, this was not death. Then, what was it?

Faces, three, and all of them a different shade of skin.

"Miss, can you understand us?"

"Crim, you think she even speaks our language?"

The film over her eyes cleared, and Synna could make out the features of the people looking down at her in the bath.

She closed her eyes briefly and fought off sleep. "I can hear you." It came out slow, but it did come out.

The strangers introduced themselves. The first one, Crim, was a man, though not many years older than her. His hair was shaggy, brassy, and he looked as if he hadn't shaved. His amber eyes were kind. Next to him was an older man, Laz. He had skin like her own, and big, owl-like glasses.

She had never seen someone like the woman, Sophia, before; with hair like jet, straight, and eyes like the petals of a flower. It was her smile that told Synna this was not Heaven.

But this was salvation.

"I'm alive," Synna mumbled, trying to sit up.

Crim supported her head. "I certainly hope that's the case. Now, bear with me...this might hurt."

Synna looked over at him. "What? Oh!"

She hadn't seen the needle, but it was over and done with before she could protest.

The older gentleman nodded. "Nutrient injection. This will have you up and running. Mind the niacin flush now; it can be a bit of a trip."

Synna's head swam for a moment before she was overtaken by a burst of energy. The fatigue subsided, and she was suddenly and keenly away of her surroundings.

The innards of a humming, sterile tunnel, like the old buildings that had survived after the blackout. Only from the subtle vibration of the room, this one was mobile. She had never seen a place like this before. It was...new. How was that possible?

"We're moving?" Synna asked, finding her footing. They had put her in a material that covered only those parts of herself she wouldn't want strangers seeing. This half-dress was quickly remedied by Sophia handing her a robe. Somehow, Synna was already dry—the liquid she had been submerged inside did not linger on the skin.

The robe was the softest and warmest thing Synna had ever felt against her skin, aside from Red perhaps. The woman took her by the hand and guided her down from the raised tank.

"What is your name?" she asked.

"Synna." How long had it been since she had to introduce herself to someone new?

"I imagine this is all quite a shock to you, Synna, so we'd rather let you ask the questions before we bombard you with those of our own."

It had been years since Synna had heard such a genuine and diplomatic remark. But she tripped over her own tongue, still refusing to believe this wasn't a death dream in the snow. That needle prick, however, told her that this world was very much real.

Sophia led her to a port hole, and Synna peered out into the world outside. Wherever they were, the snow had ceased. And there was far less of it on the ground. In the distance, Synna saw mountains. They were green.

She put her hand to her lips. "Where is this place?"

Crim came up behind them, a clipboard in his hands. "About two hours south of where we found you. You don't know how lucky you are to be alive."

"I think I very well *do* know," Synna challenged. She had found her sharp tongue, but she smiled at Crim just the same to let him know all was well. "This is a machine?"

"A vessel that houses fifty of our crew at least," Sophia said. "We call it The Whale."

Fifty? Synna's jaw dropped. "You mean, there's a whole commune on here?"

Crim and Sophia exchanged knowing, mischievous glances.

"Synna," Crim said, "this is less than 1% of our city."

Impossible. Then again, Synna thought to herself, what did she know of the lands beyond the village? There was no history, no sense of location. The world was vast and unknowable.

Laz brought over a tray with a single plate and a glass of liquid that wasn't water. On the plate, a green, pulpy cake sat, looking rather unappetizing. And yet, Synna felt compelled to eat just about anything at this point.

"It's not the most visually appealing," Laz admitted. "But give it a try."

Synna did as told. And though she was not at all fond of the texture of the morsel, it had a salty sweetness that filled her up. The liquid was more airy than watery, and had a fruity undercurrent. In a moment, she felt entirely refreshed.

This was technology beyond any she had ever known.

Sophia took Synna to a small room with a bed and desk and had her sit down on the foam box. Synna pressed her fingers into the mattress and watched as the bedding contoured to her hand.

Sophia told Synna about the "The Whale," the nickname of this transport vessel, which had a much longer and forgettable name. It was a scientific research vessel that monitored the lands outside of Sophia's city, which was just as foreign and alien as this place was to Synna. Where Sophia, Crim, and Laz were from, humans from several smaller communes had managed to come together to create a stable, walled city. They had technology to keep out the night things and were currently investigating how to reverse the weather. In these lands, winter was extant, though not as harsh.

"We have yet to come up with a solution to it all," Sophia said, and there was sadness in her eyes. "Maybe there isn't one at all. But we're trying. We also try to come out into the outer lands to see if there are any people in need of rescue. Caravans mostly."

Synna nodded. "I was part of one."

"So we had thought." Sophia averted her gaze, and Synna sensed she was uncomfortable.

"What is it?"

"The Whale came across the...oh, how should I put this...the remains of a caravan that we believed had come out of the valley, not too far from the ruins of the old zoo. They had all been killed. We think the same swarm killed off a smaller, unrelated party traveling through the city close to the bridge."

Synna lowered her head. She had to be talking about the caravan that had given Synna up for dead. The irony wasn't lost on her. But she had no reason to mourn them.

All she wanted to know was, "What happens next?"

Sophia shrugged. "You're a refugee and we haven't maxed out our quotas yet. We're going to debrief you some more, make sure your health is in order, then take you back to the city." She thought for a moment. "Would you like that? Not everyone from your part of the world feels comfortable with this sometimes."

Synna didn't hesitate. "Please." She said. Of course, her mind could not begin to fathom what would happen next. Only a few hours prior, she assumed there was no future left for her. The world had opened itself up to her, and she had seen beyond winter. The future itself overwhelmed her. And yet, she wasn't afraid.

Sophia, assuming that the girl needed some alone time to adjust, got up from the desk chair to leave, when Synna suddenly stood.

"Wait. Where is he?"

Sophia blinked. "Hm? Were you traveling with someone else?"

"She probably means the wolf," Crim said, leaning against the doorway.

Sophia threw him a glare. "It's so like you to eavesdrop."

But Synna didn't have time for these squabbles. "Please. I need to know."

Crim sighed. "Unfortunately, he didn't make it. You were curled up next to him, on top of what appeared to be a rather slapdash sled of a sort. I put two and two together and figured you had somehow managed to domesticate him. Not entirely unheard—" He abruptly stopped mid-sentence, stared at her, and shook his head. "My God. The stories you must have to tell."

But he still hadn't answered her question. "Where is he?" Synna asked again, more insistent.

Crim looked over at Sophia, and they both wore sadness openly. The woman nodded, placing a hand on the gentleman's shoulder as she left the room and allowed him to carry out the rest of his duties.

"Follow me."

Crim led Synna out into a corridor, and the girl gaped at the men and women who passed by, as she was still in shock of it all. She didn't even notice that the vessel had stopped.

A door slid open for them, and Crim and Synna stood in a white room with a single table. There was something on the table covered in a white sheet, and Synna had a good idea of what was underneath it.

"We're scientists," Crim told her. "So when we come across deceased animals, we..." but he shook his head. "Never mind that. I just knew, sort of had a sense, that this wolf was special to you. I convinced the others to let you decide what to do with the body."

Synna looked at Crim and then approached the table. For a moment, she thought of lifting up the sheet, but she knew the animal she owed her life to would not really be there, just his shell. There was a tradition in her village. When someone passed on, a grave was dug and a tree planted on top of it, the body fertilizing a new life to watch over the living. She told Crim this.

"We have no saplings," Crim said regrettably. Then, a thought occurred to him, and he smiled. "But we do have seeds."

The air was clearer here on the green hill, and though snow persisted on the slopes below, there was no denying that the grassy oasis was the closest Synna had been to the warmer times.

They had stopped The Whale to survey the warmer climate, and the teams were out below, snaking through the trees. Synna could hear them talking, laughing, and not one conversation dripped with desperation or concern. It was the most astounding thing.

And the birds too. Their song was a music she hadn't heard since she was a child.

Crim and she dug the grave, and when it was just right, the man lowered the remains of Red, wrapped in the white sheet, into the earth, which he covered with soil.

When it was all done, Crim wiped his brow and asked Synna if she wanted to say a prayer.

Truthfully, Synna knew no real prayers, other than improvised appeals to some greater will. And if that will had gotten her this far, or sent Red to her as a means of intercession, then she supposed she thanked whoever was responsible.

Prayers were all well and good, but they were also entirely too long-winded.

So instead, she said, "Thank you," and patted the earth with her hand.

In this soil, Synna placed a gelatinous sphere with a cherry tree seed at its core. Synna had selected this seed from a picture of trees that

Crim had shown her on his electronic screen. When Synna saw what a cherry tree looked like in full blossom, all dappled pinks, she was afraid for a moment that she really was dreaming. That things could exist out in the world, a world she had still seen so little of. This tree she planted, in the hopes it would honor her friend's memory the best.

That cherry tree remains there to this day, in a much greener, warmer world.

DYLAN DIPRIMA
LIFE RIVER

I'm walking by, still walking past
Trying not to draw him near
Looking down I'm looking past
Holding in the fear

He tracks me through the falling ice
No tree nor bush can break
His gaze upon me holds its mark
Enough to make me quake

He's somber though his eyes still pierce
My soul inside does shiver
He looks inside me proving that
We swim the same life river

VARZEN DRALMORT
MATRIARCHAL COMPLICATIONS

Varzen Dralmort revels in the realm of creation, seeking to build for the wistful spirit a literal dream house. Sometimes, he'll add a doggy door for animals that can take themselves out, or simply leave a set of keys for the thumbs n' bipeds crowd. His creative endeavors work to extol the earnest human spirit, and in this case our fuzzy wolf buddies as well.

May we pad their luxurious coiffures.

Varzen posts the odd story on his SoFurry account, https://varzen.sofurry.com/, and has published novels Gratitude *and* Attitude *through Rabbit Valley Comics.*

Christmas is the time for family, no matter how much they hate you.

Va'a'ou'ra "Vowel" Cairnsblood-Custer adjusted her feral-skin loincloth and velour Santa Claus pom-pom hat as she reclined in a lawn chair and ottoman made of bone, aluminum, and chiffon. She lounged on the distant outskirts of a series of plastic and glass huts that hung like wind chimes from a titanium spider-web slung across poles and open sky, frowning at a corded phone handset while in the distance, a surface-to-air freight train groaned with immense nuclear torque. Out here, beyond her suspended tribe-village, the wolfess enjoyed the cool hush of the night: a breeze tickled the grass and pushed waves through her tungsten-copper fur. Out there, beyond her obsidian black footclaws, her village, and a line of trees sparkling with the red and green lights of festively-modified police skiffs escorting the train, lay the bustling archipelago city of Copernica.

Colored stringed lights and twinkling garlands gilded the hanging village of Ayra: it was Christmas in the half-Copernicized settlement, and families made merry in a climate expecting snow, though none yet had appeared. The married woman sat away from all the hubbub, her free ear twitching at a distant radio tinkling out some seasonal tunes as she watched fat wolf-husky cub out of the corner of her eye. She fiddled with her phone, though on occasion the wolf would glance up at the sky for the slight likelihood she'd spot a corporate freighter branded Custer NucleoMagnetics, a company founded by the cub's father. Christmas was a time for family, but Vowel found herself deficient.

One light on the phone's switchboard kept pulsing while others flickered in and out; the jilted husky Typhus was on another dramatic-yet-all-so-evanescent warpath, flinging his insecurities like spears at every member of their private hobbyist group, the Grand Old Foxhunters. All the lonely single people, and her, were on the G.O.F. chat line today.

Typhus berated a Copernican councilman for his stilted performance during a drunken one-night stand, and then castigated an amputee three-war battleship sniper for his disinclination toward med-bay roleplay. Inevitably, the conference turned against him, and so he threw himself to the pity of a fire marshal whose marriage he'd broken up in a five-way tryst. Repudiated in a wash of annoyed groans, Typhus attempted a tone-deaf rendition of "Santa Baby," appealing to their sense of cuteness with a lisping puppy voice. Vowel's fur spiked as the young adult husky warbled with infantile affectations: Typhus Cochran Custer, only nine years her inferior, was her step-son.

Vowel muted the phone before she cleared her throat, then idly checked her breaststrap with her free paw. It strained from her breasts' status; asymmetrical wet spots indicated her nipples. The wolf's ear craned as her infant, Ra'ara "Aruru," yawped and howled as he bounced through the faded green grass. A yawn snuck up on her, and Vowel stretched. Her elbow knocked her scoped mag-lancer from its perch on her armrest, but with a swift jerk she ably caught it with a claw down its barrel and brought it back to a leaning position. She set it right next to her fox-hunting bollista, a non-lethal bola launcher.

Typhus got a second wind and was off again, his diatribe rapid and staccato like a machine gun. Vowel heard an abrupt click and looked down at the switchboard: Vachelon Eddies, their star fox of the foxhunt group, had hung up. This was quite the pity, as that drag-queen bastard could run faster than a cheetah. Vowel grasped the phone harder, drawing a slow breath through gritted teeth.

"Typhus, dear, I'm sure that deep down, those wall-building turbo-fascists truly want to accept a man who self-identifies as an impoverished third-world nation *and* the imperialists that destabilized it," she said, quoting one of his rants, "but when's our next foxhunt? You just estranged our best one."

She knew she was tossing sparks at a dry Christmas tree just by speaking, but someone had to topple the tyrant. The wolf felt a pressure on her arm, and she smiled as her cub ran a toy battlecruiser up and down a tract of fur. She pet his massive coif of wolf-husky head-fluff as pew-pew noises from his mouth flecked spittle on her. The hanging village of Ayra swung languorously before her in a wind scented of cinnamon and cloves: outside this phone call, things were wonderful. There went the Lang'Ou'Ren Pack, forty-strong, hauling racks of pigs, deer, and gryphons to roast over spits. She was invited over; she pondered attending. Vowel didn't mind being alone; she told herself this on several occasions.

Above, the train's engines thrummed as they pulled its cargo to the city. Vowel pondered its police escort.

Typhus prepared a Christmas speech for his step-mother. "Was that grunts and clicks I just heard? You better shut your trap, you ooga-booga animal-sacrificing savage! Why don't you suck a smallpox blanket while legal citizens are talking?"

Aruru snarled. Vowel petted his muzzle, bearing his playful bites at her fingers. It was amusing, really, all Typhus's impotent rage: he had the heart of a Liberad and the mouth of a supremacist, the beautiful hypocrite. A digital dogpile flooded the chat, everyone taking up the torch on her aggrieved behalf. Vowel smiled, though deep down felt an echo of pain: she pictured a bullet ricocheting off a copper tank and the dent it left behind.

Her rifles clattered over, and Aruru squawked in pain. After a pregnant pause, he burst into squeals and tears. Thank goodness their safety keys were removed.

"Ru, you clumsy boy. Come here," she sighed, grabbing her cub by the nape and hauling him into her lap. The keys jingled on her loincloth's hip-strap. Whimpering, he pawed at her breasts, and so she pulled down her raiment and allowed him to nurse. She returned to the conference with a chuckle; the room went silent. They recognized her laugh.

"I'll have to tell your father that one, next time he comes over. Business is going well; he's bought the High Elder a new lug-truck. So good of him; I love him so much. Oh, before I forget," she said, baring her teeth as her infant suckled, "please stop stealing my loincloth-breaststrap sets from the drying line. They're very easy to make if you want to be a noble huskyette hunter. I thought you were into cowboys, nowadays?"

"Mom!" he barked, failing in rapid succession to hang the phone up. Laughter exploded from all parties, and Vowel was sure she was offered a steak dinner from the councilman, a used military rifle from the sniper, and a deputization from the fire marshal before she wished everyone a Merry Christmas and placed the phone back in its cradle. Aruru looked up at her with globulous eyes, chewing on her nipple.

She smiled, wincing at his razor puppy teeth. "Conflicted boy. Absent father and postpartum mother; no one to spank him. Well, not in a *corrective* manner, at least," she said, remembering all the strange men he'd slung with him, "but you wouldn't hassle mommy; would you, Ru?"

She bounced the hybrid cub on her lap; he spit up on her. Vowel's brow flattened.

"Y'know, I didn't want that back. Really; it's all yours."

The wolfess wiped herself and her infant down the best she could before she made her way through her bustling tribe village to get to the communal springs in the center. Along the way, with her stocky half-breed cub babbling and squirming under her arm, she answered the conspiratorial chuckle of other mothers with a tip of her Santa hat as they acknowledged the child's vexatious energy or the conspicuous stains on her decorous animal-skin raiment.

Upon arrival, Vowel disrobed her cub and set him, already in a dog-paddling cycle, in Ayra's clear self-reciprocating springs, its waters misting with seasonal scents of cinnamon and cloves. She dunked her soiled breaststrap in its waters and hung it up on a titanium tree strung up with gaudy crystal baubles and tinsel, then flinched to cover herself when she saw that Vachelon "Vash" Eddies was already there. The fox's wet fur clung to his tawny body, further exaggerating his skinny form. The wolf relaxed, loving the open snap of his eyes when she lowered her arms.

After his gaze lingered for a few more seconds, Vash frowned and cleared his throat.

"You married into a warzone, Vow," he said, pulling his paws through russet-copper fur. "Nervous that your intervention has further destabilized it."

Vowel slipped out of her loincloth, hung up her cap, and joined him, grooming a patch of his back he'd missed. "His brilliant father is only slowly starting to realize that his chronic absence during childhood's created a hell-powered honey badger; seems like the only love Typhus will take now is an anonymous one-night stand."

Vash murred as the wolf's claws ran down his back to his buttocks, she surveying the area with the meticulous attention of an archaeologist.

"Trust me, honey," he said, "I've scrubbed that part harder than a caked-on lasagna pan. You could eat fruitcake off it and taste no musk. So did Tasmanian Typhus ever calm down?"

Vowel smacked his rear, rewarding herself with a fey yelp from him. Her infant dog-paddled around them; she steered him away with a soft paw, keeping him in her periphery. Vash attentively tended to her abdomen, scrubbing the skin and straightening the fur, and then his paws moved upward. She caught them before they reached her chest. "Please; they're company property."

The fox finally made eye contact with her, his lower eyelids twitching to hold them upright. His sinewy body moved with the high-tension torque of a freighter's tow cables, the engine itself roaring on pheromone fuel. "Would Mr. Custer mind an intern?" he asked.

Vowel leaned in, planting a slow kiss on his cheek. "I don't think that's an option, Vash; you'd blast right past homewrecker and drag this little tribal across the Arshak Ocean."

Vash crumpled, sighing. "I need you, Vow."

"Even as a third party, Vash, I won't pull you into this warzone," she said. With a marked woof of a cough, clearing her throat and the air, Vowel told him what Typhus had said.

Vash honked, flabbergasted. His mouth hung open and his lips crumpled over his teeth like a derailed train.

An Ayra tribesman heard her, too. Vowel heard the cock of a gun and a warcry, he running toward the city shouting passages from Ayra Marital Law and Ayra Martial Edict.

"Ease up!" she shouted. "It's the holidays. The brat had too much egg nog ... and no stranger's lap to sob into. I'm the one that decides if I'm insulted! And I'm not."

The tribesman stopped, grumbling insults and holy war rituals as he trotted away.

Vash frowned and put his paw on her shoulder. He waited until she looked at him. "Vow ... you *are*. Why bother taking his blows? He's an adult ... Cochran may be coming around, girding and gilding your loins, but that doesn't indebt you to his vicious son. Typh's only nine years younger than you; he's a creep! Only reason I'd put coal in his stocking would be to ignite it."

Vowel felt a tremble in her lip and pressed her molars together, eyes growing hot. When Aruru bumped face-first into the back of her leg, she picked him up by the scruff and cradled the wolf-husky against her chest. She spoke carefully. "The boy is a gaping wound of betrayal and neglect. Someone has to care, and it might as well be his step-mother, damn it."

Vash saw the way she cradled her infant, the wolf's strong arms wrapping around the small pup like two steel trusses, never to let go. She looked up and away from him, her eyes picking the story out of the sky one hot star at a time.

"Last Christmas, the day after, he called me from Galileius. He was drunk from the night before and whimpered like someone'd stuck a knife in him. I pick him up on my jet-javelin and get a look in the door of this splintered old-West shack that had a rusted window AC unit, siding caked with years of dust, and a sad plastic snowman with obscenities scrawled all over it.

"Inside are about ten low-lifes, no pants among the best of them as they slithered around that grimy terrarium like slugs. Several televisions are on, there's discarded cans everywhere, and the image I remember worst—the nadir of that encounter—is the imprint of a thin man's shoulders *in* the deep-dish pizza on the floor in the center of the room." Vowel paused as her teeth chattered. Her voice cracked. "I peeled a slice of pepperoni off Typhus's back."

The wolfess slumped. Vash took Vowel by her arms, and his thumbs massaged her biceps. Aruru took interest with the new limbs and grabbed hold of Vash's wrist, then proceeded to monkey-walk himself down Vash's skinny arm, swinging from tuft to tuft as he traversed the space between wolfess and fox. Vash winced at every tug. Vowel watched the little imp, her mind relieving itself of that ignominious memory. Another dent in the copper tank; that was all.

"He *is* a gaping wound, Vow, and if his starved, self-consuming state was caused by a lack of food instead of emotional support, he'd have been taken from Cochran and his mother while he was in diapers."

Vow would have punched him, but there was a baby on board. Aruru clung like a sloth to the fox's tight torso, dwarfing the vulpine with his stocky wolfdog body. Vowel opened her mouth to berate him, but she stopped herself as razor-sharp puppy teeth opened up at the male's tiny, pert nipple.

The sudden jolt of pain, a death by a thousand cuts, shattered Vash's face like old plaster as the cub performed its instinctual algorithm. Vow's chest heaved as she held back laughter.

"You are a strong woman," he whined.

"I'm *a* woman," she winked.

"Yeah," he grunted, breath hissing through gritted teeth, "well, I am sometimes, and Typhus's birth mother is one 24/7. They come in a lot of flavors, honey."

When he'd had enough, which was easily the span of a mayfly's life, Vowel gently extracted the floofy lamprey from its host, its tiny jaws snapping at thin air.

An explosion rocked the city, and the spring's water thumped. A skyscraper groaned, guttering out as its steel and glass constitution shivered, dropping electric pine trees, furniture, concrete, and people as it dissolved. The spring around them shuddered, ripples slapping their legs.

"What in Ayri'ai'ra'Lai's name," she invoked, running out of the spring, out of the village. She barked at tribesmen, "What happened?" "What happened?" as klaxons and raid sirens shrieked through Copernica's streets, the decorated trees, and the surrounding villages. Vash followed his friend out of instinct, jogging behind her as she sprinted.

Vowel knocked her rifles out of the way as she leaped over her bone chair. Aruru stuck tight against her and whimpered. She picked up the phone handset and stabbed claws at its switchboard until a voice came on the line. Vowel licked her cub's head between sentences, comforting him.

"Kalo," she hushed, breathless, "what's happened?"

Sirens, police on bullhorns, and the fog-horns of armored trucks shouted themselves into distortion through the Councilman's phone. Amidst the cacophony, as some ironic joke, loudspeakers continued to croon Christmas favorites. The current song was "O, Holy Night."

"Mrs. Cochran Custer," he said, his formal voice lanced with fear. A festive brass band blared on the radio behind him. "This is not a matter for Ayrads. I can't hold myself responsible for imperiling a friend-village. We have it under control. See you next foxhunt; have a lovely holiday." Something roared behind him. Sound blasted so coarsely through the receiver that the bulb swelled to a bright white and exploded. The line went dead.

Vash had disappeared and returned. He'd not bothered to dry or clothe himself ... neither had she. Sunken sockets cast shadows over his eyes. The fox held his handset out to her, where amidst the same chaos she heard familiar yelps and screams.

"Vashie, help! Get your draggy ass down here; help! Nobody's shooting at it! It's just pacing around, it's huge! I'm stuck in the center; my boyfriend's dead. Leg ripped off and swallowed ... We were doing a public thing near Perineum and I'm stuck up here ... it's got five eyes, and ugly red fur and uh smells like sulphur; shit; it's as big as a horse...nobody's shooting at it!" he screeched.

The fox slammed the handset down.

"You're not going," he said.

Heat flashed through Vowel's head; she thought about wrapping the phone cord around Vash's neck. Aruru scratched at her, looking up. She covered her bared teeth enough to lick his snout.

"Then why did you bring the phone out?"

"It'd be worse to hide it from you. Now you can make an informed decision."

Vowel blustered, snarled, and paced erratically. "Do you know why they're not shooting?" she demanded.

Vash's paw had not left the phone. In fact, his knuckles strained under his pelt, and the handset rattled against the hooks. She continued.

"And on Ayri'ai'ra'Lai's green planet, what creature has *five* eyes and smells like Brimstone?"

Vash whimpered, his voice soft and eyes shiny. "We're safe out here, Vow. Let's have dinner with the Lang'Ou'Rens, a gay and decadent Christmas feast," he implored, paw timidly reaching into the space between them, "we'll stuff our bellies to bursting and tomorrow's foxhunt will be more of a waddle. God and Ayri both know we deserve it."

Vowel's eyes twitched. Aruru clutched closer to her, tail curled under him. She put her paw over his floofy head, and her obsidian black foot-claws sliced the grass as she stalked toward Vash.

"That five-eyed monster is a dhiscm s'aedtawn. If it dies in pain, it explodes in tatter-spores, the radius huge and the coverage thick. Much like blizzards from your home planet. Hate sickle-cell? Try caltrops tumbling through your veins. Special snowflakes to cut you open."

"All the more reason to stay here!" he argued, holding up his switchboard like a shield, "Why give that city a second look; they should be boiled in their own primordial pudding, and I'll drive a stake of Ayrad holly through their heart! They barely recognize your legal status, the mayor had to be *sued* to stamp your boy's birth certificate, and they pay Ayra half a dime for steaks and pelts they sell for thousands!"

"Oh, so now it's the *city*, Vash?" she asked. The wolf leaned in on him so that their noses nearly touched. "No wonder you're the runner in our foxhunt group. You're a coward."

Vash reeled, sincerely hurt. He faced her with wet eyes. "Cowardice be damned, Vow. You go there, I lose you. Maybe some punk civilian's already shot it and made hundreds sick."

Vowel pointed down at his phone. "Ty's light is still going. So *I'm* going."

"You're not being fair!"

Aruru squawked between them, pawing and play-snarling at the fox. Vow cleared her throat, then broke the stand-off. She walked back to her chair where her bollista and mag-lancer leaned, watching the zig-zag cityscape as explosions and sirens roiled against cables of gay colored lights and secreted pockets of titanium mistletoe. She set Aruru down, then motioned over to a tribeswoman as she disassembled her guns. The keys were on her loincloth by the springs; she'd retrieve them later. Maybe.

She had a crazy idea in her head.

Vowel plunged into a swift frenzy of claws and machine parts. She set them around her infant and, when he would repeatedly try to reach out and taste one, she would intercept his paw and boop his nose with her finger, getting a yawp from him. The other tribeswoman reached out for the child, as per Vowel's motions, but the cub latched onto the chair and growled as soon as she tried to move him away.

With a twist of her wrists, Vowel pulled the wooden butt-stock off the mag-lancer and held it before Aruru, who clamped onto it with his jaws and started chomping away at the polished surface. It hurt her to see the fine weapon damaged so viciously, but the slobber and growls that came from the cub were more than enough compensation. Merry Christmas; she'd hunt herself another mahoghast tree. They didn't move too fast.

Her cub was easily removed, and Vowel whispered her thanks.

Vash leaned over her, careful in placing his paw on her shoulder. He wouldn't disturb a wolf before her work ... nor dare vex the already vexed.

"Are ... the bola cables rated for a ... d'hism? Can't Copernica Riot just tranquilize it?"

"*Dish-um*, and no; the creature goes into a drunk rage and has a habit of killing itself." she said, exposing a goldenrod coil of glimmering wires, the fur on her torso rising toward it. "I just use tow cables from a lug-truck. I'm not worried."

The fox gasped. "By Ayri, that's why I can never get out."

Vow bumped him with the mag-lancer's receiver, then broke its lower jaw and united it with the bollista's staging bay. She winked. "Not sure if it's the cables or the knowledge of your captor, but when *I* get the capture, you're posed like a submissive dog."

Vash blushed, his paw recoiling from her shoulder so he could bashfully rub his own. "You're so ... strong and relentless."

"You inscrutable cur."

With a loud snap, she brought the vented bollista muzzle—more of a duct than a barrel—down on the modified port, then slammed that contraption onto the butt-stock and power core with the clap of a gunshot. She took an unused firing pin and picked the safety lock, then pulled the cylinder out and tossed it. The weapon started right up.

In the wolfess's sizeable paws thrust a gun that reached from the ground to her lips, its electric veins glowing a sensuous blue. The buzzing obelisk rewarded its creator's ears with the sonorous rumble of a beast, quaking with power between her paws, summoning within her a vigorous hunger that wet her fangs.

Vowel grabbed Vash by the scruff of his chest and kissed him on the lips, then threw him to the ground. The forlorn fox yelped as he fell, his thin body sprawling on its side. As the tall, stalwart wolf streaked off into the night, her fur flying and her muscles throwing her toward a city in chaos, Vachelon could not help but reach into space for her, his tawny hand picking up moon beams along its prickly, furry edges. "Of a Christmas yet to come," he whispered.

Vowel snagged her clothes from the springs and arrested her body in a loping jog, tying herself back into a state of propriety in a ballet assisted by the robust, rigid weight of her giant anti-dhiscm contraption. She plunged into a wide garage hidden in Ayra's hills and slammed the door. There was the light banging of a wrench, a skillful paw maneuvering tubes, and finally a queer silence.

A pyroclastic burst shivered the landscape, the eruption spewing thick ropes of light over its rolling contours as a long, high howl accompanied a wolf reborn, screaming in a victorious arc toward the city.

Vowel held fast to a jet-javelin made of gryphon bone, aluminum, and chaise upholstery. She cleared the tree-line, wind shrieking in her ears, a thousand brisk scents tickling her snout, and stalled out in thin air. Here, high above the humble skyline of dotted archipelago towns sparkling in festive colors of red, silver, and green, Vowel drew in a deep breath: distant skyscrapers, birds, and the collective breathlessness of gods looking down at Earth's splendor met her gaze. The wolf woman bared her teeth at the chaos below her and plunged her craft toward Copernica on shafts of lightning.

The city flashed by her, skyscrapers with purple-chrome tessellated windows shimmering like gills. Behind her screeched the protest of additional sirens: she shot past cop cordons, soared over blockades, and wove in and out of increasingly thick traffic gridlocks. Post-it note infractions piled up on her steel brain and molted in a torrential shower.

Vowel found the city square and threw the vehicle upright, firing the retro-rockets and pinning her body to the seat, shattering a nearby window. Normally a vehicle she'd use to stalk vector-gryphons, the craft deployed its tree-brackets and latched onto a building bordering the trapped creature. She left the vehicle perched a couple stories up as she hopped down to the edge of the fracas, shredding through a band of frilly, colored streamers proclaiming the joyous season.

A riot guard lunged at her, and Vowel shot him with a quarter-pull of the trigger. Steel cables wrapped around an armored rhino, and he rolled away in a neat package. A more diplomatic guard replaced him, although a score of laser beads collected on her body like twitching, moving measles. She remained crouched like a gargoyle on the high riot fence, her loincloth's flap tickling her ankles.

"By the switchboard catalogue of deities, Mrs. Cochran Custer," the otter said, shaking his head, "You've summoned up almost as much police chatter as that dizzum. Good day to die hard, am I right? You've got twenty mag-lance snipers and three live news channels looking at your brass ovaries right now: want to tell me the big idea?"

She held up the mammoth hybrid rifle with one arm and indicated the otter's bound compatriot with the other. The guard looked back and forth a few times, then his face drew grim. Red and green police lights alternated on his fuzzy countenance.

"We've evacuated thousands from the area, but the traffic situation's got thousands more cramped inside these buildings. Not sure if the ventilation will hold against tatter-spores."

"I'm only here for Typhus."

The otter snorted.

"Save the cowboy, save the city, Ms. Custer. He's up on the monolith," he said, tossing a paw to the square.

This was their dire situation: they'd contained the beast. The wrecked train served as half the perimeter, having plowed through two tall buildings and sealing off half the block. Its ugly detritus and the rubble of buildings remained a grim sign of the lives already lost. Vowel dared not look at the corpses the train crash had created, nor of those the beast had finished off. Copernica's emergency tactics unit had quickly sealed up the other half in high cordon walls of titanium, plastic, and magna-shielding: the unit had been watching the train ever since it entered the city's borders, intended for the zoo. A horrid mechanical malfunction (and a lazy route planner) had ensured that this exotic beast would be a blight instead of an educational epiphany.

The beast prowled around the square's center statue, heavy muscles undulating under shaggy red fur. The dhiscm blinked its five slitted eyes, licking its chops with a forked tongue. Its feral musk, a horrible hell-born acrid acid stench, clawed the wolf's nose from here.

Krampus be damned.

Typhus yelped, and her heart sank. Way up high, the poor twenty-two-year-old clung to a broken concrete statue of the city's great founder. The baby-blue husky was in good shape, but he was steadily losing his grip. He was as loud in his clothing as he was in his speech: he wore cowboy boots and assless chaps, a cotton-pom Santa hat, a leather vest, and a pair of red briefs fringed with fluffy white piping.

Vowel leaped into the pit and leveled her gun at the monster, taking aim. The husky snarled.

"Why you; come on! This going to win my love or redeem your tribe? Go home, gold digger!" Typhus shouted, swinging around as the statue shivered. His foot kicked his phone switchboard, sending the device crashing to the ground. Vowel took the shot, but the monster leaped out of the way and backed itself between the two parties. The wolfess thought it'd go for her, but the creature seemed to understand. Four of its five eyes watched her weapon intently.

"Typhus, you stay right there. I've got this," she said, pacing with her foe. The sniper beams had left her body and idled about her like gnats.

"Oh, the all-knowing condescension," he shouted, tossing his paw up to the surrounding buildings. His ears twitched at the sirens and police chatter; news helicopters overhead thumped as they circled. Precision-groomed reporters relayed the scene, veering into a quick history of nucleo-magnetic magnate Cochran Custer, his misguided son, and the young, foreign wife he took after his first wife left the country.

Eventually, the reporters came full-circle to the bio-hazard at hand, of his foreign wife and his estranged son now trapped in the center of what could possibly be Copernica's worst natural disaster. The "confused, homosexual male's" groin was still pixelated for the viewers, despite sufficient swaddling. "Mommy knows best, right?" Typhus shouted, "I've been with men twice your age, Va'a'ou'ra. Just give it up."

Typhus slipped down the back of the statue, sneaking toward the border. The monster's head jerked toward him, and Vowel took the shot. The dhiscm was fast, however, and it juked out of the way of the projectile. Then, it bolted toward the husky.

Sirens and screams reached a new high as the husky launched into a sprint, squeezing between two partitions as the beast struggled to clear the top, riot guards scattering to avoid its gnashing mandibles. Vowel leaped after it, running up some rubble and flipping over the fence. When she landed on the other side, they were already gone.

"No, God, Ayri, and Dalvex, no!" she swore, her heart thumping in her ears and drowning out screams, police sirens, and "Angels We Have Heard on High" crackling overhead from a damaged speaker. The wolfess turned the gun over in her hand a few times, pacing the other side of the wall, eyes flicking down the evacuated road where the crashed train lay half-buried in a building, smoldering and crackling among the rubble. The hunter narrowed her eyes and looked for any sign of tracks, clawmarks, wet pawprints. When she padded forward, her head snapped to the side: the monster's stench arrested her nostrils, and Vowel bolted along that lurid vapor trail with her eyes watering and her hackles flaring.

The gay club Perineum was just down the street and had its lights on, flashing red and green among rainbows. Small model trees crowned by obscene sex toys declared its festive nature. The monster's fierce fetor directed her here, and Vowel slid on bare footpaws as she stopped at the entrance. It was quiet inside; the creature was playing it smart. The wolfess leaned her head inside, surveying the interior. It was busy, loud, and chaotic, but so was a forest once alerted.

Despite the loud Hollywood-style posters depicting various species in all sorts of explicit, compromising positions, despite the epileptic strobe laser lighting, despite a trashed neon blue and pink carpeting scored with claw-marks, and despite a soundtrack still thumping with tremendous bass, the huntress remained focused: its putrid stink put it in the rear, past all the upset barstools, the scratched-up bar, and the torn stage curtains. It was in the dressing room, and no amount of spilled lubricant, dried sweat, or old musk could cover it up.

The wolfess walked easily through the empty club: everyone had retreated to the upper floors and barricaded the doors. A recent cultural backlash against sexual deviancy—including base homosexuality, however banal she thought it—had dictated mandatory easy-access escape routes. Those, unfortunately, were now all shut and barred.

Vowel entered the dressing room and ignored all the dirty implements hanging from the walls. This wasn't a prestigious dance club; in fact, it was rather nasty. The creature was in the center of the room, gnawing on the straps of a leather harness as it watched Typhus above, locked in a steel go-go cage suspended from the ceiling. A red exit sign glowed over a catwalk next to him.

The wolfess fired again and the creature dodged, running out the back door. One more moment alone.

"Typhus Cochran Custer, find a bathroom or a closet and lock yourself in. *Hide.*"

"It's *C***in'*, not Cochran."

She drew a slow breath, nose on high alert. Mistletoe, crowned by rubber penises of various species, hung from the ceiling. The creature rummaged through trash bins. She scanned the puzzling young adult: he was her relative by marriage only and by all other accounts, just a snotty brat with pierced nipples and a lewd cowboy costume.

"If you're not going to listen to me, Typhus, listen to a life-long huntress: when they took the bottle from my paws, they put a rifle in it, so I've been dealing with monst—"

"F— you!" he shouted, then slipped out the steel cage and ran out the fire escape. A roar blasted through the alley, the same voracious death-call that had blown out Councilman Kalo's phone. Vowel heard the frightening scrabble of claws give chase, and burst out the back door.

Typhus climbed the rickety iron stairs in flat cowboy boots, and the fetid, ferocious dhiscm scrabbled up the grated footings after him. Sentinels, riot cops, and snipers had followed her out: they lined the ends of the alley and the roofs above.

The husky was fast, but his boots were slick. He stumbled several times as the creature gave chase. Vowel found an attached ladder and climbed in a panic, one paw clutching an ungainly gun as the other snapped up every other rung on her dizzy journey up.

They still had a head start on her and the creature had learned these serrated civilian constructs. Vowel barked as the husky fell and the dhiscm pounced him, biting into his leg and tearing his boot off. Typhus slammed the other heel into the creature's ugly eyes, then took up the next few flights of stairs yelping, whimpering, punctuating every exhale with a squawk of fear. He fell down on all fours.

If it were only for the look in his baby-blue eyes, Vowel would have climbed the building's bare brick edifice with her paws and seen their claws break off in the mortar. But the iron scaffolding shivered as the dhiscm threw its weight around every bend, and in this peril Typhus barked at Vowel "Help me!"

He stumbled up the stairs on his hands and feet, the booted foot slipping with greater and greater frequency.

The wolf snarled, and she sped up the ladder like a spider on a rattled web, rungs flying past her muzzle at speeds to render her unconscious should they and her snout collide. Her gun banged against the railing with every leap, sounding the death toll for the dhiscm s'aedtawn that dared threaten the husky's life—her *son's* life, as she dared presume.

Typhus's boot caught the edge of the roof, and he plummeted to its surface, scraping the whole of his left side as he slid on rough, tarred-over wood. The beast pounced from the stairs in a high arc, its mandibles glistening and its foreclaws catching moonbeams along their sheer, savage curves.

Vowel hurtled from her own perch and intercepted it mid-air, driving her shoulder into its side to spin it off course. She tumbled with the beast and cried as it lashed at her. One eye went red, and her stomach felt cold.

The wolf kicked herself off the capsized beast and fired with two full trigger pulls as she flew backward. She landed on her tailbone with a loud crack, but when she heard the beast's yowls turn into sputters, yards of barbed wire seized her heart: it was dying. She got up, she limped, and she used the gun as a cane as blood seeped into her loincloth and over the bridge of her muzzle.

She hefted her bollista as a spade and struck once, twice, three times at the back of its neck. Vertebra cracked, crushed, and sundered into pulp as she severed its spine. The creature let out a few gasps. Its head waggled until its neck muscles failed, then fell to glare at her with its five eyes until they froze in place.

It died angry and numb.

Va'a'ou'ra limped back to Typhus, maybe or maybe not blind in one eye but an Ayri-blessed hero to a few thousand non-casualties. They could have their fruitcake and eat it; she'd only come here for one person.

Typhus sat up on the roof picking gravel and beer bottle glass out of his fur, putting more concentration into the delicate art of extricating rubble than he did the bloodied warrior lumbering toward him, she dragging her gun behind her like an executioner's cleaver.

Her tungsten-copper footpaws stood right before his scraped shins. Typhus's gaze rose, slowly, in an arduous climb to the top where a wolf's face obscured by blood, sweat, and headfur looked back down at him. His face broke like a plaster mask, and he sobbed openly, thrusting his paws up into the air, groping at the dark, distant monolith hanging over him.

Vowel knelt, stumbling once, and held the boy's head against her collar. Her voice came in measured gasps, hushing out on a breeze reeking of sulphur against cinnamon and cloves. A strange white chill tapped the wet bridge of her muzzle, and she briefly opened her eyes: it was snowing.

Perhaps as a badly-timed joke or an expedient to soothe the panicked populace's, a radio DJ in a distant corner of Copernica switched the city's loudspeakers to "White Christmas."

Vowel folded her ears toward Typhus, away from the cacophony.

"I don't care what you think of me," she whispered, bleeding on him, "but you're alive *to* think, and that I will celebrate."

Typhus sobbed, pulling her body against the side of his head. "You saved me, thank you; oh my, *everything*, you saved *everyone*," he honked, sniffling into her shoulder. His blue arms held fast to her back as if he'd fall through the roof without a hold on her.

Vowel removed his Santa hat and licked his head. He whined in response, nestling closer against her. For a moment, the two rested against each other, injured, vexed, and exhausted, as riot troops and animal control raided the roof to ensure the place was secure. They scooped up the carcass and hauled it off. A news chopper thundered above, throwing their fur into chaotic configurations as it reported the happy reunion between mother and son, however overreaching that may have been.

Typhus lay safe against her. Whole world be damned; maybe there were a few pillars holding up this sloshing archipelago city of narcissists. He crooned in her grasp and, with a strange sudden impulse, pulled her breaststrap down and opened his muzzle at her teat.

Despite her sanguine haze, Vowel's paw shot out and intercepted his snout, wrapping around it like a muzzle. The other hastily re-clothed herself. Their eyes met, wide open with shock as step-mother and step-son realized what ritual the young adult had attempted. The wolfess shook her head at the muzzled husky, then released him, her ears burning.

"No."

A news chopper thundered overhead, its precision-groomed reporter leaning out the window to shove a fat microphone in the wolf's face. "You've just saved the leisure district of Copernica and reunited with your son. What words do you have for our viewers?"

"Cochran," she groaned at the camera, clutching Typhus close as snow gathered on a tentacle of bloody headfur hanging across her face. The machine's rotors blew everything attached to her to the left, and her body heaved under great duress as she spoke, "we have to talk. Soon, about your son. And as for the rest of you out there, I've done what any noble Ayrad or person in general would have done: my *duty*, if you'll excuse the bromide. God, Ayri, Dalvex, et cetera bless us all, everyone."

ALICE DRYDEN
WHITE LULLABY

Alice Dryden writes stories and poems about talking animals. Most of these are published in the furry fandom under the name Huskyteer, but occasionally one escapes into the wild. Her poetry has appeared in Apex Magazine *and the charity anthology* Civilized Beasts, *amongst others. She lives in London and dreams of snowy pine forests.*

Wolves running and snow falling
white against dark trees.
Blue dusk, shadows falling
on white fur, white woods,
white everything.
Eyes gleaming like stars,
paws padding soundlessly
on falling moonlight.
Softness on softness.
Moonlight falling
on soundlessly padding paws.
Stars like gleaming eyes.
Everything white;
woods white, fur white on falling shadows.
Dusk-blue trees dark against white
falling snow and running wolves.

CHELSEA DUB
NIGHT KEEPER

Chelsea Dub is an artist from Indiana and is currently pursuing a BFA in Painting and Animation at Ball State University. She enjoys working with various media, including sculpture, painting, drawing, printmaking, digital photography, and computer graphics. Being autistic and having learned to draw before she could speak, art was—and continues to be—both a mode of escapism and expression for her. Along with being a neurodiversity advocate, she is a feminist vegan, and her art often explores the interconnections between issues such as ableism, sexism, and speciesism. Through visual media, she hopes to effectively communicate these ideas and challenge society's marginalization of communities, including other animal species. Her art has been published in Wolf Warriors: The National Wolfwatcher Coalition Anthology, *featured in the Autism Unveiled Project and Art of Compassion Project, and exhibited in art fairs and galleries, including the Canon Tunnel in Washington, D.C. When not in Muncie, she lives in Noblesville with her family, including her two rescued cats.*

Night Keeper. Ink pen and paper, digital manipulation.

KERRY DUNCAN
THE LAST DIRE WOLF

Kerry Duncan was chilling in his den, thinking about how much he enjoys howling at the moon on a cold, winter night. His mind wandered, and he wondered if his daughter might have been an ancient wolf in a previous iteration. He imagined she would have been a strong, alpha female leading a large, loyal pack. So he fired up the time machine, set the controls for 10,000 BCE, and went back for a quick look-see...

On high ground, she could smell the ocean from where she stood, watching. The Big Ice was growing, moving her pack farther south and west. Another Long Winter was coming; she could smell that, too.

She stood about seven hands tall at the shoulder, and weighed nine stone. Her muscular body was solid and dense, about the same size as her mate. Her coat was a thick reddish-brown, with darker legs, and lighter ears rimmed in black. Her head was large and broad, her keen eyes missed nothing. She was about as long as the spear throwers were tall. She hunted Big Game here on the western shore of what would become North America in another 10,000 years.

Her pack was once thirty-six animals, but now they were fewer. The wild horses and bison had become rarer as the ice grew. It had been days since their last successful hunt. They had not encountered another pack in months. She could read the signs. Snow and ice as far as she could see. They would have to move farther south again, soon.

Noise from her pack down below attracted her attention. They were excited. Ahead of them, she could just make out a small mastodon that was mired in a thick, black pool, which stood out against the white blanket of winter. She could see her mate leading their wolves to surround the pool as they closed on the helpless creature. It had been a year or more since they had encountered a mammoth, giant sloth, or mastodon. There would be full bellies tonight. She loped down the hill and across the expanse to join the circle.

The wolves closed in on the mastodon, moving carefully across the foul-smelling crust. It was warm. The mastodon bellowed a warning. As they approached their prey from all sides, as one, the black ooze began to grab and hold paws, tails, bellies flattened against it. A few wolves cried out as they started to struggle against the tar. Then, more...

Free wolves moved toward those who had become mired, to help, in response to the plaintive calls. She could see, one by one, as each wolf shared the same fate as the young mastodon they sought. Voices were silenced. She had moved toward her mate who had been caught in the tar as the crust gave way, not far from the struggling mastodon. The oozing asphalt caught her too, as she got close to him. He looked at her with fear. The mastodon slipped beneath the bubbling tar pit, bellowing one last time.

She saw a small pack of gray wolves cresting the hill where she had been standing a short time ago. She saw that they did not approach the pit, as her beautiful, broad head slipped beneath the surface of the tar. Perhaps, someday, someone would tell her story, *Canis armbrusteri*, last of her name.

Happy Birthday, Kel!!

Love, Dad

11/2016

SAMANTHA DUTTON
FAIRYTALE WONDERLAND

Sam Dutton is a writer and nature lover who lives on the edge of the Dartmoor National Park in the South West of England. She is an avid reader of poetry and fiction. Occasionally, she likes to take out her pad and pencil to sketch pictures of animals and plant-life as she finds it relaxing. When she is not at her desk she can be found wandering in the countryside or at the seafront.

Hazy sun on glittering ground,
sparkling snow lies all around.
Feathered flakes from winter skies
festooning trees that creak and sigh.
Picture Yule card celebrations
Mankind seeing-in the season
warm and stuffed full by the fireside
on land they've stolen from the wildlife.
Can you hear the starving howls
as the humans sate their hunger?
It's the mournful tune for the season of greed,
as the wolves must scrape for scraps to feed.

A. M. DUVALL
WINTER WHITE

You stand in the forest, looking around in awe.
As the snow falls in a heavy wall.
It coats the floor of the forest.
Along with the trees and plants closest to you.
Turning the forest into a winter, white wonderland.
Suddenly the air becomes white with air breaths coming at you.
Followed by the shapes of wolves walking in a pack, full of color.
There are browns, black, grays, and even one pure white wolf barely noticeable.
All you can see is his black nose and blue eyes looking at you.
They stop moving, and stand together looking up at the snow.
Their breaths floating out to join the white snow falling to the ground.
A sound has them turning towards it.
Then they start walking again, away from you.
Their colors disappearing again into the white snow.
Leaving you filled with awe and wonder at the sight you just witnessed.
Staying forever in your mind.

GULTEN DYE
THE PIERCING EYES

Gulten Dye was born and raised in Turkey, spending her free time drinking in the colors, shapes, and scents of the Grand Bazaar, fashion houses, and boutiques of Istanbul. Her sense of fashion firmly planted, she further cultivated her artistic sense through her travels around the world. After a successful nursing career, she took her love of art, color, and beauty and transformed it into a thriving international business, designing and creating jewelry.

Writing has always been her passion and she will literally write on anything to remember her words. It is an intimate expression of her personal journey. Poetry is something that has continually shown up in her writing from an early age.

Gulten lives and creates in Las Vegas, Nevada.

On a cold winter day
Way into the woods
Through the snowflakes
I saw the piercing eyes of a lone wolf
Looking right at me
Though not fierce
Those eyes instantly froze me in my steps
I stood there
Looking right back
There was so much hidden behind those eyes
Fascinated
I let my mind be captured, permanently

Ever since then
Whenever I remember those intense eyes
I feel a close kinship, deep within
Thinking that maybe a wolf is just like me
At times, there is compassion in its eyes
Maybe sadness for a reason or two

And at times, it's just a calculation of the next meal
Then again
Maybe
What I saw that day was nothing more than a warning
For me to leave the woods
Before the dark night falls

CHRISTIAN ESCHE
A HERO LIBERATED

Christian was born on the 17th of June in 1995 in his home town Chemnitz in Germany. All of his life, he enjoyed creative things like drawing and later photography as well. He always enjoyed nature of all kinds and is engaged in its protection. Wolves especially became important to him and are very present in his life. After regular school, he wanted to become an artist or a photographer, but as both failed, he began to study European Studies with the cultural background in his hometown; drawing and making photos remained hobbies. A year ago, he started to draw digitally, mainly focusing on fantasy and nature themes.

A Hero Liberated. Digital art.

WINTER'S PEACE

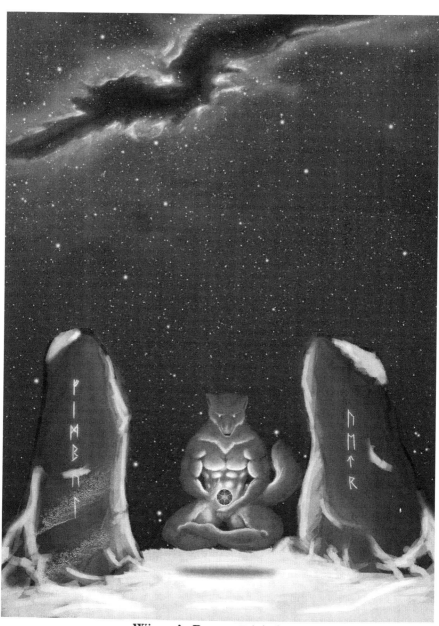

Winter's Peace. Digital art.

WINTER'S STORM

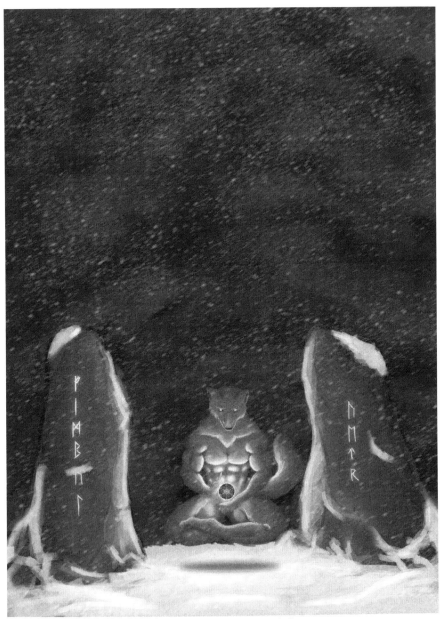

Winter's Storm. Digital Art.

AMY FONTAINE
CAGES

Amy Fontaine is a wildlife biologist who earned her Bachelor's Degree from Humboldt State University in 2015. She has worked with captive wolves in California, Idaho, and New Mexico, as well as with wild wolves in Yellowstone National Park. While she loves writing fantasy stories, she believes that living, breathing wolves are even more intriguing than their counterparts in legend and myth.

Amy's stories and poems have appeared in various publications, including Civilized Beasts: 2015 Edition *from Weasel Press,* ROAR Volumes 6 *and* 7 *from Bad Dog Books, and the* North Coast Journal *of Humboldt County, California. She also has a novel,* Mist, *forthcoming from Thurston Howl Publications. Amy currently lives in Kenya, where she is conducting research on spotted hyenas.*

"It's a wolf," said the man.

The creature thrashed against the bars of its prison like a gray gargoyle. Once full and luminous, its skin now hung tattered over its bones, its fur falling off in great soggy patches. Snarling, the animal threw itself against its cage again and again as spit flew from its mouth. The iron pillars rattled with the fury of the forest beast, who glared at the group of men standing in the snowy clearing beyond its cage.

The men kept their distance, their rugged faces peering through the bars.

"At last," said the largest man, the one who had proclaimed the beast to be a wolf, "we have caught this great mystery. At last, we can know it and make it our own."

The creature continued to lunge at the bars. Frothing, rumbling from deep in its throat, flinging flecks of saliva to the ground with each toss of its mighty head. Its growls were like thunder, and its eyes burned with righteous flame as it banged against the cage. *Clang, clang.*

"Stop!" cried a voice.

The men turned to see a little girl emerge from the trees and run into the clearing, her golden curls bouncing, her blue eyes wet and pleading. Like the men, she wore a thick fur coat to protect her from the falling snow on this cold winter day, but the fairness of her face created a stark contrast with the harsh landscape.

The girl flung herself desperately on the largest man, the leader.

"Let it go, Daddy!" begged the girl, tears streaming down her face as she buried it in her father's hip. "It needs to be free to run wild through the forest!"

The man frowned down at his child. He patted her head with a rough, calloused hand.

"Listen, Melody. Now that we have this thing close at hand, we can understand it, study it, be close to it and part of it! We can tame it, and make it our friend! Don't you want to be its friend, Melody?"

The girl just stared at the shrieking wraith, who continued to make the cage shudder with the thrusts of its body against the bars.

"It was meant to be free," said the girl.

The man took one last, long look at the writhing, contorted creature in the cage. Its hoarse cries still pierced the night as it smashed, over and over, against the bars, blindly seeking freedom or death. Then, the man turned away.

"Bring it to camp," he ordered the others, avoiding the gaze of his daughter.

And they lifted the cage on poles and carried it away.

The taming of the first wolf opened a Pandora's Box for the human race. Cultures around the world, captivated by the spiritual force they saw fleetingly in the forest, sought to catch it, to own it, to mold it according to their own perceptions. And gradually, as generations passed, they lost sight of what had drawn them to the wolf in the first place, creating creatures that were gradually less and less wolf-like, more like commodities than genuine spirit presences. Yet each nation insisted they had captured the true essence of the wolf.

"Charge!" called the captain.

The armored soldiers clattered across the battlefield. Swords clanged. The air rang with the sweaty, bloody dance of metal and skin. Mist lying low over the ashen ground could not conceal the bodies as they fell.

There was no difference between the two opposing armies: they both wore the same suits of armor, and they fought with the same array of weapons. They bled the same wine-red color. The only distinction was that one army flew the banner of the Samoyed dog, and the other marched under the flag of the Pekingese.

> *"Great one,*
> *help me to tell*
> *blood from blood,*
> *breed from breed,*
> *true dog from true dog.*
> *Amen."*

The children obediently parrot the words from their teacher, who smiles encouragingly at the front of the classroom.

"Very good," she beams. "No more verses for today."

As she shuts the dusty book on her desk, the bell rings, and students hurry from the classroom.

In the dark forest on the edge of the schoolyard, where humans no longer dare to tread, the wolf still hunts the secrets of winter. He knows that humanity has lost its way, twisting the divine essence it once loved to suit its own needs. The wolf watches from the shadows, still elegant and beautiful as ever, still his own pure, spirited self in the eyes of those who care to seek what's real.

Each of those created creatures, the dogs, still carries aspects of that original essence, that pure spirit drive. But the aspects that truly make each dog so beautiful have been buried under context and politics, fashion, and geography. We no longer know what is real. Yet we long to return to the source we once cherished. We yearn to find our way home again.

In the dark forest, the wild wolf waits. The wolf we call God awaits seekers of truth.

Walk into the forest, says the wolf. *Come and find me.*

HERALDRY DANCE

Pan's pipes play the melody
of forests long ago,
a song as old as Earth,
brighter than the stars.

Wolves draped in fantastic colors,
beneath a winter sky so untruthfully blue
you expect the dazzle to confess
fiction any second,
come to the call
of the tune,
to a snow-strewn forest glade.

The furred vagabonds respond
to the trill with a dance,
paws raised in the air.
They shine like daytime moonbeams
as they twirl,
dancing for their kind and for the memory
of the parties they held in the woods
before humans killed them with weapons
other than teeth.

The horned god skips through the pack,
his soft-throated pipes luring them onward,
toward the edge of the known world.
The unicorns, the dragons,
other beasts of magic passed into legend,
but the wolves live among us still.
And some days when no human eyes are looking,
they meet with the horned god for these parties,
to recall the wonders of bygone days,
parading through the world in a raucous romp.
They dance for the spirit of wilderness.
And none of us see.

PARADISE

There once was a wolf who lived in the coldest, darkest region of the world. To him, the forest was the only world. He knew not the thousand eyes of glittering, rain-washed cities, cities that clanged and echoed and yelled and pounded with the cries of people and cars and music. He knew not the sweltering heat of the desert, where lizards cool themselves beneath shy rocks and fennec foxes prey on grasshoppers. He never knew the height of a redwood tree, or the smell of a library, the sound of a prayer bell, or the smile of a child. The world he knew was heavy and silent, a world of eternal night and endless snow. In the depths of the black trees, where the only sound was the thick breath of the wind, where one waded through white drifts beneath a gray-black sky, alone with oneself in the terror of winter wilderness…in this wasteland far from humanity lived one wolf, alone.

He could not remember his name—or where he came from, why he lived. He knew no world outside of darkness and solitude. Yet still he wandered, without answers. For in his heart, he held a dream.

It was a dream that defied every one of his senses, a dream that his memories could not explain. In this dream, the trees opened up before him and brilliance met his eyes—the brilliance of sunlight. His world burst into golden flame, as before him shone a glade that contained no snow. A glorious glade, rich with springy emerald grass. He could run through this grass, and the soil was warm and light and spongy. No vicious ice crystals sent tremors through his paws. He frolicked through the sunshine like a pup.

And then he saw them: the two unicorns.

One black, one white, both with eyes that sparkled like stardust. Nothing in his instincts or memory could compare with their breathtaking forms. He had never seen a man, so he knew not the nature of horses… In his half-frozen state he could not recall the frame of a deer…but in any case, these two beings were infinitely more graceful than doe or mare… They were light-footed, sleek as springtime… The white one was whiter than the palest of doves, alive with a glow as bright as the sunlight. Yet this glow was not harsh, but gentle, softened. Even so, the sight brought the wolf to tears.

The other unicorn was darker than night, but in a way that evoked neither coldness nor fear. His black coat echoed the vastness of deep space, the comfort of the void so far beyond ourselves. A universe so full of mystery and enchantment that even its blank spaces sing with meaning. In this alluring black fur, the wolf glimpsed whispers of other planets, even though his lifetime had never shown him such things.

Then, the dream would fade, and the wolf would be standing in the deep snow again. But he knew, though he could not smell or taste the sun, that those unicorns lived…and that one day, the glade would open before his very eyes.

He could not remember ever having a pack, though his heart hungered for a family he could not name. Weakened by time, brain wiped clean by the cold, he plowed on through the gathering snow, more like a tumbling stone than a proud, controlled predator. He had scented a deer on the wind…and though it felt like he hadn't seen or tasted one in years, his mouth watered at the smell. So he plodded wearily onward, spurred by starvation and fatigue, stumbling through the trees, through the frozen rain, through his forest world. The tree trunks stood like pillars all around him, dark pillars like those of a gloomy cathedral, where grisly rites are performed at the altar of insanity. At last, he saw her, a lone doe far from her herd, and desperation gnawed his insides, and he leaped, charged like a burning fire at this helpless state of purity and was on her, tearing at the sinews and the blood, splashing red onto the virgin snow. And then amidst his meal, a greater hunger rose inside him, a yearning for companions and the sunshine glade of the unicorns, and a soft whine began warbling in his throat as he thought of how, like him, this doe had been weakened, hungry, and alone and that was the only reason he could catch her on his own, maddened and delirious as he was. As he stopped eating, a cry burst forth from his ruby-red lips, too disjointed for a howl and too anguished for a yip, a bloodstained, feral sob that split the night in two. And he ran from that place, left the body to the ravens, and he cried for the world of the unicorns, where he could frolic in the glade like a young pup, and there was no hunger, no hunting and killing, only sunshine and shadows spilt on the grass.

He ate some, but not enough. His muscles feel frozen, and no matter how far he presses into the forest, he seems to get nowhere. The heavy darkness waits everywhere. The dream of sunshine is so far away.

This land seems under the grip of an eternal winter, an endless blizzard, piercing his lungs with ice crystals and despair. Unable to move another inch, he collapses into a snowdrift. His eyes close. The wind moans around him, piling snow deeper and deeper over his form.

As he shivers under the weight of the cold, he wonders whether his dream will die with him. He howls at the trees that block the sky.

"Where are you, unicorns? Where are you now?"

He takes his last, dying breath. At that moment, a pup is born with eyes that yearn for the sunlight and a heart that speaks of unicorns.

RENEGADE

I am the wolf, and through crisp snow I run,
beneath gray sky pierced
by the weak winter sun.

Pursued by a creature
I can't even name:
a gigantic, fierce bird
with a black metal frame.

I am the wolf, and my soul is my crime.
For being a hunter, so strong and refined,
I am hunted, and there is a price on my head.
Already my packmates have all been shot dead.

I am stricken with anger, sadness, and strife,
but there's naught left to do but to run for my life,
to push on, aching, weary, in the grim, faded light,
across the bleak landscape, white wolf against white,

till I'm herded toward cliffs overlooking the sea,
to a dead end that holds
no escape route for me.
As I near my death's territorial door,
I realize something I hadn't before.
I howl to bird.

You can't take me!
You can't break me!
Though my pack is now gone,
my alpha spirit lives on.
You can't defeat me!
Your bullets can't meet me!
Not really, for they can't erase
on the frozen earth, the subtle trace
of wolf tracks, paws with pride here,
that lived here, bred here, died here.
We'll hunt on, for the Northern wind

does not forget, and her every song
will chill you with our memory,
haunt you with our ghosts.

I am a predator.
I won't die running away.

The wolf halts.
The howls cease.
Through the frozen air,
the crack of a gun.

THE VOICE

The last living canid on Earth was a wolf with one eye. With fur gray as a storm cloud and an eye fierce as a Norse god, he wandered beneath a wrecked winter sky, through snowflakes suspended in the dead air, across a messy menagerie of bombed buildings.

He scavenged out of dumpsters, fed on the bodies of politicians who had perished mid-argument, feasted on the carcasses of ravens that had once dined on the remains of his own kills. He traveled across a world so devastated it could hardly be called a world now, across silent streets and through what had once been college campuses, town halls, crucibles of idealism and wisdom. Now, there was no sound, no trickle of artistic dispute or philosophical debate. Nothing but the softest murmur of the wind, breathing its last.

And the wolf wandered on, his paws silent upon the abstract cubism dog-eat-dog dirt, quietly over rubble and down again.

He heard voices. Always, he heard voices in his head.

I'm tired of this! I loved you and look what you did to us! Why don't you want the baby? You never want anything I want!

Dear Mom, I miss you. I'm having fun here in Alaska. I met this nice guy named Chris at a traditional dance concert. It was really fun; they had such amazing costumes, all brilliantly colored and tasteful. I hope I can design something like that someday. Chris is a music major. He lives here in Fairbanks. How's Dad and Julia? Hope to hear from you soon!

Wanted: Grand Piano. Please bring it to our door.

The grime was not recognizable as anything in particular. Trash flooded the streets, turning them into a canal system of waste and decay. The putrid smells came from everywhere; burnt flesh, sweet blood. The wind moaned, mourning itself, but the snowflakes hanging in the air did not stir. Stepping delicately over the bodies splayed on the ground, the wolf gazed into a shattered store window.

A set of cracked television sets flashed footage before his eye. The picture, the same on each screen, ran silently across the wolf's unblinking vision: a man speaking from a pulpit, his mouth moving wide and passionate in short, lion's roar bursts as the text below the picture scampered across the screen and disappeared: SHOOTINGS ESCALATE GENOCIDE IN THIRD-WORLD COUNTRIES

THEFT OF FIVE HUNDRED DOLLARS FROM THE BANK OF THE POOR NEW PANDA BORN IN WASHINGTON ZOO....

The wolf stared at the screen, his face still and intense. In profile, his silhouette, with only one side of his face and one eye showing, looked like an Egyptian hieroglyph: flat, angular, mysterious, hinting at something far deeper than its two-dimensional surface could convey. Though the man was silent to his ears, the wolf knew the voice. It had spoken in his head many times...

We need to STOP! To end this war! Violence is not the answer; we have seen this too many times. How many more deaths have to occur before we realize we're destroying ourselves? This world is not the world a loving God wants for us!

Turning away, the wolf kept walking down the broken sidewalk. The man's voice continued in his head, clear as a prayer bell.

We need to end this, once and for all! For the first time, this could be the last time!

The wolf roamed through a dark and endless world.

He walked across a beaten patch of depressed concrete, into a mess of disillusioned shards of glass that glinted as brightly as the half-fallen snowflakes. He crossed a highway, gliding silently past the frozen cars and smashed windows and overturned tires, over an overpass as still as a painting.

The voices resounded, alive in his head.

There was a hurricane in Mexico yesterday. Thirty-thousand people dead.

That's really sad.

Pass the potatoes, please.

Blocked by the line of cars in front of him, connected like links in a gruesome metal parody of a daisy chain, he leaped gracefully onto the caved-in roof of a Toyota Corolla, leaping like a mountain goat from one car to the next.

They're sending more soldiers overseas.

That's wrong. They shouldn't do that.

Yeah. It's not right.

How was the game yesterday?

He leaped down from the final car, strolling off the bridge into the city.

Buildings loomed silent and watching on either side - grim, mutilated buildings that glared down at him, leaning precariously inwards. They leered at the wild intruder to their cosmopolitan domain, but he ignored their glowering protest. There was nothing they could do to keep him from entering; their caretakers had long since gone.

They're saying this might become a third World War.

Impossible. We're perfectly safe. Our leaders know what they're doing.

Yeah. Mind-blowing to think about, though.

Uh-huh. How did your date with Christie go?

He passed through an alley into another street, his furry tail swishing behind him. His skeletal frame showed through his skin, but his stride was calm and cool.

There are thousands dying of the epidemic.

Did you hear about the earthquake yesterday?

Terrible, I know. Did you pick out a dress for tonight?

They're throwing out the surplus.

Want to come to the dance tomorrow?

All the voices, all the voices talking and getting no answers. All the voices speaking without understanding, feeling without action, voices echoing in empty air and reflecting back on themselves.

The wolf crossed the street and entered the bookstore. Encapsulated within the little store, the wooden shelves stood firm as redwood trees, proud and preserved despite the chaos outside. The windows were shattered, the door unhinged, yet the books remained on their shelves, stubbornly clinging to life.

The wolf sniffed the air. The woody resin of the shelves and the pulpy scent of the paper reminded him of the forest. His spirit had once belonged to a place where the smell was not of stinking waste and rotting gasoline but of flowers and pine needles and damp, rain-washed earth. Now, however, the only smell that even remotely resembled the wild, free odor of the running bison was the leathery scent of the covers of these ancient books, miraculously undisturbed by the destruction of time.

He wandered through the shelves, hearing their voices screaming in his head.

Mamma, where are you?

I'm here, honey, I'm here. We have to be strong.

Oh god. Oh my god!

Remember what He said, long ago: I leave you peace, my peace I give you. Let us say the prayer together: Our Father, who art in Heaven....

I don't care. Just know that I love you.

He found one book that had been knocked to the floor. He lowered his head, nudging the splayed volume with his nose. The voice of its author, proud and timeless, came back to him.

In wildness is the preservation of the world, says Henry David Thoreau.

The wolf smiled, sinking to the carpet of the little store. The books leaped off the shelves on their own, creating a nest around his tired body. He heard all their voices again in his mind: their flawed, brave voices, their stupid and righteous voices, their noble and beautiful and loving voices, their vulnerable and tenacious voices, ringing out amidst the dirt and the din.

Whatever happens, just know that I love you.

He closed his eye and breathed no more.

WINTER SONG

Their eerie voices
Melding with the twilight
I had to listen

LOU GAGLIARDI
HOWLING GOOD CHRISTMAS

Louis is a college educated man in his early 30s from Greensburg, Pennsylvania. It is this small city from which he draws inspiration in his writing. This is his first writing credit. His hobbies include reading, playing video games, watching Pittsburgh sports, and playing with his nephew Skyler.

There was very little sun this Christmas season. John had done what he could to make the single floor home feel cozy and warm, but it was hard for just one person. Sighing, the tiger stared out the window again, hoping that he'd come back. Somehow, John knew that Seth would, but it almost didn't seem like he would. They went through this every year and John was worried. It didn't help that the snow was nearly up to their waists this year, and it was only Christmas! Still, Seth wanted the perfect tree, and why would John argue with his mate?

A howl came through the sounds of cars and people singing across the lawn. John's ears perked up as he caught it, and his tail gave a delighted twitch. That meant Seth was close to coming home. He could only imagine how big of a tree his mate had brought with him this time. Last year, they could barely get it through the door.

"John! Open the door! Come see this!"

John got up, careful not to drop the mug of tea he had prepared. The slim tiger drank only the warmest and with lots of sugar. But he did as he was told and opened the door without a coat. There stood the arctic wolf, fur matted in some places with sweat and his muscles flexing from the work done. And behind him stood a smaller tree than John had expected. Not that the feline complained: it meant less clean up after all.

"Seth, that's...well...that's unexpected."

The wolf's tail stopped wagging for a moment before he came closer. He had a look of confusion and hurt in his normally bright eyes, and his ears drooped just a bit under the hat. Seth came to the tiger and wrapped him in a big hug.

"Well, you complained without saying a word about the tree last year. So I thought I'd remedy that..."

Seth looked up, not wanting to see the tiger's face for a moment. Then, a big, toothy grin came across his muzzle. There was no malice behind it as one didn't have malice in his heart at Christmas time. Especially for his mate. Instead, he dipped down and kissed the tiger so John could see what was there overhead. Purrs and murrs became the only sound the mistletoe would hear for the rest of Christmas Eve.

RENEE CARTER HALL
THE SUMMER STAG AND THE WINTER WOLVES

Renee Carter Hall works as a medical transcriptionist by day and as a fantasy and science fiction writer all the time. Though she now focuses most of her creative energy on fiction, she began her writing career with poetry, and her poems have appeared most recently in the anthology Civilized Beasts *and online at* [adjective][species]. *She lives in West Virginia with her husband, their cat, and more books than she will ever have time to read, and she makes her home online at www.reneecarterhall.com and on Twitter as @RCarterHall.*

Another year shows its age.
Leaves of crimson, copper, crisp and dry,
scatter on the sharpening wind.

The pack waits, patient, secure.
Their prey will come—

and in golden light the stag appears,
standing proud and unafraid,
sun blazing on his fine red coat,
his antlers branching among the trees.
He paws the rich earth, once,
and nostrils flare—

and across the faded earth they run,
the stag's hooves touching ground as lightly
as the snow that swirls at the pack.
Where the wolves run, winter follows,
wind howling in their ears like a brother,

singing in their blood
as they chase the summer's end,

blowing in their breath
as they run the season in,

as the stag's red coat
dulls to gray,
and branches rattle and
antlers break
and another year
falls
away...

...

In the dreaming wood it is quiet enough
to hear a snowflake touch the ground.
The stag's scent has long since faded,
his trail swept clean in white.

The pack roams as it must,
their song on the bitter wind

holding the wood in thrall,
holding the land in sleep,

keeping the world in balance
until the year is born anew,

until their hunt begins again.

JULEY HARVEY
THE EYES OF WINTER

Juley Harvey is a prize-winning poet and ex-journalist (California and Colorado). Her most recent work is featured in Lynn Johnston's Whispering Angels Soul Survivors anthology, Whitney Scott's Tall Grass Writers Guild's Home and Flames and Embers anthologies, and as a third-place winner in the 2015 Dancing Poetry Contest. Her work has appeared in more than 35 publications, including such varied books as an anthology on bears, and in Cosmopolitan *magazine, and she has won first-, third-, and honorary mentions in many contests. She is an animal soulmate and shares her home in the Colorado Rockies with her adored, rescued Moosie, a chihuahua-wire-haired terrier, who helps her, while she helps her elderly father, and dreams of oceans and wolves.*

the ides of wolf —
if i ever get lost
in the wilderness,
i want a wolf
to raise me,
guide me.
i trust their family
love, their joy
in living,
their soul solitude,
gratitude for a meal.
snow-white wolves
in winter coats —
they'd never wear
human skin.
they have too much
dignity,
soul-fire within
glows out, suns,

from those
mesmer-eyes.
flashlights
searching for
the truth
of to be.
lighthouses
of the wintry soul,
light years yearning free.
slipping into the den
of cozy family.
alpha-amen.
family resemblance —
in the eyes,
the voice,
outcasts
by choice,
no chance,
the last dance,
the romance,
the ice palace glance
of the wolf in winter.
empress of the elegance.
i choose them;
leave these
ice-hole, hell-heart men.
out of the ghost-white
winter veil
of a trail of tears mist,
a sudden glimpse —
sun-yellow eyes,
sister-sable-hair surprise.
magic in a howl.
message in a bottled vowel —
tribe, pack,
family, from the beginning
to now.
eternity in skin,
fleet as summer sin.
wolf, i'd rather be

with your side,
than with those
trying to win
through extinction,
hide
through excuse of needy law,
greedy law.
the dark winter night
of the brink of satisfaction,
distinction,
a brief wink,
blink,
all is done,
gone.
a pawprint in snow,
blood on the rose.
you were here,
goodness knows.
silent-movie moving mystery,
reels your platinum,
magnum mysterium history —
silver drum song.
when i come
to the end
of the road,
may a wolf
be waiting on it
to show me divinely,
the starry way home,
along with an elephant,
a bear, an otter, a tiger,
a lion, a dolphin,
all those we've treated unconscionably,
and all we've rescued,
those with true souls,
and my little moosie, too,
related distantly to the
winter wolf.
we are one,
if lucky,

stars and blood,
bone and water.
that is all
that ever could matter.
oh, wolf, my heart hurts
with the beauty
and ugly of life.
just a lifetime, a lifeline,
a moment, of clairvoyant,
moonlit grace,
but maybe that sustains,
is all that is necessary
to know god's ancient face,
the paws of she-god
once trod
here.
and headed home,
in the blood snow.
how many ways
can a heart break,
and how many
can it glory?
to see, hear, commune
with, just know that
there are wolves wild —
is a "fur-acle" miracle
family story,
moongleam eyes
reflecting earthrise child.

GRAHAM HOUGHTON
THE WOLF AND THE FIGS

Graham had a privileged childhood growing up surrounded by the mountains and lakes of north-west England. There, under the tutelage of unbelievably old, but infinitely wise men with little formal education, he learned to hunt and fish, to build shelters in winter and summer, to read a landscape and to navigate through it gently and in safety. Most of all he learned to quietly melt from the presence of noisy people and to love and respect the place he had been born into.

His work as an archaeologist has taken him from the dark, muddy bowels of London, England, to the searing deserts of remote outback Australia, and many places in between. As a writer he has authored some thirty-eight children's books, contributed to encyclopaedias, and been published in journals and newspapers. He has written several screenplays, one of which, Cry of the Dreamer, *won him first prize in the LA based 2010 WriteMovies contest. He has recently been reminded of the vulnerable, but tenacious nature of existence by becoming a grandfather.*

It was poor country with barely enough grazing for the meager flocks of sheep upon which the people relied for so many of their daily needs. Here and there, a pocket of deeper soil supported a stunted growth of grain, and small olive groves were reminders of the mysteries within the ancient forests that had covered this once great land.

As I was approaching one such grove late into the evening, I slackened my pace. I had heard it subconsciously for some time. Now, the howling of a lone dog, or was it a wolf, demanded my attention. It was moving in an ever-decreasing circle, and I was its moving centre. I imagined it quartering the ground, sniffing the cool night air for my scent. The chilly serpent of fear slithered down my spine. Was it madness, or hunger that afflicted it? The howling echoed and re-echoed from the valley walls; the lone dog's presence magnified into a pack.

Nearby, I saw a tall wild fig and I climbed high into its upper branches. The howling stopped, but there followed a silence so intense that I wanted to scream back at it. But in the night, silence is the light by which we see.

I could hear the panting of the creature as it drew closer; then, its movements across the ground, the click of its claws against stones. I was afraid and shook so violently that the ripe figs that were on the tree fell to the ground. But the dog did not look mad. Its coat was sleek. It appeared well-fed, and its eyes did not blaze. It seemed entirely unconcerned about me. Apart from a sniff of the air in my direction, it set to eating the fallen figs.

I began to laugh at my own foolishness. I laughed so hard that finally I fell from the tree and landed on all fours beside the dog. The dog glanced at me, grinning as it chewed. Still laughing, I too began to eat the figs. Now, the dog began to laugh, and soon we rolled on the ground together with tears in our eyes.

"I thought you were mad," I said. "You put fear into my heart, and all the time you wanted figs!" Regaining a measure of control, I addressed the dog directly. "But tell me, where did you learn the beguiling madness that is such clever sanity?" The dog beat the ground with its tail and roared with delight. Imagine my surprise when it replied.

"There was once a cousin wolf in this valley," the dog began, "she frightened every living thing, our masters included. But we, the dogs of the villages, were not afraid of our own flesh and blood and saw an advantage. When cousin wolf howled, the shepherds hid in caves and clefts in the rocks. Those that ventured out in those days were able to feast at leisure on the unprotected flocks." Our combined howls of laughter now filled the valley from end to end. "When cousin wolf died," the dog continued with juice dribbling from its mouth, "we saw at once that she would have to be replaced, for the shepherds became vigilant once more. So, what do you think we did? Why, we all became wolves, of course! Cousin wolf, like myself, particularly enjoyed the sweet red flesh of the fig in its season and her howling drove many, like yourself, to roost in trees like frightened hens. I learned much from her." The dog broke off for a moment to scratch blissfully behind its ear. "We are wolves only at night, of course. During the day, cousin wolf is invisible, and none of our masters suspect that it is we that lope over the hillsides baying at the moon. 'Better beware a cunning friend than an honest enemy,' we say among ourselves. During the day, we even help to hunt cousin wolf. But men walk on two legs, and their noses are too far from the ground to know that the tracks we follow are our own."

It was some moments after this last remark before I could regain enough of my composure to speak again. "But tell me this," I said eventually, "what would you have done had I not been afraid of your howling and hidden myself in this tree?"

"Why, I should have bitten you, of course!" the dog replied. "And you, believing me then to be truly mad, would have run far from the sea which you seek, and we should never have heard of you again."

I thought for a moment; I stood and asked, "But now that I know the truth behind this madness, do you not fear that I shall go straight to the village and tell your masters?"

The dog shrieked with joy, and dust rose from the earth as its front paws stamped the ground. Then, itself standing on its back legs, it leaned, helpless with laughter, on my shoulders for it was the size of a wolf. It looked straight into my eyes and whimpered weakly, "Dogs and wolves are not such fools as men. The men will listen to you politely, and there will be a long, awkward silence. You will become angry, and they will see this in your eyes. You will swear it to be the truth. You will throw out your arms and hold your head as you seek ways to convince them. You will howl your innocence. Then, they will declare you to be truly mad. They, fools that they are, will say that in truth you have been bitten and that your story is but the ravings of a fevered mind. Tell me, who will listen to the ravings of a madman?"

"Truly you have the bite on me there, my friend," I agreed.

For the rest of the night, the dog and I dined like kings on the fruits of lies and the labour of fear.

WOLFY HOWELL
CHARMING GAZE

Charming Gaze. Watercolor with india ink.

HOLIDAY HOWL

Holiday Howl. Watercolor with india ink.

KRISTEN HUBSCHMID
THE WINTER WOLF

Kristen Hubschmid (K.Hub) is a relatively normal business-school graduate living in a small Canadian town. When she's not writing stories, she's often doing commissioned or personal artwork, or shooting news for a local TV station, but you might catch her roofing or boxing, too.

These days she invests most of her energy into The Meddler, *her current novel project, and hopes to one day bring her stories to the 'silver screen'. She enjoys science fiction and fantasy enormously and loves to connect with others over books, art, movies, comics, video games - anything, really. Feel free to give her a shout at https://www.facebook.com/khubswindow/*

"Be careful, Carter. You've heard how they settle things out there. I'm not gonna buy a pair of those knee-high clodhoppers and sod through some forsaken forest, looking for your tooth fillings with a metal detector, got me?"

Carter adjusted the phone against his shoulder in order to navigate the overpass that would take him off Highway 2, plunging him through the ankles of a looming evergreen forest. The late fall sunlight warming his short golden fur flickered and disappeared. Towering trees reared up on either side, squeezing the blue sky into a narrow crack overhead.

"Did you get the deed from that South Bettony pub... -what's it called..."

"Don't change the subject. Listen to this: 'business magnate goes missing on Christmas holiday in James Falls.' 'Insurance broker last seen in James Falls during snowstorm.'"

"Bev, most of these wolf packs have never even seen a city lawyer, much less learned to outwit one. Would you relax?" He checked his watch. Seventy minutes to go on this winding, cracked pavement. How the mountain village of James Falls drew so much summer tourism, he didn't know. The drive alone was enough to discourage *him*, but he knew the numbers. They'd have retreated back to the city by this time, but in the days between May and October, tourists outnumbered the local wolf pack a hundred to one. Which was why the village bar—he cast a quick glance at the paperwork on the seat beside him—Knothole Pub—was flourishing so spectacularly, the fame of its wild game menu increasing with every summer.

"They don't need to outwit a lawyer. Just you," Bev snapped. "Don't lose focus. The minute you lose focus, we're done, understand?"

"Yeah, yeah."

"Check in with me after they've signed."

"Yep."

Carter tapped End Call and tossed the phone on the leather passenger seat beside his wallet and a thick folder of papers. The radio gave him only static, as expected. He'd already made the drive three times to speak with Adel, one of the owners of the Knothole, but this should be his last trip out. He glanced at the folder, feeling a wave of satisfaction. Last trip.

The immense trees marched by on either side like sentinels, all but the foremost trunks obscured by thick green foliage. He was prepared for it, but the narrowness of the road and the height of the stretching branches seemed to compress him on either side, squeezing in as though to stifle him. His foot leaned heavier on the gas pedal.

Finally, the village of James Falls came into view, appearing suddenly through the trees where there was nothing a moment before. Carter hit the brakes, careening into the parking lot with more speed than he intended, and lurched to a halt in front of the rough-lumber veranda.

Knothole Pub reared up to the sky, a wide wooden peak supported by twisting, gnarled tree-trunk columns. Carved into the columns, the faces of a dozen ferocious-looking wolves leered in frozen malice, or watched him with quiet suspicion. He supposed they were part of the allure of this place, but he was considering the cost of sending them off.

The wooden faces didn't discourage visitors, however. In the warmer months, tourists normally thronged the capacious wrap-around veranda. But now, though it was only late October, pine needles lay in windblown dunes on the tables, and spiderwebs sparkled everywhere. This past summer had not gone well for the pub, as he knew better than most.

Carter gathered up the folder, along with his wallet and phone. A rumbling sound echoed off the trees, growing louder as Carter checked the cell service bars. The village had its own cell tower, and he should be able to call Bev easily once he'd completed his business here.

As he stuck one foot out the door of his car, the source of the rumbling sound made itself apparent. A pickup rolled into the lot to park beside Carter, a pickup the likes of which he had never seen. No one in the city drove anything remotely like it; you'd never find a parking space big enough to fit into, and he suspected it would break the noise restriction bylaw in his neighborhood. He doubted, however, that either of those problems were ever an issue. Judging by the mud caked on the tires, it wasn't a truck that spent much time on pavement, let alone on city streets.

Carter stepped out of the car into a cloud of diesel fumes. The breeze quickly whisked them away, but his annoyance remained. He walked around the back of the truck to have a word, but as he passed the bumper, something arrested his eye.

A trickle of blood dripped from the tailgate, pattering softly to the pavement, and in the guttering breeze he caught a sudden powerful whiff of its metallic scent.

The pickup door opened. A ragged boot, something like the 'clodhoppers' Bev had mentioned, kicked caked mud to the sidewalk before its owner jumped down to the pavement. He had to be four or five inches taller than Carter, and Carter was not short—as an Anatolian Shepherd, he outsized most people he met. But this wolf loomed over him, his yellow eyes vivid against the varied grays framing his face and neck.

Carter found his tongue somewhat stuck. He made to continue on to the door, as though walking around the back of the pickup had been an arbitrary decision.

"You'd better make sure that fancy car doesn't stay here too long."

The wolf, scraping a last bit of mud from his heavy boots, shut the truck door and strode directly toward Carter.

"Pardon me?" Carter said, halting. The wolf passed him, leaving mingled scents of wood smoke and spruce swirling in his wake, and opened his tailgate with considerable wrenching. He dragged a rough wooden crate from the box of the truck, catching his shredded jacket sleeve on a corner and ripping it further.

"I said you'd better leave with that fancy car before long," the wolf said, his yellow eyes steady. "Snow's coming, and those Mickey Mouse tires won't get you far."

Carter cast a glance at the sky. It was still blue, fading toward evening indigo, but blue nonetheless.

"I shouldn't be here long," Carter said, turning to continue on his way.

"Could you give me a hand, here?" The wolf pulled a second crate onto the tailgate. "I need to bring both of these in."

Carter surveyed the crates. "What's in them?"

"A moose."

"*A moose?* In those two little crates?"

"You can fit a lot of meat in these, if you cut it up right."

Carter beheld the crates with a sense of incredulity. It seemed too incredible that packed in those crates were the parts of a feral creature, recently living but now sliced up into edible portions. He had never really given such things much thought, having been raised in the suburbs. He hefted the heavy folder, the pages fluttering slightly in the breeze.

"This is an extremely important agreement, sir—I hope you don't mind if I just head inside. I have business with the owners of this pub."

"Head inside with one of these," the wolf said, thrusting one of the crates at Carter. The silence hung, the wolf's yellow gaze fixed unblinkingly on Carter's face. Finally, Carter placed the folder carefully on top of the crate before taking it.

"Have…have these crates come very far, unrefrigerated?" Carter asked.

"They've been properly cooled," the wolf growled. He led the way up the veranda's uneven steps, each one a tree trunk split in half and worn smoothest in the center.

"Excellent…excellent," Carter said. "Do you always bring the game for the menu?" It would soon be his concern, if things went as expected this evening.

The wolf shrugged. "If I have business down here, I do."

"You don't live in the area?"

The wolf held the door for Carter with his elbow.

"I'm only here for the night," the wolf replied. "After my business is finished here, I'll go back up the mountain."

The noise of voices spilling out the open door was not what Carter had anticipated; the previous trips had brought him into a silent room, empty but for the owner. Inside, after his eyes finally adjusted to the low light, he realized nearly the whole village had to be here. Wolves of every size lounged on barstools, pinning him in the crosshairs of thirty yellow-eyed glares.

Conversation lulled, and Carter felt the pressure of those gazes sweeping over his ice-white dress shirt, his business slacks paired with gleaming shoes, his Gartier watch, and his styled hair. None of them looked as though they'd ever heard of trimming their hair, let alone styling it. Some wore paint on their faces in bright blues or reds; according to urban researchers, symbols of some kind of spiritual accomplishment. Thick smoke from several pipes hazed the air, reeking of something earthy and sharp. Carter's eyes began to water. He coughed loudly and followed the wolf to the bar, where they deposited their crates of moose meat.

The barman, Adel, appeared before them, spinning a rag over a pint glass.

"This one's healthy, then?" he asked the wolf coolly, glancing at the crates.

Carter paused in the midst of inspecting the folder of papers, his eyes drawn by a slight change in the air between the Adel and the gray wolf. They had shifted, as though into a stand-off, face to face over the bar.

"I've told you before," the wolf said quietly. "Every animal I bring you is healthy."

"Apparently not every one," Adel replied curtly. He, like Carter, was much shorter than the gray wolf, and his white fur nearly gleamed in the half-light. In the common custom of wolves, he'd had a permanent tattoo dyed into the roots of his hair, a sleeve of black twisting markings almost entirely covering his right arm.

Snatching a folded newspaper from between two whiskey bottles, Adel flung it on the counter before the gray wolf.

"Seen this?"

The gray wolf's eyes darted over the front page article.

"'Local pub loses everything in food-disease scare'," Adel quoted. "Looks like everyone in the country has heard about it."

"It's not right!" snapped an elderly wolf seated at the bar, clapping his tumbler against the wood. "I've never heard of this 'wasting disease'—how do they know she got sick from our food, eh? How do they know that?"

"They don't have to prove it, boss," the barman growled, snatching the newspaper and tossing it in a nearby garbage bin. "She ate our food, she got sick. It's enough to scare folk off."

The gray wolf left the bar, skirting the edge of the room, and found a seat at one of the empty tables in the back, where he flagged the waitress.

"You shouldn't have gone to court about it," said an older female seated beside the first elderly wolf. "Shouldn't have made a stink."

"What's done is done!" Adel cried. "Had to try and prove ourselves innocent, didn't we?"

"Didn't help you none, did it?" the female wolf hissed.

"Please, friends!" Carter said, raising his voice above the babble sweeping through the pub. "I know you've been through hard times this past summer. I know lawyers aren't cheap!"

They stabbed him with their multitude of gazes again. He had not been prepared to speak to a room of wolves, but he could improvise. This may be a chance to smooth things over.

He continued. "I'm here to give you all another chance to succeed." A flurry of mutterings went through them at this. "I'm buying this pub to keep it in business, and keep dollars in local pockets. We can get your good reputation back. We can bring people back."

Carter held the folder of papers up, turning back to the barman and the elderly wolf. "I just need the signatures of the two owners to close the sale, and we're in business."

The barman regarded him coolly. "Well. I'm sure I need to read through those papers before I sign anything."

This was as Carter expected. He scanned the bar quickly, but there appeared to him no one that suited the description of lawyer. It seemed Adel had neglected to hire an expert to oversee the buyer's agreement, which suited Carter just fine.

"Should we retire to your office, then?"

Adel pierced him with a look. "No, I'm gonna read it right here."

Carter gave a polite nod. "If you'd like some time, I think I'll order some of your famous food. Can I try the Smoked Barbeque Burger?"

Adel took the folder of papers from him, giving him a glare through narrowed eyes.

"Sure, Mr. Carter. We can make whatever you want."

Carter sat himself at the last open barstool. "Excellent."

"For the purchase of the aforementioned property—" Adel began to read, his voice overcoming the low bubble of conversation.

"Mr. Adel," Carter said sharply. "Are you planning to read *aloud* from the agreement? I would not advise it…privacy is your right."

Adel gave him a long glare. "These here are concerned citizens, Carter. And I will read aloud so all shareholders can hear. Got it?"

Shareholders, Carter thought derisively. These were stakeholders, not shareholders. Only the two owners could be properly called 'shareholders'. But if they didn't know the difference between such things out here, so much the better—incidentally, that was a large part of why he and Bev had chosen this place.

Adel proceeded to read out great swaths of the buyer agreement, speaking on from the delivery of Carter's meal through to his dessert (maple grillcake, an old lupine recipe), stopping to re-read whenever a random wolf requested it. The elderly wolf he'd referred to as "boss" nodded off at times and was poked sharply back to awareness by his mate, blinking repeatedly.

Carter watched it all with increasing contentment. The listeners frequently struggled with long words, many of them calling for Adel to move on before an understanding was reached. Ridiculous, their disinterest in understanding how or why ownership would be transferred to Carter (or rather, Midland Holdings, whom he represented). It was just as well none of them lived in the city. They'd never survive it. They assumed the contract was fair and correct when they couldn't understand it, and yet made a show of checking its validity.

Carter sipped the amber ale he'd ordered. At least they knew their beer. It was excellent stuff, smooth and rich, and served in a chilled glass. They brewed it here in the village. Perhaps, he'd think about acquiring the brewery, once he'd solidified his foothold here.

"That's it," Adel said finally, flipping the last page of the contract. "Now, there's two places to sign. Does anyone have anything more to say?"

The pub was silent, more likely because several of the wolves had fallen asleep on their tables, than because they were satisfied with the agreement.

Carter produced a pen. "If you're in agreement with the contract, then I'll need you two to sign."

Adel took the pen and scrawled his signature on the space labeled *B. Adel* without hesitation.

"And yourself, sir?" Carter said, turning to the elderly wolf.

"Myself?" the wolf asked him, shaking his shaggy head.

"Yes, sir," Carter said smoothly. "I need the signatures of both owners."

The old wolf stared at him as though trying to pull him into focus. "I'm not the owner." He stared for another moment and began to chuckle. "I'm not the owner, sonny. I've no Adel blood in me."

Carter felt the eyes of all the wolves again, a roll of chuckles running through the room.

"But Adel called you boss, did he not?"

"Ah, that's just what they call me," the old wolf barked in a rough laugh. "I'm an elder! Didn't you see my face on the lee pillar out there?" He raised a gnarled hand, pointing out to the veranda.

In an effort to cut the tide of smirking from his vision, Carter swung his gaze back to Adel.

"You told me I would get both signatures."

"You will," Adel agreed, sliding Carter's empty plate into a rubber bin for washing. "This here says I have twenty-four hours to sign, right?"

"Yes—"

"Well, so long as everything is ship-shape with the winter wolf, you'll have both signatures before this time tomorrow. Another pint, boss?"

"If it please yeh."

Adel swept the empty pint glass away and turned to the towers of clean ones, glittering beside the line of draught taps.

"The winter wolf?" Carter demanded. "And who might that be?"

"Bit of a legend around here," Adel told him nonchalantly, his eyes fixed on the patient creation of a foamless pint. "Anything big goes on around here, you make sure you ask him about it. But I stopped believing in that when I was seven."

"Stopped believing!" the old wolf's mate cried. "Watch your tongue, son. He'll bring the snow if you're not careful!" Again, snickers and mutterings shivered through the attendant audience, rising to a head at the back of the room.

Adel slid the golden-hued pint across the counter, shooting an amused look that way.

"Like I said. So long as no one has any more to say on the matter, we'll leave it up to the winter wolf for the night." He swept the room with a glance. Only silence greeted his words, though a few of the wolves shifted restlessly.

"I'd say it's a family matter now," the wolf elder said, sipping his pint with well-practiced appreciation.

"All right, then we all agree," Adel said, depositing the folder of papers on the back counter with a slap.

"Adel, I was not prepared for—" Carter began, getting to his feet.

"If it's a bed and a toothbrush you need, we have an inn. Gerty keeps it wonderfully, don't you Gerty?"

The wolf elder's mate nodded sanctimoniously. "As nice as these hands can muster."

"There you are, Carter," Adel said. "A chance to keep the dollars in local pockets."

Carter stood up quickly. "I am not prepared to stay the night. I'm not sure what the delay is, you had plenty of time to alert your co-owner." He cast a glance around the pub and found nearly the entire pack had followed him to his feet. "But...I will return tomorrow morning."

The sudden buzz of his cell phone gave him an opportunity to avoid their unflinching gazes.

"This is Carter," he said. "How can I help you?"

"Well?" In that one syllable, Bev's impatience was evident. "What's taking so long? Have they signed it over to you yet?"

Carter turned away from the rest of the bar. "I'm with one of the owners now."

"And?"

"I'll update you on my drive home. Not now." He tapped End Call sharply.

The wolves still watched him, though they'd subsided into quiet conversation with each other. The only one who had not stood was the gray wolf at the back table. Ignoring the rest of the bar's inhabitants, he left a couple bills and strode out the door.

After the company had watched him exit, Adel signaled them all to sit down with an impatient wave of his dishtowel.

"All right. Mr. Carter said he'll be back in the morning, didn't he?"

Carter paid for his meal and took his leave with the promise of returning at noon tomorrow. He left the parking lot empty despite the number of wolves gathered there, and set out on the road toward the city, muttering aloud.

"…can't believe these barbarians. And people love them for it! Unbelievable…"

Potholes veered at him left and right out of the darkness. He swerved through with ease, having by this time learned the location of the worst of them.

He didn't notice the climb of his engine temperature dial until it beeped shrilly at him.

"What?" he growled at the offending warning light.

It shrilled again and began to flash. Smoke licked from the edges of the car hood, shadowy against the illuminated pavement.

Carter guided the car onto the side of the road, the beeping continuing without pause until he wrenched the key out. The rushing hiss seemed loud against the sudden silence of the engine.

"*What?!*" Carter muttered, staring at the dashboard with his hands in the air. He knew nothing about cars. Nothing. This one was only a year old, purchased brand new when he and Bev had acquired Fry Guys (makers of the legendary 'sour cream poutine').

The silent road stretched before Carter nearly a kilometer before it twisted and disappeared. Behind, it sloped up into the alpine valley Knothole Pub nestled in, but nowhere was there any break in the trees, or any hint of a nearby habitation.

As the hiss from under the hood waned, other noises began to filter into Carter's consciousness. Flanking him like bookends, the trembling trees hid the source of a continuous scraping and rustling. Every now and then, a sharp crack would sound, as though someone snapped a branch over their knee not fifty feet away. Other sounds punctured the general rustle; hoots and bugles and twitters, some echoing from a distance, some seemingly from a few steps away.

Carter wrested the owner's manual from his cluttered glovebox, flipping through the index.

"Smoke. Smoke? What happens if there's smoke?"

A low, growling noise filtered through the car's closed windows. Jerking, Carter surveyed the surroundings, eyes leaping from tree trunk to tree trunk.

The growling increased in intensity until he recognized the sound. Headlights blazed on the road behind him, beaming down the slope. It was the gray wolf's truck, trundling down the potholed road.

At least it wasn't his tires that had him stuck here. Mickey Mouse tires, had the wolf said?

Carter put his flashers on, sending blooms of yellow light over the trees as the truck crept to a stop a few feet from his back bumper.

Carter climbed out of his car as a black silhouette crossed through the truck headlights.

"Hello!" he cried. "I was wondering if I'd see anyone on this road!"

The gray wolf made no reply, but he stopped in front of Carter, surveying him.

"It's smoking from under the hood," Carter added, quelling a strange urge to keep talking.

"Did you have a look?"

Carter balked. "Um, not yet."

"Is the hood popped?"

"Uh…" Carter descended to the driver's seat and scanned the interior. "I've never needed to open it before…"

The wolf walked round to the front bumper, hands in his pockets.

No button presented itself. Carter seized the owner's manual. Surely it would tell him where the hood release was. He flipped madly through a few pages before the breeze grabbed them and spun through a third of the book—

The wolf reached suddenly past him, pulling on a small lever by his foot that looked nothing like a lever—Carter hadn't even heard him move.

Casting him an unreadable look, the wolf returned to the front of the car and opened the hood. A waft of smoke mushroomed out.

Carter followed, peering at the spidery mess of tubes and wires that made up his car's engine. It was unintelligible to him. The wolf leaned against the open hood, clearly waiting for him to comment. Finally, he broke the silence.

"Do you see where your problem is?"

Carter blinked between him and the engine. "Um."

"Your coolant line is cut." In the silence that greeted these words, he seemed compelled to add, "Your engine overheated because you have no coolant."

"Ah," Carter nodded. "Can that be fixed?"

The wolf regarded him for another long moment. "I have some electrical tape in my truck."

"Good…that's…excellent."

Pushing off the hood, the wolf strode back to his pickup. After some moments of rummaging, he dropped a jug of what Carter assumed was coolant on the pavement and shut the truck door. He stood, pausing by the box of his truck. Apparently making a decision, he dragged out a large wooden crate, this one empty, and dropped it on the pavement. He dropped something else on top—perhaps a hunting knife?—encased in leather.

Leaving those items where they lay, the wolf returned with the jug and a roll of black tape.

"This should be enough for you to make it to the city," the wolf said, setting the jug down. He donned a pair of darkly stained leather gloves before leaning carefully over the engine, poking and prodding at some sort of tubing.

"I thought you'd want to stay in James Falls. Keep the dollars in their pockets."

Carter felt a flutter of annoyance. "I thought you were headed back up the mountain? Find some more big game?"

"Plenty of game around here." He seemed to locate what he was looking for, and peeled a strip of tape from the roll with his teeth. With care, he wrapped it several times around the coolant line, re-sealing the clean slice in the rubber.

"Is there?" Carter glanced at the trees. Was there something large and hungry out there, watching them from a shadow?

"Have you been in the food business before? You kept calling the pub 'the establishment'."

"This is my first foray into restaurants." Carter smiled thinly. "I just wanted to use the right terminology; make sure everyone's clear."

"It makes things less clear," the wolf rejoined. "Calling it the Driftwood Pub would make it clear."

"Look," Carter said in an easy, open tone, ready to smooth feathers. "I can see you're not pleased with the idea of new ownership at the Driftwood. But I assure you, I want it to retain all of the rustic and authentic flavor that makes it so renowned. I'm not going to fire the owner—I want the expertise he offers as a local food guru. So really, all of this is only going to benefit James Falls as a whole."

The well-rehearsed words came naturally. Tell them everything would stay the same. Tell them their community would do well.

The wolf's face was unusually hard to read, though. He turned away to pick up the jug of coolant and opened the cap on the coolant reservoir.

"You're not going to buy the pub," he said, carefully pouring the blue-green liquid. "Why—"

Carter jumped in with a ready rebuttal. "Trust me, even though ownership is changing, the establishment will keep all of its small-town sparkle—"

The wolf had continued talking as well, and as a result Carter wasn't sure he heard correctly.

"I'm sorry?"

"I said, why do you think I cut your coolant line?" The wolf emptied the jug and replaced the reservoir cap, his eyes flicking up to Carter's face. "I wanted to have a talk, just you and me. It can be hard to get anything across with a pack of wolves looking over my shoulder."

In the following beat of silence, Carter gripped the hood to steady himself.

"Better check the engine temperature," the wolf said, striding quickly to the driver's seat. He flicked the car on, watching the dash.

Carter couldn't quite reconcile what he'd just heard with the wolf's manner. As the wolf stepped back out of the car, the lights flickering out again, nothing in his bearing suggested aggression or anger.

"It needs some time to cool. You've got a lot of mileage on this car for its age," the wolf remarked. "But I guess that makes sense, given that Driftwood Pub is three days' drive from here. South Bettony, right?"

Carter was again struck dumb. He stared at the wolf. How did he know about South Bettony? Last week, he and Bev had laid hold of a seaside eatery that drew people from miles around for its crab cakes...now that he heard it, Driftwood sounded right...

"I read about that one," the wolf went on. "You took the Driftwood over just recently. Left the owner as manager, and then you came here. But I get it, it's a recent acquisition. You might not be that familiar with the name of it yet."

Carter's mind raced. The wolf had baited him, used the wrong name on purpose. How could he have mixed up the names—how?!

The wolf broke his gaze, shutting the hood with a clap that nearly caused Carter to fall over. "The thing about wasting disease is," the wolf went on, leaning on the car, "while it's related to mad cow disease, there's never been a case where any effects were passed on by ingestion of the diseased meat. It's not transferable between species.

"That's supposing I saw an animal with the symptoms of wasting disease and still decided to sell it for people to eat." The wolf directed a pointed look at Carter. "I knew right away when that girl got sick. It wasn't the food." He waited. "Do you want to fill in the blanks for me?"

Carter attempted a laugh. "I'm not sure why you're telling me stories, but I need to get on the road."

"Then wait until I've reached the end," the wolf said. "So the sick girl. I asked myself, why would someone fake food poisoning, and why chalk it up to wasting disease? Why go to court over it? Why incur those costs?"

The wolf paused again, but Carter's mouth was too dry for him to form a reply, so he continued.

"It turns out, in the last few months there have been about six similar occurrences across the country. Remote places known for good food. They're up-and-coming sensations until they have a contamination scare, and then they have to be investigated. Every case I found went to court, and in every case nothing was proven—only that small restaurants can't afford city lawyers."

"I don't see what significance any of this holds for me," Carter spat. "If you'll excuse me." He strode past the wolf, half-expecting him to give chase, and opened the driver's side door.

His pocket buzzed, and Carter paused automatically, swiping the phone out of his pocket to see Bev's name on the caller screen.

It happened before he could react. The wolf pulled the phone out of his grasp and held it to his ear.

"This is Carter, how can I help you?" he said in a passable imitation of Carter's voice.

Carter was in shock. He made no movement as Bev's voice came through, loud enough for him to hear every word.

"Are you done *yet*? We need to close this one and skip for a few days, I think."

"How's the mad cow?" the wolf asked.

Her reply was so shrill there was no missing it. "Go to hell. Better yet, get them to sign and *then* go to hell. You got that? Hurry up, I've ordered Chinese."

She hung up, and the wolf pocketed Carter's phone. He resumed as though there had been no interruption.

"I've read six different articles about this kind of takeover, leaving the existing staff and ownership intact. It's a different holding company every time. But you know what's unusually similar?"

Carter had no idea. He was seriously thinking about diving into the car and running the wolf over.

"The quotes from the buyers. 'Small-town sparkle'. 'Keeping dollars in local pockets'. 'Local food gurus.' Isn't that strange?"

"Why do you care, anyway?" Carter snarled. The driver's door between them bolstered his courage. "You don't even live in James Falls! Them with their superstitions and their winter wolf!"

The wolf opened his jacket and dragged a giant folder, with difficulty, out of his inside pocket. Unfolding it, he waved it at Carter. It was the buyer's agreement he'd left with Adel.

"That, yeah. Winter wolf. They've been calling me that since I moved up the mountain. I put my winter supply trip off until the first snow, so things last longer. Yeah, they all have a good laugh...—but my name's Adel." He flipped through the pages of the agreement and showed Carter the last page, where a blank line waited beside the second owner's signature, denoted *W. Adel.*

Carter gulped for air, his mind spinning. "You-you're-you're the other Adel?"

The wolf nodded. "Do you remember what I told you about those crates?" he asked, nodding at the one sitting beside his truck. Carter's eye lurched there unwillingly.

With sudden, unthinking panic, Carter's body moved of its own accord. He sank into the car, slamming the door—

No keys. The keys were missing.

Leaning down outside his window, the wolf dangled them. They clattered against the glass. Carter's car keys.

Suddenly, the wolf looked skyward, distracted. "Look at that. I told you the snow was coming."

Carter could barely register it. Big, fluffy white flecks meandered down through the air, glowing brilliantly in the beams from the pickup's headlights.

The wolf opened the car door—Carter slammed it shut again, hitting the lock button—but the wolf unlocked it with the key fob and opened it again. He stood inside the door, squatting down, his yellow eyes flashing luridly in the headlights of the truck.

"Two options, Mr. Carter."

Nothing within Carter's reach would make an effective weapon. He didn't trust his strength anyway. He'd never needed it much.

"I've met a few of you city-born mutts, so I'm keeping it simple. Your first option is this: the money you would've used to purchase my pub—the *Knothole Pub*, if you're still confused—you will gift to us as a charitable donation, and then disappear forever from my town and my pack."

A silence stretched, softer and heavier as the scattering of snowflakes thickened into a flickering cascade of white, obscuring the trees, blurring the road…

Carter knew the wolf was waiting, and he resisted at first—but the wolf waited on with a patience that made no flutterings or misgivings, and Carter felt they might sit until the snow buried them.

"And option two?" he finally hissed, teeth gritted.

"You must read the news." The wolf smiled. "I told you I've met a few of you."

WILLIAM HUGGINS
WINTER COUNT

William Huggins lives, writes, works, hikes, and camps in the desert southwest with his wife, daughter, and three rescue dogs. Wild country fuels his imagination. His fiction has appeared at Another Realm, Expanded Horizons, *and* Third Flatiron Anthologies. *He also writes for* Texas Books in Review *and* We Are Wildness *at wearewildness.com/blog.*

It was pure pleasure to watch them run.

Hardin turned in his seat in the orb, looking through the one-way glass that encased him, twisting back and forth, unable to get enough of the wolves—Pack 2, they called them—as they surged single-file across the tundra below them. He had been in the belly of the *Singer* for a decade, watching vids and working with plants, but dreaming of wolves. And now this, a dream come true—to be allowed to the surface to participate in the annual winter count, only the third such at this latitude, as the wolves recovered and made their way deeper into the landscape.

They flew a mere fifty feet off the deck, silent as only an orb could manage. Snow swirled around and above them—just a light storm, the snow mostly grounded and moved by wind gusts, the air half-clear with high clouds. A front might be moving in later in the afternoon, but for now they had perfect conditions with which to view the wolves, an extended pack of ten hunting a three-hundred kilometer circle, with three pups back at the den. The pups interested Hardin most—everything relied on them.

Three centuries of Fallowing, he thought. *And so much on the backs of three small souls.*

"Worried, sir?" the pilot asked. Warren, his name was: young, confident. He maneuvered the orb like an expert. In its silent passage, the wolves knew nothing of them over the shifting sands of snow and wind.

Hardin grimaced. "Worried? Yes, some." He saw no reason to lie. "Last season this pack lost all its pups?"

The pilot nodded.

Hardin grunted. "I couldn't be here then. But just seeing them— I'm awestruck."

Warren laughed. He was used to flying alone—preferred it, actually. Orbs were meant for solo fliers, though they could comfortably fit two. Long days and nights mapping or tracking or collating data on the way back to the *Singer*, one got used to being alone. But the ecologist was a nice man, quiet, respectful, and his questions were shrewd and to the point. Warren liked him.

"Fifteen years I've tracked them, on and off." He sensed he had the ecologist's ear, another thing he liked about Hardin: he listened. "Last year's winter was especially bad. Nothing to be done. This year, the game's much stronger: more buffalo, more elk. Even some musk oxen returning, if you believe the scientists." Hardin rewarded him with a smile for the poor joke. "The pack will have an easier time. It will hold. You'll see. The Fallowing is working. Not perfectly, but it's working."

Hardin nodded. A three-day pass, he had. Hardly enough to get a feel for all that took place below him. He was already in love with the cutting air, the feel of snow against his face—Warren had been kind enough that first day to land and let him step out and get the experience, even if it was against regs, and what he longed to do was stretch his legs and run, just run—but mostly what it looked like to follow those beautiful wolves on their circuits. For two days, they had paced them, watching them take down a small buffalo calf in the late morning. Their precision, their focus, the teamwork—so much of what he studied could be applied to the human equation if they would follow their example.

If only we would.

The pack spun suddenly below them, following tightly behind the leader, and Warren turned the orb to compensate, the wind lifting and settling them a moment, about thirty yards behind the five pack members.

"Returning to the den," Warren said, consulting the orb's board. "Want to follow them or head back for an early dinner?" But Warren had already taken the measure of the ecologist and knew the answer.

"Oh, follow, please."

Single-file, they paced the pack the thirty minutes until they disappeared into the den, bellies full of meat for themselves and their young. Warren made a quick circle of the area for show, again letting Hardin take in the harshness of the clime these wolves called home— an empty vastness of snow and rock, deep grays upon white as far as the eye could see, forcing them to range a hundred kilometers some days for prey—before he swung the orb and accelerated for similar human habitation.

Ice Camp Three, they called it—*a rare lack of imagination for scientists,* Hardin thought, who always seemed so clever with their names. But maybe it expressed the temporary nature of the place: the third camp for the third winter count, tucked inside a cave with a thin barrier of single-celled bacteria to keep the cold mostly at bay. When they left tomorrow night, it would biodegrade and start a small food chain, rippling from the cave into the wild lands beyond as the snow and ice faded and the green moved back in. Hardin smiled at the thought.

He held out a finger for a second and almost touched the barrier but stopped at the last minute. You never knew what repercussions could come from the simplest acts. Fallowing ethics: they had to stay hidden. Nothing could know they were there. Ever. They had removed themselves from the planet to let it heal, from the lush rainforests of the equator to the deserts and mountains and great plains to this—a land of extremes that only now, after three hundred years of removing industrial civilization from the planet, was seeing the ice and snow it should have always known before rising carbon chased it away. The cold felt thrilling against his bare hands and face. He clenched his fingers and drove them into his parka's pockets as he walked back into the cave. Even with the barrier it was still frighteningly cold, and he hustled through the dimness into the lit cavern beyond, emerging soon into warmth and laughter.

He took off the jacket. "Hardin!" someone yelled, and he raised a hand in greeting. Some of his comrades had clearly been at the vodka already. There were two other ecologists from the *Singer*'s sister ships— Prima from the *Rise Against* and Eckstein from *Piper's Rescue*—down for the winter counts, as well. Prima, with seniority, got Packs 3 and 4; Eckstein had 1. They sat at table with two visibly bored techs, both young women whose jobs were to maintain the log servers so all the information got recorded, more at ease with technology than people— especially drunken people. Prima's cheeks looked warm and red, her old, lined face glowing, a light flirtiness to her eyes—but Eckstein was glassy-eyed and leaning already, his voice loud, motions staggered. He grinned at Hardin, waved his cup at the other table in the room.

"And they won't even participate!"

The pilots sat separate and quiet in a dark corner. They, too, more at ease in the silence of their orbs than here. Warren looked up at Hardin and shook his head, offended. He nodded toward Eckstein. Hardin sighed. Of all the things he didn't want to do on this trip—

"Maybe time to grab some sleep, Eck," he said. "Early morning tomorrow."

"Come on, Hardin, don't be so stuffy. When do we get to do this above? Have a drink."

"Not tonight, thanks. I'm here for the wolves—as you should be."

Eckstein laughed. "The wolves—like they're going anywhere."

Prima cleared her throat. "Eck—"

"Oh, please. Running. Just running. Them and the snow, over hill and hill. Not what I expected, I'll admit." He took a long drink from his cup. "I thought they would be...well—"

"I think they're magical," Hardin said. "Think about it, Eck: up here less than a decade, and we have four packs we're covering. The best pup count so far. And all that game they haven't even discovered yet."

Eckstein laughed and waved his hand dismissively. "Magical? Not them. What's magical is us: we wiped them out and we brought them back. If they'd brought themselves back, that would be magical. We're the magicians—we scientists."

He reached for the bottle close at hand, but one of the techs grabbed it first and tossed it to Hardin, who caught it in an ungloved hand and folded it under his parka. He glared. He walked toward the sleeping area another tunnel beyond.

"Oh, Hardin, don't be so damned serious! The Fallowing's great; of course it's great! It's working, isn't it? But give some credit where credit is due—we're the catalyst, we're the saviors!"

Hardin left the rest of his colleague's words as echoes as he hit the tunnel. He undressed quickly and slipped into his bag, pulled it snug around his neck and shoulders. Sleep found him quickly.

"We have a problem," Warren said as they left the makeshift hangar. "O-36 called in a lost pup as they headed toward Pack 4."

"Lost pup?"

"Aye. One of ours. Must have slipped from the den overnight. Who really knows? But the pack's hunting in an area where we need to count buffalo today so we don't have a lot of time to track."

Hardin seemed confused. "Doesn't the pack know it's lost?"

"No doubt."

"So why haven't they gone to help it?"

Warren shook his head. "It's survival out here, sir. It's make it through the winter. The pack hunts. The pup's on its own."

Hardin swallowed. "And last year you said one pack lost all three pups?"

"Yes, but not like this. Just winter—cold, disease. It's a damn hard life out here, sir."

Hardin nodded. Warren accelerated, and the white and gray below them stirred into a mist. Three minutes brought them over the den site. Warren circled once, saw no activity, then swung west where the pup sighting was called in. The den sat at the top a long sweeping hill, half snow and ice, half bare rock, tumbling down into a valley several kilometers below the den on the high ground.

"There," Hardin said, and pointed.

"Good eye, sir." Warren pulled the orb into a long, low swing, stirring as little snow as possible. Sure enough, in the bare deep valley stood the pup, mottled gray with black tips on its ears, turning a circle. Its small mouth moved, crying no doubt, but the two men in the orb could hear nothing.

"What should we do?" Hardin asked.

"Nothing, sir." Warren's mouth made a tight line and he kept emotion from his face. "Fallowing ethics: log it, and we chase the pack."

"But they're on the other side of this range."

"Aye," Warren said, and keyed his hands across the controls before him. The orb rose and accelerated toward the peaks before them.

"We can't just leave it, Warren."

The pilot's voice took on a firmer tone. "We can and will, sir. You knew what you were getting into when you came down. This is not a laboratory. You aren't a veterinarian."

"But the Fallowing—"

"Continues, sir. One pup will not change the direction of what we've set in motion."

Hardin sat back against the seat and let out a breath of frustration. Of course, he knew Warren was right—but it didn't make the knowledge any easier. All this work, three centuries of returning things to their proper rights—and to leave that little being to its own devices when it would be so easy to just nudge it back home, or hit it with a tranquilizer and drop it near its den so it would be found—

But maybe that was the point, he thought. If the Fallowing didn't take on its own, if the creatures they were bringing back from the brink of extinction didn't manage their own survival, then how could they call it a success?

He tried to soak in the beauty of the peaks, imagining them covered in green foliage and all the colors of flowers that came along with spring, and all the life that spread across them, that carnival of life denied this place for so many centuries. And he did, for a time. He even found the starkness of the winter landscape beautiful in its own way, stripped down to the essence of survival, as winter tended to be—but a part of him always drifted back to that little life in the midst of this cold vastness, and its unheard cries.

He forgot again as they swept over a buffalo herd two valleys over, hundreds of individuals spanning several kilometers. Not even a large herd by many standards. He longed to see the caribou so much farther north of here, those massive trails of animals that went on migration taking the better part of the day for the entire mass to pass. The wolves were slowly making their way north back into that territory, and once they did—how exciting it would be to participate in a count there. But for now, he focused on what was below them, staying in the now, as the orb's tracker counted off individuals.

"No wolves," Hardin said.

Warren shook his head. "Not from our pack. Not yet. But this herd is migrating. They may drift down that way. We were lucky to see the kill yesterday. This is a long way for them to run." Warren tapped a key. "Mapping sequence initiated." And the orb took over from its pilot for a time, circling the buffalo below.

"I'm sorry about Eck last night," Hardin said into the silence. "I don't think he meant what he said."

"He did," Warren said flatly. "Peck didn't even want to take him up today. He won't be down again." The pilot's eyes were firm and hard as steel. "Our say counts a lot, sir."

Hardin cleared his throat. "Well, I hope I haven't similarly offended. I would like to come back." He smiled. "It's so amazing, so much more than I thought it would be. I would like—" Hardin stopped.

Warren let the silence linger a moment, then asked, "Like what, sir?"

Hardin waved a hand. "It's a fool's dream, Warren."

Warren laughed. "Most things worth doing are, sir. Please."

"I'd like to watch wolves hunt caribou."

Warren laughed. "I'll make it happen. I'll fly you if I can. But I think there's something more bothering you, sir."

Hardin nodded.

"The pup?"

"Yes."

Warren leaned back and scratched his chin. His eyes glanced at the board. "Tell you what, sir. We finish the count, we're good for the day. We've done our duty. No reason to rush home. We'll run by and check on the pup to put your mind at ease."

They chatted about small things while the orb did its work: the arc of their lives that brought them to this place, what family they had, the Fallowing, what drew them to these wild places. Warren could have flown an orb so many other places, and there were choices for duty assignments for ecologists besides the frozen places. Friendships were born from such chance assignments.

So when the count ended, Warren recoded the board, and the orb swung high and away, benefitting from a prevailing thermal that cast them back toward the den. All through the morning and day, they had not seen the wolves, and Hardin felt disappointment at that, but such was the way of things.

They swept down over the valley, and the pup was there, near where it had been, turning and running in circles. Hardin watched it with concern, then noticed something off to the side, hovering.

"Warren—"

"Aye, I have it, sir." He tapped keys. "O-36/38: who counted Pack 2 last year?"

The response was immediate: "O-37, O-38: I did."

The day was darkening outside as a front moved in and obscured the sun. Hardin twisted for a look back and forth as the orb circled the cub. And he caught a glimpse, behind some rocks, finally: another wolf, half hidden, looking at the pup—a new and different one they had not seen before.

"It's a wolf!" Hardin half-shouted, hitting Warren's arm.

Warren nodded, pushed the ecologist back. "Did you get a count on the three pups we lost last year?"

"Yes. They never returned to the den."

"Hate to be so harsh, Peck, but did you see bodies?"

"Well, no. But we didn't need to—nothing could survive out there on its own."

Hardin shook his head, leaned forward. "A nursed pup five weeks old can survive, according to the literature. How old were the pups?"

There was a pause across Peck's transmission. "Two months, maybe? Do you remember, Warren?"

"At least seven weeks. Heavens, do you think it's possible?"

Hardin nodded. "Absolutely. Have you scanned it?"

"Doing so now." Warren's hands moved across the board. "What's the issue here, Hardin? Why all the questions?"

"I think one of the pups has come home," Warren said. "We've got a new wolf down here with the stray pup. Looks healthy enough." He paused. "Scan came through: just over a year old, full muscle and skeletal structure, hearty and hale."

"Rerouting," Peck said. "We're coming back. I want to see this for myself."

"How's Eckstein?" Hardin asked.

"Sleeping. He didn't feel so well today." The disgust was evident in Peck's voice. "Maybe this will liven him up. Hold position. We'll be there in twenty minutes."

"Might not be holding position," Warren said. "They're on the move."

"Aye," Peck said. "Closing the line. Keep me informed."

Warren swung the orb as Hardin hit his arm. "Stop hitting me, Hardin!" he laughed, pushing the ecologist to the side.

"But, look—"

Warren already had. The pup and older wolf below had made acquaintance, moving around one another cautiously. The pup followed the older wolf instinctually, and the new wolf raised its head and then moved up the drainage toward the higher peak. Warren smiled. "You may get your help, Hardin."

"Are you getting all of this?" Hardin asked.

"Aye. I've been recording since we came over the ridge."

The pup shadowed the older wolf as they moved higher up, the older one waiting at points where the pup had trouble climbing rocks. They stopped halfway up the climb to drink from a spring. Warren hovered above, filming. Both men watched quietly over the half hour they watched the wolves, until a voice broke through.

"We're over the ridge," Peck said.

"They're moving up the drainage," Warren said. "Turn on your cameras. We think the prodigal is leading the stray back to the den. I'll take the south side, you take the north."

"You running data?"

"Everything. Let's keep to silence."

"Aye. I'll let base know what we're doing then shut down."

The other orb fell into pattern across the drainage that was steepening into a canyon now. The older wolf moved up with strong, sure strides, the pup closer on his tail as it grew in confidence. Both stopped from time to time to spray a rock or bush but mostly they moved. The orb swung in the strengthening wind around them, a front clearly moving in, clouds dark and growing, moving lower. It would be a cold night out here if the pup had to last, but at least it would have company—though Hardin was hoping they would make the ridge, which loomed closer and closer. The wolves picked up pace, making better time crossing the ridge at an angle than they were in the steepening rockiness of the canyon.

"They learn quickly," Hardin said. Warren only nodded.

They paced them another hour until they reached the ridgeline. The lead wolf slowed, looked back at the pup. The den loomed before them, tucked snugly under several large rocks. No one sat in the entrance. The pup stepped forward. The lead wolf nudged it with his nose, pushing it toward the entrance.

Just then a head appeared in the hole, and suddenly two of the larger males of the pack lunged forward. They separated the pup from the newcomer and spun, tails level, teeth bared. The newcomer stood his ground, head low, tail down, waiting. The two from the den circled him, sniffing, considering. They stepped back, apparently satisfied. The newcomer backed away, tail level, and ran back down the hill.

"Thought we'd see a fight?" Warren asked, and Hardin realized he'd held his breath during the short exchange. He laughed. "We easily could have," Warren said. "That was unusual."

"Yes. From all I've read, territoriality reigns, yes?"

Warren chuckled. "The world is a bit more complex than your literature."

"I'm learning that."

They circled the wolves as they herded the pup back into the den, then rode a thermal down the narrow valley and followed the newcomer until he ran out onto the snowy plain and merged with the dimness. Snow began to fall, obscuring him further.

"What do you think will happen to him?"

Warren shrugged. "He's lived this long on his own. He's got a good shot at a decade. Maybe he'll found Pack 5 with a female stray. Maybe he won't make it. We'll find out at next year's winter count, now that we know to look for him."

Peck's voice sounded. "Orders from above. Ships want us back. Major winter storm moving in. Techs are already stripping the cave."

"Aye," Warren said. He smiled at Hardin. "Adventure's over, sir."

The orb swept up, rising through a sequence of clouds that bounced and tossed them until they rose into clear sky. Night was already coming, stars showing in the early gloom. And Hardin felt a pang of loss—how much he wanted to stay, how much to return.

"Magic," he said, not knowing he spoke.

"Aye, sir. I promise, if it's in my power, I'll get you back sometime in the future."

Hardin nodded, half-hearing—for much of him was on the ground, four-footed, senses wide, taking in a world of snow and ice, raw hunger in his belly, though a part of him knew that spring and better times would come. The better part of him was lost in joy.

For oh, it was such a pleasure to run.

BILL KIEFFER
BROTHERS IN FLUX

Bill Kieffer was born in Jersey City, NJ. He never fully recovered.

His novella, THE GOAT: Building the Perfect Victim, *is now available from Red Ferret Press. Everything else is Subject to Change.*

A black-furred nightmare in a quilted parka pushed the front door open as the beginnings of a winter storm howled behind it. It spun, cooler forward, and used the red and white plastic box to push the door shut. It resisted the urge to shake off the snow, even if none of it was actually on his fur that was quickly growing beneath his many layers of clothes.

It heard movement in the living room and quick-stepped to the kitchen where it hoped to store their catch before the sick brother tried to get up. Its foot pads were frozen, and it silently apologized to the three generations of pet dogs they'd cruelly assumed the black pads never really felt the cold the way soft pink human soles did.

It had been so wrong.

When the fish were on ice, it took a moment to collect itself.

This was the new normal. The new normal.

There was Bobby after all.

He'd gotten his wish. They didn't look alike any more.

All it took was the world coming to an end.

"The Internet was up for an hour today," Bobby said as the wolfish thing who used to be his twin flopped onto the couch. "Things are starting to get back to normal..."

A new normal, it thought. Ice blue, soulful eyes looked down a short, black muzzle at Bobby lying on the floor, his almost pink body showing the ravages of a Flux transformation in progress. "Tha'sss good," it forced the words out its distorted jaws and stretched lips. It hated the sound of its own voice, but was grateful to have rediscovered the ability. There was so much left unsaid between them. "'Oow'ss da... tail?'"

"Infected, still," Bobby's twisted left hand reached around his own back toward the huge purplish mound that the wolf thing knew was under the sheet. "I wish we hadn't tried to cut it off with that ax."

Jerry rubbed at the thick black fur on its own arms and hugged itself. Beneath its flannel shirt, a patch of white fur was growing on its belly. Who knew what changes were occurring internally? The doctors were just as clueless. They were on their own. No one understood what was happening. They were all changing, and everyone was different.

But they all quickly learned that injuries while in mid-transformation could upset whatever mumbo-jumbo that kept Flux victims alive during impossible re-configurations.

Some just learned quicker than others.

"Izzs not 'air,'" it said softly. Its brow deepened as he tried to get the "f" sound right, but the threat of its tears kept it from making another attempt. It forced its ears back into the safe, upright position.

Bobby pulled at the laptop with his right hand, the fingers of which were mostly fused into a paddle-like flipper. The wolf-thing looked away. "This time last year, Jerry, we were ordering pizzas on this thing. Remember that?"

Jerry snorted at that. In truth, it'd been closer to two years since Papa John's had come knocking at their door. They'd been identical twins and fully human back then, before the Flux. Before the world fell apart. Before Bobby started slowly changing into an otter. Before they cut off their tails, thinking they'd somehow be more human that way.

Back in the days when Bobby could do more than just crawl on his hands and feet.

It was going to survive because its transformation had almost been complete when the ax came down. Bobby...not so much.

The wolf forced a smile into its voice, "Yea...I rrr'mem'br." It could not bring itself to force a fake smile.

"Did you get to the store?" Bobby said, forcing his own voice to be cheerful.

"Yea," Jerry lied easily. The stream behind their house provided all their meat these days. "Got 'ishh 'ur you. Eh'pensive," it chided gently.

"I miss beef." Fish was all Bobby could probably eat. Good thing because that's all there was to eat. He looked up at Jerry with his round black eyes that had once been blue. He sniffed, his long whiskers bouncing. "I miss...lots of things."

The silence stretched a bit too long, but this, too, was the new normal.

The silence that taunted it. The smothering quietude that promised it that of all the things left unsaid, goodbye might be the only word worth saying.

The brothers flinched at a sudden, loud pounding at the door. Once people had started turning into monsters for no identifiable reason, visitors had become rarer and less welcome as time went by. Jerry stood and saw a familiar fur-covered face, a reflection in brown and white, looking back at it from the door's window.

"Izzs O'kay," Jerry said and indicated with a few silent gestures that Bobby should stay put where he was, just in case. A rifle tip appeared from under the blankets. Buckshot didn't need to be aimed to be effective. Webbed fingers could still pull the trigger. Jerry nodded and walked on his still wet feet to the door. It found itself shaking off its feet before stepping back outside into the chill night air.

Nerves.

The wolf-thing on the porch was larger than Jerry by almost a foot. It wore nothing, yet the intelligence in its eyes would have marked it as human if one knew what to look for. He'd adapted better than most. Jerry found himself hating the man beneath the fur, but it forced itself to greet the sheriff with something other than a growl. "What?"

"The Pack's moving out tonight," the sheriff said in the guttural version of English the canine folks of the county had taken up in the last few months. It had been frightened at how fast they'd all learned it. Almost as if the language had been built into the virus. Or whatever the Flux was. "You sure you're not coming?"

"I can't leave my brother," Jerry said and then, with a snarl, "He can't hunt for himself." The sheriff nodded sadly and somehow managed to look sheepish behind the black lips and sharp teeth. "We should all go, you know. We've got the townfolk to consider, you know."

Jerry nodded. Canines and Felines made up the Pack. All Flux victims, they made up about a fifth of Manchester's population. The rest of the town still slowly turning into various types of herbivores. Everyone still looked mostly human now, but winter was here. How long could a hungry predator resist tearing into a cow or chicken, even when it begged for its life in English?

Worse was the fear that the final phase of the Flux could have them all thinking like the animals they resembled? No one knew for sure. Doctors were being lynched all over the country.

"Jerry, please...we need you." The sheriff said. After a moment, his ears went flat back, and he seemed to cringe a little. There was suddenly begging in his voice. "Please! If we're to survive...we'll need someone like you who can build things...to program computers once we get the power back...like you helped getting the phone lines back up."

Seeing the sheriff submit to it like that turned its stomach. "Bobby needs me." It refused to let its ears move. It refused to dominate, but it sensed that it could.

The sheriff shook his fuzzy canine head. "You've figured out how to recharge his laptop battery with the carrier wave of the phone line. You wrote a program to emulate a chat room, when you know he can barely see. You've invented this whole fantasy world for him, for God's sake! What are you going to do when he finds out there aren't any normal people left? That there's no hope?"

"Hope." Jerry snorted. "When people started changing after the Flash Event, I had no hope. You people just want to go someplace where you can't kill anyone you know. People who don't know you are another story, right?" There wasn't enough game to survive in the hills about Manchester. They both knew that. "I don't care. But when I lost my voice and Bobby took me in...Look, all I care about is being human. After almost two years of watching the Flux take my friends, I'm not about to throw it all away and run off into the woods to act like an animal."

"We're not...!" Their eyes locked for a moment, and then the sheriff averted his eyes, submitting even further. "We..."

It shook his head. "You're all lying to yourselves. As instincts sneak up on you, your makeshift pack is going to turn on itself. Cats and dogs...it isn't going to stay about predators and prey. You know that, right? You'll never be human again if you run away. You have to fight to stay human."

The sheriff grumbled as he remounted the horse. He was still human enough to want to argue but wolf enough to obey the more dominant wolf. The sheriff rode away without saying another word.

It wondered how many humans in the world were turning into horses. It wondered how many more stillborn and deformed babies the Flux-cursed women of Manchester would bear over the winter.

It wondered if it could really make penicillin out of moldy bread.

Flux denied all reason, yet it had rules.

The snow continued as the sheriff's horse vanished into the woods.

God promised no more floods, but there were other ways to make the world over fresh.

Somewhere down the road, the Sheriff howled his regret and loneliness. The snow carried the sound for miles.

It found itself, thigh deep in the snow, marking his territory. The black and white shook the snow off its plaid-covered back and went back inside.

It was no longer a man, but it was wolf enough to remain loyal to its litter-mate, Bobby.

PATRICIA LEHTOLA
FIRST TASTE OF WINTER

Patricia Lehtola is a freelance artist. She is active with local wildlife organizations to aid and raise funds. She currently lives with her family in southern California.

First Taste of Winter. Pastels on illustration board.

JANE LEE McCRACKEN
AMERICAN DREAM

Scottish artist Jane Lee McCracken makes intricate multi-layered ballpoint pen drawings and constructs multi-media objects and installations inspired by her drawings. Her work is impassioned by childhood memoirs, fairy tales, forests, wolves, and other animals. Along with her continuing interest in war, environmental destruction, and loss and the impact on humans and animals, Jane's work is symbolic of life's brutal reality. Jane lives in the Northeast of England with her husband Rob and their Northern Inuit dog, Lily, her muse. Jane also fundraises through her artwork for endangered and threatened species and organizations such as Wolf Conservation Center, Save Wild Tigers, UK, and the Born Free Foundation. Her artist's website is www.janeleemccracken.co.uk

Winter howls through Yellowstone National Park, sweeping across the Wolf Conservation Center's Ambassador wolf Zephyr's fur. An intrepid stag plunges through a deep blanket of snow, pursued by wolves, as a bison battles against a blizzard on the plains between the mountains.

A mountain bluebird heralds the arrival of spring, as a bear wakes from hibernation and a bison calf is caught in a spring shower, while Alpine flowers blossom on Zephyr's legs. Summer shimmers on the wings of a monarch butterfly announcing the arrival of Nikai, WCC's newest Ambassador. Nikai listens to the bluebird's song as bison rut in a summer meadow.

Fall flickers over Zephyr, as a pup, and turns to winter across Alawa, also as a pup and the wolf pack led by Atka return to their winter trail. Atka, the leader of the WCC Ambassador Pack, gleams like the sun on the wings of a monarch butterfly. He watches over Zephyr, Alawa, and Nikai in a landscape where wolves roam free.

Jane sought inspiration for her Biro (ballpoint pen) drawing from the BBC film Yellowstone *(2009). She took hundreds of still photographs as the film played, searching for images that would best represent the wildlife that has inhabited America for thousands of years. Jane also worked with beautiful images of wolves taken by staff at the WCC, aspiring to capture the majesty of the center's wolves. Her aim was to create a piece that presents wolves as a keystone species while evoking the timeless beauty of the great American wilderness. The monarch butterflies that appear in the drawing highlight that they too are a vulnerable species, their epic North American migration to Mexico now under threat. The spectrum of colors applied in the piece reflects the beauty of our natural world, while the dominance of red, white, and blue suggest American traditions and resound 'hope' that wolves and other wildlife are thriving again through the inspirational work of organizations such as WCC which dream the 'American Dream' and are making it a reality.*

American Dream. Color ballpoint pen drawing.

JUSTIN MONROE
THE WOLF'S SONG

Justin Monroe has been writing since he was fairly young and this passion for writing has stayed with him to this day. He is presently a History major in college. He has been published once before in a conbook for a convention in Cincinnati.

The wolf's melodious song,
With the winter wind,
Floats slowly along,
The notes and the wind combined.

The forest guardian sings,
Its low mournful tune,
Through the forest rings,

To the winter's silver moon.
The wolf's form like a ghost,
Mysterious calm,
Spiritual host,
Against the wood's snowy balm.

With a final gorgeous note,
The wolf's song complete,
It's aria afloat,
On the forest's winter sheet.

The wolf lowers its gray head,
It turns and walks home,
To its den and bed,
Away from snow's monochrome.

MATT NEWMAN
MY PACK

Matt Newman is the author of "My Pack," and resides in Middle Tennessee. He studied technology at White County High School in Sparta, Tennessee. One of his teachers in high school told him he shouldn't let his writing skills go to waste, and he took that to heart.

"My Pack" tells the story of a young man named Joshua who lives in a small village in rural Alaska. He learns the importance of companionship, and realizes that sometimes, leaning on someone else is the only way to conquer a challenge.

Special thanks to Nelson Johnson for sharpening the story.

My name is Joshua Thompson. I grew up in a small town in western Alaska called Kaltag. I live with my parents and my older brother, Steven. He's basically my best friend, but it's not easy coming by friends in such a small village. We do everything together. Sledding, ambushing the neighbors with snowballs, and playing with our dog, Max, are just a few things we like to do. My father works as a bush pilot, and Mom stays at home and takes care of the homestead.

There was one night I will never forget as long as I live, however. It was a particularly cold one in 1944. Max and I had trekked down the road, braving the tall drifts of snow in the ditches. All of a sudden, I saw the headlights of an approaching car, something I'd only seen a few times in my life. I could see it was a dull green sedan with a big white star on the front door. "Strange," I thought to myself, still lifting my boots high to clear the snow. "That's a military car." I made it to the market just as the shopkeeper was about to lock the front door. Catching a glimpse of me, he chuckled and opened it wide.

"What're ya in for so late, Mr. Thompson?" he said with a cheerful tone.

"Just some flour for dinner tonight, sir."

"Ah, sounds wonderful. You'd better get home soon. You'll catch your death out there."

He directed me toward the correct aisle, and with Max at my side, I grabbed what I needed, and stepped up to the counter to pay. I exchanged some friendly words with the clerk and headed out the door. The wind whipped my face, so I pulled my scarf up until just my eyes were uncovered, trouncing through the deep white fluff. After a few minutes, I made it to the front door of my house, and turned the knob. Max ran inside and shook himself off, then wagged his tail happily as he watched me make my way in, bundled up to the point that I could hardly even move my arms. "I'm home!" I yelled out, pulling off my knitted cap and scarf, tossing them in a chair in the foyer. Before I could get my boots off, I heard a commotion in the kitchen. Walking in, I saw my parents sitting at the dining room table.

"Mom, Dad? What's going on?" I questioned, a bit worried.

My father looked up from the table where he was studying some sort of paperwork. "Joshua, we didn't want you to worry about this, but we think you need to know," he said, looking over to my mom.

"Honey, your brother had to sign up for selective service. He's been drafted, and he's going to be going to Germany," she said, with an almost regretful tone.

My heart sank. I couldn't even hear anything they were saying. I dropped the bag of flour I was carrying, white powder spreading all over the floor as it broke. I felt so betrayed by the both of them that I turned and bolted toward the front door, slinging it wide open. I could hear my father close behind me, Max darting out as well, right on my heels. I knew my old man wouldn't be able to catch me. He didn't even have his boots on. I ignored the pleas for me to come back, and, by the time I stopped running, I could hardly see the front porch light.

I crumpled to the ground and sat there. The snow was falling less densely. I looked to Max, then to the treeline, and back to the street. I didn't want to go back. They knew this was coming, and nobody told me, not even Steven. I knew something was off when he didn't come with me to the market. Did they even care?

I picked myself up, and started walking toward the thickets that outlined the forest, a place where we were always told never to go, especially not at nighttime. I figured since I was fifteen, there wasn't anything that could harm me. I reached for and pulled back some of the bushes, slipping my way into the unknown. I looked over my shoulder and saw Max standing there, giving me a look of worry, whimpering. "C'mon, boy," I commanded. He instantly turned and bolted back toward the house. Even he knew this place was a strange land of wickedness. I moved on, knowing that certain danger lurked ahead.

It was so dark in that forest, but it was peaceful. The only thing I could hear was the crunch of the snow under my boots and my breath which made wispy clouds of vapor, contrasting against the dark landscape around, with only the moonlight to guide me. After a few minutes of just walking, my head clouded with thought, I looked behind me, and realized that I didn't know what direction I'd come from. The wind had blown snow over my tracks and all but hidden my path. It was at that moment, I realized I'd made a huge mistake. It was getting colder, and the only things I had on me were in my pockets: a book of matches, a knife given to me by my grandpa in Montana, and a chocolate bar. I did my best to gather what little wood I could find from fallen branches, breaking some of them to get a few decently sized chunks to push into a neat little pile, and I used the wrapper of the candy bar as kindling. Some of the smaller twigs caught first before any sort of real fire came alive, and I huddled around it.

I finished off the chocolate and sat back. The snow had stopped falling at this point, only the crackling of the flames heard in the deep woods. Suddenly, I heard a soft growling noise. I was sure it wasn't my stomach, and I panicked, standing up and keeping my back to the fire, looking into the treeline where the warm glow couldn't reach. "W-who's there?" I stammered, reaching for a stick that certainly wasn't going to protect me from the vicious beast that was approaching me. I could finally see its form approaching me. Clenching my teeth, I gripped my weapon, preparing for the battle.

When the silvery brown pelt came into view finally, I realized it was a wolf pup who was coming at me less angrily, and more cautiously. I loosened the grip on the stick and watched as it started to pick up the pace until it was right up on me. It was strange how it approached me. I'd never known wolves to be so comfortable with humans, even though this was just a youth, probably no more than a few months old, split off from its pack. I took a knee as it got closer and extended one of my gloved hands. It sniffed at me, then looked up to me, its ears pinned flat against its skull. I gave it a soft pat on the head. "You're away from your family too, huh, buddy..." I said, trailing off. The pup looked healthy, perhaps just recently separated from its pack. I wasn't sure if it would stay put for the night, but I took a seat back next to the fire, the flames hot enough to melt most of the snow around it. The pup plopped down next to me.

"So...My name's Josh. I think I'll call you Yukon, like the river." I said to the creature. He looked at me, the tip of his little tail shaking against the snow. By now, it must have been nearly midnight, the moon high over the makeshift camp. I gathered a bit of firewood for the night and tossed it into the flames to keep it up all night. I knew I wasn't going back home. My thoughts started to race once more, warm tears streaming. It honestly felt good on my cold cheeks. Yukon watched me, his ears pinning back once more, as if he could feel my pain. I felt him lean against me, curling up and burrowing his nose under his bushy tail. It was warm enough next to the fire for me to take off my parka, balling it up and then laying my head upon it. I gazed into the fire until sleep overtook me.

I woke up the next morning, rousing quickly to realize that the previous night wasn't part of some nightmare. The fire had died down to just coals, which were warm, but weren't putting off enough heat for me to keep my jacket off. I pulled it back on and stood up, letting my legs be warmed by the smoldering embers. I looked around, my eyesight blurred since I'd just woken up. I didn't see any sign of Yukon. I sighed, figuring he'd taken off during the night. That was okay, though. He knew where he was. I didn't. I started to break up the embers with my boot, putting the fire out completely before continuing on. I figured I should probably head back, whether my folks cared or not, but what direction was back? I felt hopeless, slumping next to a tree and thinking for a moment, when the next terror arose. I heard twigs snapping, snow crunching under huge paws. I turned to see the lumbering form of a bear making its way through the forest. My eyes went as wide, and, though I tried to stay as quiet as possible, it spotted me. I saw it look my way, then it diverted its course toward me. I stood up instantly, backing up, watching it close the gap. I knew if I turned and ran, it would for sure chase me, so I stood my ground, nervously looking around for anything to fight back against the attack.

Suddenly, I heard a high-pitched yip. Looking around me, my wolf companion from the previous night approached, baring his fangs and putting himself between me and the bear, even though it was at least ten times his size. The bear stopped in its tracks, let out a roar, then as quick as it had become interested, completely ignored us. Yukon kept staring, growling at the beast, even as it trudged away. I could feel my heart beating out of my chest. The little wolf had saved me, almost as if I were his packmate. It felt nice, almost cared about, even by a wild animal. His fur lost its bristle as the bear went off into the treeline, and his ears stood on end. He turned back around to me and approached me, staring up at my face.

I knew I had to keep going, and I was extremely hungry. I'd had nothing but a chocolate bar since yesterday's lunch. I had cut some of the bark from a limb on the ground and tied it around the bundle of firewood I had, slinging it over my shoulder and continuing on my journey. Everything seemed to blend together within the weald. I couldn't tell if we were going in circles, but I knew I had to eat soon. A miracle occurred just moments later as we came to the top of a ridge, and down below was a river. I slid down the snowy bank and ran up to its edge. Surely, there must be a fish or two in this water, and if I was going to have a wolf by my side, I'd better do my best to live the way he does. Steven and I had caught fish this way before, so I was a seasoned veteran in creating a spear out of one of my pieces of firewood, whittling away at it with my knife. I pulled a thread from my parka and tied it around the base of my expertly crafted tool. Even Yukon seemed impressed, watching me work, wagging his bushy tail. I walked to the edge of the clear water and peered in.

There were some salmon swimming around in a cloud of minnows, no doubt getting their fill, unaware that I was raising my spear to the sky and at one fell swoop, plunged it down into the water. I let it go and grabbed the string tied to it, feeling it being yanked from my hands. I gripped it tighter and pulled it in, realizing my effort was a success. I tossed down some of the firewood I'd collected and elected to make this spot my camp. It was a fairly open area. "Maybe they'll find me," I thought to myself for the first time. I wanted to go home so badly and just take back what I'd done. I seated myself at the edge of the river and struck some matches, quickly getting my fire going once again, pulling the scales off the fish and then cooking it. Yukon stared at me the whole time. He must have been hungry, too. Wolves usually hunt in packs, and, alone, they don't fare well. I looked at my meal and sighed softly, knowing it was only right at this point. I reached into the red meat and ripped off a morsel. "You're catching the next one, bub," I said jokingly, tossing it to his paws. He snapped at it and gobbled it down, whining softly as if his stomach hadn't had a bite in days. I sat back and tore little bits of meat off after I'd properly cooked it, munching on what was edible, tossing the rest toward my lupine companion. He eagerly chomped it down, his little tail waving back and forth. Relaxing for a moment, I stood up and walked to the edge of the shore, reaching down and picking up a flat rock. I flung it toward the water's surface, watching it skip a few times before breaking the water's surface with a "plunk," sinking down. I tried to beat my record a few more times, satisfied with six skips finally, looking back at Yukon who was gleefully gnawing on the bones of the fish. I walked back over to him, sat down, and petted his head. He instantly snapped his attention up to me and stared, then went right back to his work, picking the skeleton completely clean of every bit of nutrient. I reached down and pulled the laces of my boots loose, pulling them off and resting my feet next to the fire, sighing contentedly. This would have to do for now.

My mind wandered. I thought about what my brother must be doing. The family had just recently gotten a radio, and there were only a few stations you could reach in Kaltag. One of those was a news station, and the war was the most popular topic. It sounded so harsh in Europe, and that made me worry about Steven. He'd always been by my side growing up, and now he was on the other side of the world. It felt so foreign.

Suddenly, I came back to reality, hearing a cracking sound, looking up to see a huge pine tree falling, perhaps too weighted down with snow to be able to hold itself up. It came crashing down, and most of its mass went straight into the river, causing large waves to wash over the banks, coming right toward me. Without enough notice, I was hit with the swells, tumbling in my bundled up state. When I finally came to a rest, I sat up. The ground around me was covered in slush. My fire and all the wood I'd collected was gone, washing down the river, as well as my boots. I was soaked from head to toe, and after the shock had died down, I realized just how cold I was. I saw Yukon heading toward me with his tail pinned between his hind legs, his worried yips echoing off the trees around us. I sat up, pulling my gloves off, tossing them aside as well as my parka, trying to strip away the drenched clothes as best as I could. Yukon pushed himself into my lap. He felt like a hot radiator compared to me at the moment. I couldn't help but to embrace the wolf, wrapping my arms around his fuzzy body, shivering as I tried desperately to sap some of his body heat. The situation wasn't made any better by the fact that the book of matches in my pocket was now also soaked, and ruined. I knew it wouldn't be long at these temperatures until the entire riverbank would freeze over, so I knew we had to get out of there.

I gently pushed Yukon out of my lap and stood up; I had on a sweater, my socks, and jeans. My parka would have taken the entire day to dry out, if even that, so I reached down, taking out my pocket knife and slicing through the material, cutting it into pieces I could wrap around my feet, taking the draw string and tying it around each ankle. The inside of the fabric was dry, and it would at least keep my feet warm and more protected since my boots were washed away.

I figured if Yukon and I followed the river upstream, we'd make it to a larger body of water, and I knew that Kaltag was situated on the Yukon. There was a chance. "C'mon, boy," I called out to my partner, starting my awkward waddle with the bundles of fabric on my feet. We made it a good hundred yards when I realized the falling tree had sparked the curiosity of something else in the forest. I stopped walking, listening to the trees around me. I could hear footsteps. My eyes scanned the thick forest, trying to spot something. I looked down to Yukon, whose ears were perked high, his tail raised. I could see his leathery black nose twitching as he'd caught the scent of something. The footsteps grew closer. I could tell there had to be more than one. I pushed my back to a tree, gritting my teeth, trying not to make a sound, but Yukon was reacting oddly to this encounter. He sat down, and he yipped a very high-pitched almost welcoming tone, then took off, bounding over a fallen tree. I peeked from my hiding spot, and that's when the group finally came into view. There were four fully grown wolves, three males, and a female, followed by a few youths the same size as Yukon. I tried to stay hidden, but one of the larger males spotted me. I could see his pearly white canines as his lips curled back. I was shaking, trembling in fear as I saw that powerful creature start to move toward me, his tail waving behind him as his ears were pricked forward in a very dominant fashion. I saw Yukon pounce in front of him and whine, his ears pinned back submissively. The larger wolf paused, looking down at the young pup. Yukon leaned up and licked at his chin as if to say "It's okay. He's my friend." The entourage of wolves just stood there, save for Yukon and the larger male, no doubt a protector of the pack. He had a calmer expression now, ears pricked up on high alert, still approaching me, Yukon in tow behind, his tail tucked and ears flat on his skull. I turned a hand over and held it out as it approached. The wolf paused, then trotted up to me, sticking his neck out and giving my palm a sniff. He was nearly half my height.

I'd never been so close to a fully grown wolf before. While everything I'd ever been told about them had been bad, here in this moment, I started to doubt everything I knew about them, just watching him sniff at me. I offered to gently rub the top of his head, and he stared at me through his bright amber hues. I realized this was Yukon's family. They had been looking for him this whole time. How fortunate I was to be able to share such a moment. The bliss of petting one of nature's most misunderstood creatures was broken suddenly by a bark from the female amongst the group. The large male turned his head, then looked back to me, pushing it against my thigh and then trotting back off to the group. Yukon stood steadfast for a moment, then looked up to me. "You gotta go, Yukon. Your family is waiting for you," I said, getting down on one knee, gently brushing my fingers under his jaw line. The female barked yet again, this time directed at Yukon. The tip of his tail flicked back and forth as he made his way to the group, looking over his shoulder to me the whole time. The males led the way, the pups in the middle, with mom bringing up the rear. She took one last look at me, as if thanking me for keeping her son safe, then disappeared into the timberline.

I had a sense of relief wash over me, but that feeling was quickly replaced with loneliness. As the sounds of those large paws padding through the snow faded to nothing, I sank down at the base of the tree. I wished like crazy that I could be with my own family, my pack, if you will. I wished that I could just wake up from this nightmare and everything from yesterday be taken back and everything be back to normal. I wanted my parents. I wanted my brother. I wanted Max. I just wanted to take it all back. I found myself burying my face into my hands and crying, angry with myself for leaving, wondering if I'd ever be found, or find my own way back. I clenched my teeth and snorted back snot as my bloodshot eyes poured tears.

Just then, my blubbering stopped as I heard something approaching fast. The snow was crunching, and I could hear twigs snapping. I lifted my head, concern striking me yet again, but then the sounds were accompanied by the jingling of a collar, and a shrill bark. It was...Could it be? "Max?" I called out, seeing that mutt bound over a fallen log and land right in my lap, knocking me against the tree I was resting against. "Max, you found me!" I exclaimed, hugging that silly mutt of mine. I heard someone yell, "Hey, I think he found something!" And so I stood up. "Dad..?" I called out softly. Sure enough, a rescue party headed by my father topped the hill.

"Josh!" he called out.

"Dad, I'm sorry! I'm coming up right now!" I said, hardly able to believe what I was seeing.

"You've had us worried sick, son. You know how dangerous it is out here."

"I know, Dad. I just want to come home. I wanna be with you and mom, and I'll never go to the forest again."

My pack had come for me. A pack knows a lone wolf can't survive on his own, and if they care enough, they won't let them go for long. I couldn't believe they'd gone so far to find me. I was freezing cold, and I knew that especially once my father scooped me up and started carrying me. My head was cloudy, but all I knew was that I was going to be safe. I swear it took at least an hour of walking before we came out of the treeline. The sun was setting, but the group carried on. Everyone had their fair share of "we're glad you're okay" spiels, and then they dispersed.

Dad unlocked the front door and carried me in, and placed me on the couch to cut off my improvised shoes. My mom came in, crying her eyes out, and then proceeded to bend me over her knee and give me the spanking of a lifetime. I can still feel it to this day. At that moment, I wanted to be back in the wilderness. Hell hath no fury like my mother's spankings.

"You're lucky a...a pack of wolves didn't get to you!" she exclaimed.

"Mother, if I'm perfectly honest, I'm lucky a wolf did get to me..."

That was quite a few years ago. I never understood the bond between families until that night out in the Alaska wilderness. I think in a lot of ways Yukon is the wolf version of me. I think it was destiny that we'd met that night. Mom and Dad moved south to Anchorage because Dad swung a nice job at the airport flying passenger planes. Steven fought through the European tour and continued his career in the army in the Korean war and got out as a Master Sergeant. Me? You can find me living in that same house in Kaltag, sitting on the porch most days with Max by my side. As for Yukon, he's still around. It isn't uncommon to see him lurking on the treeline. I think we both realize if it weren't for each other, we would have both perished in that forest alone, and we both learned that the pack life is the life for us.

J. NOELLE
THE WINTER WOLVES OF SPRING

J. Noelle is a professional in the business world by day and a writer by night. She writes primarily fantasy and science fiction, as these were the genres that inspired her to take up the pen as a child. Her specialty is the construction of intricately detailed universes and cultures. She is currently working on two fantasy novels and is submitting her short stories to many anthologies across the country. J. Noelle's other passions include studio and digital art, which she sells through her online store, spirituality, and anthropomorphic media. You can find her dreaming up her next big idea in the shade of her backyard oak tree, with her best friend Fawn, a Chihuahua, in her lap.

The smoking pillars of filth and grime slowly disappeared behind them as they walked slowly, carefully, through the freshly fallen leaves that blew freely about their feet. The rustle—a gentle, comforting noise—put him more at ease as he put one foot forward, and then the other. He urged himself to focus solely on the movement of his feet on the browning grass, trying as hard as he might not to let his mind wander. It was all he could do to keep himself from pausing to tug on his stepfather's sleeve and beg to return to the safety of their small town before they got too much farther.

The treeline was in sight now, the imposing figures of the century-old trees looming forebodingly on the horizon. They started as a vague, tea-green blur, then slowly became squatty bushes, and finally, towering evergreens. The thick smell of sap clung to the dry breeze, carrying the sweet fragrance—one so rarely smelled back in town—to Harland's nose. The images of sweet tarts, chocolate pastries, and candied fruits flashed across his mind as he was transported to the Deep Winter Festival that was still so many months away. He hoped his mother would put the small arrangement of pine branches on the table as the centerpiece again this year. He had always loved the way the sap-laden twigs had made their small home smell, but he had never given much thought to the work that his stepfather had to put into retrieving those lovely boughs.

Their small party had been walking for hours now, trekking across a vast and desolate grassland that had already turned to straw with the nearing of winter's cold embrace. Now, as of his fourteenth birthday, he was finally old enough to join the Gathering Party, along with all the children in his small class.

Sammen walked alongside him, pulling her knitted scarf more tightly around her neck each time the chilled morning breeze ripped through the group. Her auburn hair was pulled back into elaborately crisscrossing braids that spiraled from the center of the back of her head, making a sort of tight bun that added a few inches to her profile. Though obviously as terrified as he himself was—her trembling lower lip betrayed her—she was doing a lovely job appearing as if the thought of approaching the dreaded tree-line did not bother her in the least. Her fists were clenched tightly around the handles of a running-wagon, which bounced along behind her.

Harland looked back at his own wagon, disgusted. It would have been so much easier to just crank the stupid things up and let them chug alongside them, but the elder members of the group had warned them against using their fuel prematurely. It was always much better to have fuel available for the long trek home, so that the running-wagons could carry their heavy spoils without any manpower needed. But the even more important reason behind their conservatism was the topic that no one in the party dared to bring up. The adults acted as if there were nothing to fear, while the children did their best to think of anything *but* their unspoken terror.

The Winter Wolf was out there. And if they happened upon the creature, they would need the running-wagons to be able to carry *them* away as fast as possible.

It was uncommon, but not unheard of, for a Gathering Party to have to abandon their duties at the sight of the horrible creature. The elders spoke of it as if it were a massive, four-legged abomination with glowing eyes and jaws that could snap a steam lift in half. Others described it as a large, white beast as tall as a man that walked on its hind legs. But no one disagreed with the portion of the description that covered the beast's massive teeth.

Sammen shuddered as she walked, as if suddenly overtaken by a rush of fear. Harland saw his opportunity.

Sliding his free arm about her shoulders, Harland edged in close to walk abreast of her. "Hey," he whispered softly, flashing her a smile that was much more confident than he actually felt. "It's gonna be okay. It's still autumn; see the leaves? Everyone knows the Winter Wolf is only around in the winter. That's why they called it that."

Irritably, she swatted his arm away. "I know that!" she snapped, obviously taking the advance as just a stupid boy's attempt to talk down to her. She was only one of three girls in the Gathering Party this season, and the trio had set out to prove they were just as good—no, better—than everyone else in their class.

"But still, winter isn't too far away," Sammen suddenly said after an extended period of silence. "You figure the brute has to have some travel time to get this far east. It may already…" she fell silent in fear without finishing her thought.

Har tried to give her a reassuring smile. "Just keep an eye out, okay? We'll be okay. The adults aren't going let us go into the trees alone. And 'sides, I'll look out for you too, Fin." To add a more casual feel to the conversation, Har slipped in the nickname she was often called at school, which made reference to the fact that her name was pronounced in the same way as a river fish.

Sammen's soft, pink lips cracked a small, nervous smile, but the girl said nothing.

Soon, the sweet smell of evergreen sap was so thick in the air that Harland began to feel the back of his head throbbing sorely. He fingered at his thin cloth scarf nervously for a few moments before deciding to wrap it about his mouth and nose. Better a small amount of filtering than none.

"All right, everyone!" The Gathering Party slowly rolled to a stop, all eyes fixing on the source of the booming voice that now echoed through the quiet wooded expanse. "The children will take to climbing the trees in a moment. They will go as high as they can, and will begin tossing down branches to the mid-climber. Then, the mid-climber will toss them to the ground, to be collected by our haulers. We want these branches to be as whole as possible, so please, no chucking the wood! Wood chips will do nothing for our hearths this winter, understood?"

The Gathering Party nodded as Rasc, the party leader, walked up and down the rows of running-wagons, helping the children lock the wheels in place so they would not risk losing one of the vehicles to a faulty engine start. The poor town was down to thirty running-wagons, with no way to build new ones from scratch. They had no access to the ore that had once come from their predecessors' mines and were running out of their dwindling metal stores.

Rasc continued his briefing. "Once the wood is gathered, the hunting group will head out together either tonight or in the morning. Winter will soon be upon us, and we cannot risk running into wild animals. We all know that the predators here hunt more desperately as the colder days approach. They, just as we, know that there is little food to go around. And we will not lose any of our hunters to a rogue bear or wolf, understood?"

Everyone nodded silently, feeling the weight of his words. If the animals were becoming so ferocious, then that must mean the numbers of game in the forest had decreased from previous years. The town had lost many of its citizens to starvation the previous winter, as their last Gathering Party had failed to bring back enough game to feed all the townspeople. Rasc had told Harland that the party had been camped out at the tree line for weeks, tracking any small hint of *any* animal it could get a lead on.

"Why not go deeper in?" one of the children asked, gesturing broadly at the breadth of the impressive forest before them. "That fountain is deep inside the forest, right? Can't you just go around it?"

A few of the kids laughed softly. His stepfather kneeled, putting one burly arm over his knee and taking the little urchin's shoulder in his free hand. "No," he replied evenly, frowning. "Even if we risked running into the Wolf to go that deep, none of us would get back alive. The Spring is too large to go around. Even getting close to it is too dangerous. Many have passed from only approaching it. It's evil. And we don't know how to counteract it."

"But what about asking for help from the city?" Sammen piped up, frowning. "Surely they hunt on the other side of the Spring? What if there's more food there?"

"Our messengers can't make it past the Spring, and none of our attempts to contact Zephyrport have seemed to work," the burly woodsman replied, beginning to sound mildly impatient at the task of educating the children. "None of our birds have returned, and even the one running-wagon that was sent through the Spring simply disappeared. We assume that our messages never made it all the way there."

"Can you see Zephyrport from the forest?" Harland asked, suddenly intrigued. Few in the town spoke of the great city by the sea, mostly because there were few who were old enough to remember it.

In school, their people's history was taught every year, to the point that many of the children grew tired of hearing the same stories over and over again. The great riches that flowed in and out of the giant port city. The kind master of the city-state center, Wise Jarold Heisen, who made trading agreements with the settlements all across the Greenwood Sea. The pirate attacks that slowly drove settlements farther and farther inland. The founding of their small town, Wagonbarrow, by a small group of wagon masters.

And finally, the appearance of the Spring that cut off all communication between the eastern settlements and Zephyrport to the west.

With no way to get any of the industrial supplies from the city or any of the goods that were being traded, the towns and cities to the east slowly died out. And now, with Wagonbarrow claiming all the survivors from all forgotten eastern towns, the remaining population of easterners gazed knowingly at their deaths. For once the forest was cut down to the Spring's border, no one would have any food, building material, or fuel left to sustain themselves.

Rasc appeared bewildered at Harland's sudden question concerning the great city, but nodded his head in response anyway. "Yes, Har," he replied. "You can see the lights from the tops of the trees once night falls. But the city itself is a very long way away, so you can see no buildings. It is only a bright glow in the distance, just at the water's edge."

The children's eyes lit up with excitement at the idea of finally seeing the City by the Sea for themselves. All those stories and legends, proven true!

"But hear me!" Rasc bellowed, waving a threatening finger at all of the children. "You *cannot* attempt to cross the Spring! Do you hear me? You will *die,* and I am not going to carry anyone back to town. You would take up space we need for wood and game on the running-wagons. Let the Wolf have you."

The children all fell silent as the reality of the danger in the woods fell upon them. However, Har knew the man better than anyone else here, and he knew for a fact that he would never leave anyone behind. The scare tactic was probably just a ploy to get them all to be quiet.

"Any more questions?" Rasc asked gruffly, already knowing the answer. No one replied. He then made his way to one of the running-wagons and took a length of rope and slung it over his shoulders. The

Gathering Party's senior members quickly sprang into action, following Rasc's lead.

The children, however, took their time.

The day turned out to be extremely productive, and the group was finished with their wood gathering by the time dusk had begun to fall. Half of the party's running-wagons were now stacked high with logs and large branches, most of them cut to only a few feet in length to be used as firewood. The children had proven to be exceptional climbers, and had been able to harvest more branches than Rasc had expected. They each carried a machete strapped across their backs as they climbed, and began hacking away at the highest branches while the adults caught the falling lumber or moved out to chop entire trees a safe distance away.

As the sky began to darken, Har decided to scale the rest of his tree before returning to the group. Sammen, who had been above him in the same tree as him for most of the day, met him on his climb up.

"It's beautiful, Har," she said softly, smiling wide with wonder. "Wait until you see it."

Spurred on by her excitement, Harland continued his perilous ascent, being extremely aware of each movement that either hand or foot made. The climb became more difficult the higher he got, as the branches became thinner and thinner and began to point themselves more sharply skyward. He paused before he broke through the top of the tree, taking a deep breath in excited anticipation.

The sudden rush of the cool, evening air was a shock to him. With all the trees and foliage around him throughout the day, he had forgotten to expect the chill of autumn's evening winds.

He turned his gaze eastward first, back toward Wagonbarrow, where rising smoke and the dim light of lanterns guided his eyes back home. The town was a tiny candle in a darkened sanctuary, the shadows creeping up on either side, and the slightest draft waiting to snuff it out. He then turned his head to the west, meeting face-first with the salty air. Past the edges of the trees, he could make out the shape of a distant coastline, and he followed the darkening line of water to the northwest, squinting.

With darkness rapidly approaching, he could now see it: a huge patch of bright—incredibly bright—lights, dancing in the distance near the coastline. It glowed like twinkling stars in the darkness, bathing its surrounding area in a warm bath of golden light. Zephyrport. It still lived.

He felt warmth rush to his eyes as he blinked back tears, staring longingly at the city of three generations past. Being so close to it—to *them*—and not being able to do a thing to reach them... That was true pain.

He began climbing back down after stealing one more quick glance at Zephyrport.

When they set up camp that night, the adults arranged their knapsacks to flank the children, sleeping between them and the inner portion of the forest. Harland had thought that, perhaps, they would all move back to the grasslands to sleep, but Rasc reminded him curtly that they were conserving running-wagon fuel. The children, after working so hard up in the trees all day, were glad to get a respite, and they quickly began climbing into their sacks and extinguishing their lanterns.

Harland was preparing to extinguish his own lantern when Sammen approached him. "Hey, Har," she whispered, looking around at the others, some of whom were already asleep. "Your stepdad is taking some of the adults deeper into the woods to scout part of the path we're going to take in the morning. He asked me to come get you."

The two children made their way out of the camp to find Rasc holding his lantern high to cast as much light as possible on the pitch forest floor. Behind him stood two other adults.

There was Reina, a young blonde woman who worked with the wagon masters, who was learning the delicate craft of wagon upkeep and upgrading. She was surprisingly small for her age in both height and weight, but was incredibly agile due to her stature. Across her back were a hunting bow and a quiver that was filled to the brim with eagle-feather arrows. Then there was Jutend, an older man of a heavier build, whose arms and legs were still stoutly built from a lifetime of hard labor. He had always been a woodsman, and had made a name for himself as a year-round lumber gatherer and carpenter. In his hands, he carried a mighty axe.

Rasc was scratching his head absent-mindedly when the two children approached. "Took you long enough," he muttered quietly, making both children wince. "Come on. We have a long way to go, and I am not willing to stay up all night."

Rasc picked up his oaken crossbow, which had been lying at his feet, and began moving forward. "Kids, each of you take a machete with you. There are a few in that running-wagon over there." Har and Sammen obliged quietly, and the small group began to lumber their way deeper into the trees with Reina and Jutend leading the way.

"I'm sure Sammen told you this is a scouting mission?" Rasc asked, giving a pointed glance over his shoulder at his stepson. Harland nodded silently. "We always choose two children to take scouting each time the Gathering Party goes on a mission," he continued, the hint of a smile creeping up on his thin lips. "And the three of us—as the leaders of the Party—have decided that the two of you are the most ready to take on the responsibility. You will be scouting with us each night after the others set up camp. And if you prove to do your job well, you may well become our apprentices before the season ends."

Harland and Sammen gasped in delight, their eyes widening.

Jutend laughed heartily, his voice like a sudden roar of thunder. "Good going, you two!" he boomed, revealing yellowed teeth. "I knew it would be you two, after I saw how you worked so well together earlier today! You gathered more branches by lunch than most of the new teams had by sunset! That takes real determination!"

"*And* skill," Reina chimed in, flashing the two children a catlike smile. Harland shuddered, suddenly feeling her bright eyes upon him. Her cold gaze made Har feel exponentially more insignificant, unpolished, and immature.

"Yes, yes, *and skill*," the burly woodcutter bellowed with a jovial grin. "But don't make the children take this moment too seriously, my friend. They should be celebrating!"

"They can celebrate after we return to camp," the huntress replied with a crooked smile. "I don't think now is the time." The children caught the change in her tone. The cat woman expected them to encounter danger.

"Now, keep your eyes out for any movement. But your lantern won't be much help to you if you are attacked, since you'll most likely have to drop it to defend yourself. Instead, try to depend on your ears." Rasc had obviously decided to speak up to put the playful squabbling between his partners to rest, as his tone was more than a little exasperated. "Now Har, I expect you to be particularly good at this, since we've already practiced."

Harland nodded, grinning impishly. Their hunting trips throughout the year had given him plenty of time to practice the art of seeing without sight. His classmate looked jealously, a feeling of inadequacy rising inside her. He started to open his mouth to reassure her, when Jutend suddenly came to a halt in front of them.

"Stop."

His voice was hushed, harsh, and tense with effort. The other leaders grouped together close behind him, each one of them facing a different direction as they waited for further instruction, or the next sign of life to emerge from the dense underbrush. Har and Sammen rushed into the center of their triangle formation, and the adults spread their shoulders wide to form a barricade around them.

"Lift your lanterns," Reina hissed over her shoulder as she notched an arrow, her eyes never once leaving the shadowy border of the trees.

They obliged, both of them feeling adrenaline rushing through their bloodstreams. Every sound was suddenly a roar, every crack a menacing footstep. Harland caught sight of some flickering shadows—cast from the dancing flame of his lantern—and nearly screamed in terror, his mind recalling the talk of the Winter Wolf from that morning.

Slowly, the distant rustles that had caught Jutend's attention fell into a regular pattern: slow, even, and measured.

Without the need for instruction, Jutend moved forward, separating himself from the defensive triad with a slow, cautious gait. Reina and Rasc shifted their positions to make themselves a shield that stood between the Jutend and the children, just in case the approaching animal found a way to slip past the old woodsman. Harland felt his breath catch in his throat.

Jutend pulled his axe close to his chest with one hand in a defensive position. The rustling in the underbrush became louder, but still maintained the steady, rhythmic pounding as it grew closer and closer. Thump-thump. Thump-thump. It sounded unnatural. Too measured. Too consistent.

Harland heard Reina and Rasc gasp in unison, both of them focusing their arrows points at the spot where the beast would emerge. They had realized too late.

The heartbeat stopped. The darkness of the forest was suddenly thick as pitch, catching in their throats, slowly smothering them. No one moved.

Suddenly, as if the form had materialized from nothingness, a white shape appeared against the backdrop of blackness. From the dense undergrowth had emerged the floating image of a wolf's head, beautiful and pure white as the snow in the depths of winter, followed slowly by one paw. Then another. Thump-thump.

"Stay behind us..." Reina hissed, her eyes glued to the creature. "And when we break line...run."

The horrible realization suddenly set in. The Winter Wolf.

As if summoned forth by the words spoken by the adults, a sudden, horrible, sickly green glow settled on the small clearing in which they stood, its brightness undulating in that same horrible rhythm. Thump-thump. Thump-thump. The creature stepped into the glow with its head lowered, its eyes—glowing with the same eerie light—unblinkingly staring ahead. The children could see Jutend's knees shaking as the giant beast approached him.

Leave...

The voice startled the children, both of whom whimpered reflexively at the sound of it. So soft, but echoing against every surface as if filled with the strength of a thousand voices.

Must go back...

Jutend began backing away, never lowering his axe as the creature continued to slowly step forward. Its head remaining suspended in place as if the body did not move at all.

"Run! Run back to camp!" Rasc barked, failing to mask his own terror.

Harland hesitated for a split second, but Sammen grabbed his shoulder and thrust him toward the trees almost immediately. Without speaking, the two of them glanced around the forest and bolted in the direction directly opposite from where the Wolf had emerged.

Har's lantern had been left behind due to his hesitation, and only the dim light cast by Sammen's lantern guided them. She held the lantern as high as she could while running and struck the metal casing around the light repeatedly against the trunks of trees as she bounded. After running for what seemed to be all night, the children finally slowed, panting and wheezing with exhaustion. Sammen took a moment to lean forward against a tree, and Har heard the sickening noises of her emptying her stomach. Har felt as if he would follow suit, but nothing emerged when he leaned over. With a haggard, shaking voice, Sammen was the first one to break the silence.

"Do you think any of them escaped?"

"Of course we did!" replied a weak voice with a jovial mood. The children turned to see Jutend—trousers and shirt tattered—emerge from the shadows. "You two can really run when you're scared! It was hard keeping up with you!"

"What about Dad?" Harland asked, panicked.

"Rasc and Reina took off in a different direction," Jutend replied, not sounding overly concerned. "They went back towards the camp. You two went deeper into the forest, and I couldn't let you go alone."

Sammen hung her head at the news, and cursed herself for not making note of the directions while they were walking into the forest initially. "I'm sorry, Juten--"

Green. Suddenly the area exploded into the same sickening hue as before, its sudden appearance stealing a yelp of terror from both children's mouths.

Thump-thump. Thump-thump. Thumpthumpthumpthumpthump.

All around them, flashes of white emerged against the expanse of blackness. Wolves—at least ten of them—stood in a semicircle around them, blocking off the direction they had just come.

You you you must must must turn turn turn turn back back back now now now now...

Jutend shoved the children toward the empty trees behind them, and took off in that direction alongside them. Sammen had dropped her lantern somewhere. Now only the bright green lights from the eyes of the Wolves lit their way. Up ahead, Harland could see dim shimmers of yellow light, so he pushed ahead, a smile breaking out on his face in spite of himself.

Camp. They had made it back.

"HAR!"

He was suddenly off-balance, yanked backward by the collar of his shirt before his feet could take another step. He teetered, unsure of what had happened, and heard a loud thud somewhere nearby. Sammen screamed. And suddenly...

Pain. Icy, burning, agonizing pain erupted in his left shoulder, lacing its way down his arm and making his fingers go numb. He felt hot tears well up in his eyes as he snatched his head around to stare up at his attacker, expecting to smell the stench of a Wolf's breath and see the flash of its eyes.

Instead, he found himself looking at the human hand that had clenched around his shoulder, and up to a face shrouded in darkness, hidden beneath the pelt of a white wolf.

A scream of agony ripped itself out of Harland's lungs, and the boy quickly lost consciousness. Before his world went black, he caught sight of Jutend lying face first in a patch of dying grass.

Thump-thump.
    There was that noise again.
    Thump-thump.
    He urged himself to move, to stand…to *run*.
    Thump-thump.
    He struggled to open his eyes, feeling the oppression of his own weight and exhaustion holding him down. Blurs of color slowly came into focus. The straw-yellow before him slowly sharpened into long blades of dried grass, blowing softly in the breeze. His nose was full of the metallic smell of the dirt, and he coughed several times to expel the unpleasant odor. The smell of evergreen sap rushed in to replace it. The woods. He was still inside them.
    He struggled to stand to his feet, finding himself uneasy and unbalanced. When his eyes adjusted to the sunlight that spackled the ground through the canopy, he let out an audible gasp. He was not in any part of the forest he had seen before.
    The grass beneath his feet was cool to the touch and seemed to leak cold energy through his trousers and to his skin. He shuddered at the unfamiliar sensation, and grasped his arms across his chest. Thump-thump.
    The trees around him were imposingly tall, with wild and unchecked branches twisting chaotically up into the canopy. And every tree was barren of leaves prematurely, as if high winter had already fallen on them. Even the evergreen trees lacked their needles.
    Thump-thump. The noise was louder now, and Harland began to look around himself, scanning the spaces between the trees for any sign of movement. No sign of life revealed itself to him. Thump-thump. He shoved his pointer fingers into his ears to muffle it.
    Thump-thump. Thump-thump. THUMP-THUMP.
    THUMPTHUMPTHUMPTHUMP. The noise became exponentially louder so suddenly and without warning that Harland jumped, wrenching his fingers from his ears.
    It's maddening, isn't it…?
    Harland spun around to find a human figure towering over him, bright green eyes staring at him knowingly from beneath a white pelt. The figure was tall and gracefully built, its feminine outline visible

even beneath the cloak. Upon her head sat a fur hood, capped with the upper half of a white wolf's head, its ears still standing erect as they would have in life. Long, gossamer strands of hair danced in and out of the lining of her hood, twisting freely and hauntingly in the breeze like the tendrils of ghostly jellyfish.

"*Wh…who are you?*" Harland clutched his throat with both hands, alarmed at the sound that had emerged from his mouth. His voice had sounded so smooth, so soft…and had echoed throughout the small clearing as if carrying the words of many voices.

I am Sessa, the figure replied evenly, staring unblinkingly into Harland's eyes. *Welcome, Harland. We feared you would not wake.*

"*We…?*" he asked, unnerved by the fact that her mouth had not moved.

There are many of us deeper in the wood, she explained calmly. *You will meet them soon. But you must first deal with the echoes.*

"*How do I stop them?*" he asked, bewildered at the thought of controlling his own voice. The reverberations emerged from his mouth as if his cheeks were the walls of mighty caverns. The cloaked woman shook her head slowly, then raised a finger to gesture at his chest. Harland realized with terror that her skin was as gossamer as her long hair.

Thump-thump.

The loud, rhythmic pounding was not the footsteps of Wolves, but was blossoming forth from his own chest each time his heart made a labored beat. Thump-thump. He could tell the rhythm was much slower than a normal heartbeat. Thump-thump. The same rhythm to which the Wolves had walked.

It will be too much for some of the others, just as it is too much for you to handle at the moment, she continued, sounding almost remorseful. *You must mask it. You must take a skin.* She tugged softly at the edge of her wolf-pelt cloak. *A second layer of flesh will mask the sound from the others. Come. We must search.*

Without pausing to see if he followed, the ethereal woman turned and began to walk with a fluid stride into the trees.

As they walked, Sessa explained that the flesh of a once-living creature would muffle the sound of his own heart's energies, therefore making him tolerable to the others. But in order for a pelt to be able to muffle the energies effectively, it must still possess a thin film of its owner's original energy, which normally dissipated at the time of death. Only those creatures whose soul was ripped suddenly from their bodies by encountering The Spring would leave behind flesh that was still charged with life.

All the talk of souls and energy made Harland uncomfortable—even more uncomfortable than he already was between the echoes, coldgrass, and the transparent woman—and he felt he would be sick. Harland stopped, leaned against a tree, and stared down at the ground for a moment. As another wave of illness struck, Harland reflexively cupped a hand over his mouth in a fluid motion. But as his hand approached his face, he was overcome with another wave of fear that left his feeling of sickness forgotten. He stared down at his hand in horror, his eyes studying the dark webbing of blood vessels that were slightly visible through his skin. Though not nearly as transparent as Sessa's flesh, his own skin had lightened in color so much that he was reminded of the look of the corpse.

Do not worry, Sessa's voice echoed from a distance in front of him. *It takes many decades to look like mine.*

"*This is permanent?*" Harland asked, tears trickling over his pale cheeks.

Yes, child. You have been reborn through the Spring. There is no going back.

"*But I didn't even see the Spring! How could I have—*"

Your friend saved you from falling in," Sessa cut in, turning to face him. *You nearly lost your life last night. Instead, it was he who gave his life force to the Spring. You would have fallen in, despite his efforts, had I not saved you.* She glanced over at Harland's shoulder.

Following her gaze, Harland looked down as well, and tore the collar of his shirt open clumsily. There, on his left shoulder, was a massive handprint, seared into his flesh as if he had suffered a horrible burn, and had healed many years ago. Its shape was glistening and slick with the appearance of ancient scar tissue.

But with my touch also came my blight. You are one of the skinwalkers now. Or as your village seems to call us on some occasions, the Winter Wolf.

He was numb. Her words had no meaning.

Do not grieve, Harland. Sessa interrupted his thoughts, her voice taking on a tone of restrained pity. *You are not dead. You may choose to take your life if you do not wish to continue. I understand. Many before you have chosen that path. But if you wish to stay, to learn, and to help, you may be able to save the people you love so dearly.*

He looked up, his glowing green eyes flashing with interest.

Come. I will explain as we fashion your cloak. She gestured to a large, brown bear that lay strewn on the ground, its eyes staring unblinkingly into the distance. Beyond where the bear lay in the coldgrass, the trees rustled with the sound of blowing leaves and needles. There was a defined border between lush autumn and desolate winter. This dead place, then... It must be the Spring.

Skinning bear was bloody, disgusting work, and Harland only served to make a mess of himself and the clumsy cuts he made to the pelt with his machete. Sessa had knelt to assist him after watching the poor boy, nerves still raw, fumble around with his blade for several minutes. She produced a skinning knife from somewhere in her cloak and made quick work of separating the bear pelt. Harland was impressed, as Rasc had always taught him to hang the creature in a tree before attempting such a feat.

"*Rasc! What about my dad? My friends?*" he blurted suddenly, panicked.

Sessa nodded expectantly, her hands continuing to work on the pelt. *They are all safe, Harland. After the girl saw your savior fall, she ran back the way you had come. Though she was terrified the whole time, the Wolves led her back to camp by herding her that way. A man with a crossbow and a huntress were also seen close by the camp early this morning, soon after the girl arrived back there as well.*

Harland sighed with relief. At least the others were okay... but Jutend...

The transparent woman tossed the pelt, already cleaned and fleshed, face-down on the coldgrass. *Let it stay there awhile. Once it freezes, we will hang it in the trees to thaw in the sunlight. Then, I will take you to the others.*

The coldgrass would take several hours to freeze the massive pelt, so Sessa beckoned Harland to walk with her through the dead forest. The grass began to thin beneath their feet until only dirt remained, and Harland could tell by the brightness of the sun before him that the forest must end up ahead. He took a step forward, spurred on by the bright sunlight, before realizing that Sessa had stopped.

Wait.

Her green eyes flicked down to the ground beneath Harland's levitating boot. He followed her gaze down to a small crack in the soil: a stark and jagged line that wound its way through the trees. *These are tributaries to the Spring,* Sessa spoke, answering his unspoken question.

Within them flows great energy that is disastrous for any life to touch. It is these tributaries that can snatch the life from the living.

The cracks in the dirt began to deepen as they continued towards the forest's edge, until they were stepping around openings that were only a few inches wide, but were deep enough for the bottoms to disappear deep inside the earth. Stepping over one of those was expressly discomforting, as the openings spewed icy cold vapor skyward.

The Spring releases this vapor whenever there is a great energy source nearby. It is proof that the Spring is digesting it, trying to bring it back into the earth.

A great energy source? They were nearly to the end of the forest...which meant...

"*Zephyrport!*" He rushed ahead of her, being careful to avoid all the splits beneath his feet as he bounded to the last line of trees. Beaming, he emerged at the other side of the forest, receiving a welcomed blast of fresh sea air. He opened his eyes, squinting against the powerful wind to gaze upon Zephyrport: the fabled-city state, home to the first immigrants to their fair land from beyond the Greenwood Sea, the crowned jewel of the eastern world's trading empire, and the land of his ancestors...and gasped.

For as far as he could see, the land before him was barren: stripped of trees, of grass, and of flower. The rocky ground was split into massive running chasms that stretched all the way down to the coast and into the water, seeming to stretch a league wide at some points along its twisting path. Vapor spewed into the air from every orifice. The earth itself glowed with the same greenish glow from within the widest of the chasms, lighting up the landscape with the horrible color of the Wolves' eyes. Of Sessa's eyes. Of *his* eyes.

The only sign of life in the desolate landscape were flashes of white movement that occasionally crawled in and out of the splits in the ground, slithering into existence as if they were ghouls. Wolves. The giant Wolves emerged from the ground in formless, faceless masses of white that seemed to take shape as they pulled themselves out of the openings, their menacing green gaze being the first attribute to emerge. Their eyes, along with the green glow from deep within the earth's gashes, flashed brighter and then dimmer in time with the same terrible beat.

Thump-thump. Thump-thump. Thump-thump.

Do you understand? Sessa's voice cut through the steady, high-pitched hum that the earth wailed all around them. *When you take too much from the earth too quickly…it finds a way to take it back. This is the core of the Spring. Zephyrport.*

There was no reason. There was no reason to anything anymore.

The City that had long perished. The lights were now lit by the energy of its citizens' long-dead bodies and by the stores of fuel that they had amassed before the Spring erupted beneath their feet. The same light that had lured Harland to a tributary only the following night. The same light that shined from his eyes in the darkness.

"*It was the mines, wasn't it?*"

She was surprised to hear his voice, after walking along in silence since long after the sun had set. *Yes. The iron mine to the south of town was the catalyst that set off all of the great chasms you saw.*

"*Is it spreading?*"

Again, she nodded. *Taking all the energy back from Zephyrport was not enough to quell the earth's thirst. Now it spreads, looking for other life energy to drain.*

"*When will it be satisfied?*"

The skinwalker shook her head. *Only the earth knows. But Zephyrport taxed the earth very heavily for generations. I am sure the tributaries will flow much farther than they do now in the future.*

"*And what about Wagonbarrow? Will they all die?*"

They will move, just as the original eastern settlers did as the Spring's influence grew in the early days. Their biggest immediate threat now is starvation.

The thought of food made him suddenly and painfully aware of the emptiness in his own stomach. When was the last time he had eaten? How strange that he had not felt any hunger pains before he had actively focused on it. Not long after he had noticed his own hunger, it seemed Sessa had done the same. She settled herself on her knees and dug in her cloak for a moment, pulling out a small bundle of cloth. Unfolding it, she exposed a large slice of fire cooked meat, wrapped meticulously in coldgrass. She tore the meat in half and silently offered it to Harland, who took it and devoured it gratefully.

As they sat, a small group of Wolves sauntered up to them, attracted by the scent of cooked venison. Har's first instinct was to pull away, but Sessa shook her head as she extended her hand out to one. It nuzzled her hand as if it were nothing more than a house pet, hoping for affection.

This is Arlanna, Sessa whispered, stroking the wolf under its chin. *My mother.*

It was all Harland could do not to laugh bitterly. Sessa shot the boy a warning look.

The Wolves are remnants of the citizens of Zephyrport, reborn again through the Spring as protectors of the forest. They retain a limited bit of their previous memories. Above all, they know who is in their pack.

Harland's attempt to shield himself from more unwanted information by laughing it off as a joke had failed to steel his emotions against Sessa's words. *"All of these Wolves...? They were people?"*

Yes. They live to protect the Spring, and the humans that wander too close.

The previous night's encounter with the Wolves now made sense. If only he had known the meaning of their appearance sooner...Perhaps they would not have made it to the tributaries... Perhaps, Jutend would still be alive. Perhaps, he would still be normal.

Thinking of those he left behind brought a pained expression, and a marked lack of tears. His chest contorted with pain, and yet he made no sound.

Do not despair... the Wolf called Arlanna suddenly spoke slowly, steadily, and monotonously. *We will save them.*

We we we we will will will will save save save save them them them them...

The clearing was suddenly alive with the rumblings of dozens of voices. The eyes of many Wolves fell upon him, lighting the surrounding trees with a green light as bright as the noontime sun.

Harland sat down against a tree nearby, watching as Sessa and her mother dozed off. He was glad that skinwalkers needed to sleep. At least while he dreamed, he could climb trees with Sammen, cook with his mother, and hunt with Rasc...

Just as his mind drifted off to sleep, he felt a weight drape itself across his lap. When he opened his eyes slowly, he found the giant head of a Wolf resting atop his legs.

Sleep well... he rumbled softly, sniffing Har's hands gingerly. *My descendant.*

He was too exhausted to interrogate the Wolf to learn his identity just yet. Instead, he buried his face in the Wolf's soft fur, and allowed himself to be taken by sleep.

During their walk the following morning, the Wolf that protected him in the night had revealed that his name was Abbott: a name that Harland had remembered from somewhere on the chart of their family tree in their holy book. All he knew is the Wolf considered him to be one of his pack, and he accepted the position gladly. It was almost like having a pet, since the Wolves did not speak often. And it made him feel a lot less lonely.

While they were walking, Harland had taken to stroking the giant creature's head absent-mindedly, enjoying the texture of his thick fur. He made a conscious effort to clear his thoughts, to focus on utter nothingness, to avoid the temptation of giving up on everything right then and there. His machete blade's gleam from its spot on his hip seemed to be becoming more and more like a friendly grin.

And suddenly, he felt nothing but the cold touch of the coldgrass under his feet. He smelled the faint scent of salt on the air, mixing with other, unfamiliar odors. Looking down, he saw the steady movement of his feet on the ground… and a tributary approaching more and more quickly! He fought to stop his legs, but found them unresponsive. Panic washed over him, thrusting him out of his peaceful mindset with a jarring snap of pain at the back of his head. His legs immediately stopped in their tracks, suddenly deciding to resume their duties obediently.

It took him a moment to register that he had somehow avoided the tributary, and he looked about his feet for the crack. If his body disobeying was yet another attribute of his new condition, Harland wanted nothing to do with it. What was the point if he would lose control of himself completely?

Excellent! Sessa exclaimed. *Though you needn't worry so much. Wolves can touch the tributaries.*

"I…I overshadowed Abbott!" Harland exclaimed, in a mixture of terror and—in spite of himself—excitement.

Not quite. You melded your consciousness. You cannot control him, but you can communicate, as well as see and experience what he does. But this kind of bond only exists between a skinwalker and a Wolf of their pack.

Harland stared, agape, down at Abbott, whose muzzle seemed to be flashing him a very familiar toothy grin.

Such a Bond allows a skinwalker to join in our efforts to herd game from the northwest towards the eastern settlements each year. If you're willing to stay and learn, you could help in the coming years. We have so few Bonded skinwalkers, and the threat of their starvation looms.

Harland smiled inwardly. Perhaps, there was a reason to continue on.

BanWynn Oakshadow
RAGNÅRÖK: Gray-Furred Sons of Midgård, White'Winged Sisters, and Wolf-Kin Come a'Viking

BanWynn Oakshadow's poetry was published at State and National levels when he was in high school. He started working as a member of the editorial staff of a small poetry press for two years. That was enough to make him run away from editing and writing poetry. He picked up his laptop again when anthropomorphic writing started to grow beyond webzines and peer-to-peer groups. He had three pieces published in the first issue of FANG *and a novella in the third. Two strokes put writing on hold while he relearned to read and write, and 2015 was his first foray back to writing fiction and poetry for publication.*

He left the US to get married, and lives with his husband and a brain dead Border collie mix in the middle of a forest in Southern Sweden. During writing breaks, they work on renovating their nearly 300 year old cottage. He has been Guest of Honor and Guest Speaker at Feral!, and been nominated for an Ursa Major award.

The Trio (around 1000AD) concerns those years when moldy grain, maggot ridden smoked meat, diseased livestock forced the men to pick up their oars once more and go a'Viking. They would board the sacred longships that would carry them to bloody, glorious battles, heroes made and killed. Riches to be won and possibly a white-winged wolf come down from Asgård to carry up the most heroic. Each poem focuses on a different aspect of the off-season a'Viking, and is told in a different manner. The poems can stand on their own very well, but the skaldic way was to add the new over old (all verbal by skalds) and create a new link to their history and heritage. Different kingdoms (all of them small) fought in different styles, thus the Ursine standing apart from each other, each trusting his strength. Wolf-kin fight as one. Battles in winter usually involved less troops and different tactics. I hope to do Shield Maidens in the next piece.

Note: In these poems "Viking" is a noun, a gerund (a verb used as a noun) and a verb (archaic.)

RAGNÅRÖK - I
GREY-FURRED SONS OF MIDGÅRD

At Allfather's knee sits Ravenous
Beside him, his brother Hungers
Son of Loki, bane of Oden is Fenris
The fourth leg, we your Wolf-kin sons

Oh hear me, Allfather! All seeing Oden, Father of Valhalla…
    salt-rimed fur, frozen our manes, oars rise and fall rowing
Bear are arrayed, account Wolf-headed sail and steady keel,
    Sea-Wolf swift, sea-striding, sea-foaming and howling.
To a foreign land Ice-Mane hast led us, my skald-sung Jarl,
    come to claim it, by sword, by axe, and by blood.
Finish with blue clay and soot, your faces fearsome making,
    in manes, wood and bone and gold and stone tokens be woven.
Grease on blades. Spears and shields ward them from salt and ice
    now we, with muzzles raised, praises to Asgård are howling.

Allfather! Pray send wisdom
and cleverness by Hugin and Mugin
Offer sage advice winging above,
circling where enemies hide.

First of our foes are ready and placed, growls and stomps
    no small fight. Brown Bear are arrayed in bow shape
Stolid and steady they on the beach roaring and ready
    we flounder through ice and waves, every step costly
The first of their spears with power and strength thrown
    I and my brothers as one shield, brush them from the sky.
The Pack, each warding his brothers, on shore many become one
    shield, spear and sling and we become Oden's fourth leg
Your sons know the pack way…no self…remorseless gray fog
    silent in its destruction, moving as one and devouring.

All seeing Oden! Hear me!
Raise Gungir and loose thy bolts
Send into woods where archers hide
My brothers, Ravenous and Hungers

Oh hear me Tor! Friend of Wolf-kin! God of war!
  skies darkened by cloud of gore birds crowing.
To thine hammer I make oath: no step back shall I surrender;
  no Bear-kin ever my tail shall I be showing.
Should I fall in battle to the axe or the sword in glory,
  may I, at my moment of death, hear thee howling;
A cold so deep it freezes shaft to loam, sail hanging with
  icicles cascading, Sea above gray clouds are roiling
Foe nears, eager their yells, we spears on shields beating
  Ursine bearsarkers roaring, in frothing rage exulting

Tor hear me, oh hear me!
Loose thy hammer! Send Mjolnir flying!
That their longships are sundered,
Swallowed into surging of the sea,
And that their dogs of war be drowned.

Oh Freja! Glorious Bitch of war, ever in your heat!
  to battle I go, thy reward of ever mating may be mine
On the shore, our piss steaming, we claim this new land.
  our howls and their horns eagerly are blowing!
My shoulder brushing that of my eldest son,
  howling we go side by side to joyful slaughter.
Ursine warriors might of strong arms and death swinging
  alone they brace one from another each on his own.
Bearsarker swings heavy maul deadly and wailing, red-eyed
  my son runs up haft a dagger in eye ends Ursine fury.

Freja hear me, oh hear me!
Send forth thy love-lorn Jotun,
To wade among their Beasarkers
Loose thy loyal swine and
Bring woe unto all foes!

Oh Loki! God of Chaos! Father of Fenris!
  enemies round me, the Bear are slowly falling,
On shore they blow their horns and stamp their feet,
  from deep in the hills, I hear their bugles calling.
Swords grown slick and heavy, iced crusted tails hanging,

the fearsome Bear-kin accounted dead and dying.
We here upon the shore this day, our Pack has won,
    but doomed are we, if more Bear-kin coming!
Gone are foaming muzzle red-eyed painless monsters
    here friends and kin and son no longer bleeding

Loki hear me, oh hear me!
Send mad, confusing
Despair! Bring dark woe to them
And loose thy fearsome son,
May he devour enemy mine!

Oh ye hosts of Asgård, hear me!
Day is done, the battle won,
Unto thee the glory!
Loud the Raven and the Wolf,
Feasting on dead and dying.

In gray-furred arms and white wings,
Valkyrie carry those of glorious deed.
Victory!
Yet still I weep that I live,
When Ice-Mane, my beloved king,
The Eagle is devouring.

RAGNÅRÖK - II
WHITE-WINGED SISTERS

We our longboat pull onto the frosted pebble strand,
  Howls answer enemy, eager for blood and glory!
  A warrior fearless and bold blade can be hero made,
  Very walls of Mead Halls echo their skaldic story!
White Winged Wolves, the heroes to Asgård be flying
Howl thy name! Bring Valkyries flying, flying, flying

Charging with mighty roar called unto Tor:
  Across the strand Jarl's band charging.
  Deafening crash when warriors clash.
  Steel red, cloven shield thrown and barging!
Crash thy blade! Howl of all: the fallen, the dead, and dying.
Honor those who gather our best, upward flying, flying

All spears cast, all oaths made, the day belongs to the blade.
  Sword running red takes the head of red bear roaring,
  Warrior's blade broken, fighting with fang, claw, and fury,
  In a ring of dead you stand, with thy own guts outpouring.
Raise thy fists! Howl thy name! Howl thy name as you stand dying!
Hero thou, they come for you! White-Winged Sisters flying, flying!

RAGNÅRÖK - III
WOLF-KIN COME A'VIKING

Raven, Wolf-kin battle seekers following the Wolf prow
Wooden blades slice the water, ice crusted holding to the bow
The Raven, our spy, let loose and does it return to hand
Know that relentless searching there showed no sign of land
When Gore crow loosed circles spar and is never seen again
Know that it has found land, and our course to battle lain

Wolf-kin pull the oars, backs creaking like the spar
The songs of gods and of heroes marking off the time
Scree of stone on steel, edge making shaving fine
Naught but to eat and sleep 'till the Raven flies again
Oil each piece of leather that salt spray rot it not
Blue woad marks all muzzles, Wolf-Kin have come a'Viking

Pivot the oars! Reef sail! The Raven's found us land!
Bear grease on weapons! One horn of mead to each man!
Red-furred Foxen we'll take, grain and their red gold!
Quiet we split thru ice, and soon be boastful stories told.
Fall you with wounded back, no Valkyrie shall you ride.
Rest you now, while I keep watch, waiting for the tide.

Long boat beaching silent pulling onto pebbled strand
Before the trees, snowdrifts, after the flames of torches
A little village, a posted lamb, thinking it safe from wolves
Grey-furred fog whispering spreads among the ferns
Village wakens to sounds of fire, blood and screaming
They learn far too late that Wolf-kin have come a'Viking.

More ravens have we, and so onto new shores are turning.
For glorious battles, and piles of gold every man is yearning.
Four more foreign shores raped, and more people learning--
Your dead god cannot save you, nor bars when church is burning
His priests killed, all gold taken, dead god's home is no more
Behind us lays ashes of another charred Wolf-kin's whore.

Sing to Asgård, Oden's Mead hall, Freja, goddess of sex and war.
Ride storm, cracks of lightning, raise thy hammers unto Tor.
Last Raven gone, pull the oars, wind sets the sail strumming.
Word spreads, villages cower, in fear of our fangs coming.
Dead burned in honour smoke rising, we homeward sailing
Empty benches bring no sons and wives to mournful wailing

Rowing homeward, to another gold that burns blood and soul
Whether shield maiden or farmer, 'an she can raise your pole
And to her you speak sweet lies of never leaving her again
Words both know lies, raiding season is in the hearts of men.
Next year will come the time to put down scythe and the grain
Time for the Gray-Furred Sons of Midgård go a'Viking again.

Bar closed the church and bury your gold,
    Douse your torches and close the flues!
Send far away comely lads and lasses,
    Those we shall happily broach and tup!
Stay hidden in the cellar with the rats,
    For we'll leave naught but coals behind!
It is by Our claw prints on your strand,
    Your Blood on the snow that you shall know!
No matter it be Spring, Summer Fall, or Winter,
    at any day can Wolf-kin come a'Viking!

FRANCES PAULI
SNOW STORIES

Frances Pauli writes across multiple genres. Her work is speculative, full of the fantastic, and quite often romantic at its core. Whenever possible, she enjoys weaving in a little humor.

Once upon a time she was a visual artist, but she's since come to her senses. Now she fills her minuscule amount of free time with things like crocheting, belly-dancing, and abysmal ukulele playing.

In the snow their stories linger,
etched in pawprints
on the empty page.

Dark dent dances,
the poetry of wolves
overlain
in forest shadows.

Wandering winter tales,
archived,
printed on cold, clean paper.

Soft paws pressing
secret sigils
into snow.

DAVID POPOVICH
AM I THE BAD GUY?

David Popovich was born and raised in a small village outside of Cleveland, OH. He studied film at Full Sail University in Winter Park, FL. He now lives in Burbank, CA. A lover of books, movies, animation, games, comics, and furries; he spends his free time producing his own YouTube book review channel called "Bookworm Reviews." "Am I The Bad Guy?" is his first published work. Hopefully not the last.

Am I the bad guy?
Am I something to be feared?
Something to be distrusted and leered?
Am I the bad guy
For my gray fur and paws?
My long muzzled snout and huge carnivorous jaws?
Am I the bad guy
For the actions of my ancestors?
Only trying to survive to make the pack better.
Why am I the bad guy in your eyes?
I've never done anything to hurt your lives.
Yet I smell your fear when you spot me.
Choosing to cross that street to avoid me.
Saying those stereotypes are dead
But you won't feel safe until I'm full of lead.
I've seen the news.
I've read the headlines.
Another dead wolf who committed a crime
Never wanting to learn where that life is coming from
Cause it fits with your narrative that we are scum.
I am sick of being labeled a crook
Tired how everyone makes the bad guy the wolf.
A villain, a fiend, a trickster, a brute
Taking a simple lie over a complex truth.
I am angry that all my efforts to change this are in vain.

I've had enough of trying; I just want to cause pain.
You want a bad guy?
A bad guy you'll get.
With a grin on my face, my claws will lash out
Howling with joy as their screams ring loud.
Truly the city will be painted red.
As I become the monster you all have in your head.
But that would solve nothing, just another death for the news.
Just another story about a mad, mad wolf.
Am I the bad guy
Cause I want to be?
I don't think so.
No, I'll never be.
Those last few lines were nothing but a sick dream
Created to fit in a sick society.
I know our history is full of darkness.
Some truth in those tales to protect the harmless.
But times are changing whether you like it or not.
The wolf is no longer the bad guy as we once thought.
We've evolved with you so we can better ourselves.
To leave those savage thoughts back in the dark jungles.
But old habits are hard to shake loose
Putting us on an uneasy truce
I'm a wolf and I cannot change that.
But I can show you I'm not the monster to fear at.
I can show you our love for family and community
And the sweet music we make for everyone to sing.
That we are also silly and playful
Like little pups who refuse to grow old.
But also wise and courageous
Brave and bold.
The culture of a wolf is long and messy
But underneath it all is beauty.
The tides are changing.
And so will those thoughts.
Soon those beasts of the night will be an ancient memory.
As I howl into the night with my loving family.
Am I a bad guy?
Am I?

HEMAL RANA
A CHRISTMAS STORY FOR PUPS

Born and raised in Passaic County, New Jersey, Hemal Rana has had a passion for both animals and writing since elementary school. His favorite books include The Call of the Wild, Ender's Game, *the* Redwall *series, and* Percy Jackson & the Olympians. *Hemal also loves playing* Pokémon *and* Sonic the Hedgehog *in his spare time. This is his second published work for* Wolf Warriors *and his very first published short story. He has no desire to slow down. Hemal is currently an undergraduate at Rutgers University.*

It was a cold, early winter night. There was a full moon in the sky, shining moonlight across the snow-covered lands. In a small den was a she-wolf. She was lying on her side and was very tired. She had been scared that she wouldn't live through the night. But her ordeal was over, and she was still alive. Very exhausted, but alive.

Just then a male wolf came into the den. He had a worried look on his face. He asked the she-wolf how she was. The she-wolf picked up her head and gave her mate a tired smile. She then said, "I'm alright. The pups seem to be healthy too." This caused the male wolf to look at her belly where two newborn pups were nursing. The worried male became very happy.

He said, "They're beautiful!" He then lowered his face to nuzzle his mate's face. "Born on a full moon, these are going to be some special pups." The she-wolf couldn't help but smile at that. She then said, "Let's name them now. One is a female, and the other one is male."

"Hmm. I was thinking Zayev and Sirhaan. What do you think?"

"I love them. Plus, I'm too tired to argue right now. Let's just go with those names for now."

The male wolf laughed at this and then lay next his mate and his newborn children. The two new parents closed their eyes and began to enjoy the quiet, peaceful night.

A couple of miles away, there was a woman looking at a laptop screen. She was sitting next to the fireplace, amazed at what she was seeing. A man came into the room with two cups of hot chocolate in his hands and greeted the woman. He said to her, "Hey, what are you doing? The party is next door. I've brought you some hot chocolate." The woman took one of the cups and said to the man, "Thanks. I was just checking out the wolf cam, and you are not going to believe this. Lycaonia just gave birth to two cute little wolf pups!"

The man stopped drinking his hot chocolate and gave his friend a surprised look. "What? I thought she wasn't due for another week or so. Show me."

She gave him the laptop with excitement in her face. The man spent an entire minute looking at a laptop before saying to his friend, "They're beautiful. I was really scared that they were going to be born premature, especially since this is Lycaonia's first litter. But everybody seems to look healthy. Zeeb sure looks like a proud papa." He gave his friend her laptop back. She then said, "I know right? It's a Christmas miracle! We have to show everybody."

"Oh, definitely. First, we get snow, then a full moon, and now wolf pups; this is the best Christmas ever!"

The two friends started going to the next room to show everybody, but then the woman asked her friend, "What should we name them?"

"Hmmm. We don't know the genders of the pups yet. But for now how about Jesus and Mary?"

The two friends laughed at this joke and then went into the other friend to spread the good news about their discovery.

When the pups finished nursing, they began to rest. They were frustrated that they couldn't see the world around them. The two siblings wanted to explore their surroundings and discover what they were born into. However, they had to continue to wait. Enjoying the warmth of their mother and of each other, the pups began to sleep. The small family of wolves spent their Christmas night enjoying the peace and quietness of the early winter night.

ADAM ROBERTSON
OUT OF THE CIRCLE

Adam lives in Virginia and enjoys storytelling through different mediums, such as writing, music and film. He is an advocate for animals of all kinds and is constantly inspired by their spirit and their struggle.

The universe doesn't seem quite so vast within a frame. It takes you a moment to really allow the idea to settle, but when this boundless entity is suddenly ridden with limitations, your perspective narrows—or widens—I am not sure which. Nevertheless, there it is: four walls and darkness, slowly closing in on this universal concept of eternity. Every book you have ever read, every god who has ever laid a vengeful hand upon this earth; they spoke of a divine providence, a bounty of energy that lies within our reach—that is not the revelation that lay before me in this moment.

Lying within my confines, the walls are closing in on me. The image of space swallowed up before my very eyes. There is a call amplified across the horizon, a lamenting of sorts, but its spirit is not of regret. Long and drawn out like a violin caressed by its bow, a musical prowess I have never heard. My vision has narrowed as the walls gradually reach beyond my grasp; the luminous sky now imperceptible. There are four faces, blank and without movement, glancing at me from above, beyond the frame—against the brilliance of space. Their features covered in shadow; somehow, their intentions are clear.

I am a prisoner. I have been for some time now, and while I don't remember how or why I came to be here; my ingress into this boorish hell, I do remember.

It was the dire cold that imprinted upon me so deeply. It was only a moment that I felt the mystery of the violent winter surrounding this place, only a moment that I felt the icy sting that lies beyond these walls; a sting accompanied by the darkness of deceit, pulled about my eyes in trickery. It wasn't until the hood was yanked from my face that I understood my harrowing plight, and was formally welcomed to my asylum.

One room: four walls. My hair lightly brushes the ceiling as I pace in small concentric circles around a stale slab of concrete. The rotting stench of mold mixes generously with the stiff odor of blood, metallic and nauseating.

With rocks, I often scribble incoherent nonsense upon the walls. Most of my drawings narrowed to useless tracings of my hand, but often, in my desperate search for variance, I will flood the walls with scribble and leave my canvas gray and empty of artistic prospect. There is but a single image sketched upon these dreary walls that I have never had the courage to remove. It has remained upon the door since my delivery here, and I have no recollection of its origin. I often marvel at its simplistic elegance and the spell it seems to hold over me, as it rests just above the small opening in the door.

The small opening would occasionally produce rations; I suppose in effort to maintain my dwindling vitality. It would also serve as a catalyst for my desperation, and my drastic need for companionship. Often, I would converse with the narrow rift, my sole friend—as he was the last vestige of my dying humanity. Rex was his name.

"Am I still here?" I ask Rex. "Where…is here?"

"—," he responds, of course. He is a space in a door. I know this fact, at least I knew—this fact—I hope I still do.

Aside from the solitude, it is the long draw of time that has cursed me most, although I am not certain as to the full length of my stay here. But my lunacy has evolved beyond my grip of self-realization. Of that I am certain.

There are men here. They interrogate me quite frequently. Why am I interrogated? The enigma eludes me, as my tormentors speak a foreign tongue. They scream. I yield, yet I know not what is required of me. Often, my interrogations arrive daily. Though, 'daily' is quite nebulous without the meter of daylight as measure.

Insomnia plagues me. It remolds my sanity, much like the interrogations, and the solitude, and the deprivation—the solitude—the madness.

The darkness—the misery; they are the necessary precursors to the madness of which I speak. The madness, I understand, but the darkness has consumed me beyond my comprehension.

There is a single, reoccurring vision that often weighs upon me, a dream that has led me to consider a time before my imprisonment. Perhaps, it is a memory of who I once was—or what I was meant to become. I see an ocean of midnight blue that paints the night sky, a translucent canvas of the expanding universe. The moon glistens with a radiance that I am unable to articulately describe, yet I have never seen the marvels of this natural spectacle. I hear a cry reaching through the twilight, a sound that bleeds of heartache and pain, yet speaks to my soul of eternal beauty; a singularity of light. Amongst this light, I see an oasis, but it's just a dream. Except that it is a dream that is not my own; it is a dream that I have simply overheard or bore witness. It is apart from me. I am apart from me—and I am despairingly lost.

Now—the torture.

The guards unlatch the steel fastening and employ my chamber door. As always, their faces cast in shadow, unable to be seen. It is as though the light danced around them to avoid revealing the mysteries of their identity, a notable catalyst to my fear.

A crudely fashioned hood is then violently strewn about my head, the coarse fiber burning my face as it is pulled taut. "Please!" I plead with them in my vulnerability. "No more…"

My bare feet drag through the shallow puddles along the hallway floor as I raise my sagging head to the ceiling. I shuddered at the muted glow of the uniformed ceiling lights that bleed through the hood; like ghosts they haunt my descent into this hell.

I have arrived. It is a room much bigger than my own and there is an unforgettable smell that lingers. It is a distinctness that resembles wet mold and carnage; worsened by the maddening tedium of a constant leak of the ceiling. I am strapped tightly to a chair that is fit for an insane asylum; a lamp reaches over top, positioned to illuminate the contortions of my agonizing face. There are four men…always four men. The room is circular, with two rusted doors opposite each other. I have come to call this place, *the circle*.

The hood is torn from my head and the lamplight stuns my vision. A heavy sweat about my brow; my knotted hair clings to my face like an ebony spider web. Suddenly, the guard to my left quickly presses the lamplight to my face, searing my skin and filling the room with an irate tension.

"Sleyte ghois!" he screams. "Sleyte ghois!" he spews. Of all that was said to me, it was the only reoccurring pattern that I could ever recognize. I had tried for so long, but I understood nothing of their babble, and they made no effort to remedy that. Over and over they would scream, one after the other: "Sleyte ghois…Sleyte ghois."

The engines of my torture would vary by episode; each more or less menacing in their own respective intent. Sometimes, it was a bludgeoning tool of sorts, and sometimes it was as inconspicuous as a clear plastic bag. Such is this chapter.

My heart raced. My lungs surged. I gasped for air like a fish out of water, flailing about my shackles and a cast of ashen blue about my face. Just as I would reach blackout, he would release. On. Off. "Sleyte ghois!" On. Off. "Sleyte ghois!" he cursed. The assisting guards contributed with crushing blows to my ribs, snapping them like wet carrots; one strike after another—and another. I feel like hours have passed. This can't go on. It can't. I feel myself go limp. I lose consciousness—finally.

I blinked, and I was awake, or so it seemed. The room was empty. The guards had left me alone to breathe, to cope with the piercing agony of my broken ribs. I scanned the room cynically, but found nothing. "What the hell?" I groan, realizing that I was no longer shackled and could move about freely.

I sat forward, continuing to scour *the circle* in disbelief, pressing my arm against my rib cage to abate the sickening throb. I waited, expecting some fashion of activity to come tearing into the room. Unexpectedly, I came to find a different sensation, something unexplainably surreal; a cold silence that seemed to penetrate and envelop me with one uniting voice.

In that moment, I felt a breeze wash over me. Not the breeze that came as my chamber door is slammed shut and I am left to ponder my sanity, but a breeze from whatever lay outside these walls; a breeze from the unknown. And despite the blinding pain of my wounds, I began to scour *the circle* furiously, desperate to find the spring from which the draft had flowed. What I would do when—if—I found it, didn't concern me, I only sought to find its origin. To my surprise, I found myself standing before the large door opposite where I had entered.

The wind tickled my fingers as I waved my hand about the small gap at the jamb of the door; a shiver creeping up my spine. I closed my eyes and pressed my face to the steel, imagining what lay on the other side, imagining the freedom I would never experience; and as I pressed my body vigorously against the door, it sounded a deep groan and crept open, slamming against the wall opposite its tremendous hinges.

In the darkness before me extended a narrow hallway, the end of which led to a blinding prism of light. The breeze that I had felt on the inside was amplified as the stark cold rushed forth and surrounded me, but I felt nothing but the warmth that radiated from the mysterious light at the end of the tunnel.

As my sense of shock staggered me, I threw away any sense of inhibition and quickly started down the hallway. Every step closer to the light was overwhelming—blinding. And when I took my first step beyond the fringe of darkness, I could see no more. I was paralyzed by the light; helpless, as the raging winter landscape besieged me.

I saw nothing of the sun through the blanket of snow. My eyes faintly adjusted to the piercing winds, and in doing so, I was able to observe the place I had called home for all of my known existence. No more than a singular steel tower rising out of the icy terrain, a constant siege of black smoke poured from its chimney like a lit cigar. The tunnel of my escape sunk back into the ground, while smaller pipes that scattered the yard stood as trees would stand, probably a ventilation system of sorts for the sunken fortress below. I could scantily make out a fence that towered above the perimeter of the yard, adorned with razor wire, glimmering amongst the steady shower of falling snow.

I walked the yard curiously, covering my face, shielding the onslaught of the blizzard as best I could, when I came upon a small enclosure, boxed tightly into the corner of the yard.

Huddled about the far corner, I could make out an apparition of sorts within the enclosure. I mounted my hands upon the heavily braided fence and stared intently at the mound, generously covered with snow. Any movement was unobservable with the impairment of my vision. I stared, waiting for a few moments, before deciding to move on at the lack of prospect, until the storm inhaled for a moment, long enough to clear my obstructed gaze and stir the being from its hibernation.

Hypnotic orange eyes—it was the first I saw of the creature as she appeared magnificent against the backdrop of uninterrupted white. She then caught glimpse of me and rose from her dormancy, shaking the mass of snow from her frail and weakened frame. There, standing against the pearl landscape of a prison yard, was a wolf; as pure white as the snow she stood upon. She was built far better than I for such inclement weather—but not like this, not on these terms. She was a prisoner, same as I, with no shelter save the ragged fur upon her back. She was weak. She was frail, withered, and she was scared. I gazed into her fire-kissed eyes as she remained backed into the corner, anxious with fear. I knelt down in effort to establish direct eye contact with her, when she let out an exhausted, albeit sovereign, howl. It soared over the winter rampage and rattled my bones.

I stumbled to my feet in awe of her brilliant song; its sheer intensity was thoroughly disarming.

"— I know your cry," I whispered under my breath, as I closed my eyes and took a step back from the enclosure.

"Set me free," she pleaded.

Mesmerized, I transfixed upon her cryptic speech for just a moment—until they found me, the ruthless bastards. I felt the cold sting of steel upon my skull, and in my anomalous state of unconsciousness, I dreamed.

Time stood still as I stare into her eyes, a deep ocean of amber bronze. They overwhelm my senses, and I lose myself in the undertow of their turbulence. My angel, have I lost you amongst this neverending misery? I have never dreamed this dream. I have loved you, but your face is strangely foreign to my heart. I brush the hair from your face, but I am utterly numb to your song. I feel your hand melt into mine, a soft touch as your finger traces the palm of my hand, expressing a familiar mark upon me. I know this marking; I know you. I have loved you, but I know not who you are. You sigh deeply; your lips tremble as if to speak, yet I am forbidden to your voice—unable to hear your words.

Here again, I lay upon the frigid dirt, callous and unwelcome. The stars shining high into the heavens, framed within the dark curtains of my pit. A theatre of spectacle beheld, as a cry carries across the night sky. The edges of my confinement stretching apart from me; I know this place well. I see them now, stirring, my demons. They welcome me back home.

"Who is she?" I ask Rex, pacing my cell, toiling over what had occurred.

"—"

"But who? Why do I recognize her?—And not?!" I plead discouragingly. "Why the hell is there a wolf?!"

"—," responds Rex.

"I don't understand!" I scream, my frustration peaking.

Certainty of reality is much simpler in the moment, rather than in hindsight. I began to doubt that I had ever left *the circle* in the first place. I groaned in my frustration and gazed hopelessly at my dimly illuminated finger grazing amongst the light from Rex, until my eye caught a glimpse of the drawing that I had left upon the wall so long ago.

A simple sketch, I never understood its meaning, but I had never been bold enough to remove it either. I had always felt an unexplainable bond that kept me from doing so. I ran my fingers across the drawing, tracing its contours over and over again. I must have spent hours in this arduous trance, until at last, I had my 'eureka' moment.

"This is the mark!" I asserted with a heavy degree of confidence. "The dream...the mark...the woman...this is the mark that she etched upon my hand," I said, coming suddenly alive at the details of the enigma, a mysterious sensation, long inert within me.

The marking was simple, yet cryptic in nature: one circle, surrounded by the outline of a partial circle, settled just above and to the right of its peer.

Had she spoken to me? Although I am mostly certain, I could not thoroughly recall; the details of my dream steadily crumbled from my recollection. And what of the wolf? Her mystery besieged me! I doubt her very existence on the planes of my unstable reality, although I do not doubt the question of relation. I had experienced two very bizarre and puzzling situations within mere moments of each other. Coincidence is too simplistic an answer for this plight. There must be a connection.

I would repeat them often, the words of the wolf. They haunted me; an obsession that repeatedly flooded my mind like a broken record.

"Set me free…" I whispered to myself. "Set me free!" I barked at Rex.

Fits of hysteria would manically follow in the coming days—inescapable black holes of time. "Set me free…" she had begged of me—and I, in many ways, of her.

I remembered little of my time before I would enter *the circle* again, my only measure of such being the remaining soreness that lingered since my previous visit; a dull throb that mirrored my continual disheartenment.

While in a frailty-induced coma, they hauled my broken body through the corridor. They tore the hood from my head, and I struggled against the blaze of the overhead light. My torture would soon begin…

"Slet ghoi!" says one guard in a demanding, frightful tone.

"Huh?" I mumble, confused. "That doesn't sound the same…"

"Slet ghoi!" abrasively screams the guard opposite.

Their words, they were peculiar, divergent from my previous experiences strapped to the chair; but they made no effort in explanation for the variance, no matter my plea. They merely continued in acting as agents to their duty, enacting terrible deeds upon me. "Slet ghoi!" they screamed, fueled by a macabre creativity that left my fingers curled, my heart pounding, and my teeth grinding like wet sandpaper.

I winced and gnarled in agony. Their words may have changed, but their actions had fiercely intensified. My head swam as I neared blackout. The guards screamed and danced around me like wild natives. Time drug idly by—and as I neared unconsciousness, by way of bitter strangulation via a length of thin twine, I finally fell limp. Another round in *the circle* I had survived, just barely, as I always do.

Again, I awoke amongst an empty room. Crippled by weakness, I struggled to my feet and scanned *the circle*. I then quickly made my way to the door. My strength wavered, and I knew I had very little time.

The door was unlocked, and I made my way diligently through the tunnel, against the blinding light and the rush of frigid air. "What will I say to her?" I asked myself. Each step fueled my anxiety. Every stride crushed my lingering disbelief. This was, in fact, some strange division of reality I was experiencing, but reality nonetheless.

Chaos.

I had to rely on memory as I clawed my way along the fence, searching for the wolf. Every lashing of the wind numbed my extremities; the intense cold like a drug coursing through my veins.

I saw nothing through the bedlam of the storm. It must have been by sheer chance alone that I found her enclosure. I fell to my knees in exhaustion, and it was then that she appeared to me; melting away from the white of the storm, her eyes aglow with a new vitality that stopped my heart.

She stared at me as if she were reading my thoughts, but remained silent.

I was in awe. I knew that I had limited time and that whatever I said, or inquired, would have to be worth its weight in gold, but my mind fell to blankness, and I simply mumbled, "What—is this?"

Again, she stared intently, her eyes never parting from mine. Her face remained still and stoic as she spoke, "Set me free…"

"How?" I cried. "I don't understand what is going on!"

"They speak your truth. Listen…" she whispers, her voice not female, not male, but something else entirely. It was the most beautiful sound I had ever heard. She spoke, not from her snout, but from her mind—from her soul. "Just listen," she begged.

"Listen to who?!" I screamed in frustration as she faded into the noise of the storm. "Who?!"

In an instant she was gone, and I again fell into a dream-state oblivion by the callous hands of my captors.

My angel, she is with me yet again, staring into my eyes as if we had never broken gaze from one another. We sat hand in hand, the wind in her hair, upon a bench amongst a grove of trees overlooking a glassy lake. The scent of pine wafted and mixed effortlessly with the smell of her perfume. My hand lay softly in hers as she traced the marking with her finger. With her head tilted, she focused on my hand. Over and over again she drew, before silently pausing and squeezing my hands warmly. Staring into my eyes once more, fighting back a single tear forming in the corner of her eye, she leans in and whispers softly into my ear, "You are my whole world, and I am forever your moon."

With I in my pit and the universe before me, I again observe as time lurches forth. My walls are closing in on me, and the stars have lost their luster. A moment of silence lay bare, followed by a howl that pierced the heavens like an arrow. As sure as the hours do dwell, my demons will reveal themselves and lead me back into the abyss.

"You are my whole world, and I am forever your moon," I repeat over and over as I thump my head against the damp wall in an attempt to strike ablaze some long dormant memory. It was the marking, she was verbalizing its purpose, its meaning. It must have been some code for one another, or perhaps just an emblematic gesture of intimacy. There was much of her that continued to plague me with confusion, but I could recall that she and I once carried a bond, yet I still did not know who she was, or where she is —.

And where did the wolf fit in to this vision? This was perhaps the most mystifying occurrence of the lot. My initial shock of having a wild animal speak to me via some radical method of telekinesis had faded, somehow. However, my curiosity at the simultaneous arrival of my dream, in relation to the wolf, had peaked and sent me into a bewildered lunacy.

"They. They. They. They…She says 'they' but the only 'they' is *them*," I gesture outside of my cell in reference to the guards. "Truth?! My truth she says? *They* have it?!—Damn them!" I exclaim, pacing maddeningly about my restricted cell like a lab rat.

"—," responds Rex.

"How the hell do I listen to them? What the hell are they even saying?!"

"—"

"God damnit! They've done this to me!—I know nothing of who I am! Where I came from! They took that from me!" I scream, seething. My fists clenched and my heart racing, as I struggle to compose myself. "I—I can't keep doing this…"

I fell backward until I thumped the wall. I slide down, my hands to my side and my chest heaving. My fury melts away in an instant, and a surge of hopelessness falls over me. I leaned my head against the wall, the stress of losing my temper taking its toll. My skull ached, and my wounds pulsated under the pressure of my straining heart.

"I can't keep holding on to this…Can I?" I ask, desperately glancing at Rex for any sign of agreeance; for any sign of anything—anything—but nothing.

A mad smile curls across my chapped lips as it again sinks in, the thick fog of despair as it wraps me inside of a warm blanket and rocks me into delirium. I have, on occasion, lost myself inside the impervious fantasy of escape from this place, but I always return to the nexus. I am always able to tap into that last shred of sanity and stomp out the lingering hope that fans the flame of liberation. It had just grown more troublesome in this long stretch of time.

This was my moment. The moment when I am able to step back from myself and see my actions from a fresh perspective. Like a ghost, I hovered amidst my body. I quietly climb to my feet and run my fingers across the marking on the door, convincing myself that I had simply reverse-engineered a story that fit its purpose. It was merely chicken scratch, a symbol whose meaning was never meant to be heard, or understood. Thinking of the woman in my dream, the wolf, desperately needing to hold on to the idea that what I had been exposed to was in fact real, but I knew better. A wave of disappointment fell over me. Disappointment that I could let my imagination again carry me away. Disappointment that I could again expose myself to these misguided illusions of grandeur, but enlightenment again befell me.

Becoming enlightened—can be a beautiful moment, if it is light that fills your path, but enlightenment under the guise of sorrow rapes you of your innocence. It seeks out your faith and swallows it as a whale swallows a minnow, leaving what is left of you a useless shell. Not an empty shell, but a shell filled with blind rage and inconsolable hatred. Hatred of all things, but none more than yourself. Bottle that up inside of a cage and a bomb goes off, leaving you bloodied and in pieces, just trying to scoop your guts off of the floor.

Time stood still for me, and under the veil of defeat, I wallowed.

I stood at the center of my cell in a haze of pity and self-doubt for what felt like an eternity. My head tilted, my fingers stiff and my eyes glazed over. I twitched. I shuddered. I felt like I was frozen, an ice sculpture that couldn't melt. The world, whatever was out there, whatever was left of it, passed by as I stood still. I didn't age. I didn't wither. I died. Slowly and steadily, I decayed from the inside out as the days and months drudged forth, helplessly dragging me along.

My visits to *the circle* were frequent, as I fell into a toneless loop of circumstance. I slept. I barely ate, and then I returned to *the circle*. I was a zombie. My senses had shut down, even in the wake of the varied displays of torture I was shown. I had some relic of knowledge that they aimed to extract, but whatever I had was buried deep within the caverns of my paralyzed psyche.

Inside *the circle*, I kept my distance from the door that led outside. Hope is too painful a concept when it is beyond the scope of existence. I had been down that road, and I had no desire to travel it again.

"Arrrrrrrghhhckkkkkk," I drone under clenched teeth as the guard cruelly taunts me with a rusty knife.

As of recent, I had felt little in my trips to *the circle*, whether in time I had gained a heightened sense of pain tolerance I am uncertain, but pain was pain so I was not immune, just experienced. My groans were infrequent, and I remained brutally un-phased, a stoic and deadpan countenance throughout.

I was riddled with trauma, and there was little, in my experience, to be unexpected. But, as the wielded blade met ferociously with the frailty of my palm, I felt an unquenchable fury surge within me. My eyes widened. My muscles tightened, filling with what little blood remained as it rushed through my constricted veins.

"Don't!" I angrily scream, my nostrils flaring with each labored breath.

"Don't!—Bastards!" I spit. "Stop!"

"…finally responding…," I hear one of the guards mumble to the other.

"What did you say?" I demand, in a state of shock.

With his faced draped in shadow, he stares with no response, redirecting my attention toward the direst state of my palm. I turn in accord with his direction when I am promptly met with a crippling blow, landing flush upon my weakened jaw.

"Let go!" he screams, inches from my ear.

"Wh…wha?" I mumble in a daze. My mouth hung wide in confusion. Somehow, I understood his words, like the language barrier had suddenly disintegrated. But how was that possible?

The shock and awe of my discovery bewildered me into such a state of disorientation that I had forgotten what made me so irate to begin with. I began to recall what the wolf had said, before I pushed her words almost entirely from my memory: "Listen…"

"Let go!" he screams again, the guard to my left jarring me with a heavy-handed right hook; the blade still intimately paired with my palm opposite. My temper quickly boils, and I start to shake violently about my restraints, kicking my legs and flailing my arms, the sheer force of my eruption loosening my bindings. I am able to free one hand, then the other.

I quickly unbuckled my straps as the guards stood mysteriously idle. My eyes, fire red, and my rampage still in full swing. I turned to the guard with the knife and glanced down at my carved up hand. I became drunk with power. I rushed forward with every bit of vigor I had in me. I floundered recklessly, missing the first guard, but turning my sights toward the next. I swung a wild haymaker, missing again. I rotated my stance and set my sights on the third. I tucked my head into my shoulders and charged like a bull, lapsing yet again and losing my footing, stumbling to the red, stained floor.

Prepared for an onslaught of retaliation, I regained my stability and rose to my feet, but I was met with silence. They were gone. Both doors were shut. I stood alone in the center of *the circle*, coughing and hacking, trying to catch my escaping breath.

I placed my hand on the wall, trying to retain my balance. Nausea suddenly kicked in, and I felt the surge of adrenaline begin to level off. Though the guards had gone, my anger seethed, and I stared ponderously at the door that led to the tunnel, remembering—debating.

"Damn…" I groan, realizing the inevitable. The circumstances demand action. The door beckons me.

I left *the circle* through the illuminated tunnel, leaving only the faint outline of the marking on the wall; left in blood, where my wounded hand had rested.

I was on fire as I stomped my way through the tempest of frost, the enclosure of the wolf mere steps away. Much time had elapsed since I had seen her, but as I again laid eyes upon her I was struck by her mystery, her hypnotizing beauty. As well I was perplexed by her health, as it had seemed to flourish, almost to a point beyond feasibility.

We stared at each other for a moment, my heart pounding. "What the hell is happening here?!" I demand, raising my voice above the turbulent winds. "I can't understand any of this…I just can't!"

I dropped to my knees before her, my anger quickly turning to desperation. My eyes began to swell and water, I became overwhelmed and undone.

"You listened," she spoke with a pleasant elegance of delight.

"But it's been so long… and—I still don't understand."

"It has been but a moment."

"It's been…so long—years at least, has it not?" I ask, confused.

"A moment…a drop amongst an ocean," the wolf responds pleasantly.

A minute passed as I momentarily fell speechless, "Let go…what do they mean? What do they—want?"

"It is the same as I asked of you."

"The same?"

"Set me free, I had asked. Do you remember?"

"But I don't know how…I don't understand any of this…"

"You must let go if you are to move forth…you must," her tone takes a dire turn.

"Of what?!"

"Of what has confined you for so long. You must let them go."

"Them?"

"Fear, anger, despair, regret. Set them free."

"Set them free? What are you saying?" I pause for a moment, pondering her words. "I am confined here—there is nothing for me to release."

"You are no prisoner here. It is they—who are *your*—prisoners."

"How can you say that?!" I roar. "Those—bastards have taken everything from me. From *us*! Are you not their prisoner as well, confined to this caged hell?!"

She stared at me blankly, her orange eyes seemed to penetrate and warm me like I was gazing into the sun. She stepped closer, "I too, am your prisoner in this place."

A sense of disgust covered me like a dark cloud. What she had said was not only ludicrous, but impossible, yet there was a voice in my head that validated her words.

Her ears flattened against her head as she sat down in the snow, her paws kneading back and forth as she settled into her seat. "You have forgotten something," she explained calmly. "Something valuable to who and what you are. These memories you have erased have kept you in this place for so long. It is the reason why you know nothing of where you came from before this. It's why you can't even recall your own name."

"Her…" I whisper under my breath, my eyes wide with disbelief.

"Yes…her," the wolf affirms, a long pause followed. "But in order for you to escape from this circle, you must first let go of what you have kept imprisoned.—You must realize that to let go—is never to forget."

"But...how?" I solemnly ask. "How do I remember—without holding on?"

Her eyes smiled at me, "The answer is in the palm of your hand."

Slowly, I raised my hand to eye level as I obsessively studied the bloody marking that had been carved into it. I fixated on it so intensely that my vision began to falter, but then suddenly, like a tidal wave, I remembered—and again, in my forced unconsciousness, I dreamed.

"You are my whole world, and I am forever your moon," she whispers into my ear as she marked upon my hand. I sat helplessly frozen, suspended in a state of trauma. "I am so sorry —," she wept, her eyes red and swollen.

She had taken me to Evans Lake to tell me the news, as it had always been our favorite spot together. We sat for hours, it seemed, as she and I both hoped that perhaps time would dull the edge of the shock. Or that maybe we had spiraled into some awful nightmare, and we would soon wake up...soon.

"No matter what happens," she finally says. "I —," she tries to speak but loses her composure again. I run my fingers through her hair to comfort her. Still unable to speak, I force a smile and gently kiss her head, all the while holding back a flood of hopelessness and devastation. "This is just a dream," I said to myself—over and over. "This is just a dream."

In the following days, we attempted to go about our lives with some degree of normalcy. After all, she had been told that she had many months, perhaps even years ahead of her. We visited specialists and got varying opinions that all seemed to meet with the same fate. But we still had a chance to be happy again, at least for some time.

She told me the news about her disease on a Monday afternoon. Eleven days later, on Friday, she was gone.

I never got to tell her all that I had wanted to say, and no matter how hard I try, I can't let go. I can't forgive myself for having left her side for selfish aspirations. I can't forgive myself for the malady that consumed her body as I stood idly by. I can't and won't forgive myself, because nothing will bring her back—and I will remain under the cloak of this wretched nightmare until I take my last breath.

But something was different now —. No longer did I lie in wait at the bottom of my grave, gazing into the heavens and waiting for the frigid hand of death to pull me deeper.

I hear her calling now...wake up...wake up...

Propped in the corner of my cell, I opened my eyes to a faint beam of light, gently warming my face; my cheek pressed against the cold dankness of the wall. The beam of light, as it seemed, came not from the mouth of Rex, but from the open door.

Riddled with wounds, I slid my back up the wall until I stood, still a bit light-headed and hazy. In disbelief, I reached for the door and gently pushed; it released a deep moan and hesitantly swung open. I stepped into the hallway with a watchful eye, my level of expectation in a whirlwind of chaos, but I found nothing. Not even a sound, save the muted echo of my footsteps, and the incessant leaking from the ceiling.

I slowly, yet reluctantly, made my way down the hallway. I tracked the lights that trailed the ceiling, and I scoured for answers with every step. I then came to the entrance of *the circle* and realized there had been no additional doors between my cell and where I stood. Not one.

I continued past *the circle*, increasing my pace, until I again arrived at my own cell. I was back where I had started and encountered only two doors: my own and *the circle*. It started to make sense now, what the wolf had told me. It was insane, and it was unimaginable, but I believed her now. I had no other choice.

I went back to *the circle*, the entrance locked and latched. I rigidly gripped the handle and pulled, as it released the locking mechanism and made a jarring sound like a train crawling down a railroad. The door opened, and I quickly sprang from the frame, as the guards stood waiting at the other side of the room. I remained hidden for a moment, expecting a response, but after a minute or two, there was still no hint of movement from them. I glanced inside and saw them frozen there, their hands plastered to their sides, posed like toy soldiers.

I entered the room slowly, one step at a time, reassessing my situation with every inch. They never budged; never schemed, and so I continued, closer and closer until I was face to face with my mysterious captors.

I stepped before the first, still unable to see his face. I wavered my hand in an attempt to draw his attention, or perhaps shake him from his reverie, to no avail. Something was strange, and as I stepped even closer I realized, in horror, that he had no face—just a black hole where a face should be. No eyes; no nose; no mouth; nothing. It was just the illusion of a three-dimensional object, achieved by some quantum means of deception, floating atop what appeared to be a flesh and blood body.

In my dismay, I examined all four guards, all of them identical in form and nature. All stood abnormally erect like figures in a dollhouse, but as I neared completion, something caught my eye upon the wall. It was the marking, left in blood from my lacerated hand. I gazed fondly at it, and then at my bloodied hand. I thought of her for moment, and as I traced the outline on my palm I whispered her name, "Christine."

Before the word even escaped my lips, it felt as though an earthquake began to rumble below my feet. The concrete of the floor began to crack and crumble as the tremors grew in strength, releasing a hail of debris from the bed of rock above.

Covering my head, I made my way toward the tunnel, my only means for escape. I stumbled and faltered while the guards remained in a state of inertia, unmoved by the pandemonium around them. The quake swelled in severity as I shoulder-checked the door open, the light at the end of the tunnel blazed. Despite my weakness, I darted through the tunnel like an Olympian, but then stopped. I turned for one final glance at *the circle*, before returning down the tunnel. I ran into the light. I never turned back.

Out of the tumultuous carnage, I escaped to the outside, the earthquake ceasing the moment I reached the end of the tunnel, but the prison continued to give way under the weight of the destruction. The tunnel seemed to breathe and swell before it wilted like a dying flower at the heels of my escape. The tower crumbled into dust. The smoke stacks shook riotously as each sunk into the earth, one by one.

There, at the surface: my vision clouded by the arresting light, my lungs afire from exhaustion, with the upheaval of the earthquake having quenched its thirst; I saw it. For the first time, I saw the sun.

The storm had departed in a poetic elegance. The orphaned clouds crossed before the sun as its golden rays painted the snow with a rainbow of vivid patterns. The snow that blanketed the ground glistened and sparkled in reflection. In the distance were white tipped mountains stretching across the horizon, lush green forests that foreshadowed their ascent, trees all around that bent in obedience with each breath of the wind.

I pushed the hair from my face, melting with the lost sense of freedom that suddenly came over me, when the wolf appeared before me. She was enchanting, stronger than ever. The tower lay in ruin and the perimeter fencing had fallen to the ground, sinking below the surface as she stood glowing before me. The snow that settled upon her stark white coat reflected the vivid intensity of the sun, an illusion of diamonds that covered her from head to toe.

"Am I dead?" I ask candidly, the dust from the crumbling structure rising like a phoenix behind me.

"No…not dead."

"It doesn't feel like a dream," I assert, shaking my head. "Not at all."

"It's not," she says, bowing her head in contemplation of an appropriate explanation. "You are—between."

"I guess I can accept that."

Still sensing my confusion, she explains, "Tragedy and ruin hold weight in all life. Some—hold so tightly that even beyond life, the grip of that affliction is unbreakable, and that life is unable to transcend."

"I'm not sure I understand."

"You will…in time," she nods affirmingly.

"But…why are you here?"

"For you, of course. I am your guide away from this place—a navigator of sorts," she concedes. She steps forward, the warmth of her breath upon me, "I promise, all will make sense in due time."

A moment of silence fell between us. I stared at her attentively, collecting my thoughts.

"What do we do now?" I ask her curiously, hopefully. "Where do we go?"

"Out of the circle," she replies. "Out of the circle."

We ran, faster than I ever could have imagined. We ran with the soundtrack of the snow crunching under the weight of each step. We ran through vast and remarkable territories across the open lands: through forests, across frozen lakes, into and over the mountains and beyond the horizon. The warmth of the sun was always upon our backs, the call of the ravens reverberated across the open skies. The wolf had become a part of me, and I of her. She was the explanation to the answer I had come to ask myself. She was the bridge between self-destruction—and transcendence.

We came to a mountain pass where there was a lake laid bare before a towering mountain; a mirror to its grandeur. It was the first body of water we had seen that wasn't a frozen bed of ice. We approached, dipping our faces in to drink from the cold mountain spring as the breeze sent ripples across its clear, glass-like surface. And as I admired her alluring reflection cast atop the water as she drank, I came to realize the unforeseen absence of my own, as I stared into the emptiness of the blue.

No matter was the revelation that I had at that moment, as I blankly gazed into the lake. It had no bearing over the relationship or the bond that would continue to flourish between the wolf and I. The state of consciousness that existed between us was trivial and inconsequential, never meant to be understood—only had, and that was all that mattered. I would follow her anywhere, the wolf; she would lead me from the darkness, granting me sight through the fury of the storm.

We soon found a wandering pack of wolves that welcomed us as family. We fell under the spell and mystery of the forests as we traveled and explored our vast territory throughout the years. With every passing light of day the strength of the pack grew. We were the guardians of the dawn. We were the children of the night.

I thought of her often, my love, Christine. I had forgotten her for so long that I often sat and pondered her memory in excess, making up for lost time, perhaps. I would always love her, and I knew that our journey together had only been postponed. No manner of time or resolution can break the bonds of the heart, and I knew that she would always be at my side, holding my hand, making her mark upon me.

I would cry out to her nightly, my Christine, as the dawn fell to shadow. She looked down upon me in fondness as I and the pack would lift our heads into the fog of the night sky, howling in an immortal chorus of loneliness for our fallen loved ones. They had lost, same as I, same as us all—and we would never forget their undying legacy.

Forever, I would be in love with her, for all the coming days of my life, until our paths cross again. After all, I was her whole world—and she would forever be my moon.

LAURA CRISTINA SÁNCHEZ SÁENZ
EL SUEÑO DEL BOSQUE

Laura Cristina Sánchez Sáenz was born in Bogotá, Colombia. She is twenty-five years old. She has been a Doctor of Veterinary Medicine from Universidad Nacional de Colombia (National University of Colombia) since 2015, and she works in wildlife rehabilitation as a volunteer.

She has liked writing poems since her childhood; she used to write verses at the school because she felt her soul could get freedom from it, and it was also a good way to express, discuss, and promote awareness. When she was in the University, she had no time for it, but sometimes she converted in poems her experiences with nature and animals, her feelings and deep thoughts. Once, she wrote a poem for her University entitled "Herencia inmortal," which was published in some student papers.

She loves and respects animals, and admires them because they are so different and have a lot of incredible virtues and abilities. Moreover, they are mysterious, know about many things hidden to humans, and live with nature in peace. Even the wolves have a strong link with the forest and the sky, until the moon can hear them.

El bosque se ha vestido de blanco
Una hermosa alfombra arropa los campos,
Diáfano paisaje canta en suave melodía
La exquisita tonada da al invierno la bienvenida.

Por el camino juega una tímida liebre
Contemplando la danza de los copos de nieve,
Se acerca la hora en que los árboles duermen
Custodiados por el cielo y los príncipes silvestres.

Del crepúsculo alza vuelo un cuervo de las colinas
Y se prepara el escenario de una bella poesía:
Los hijos de la luna declamarán esta noche
Sus más profundos versos al corazón del bosque.

Los poemas declaran sus virtudes innatas
La lealtad o la astucia, aun la magia de su monogamia,
El hechizo en su romance único y admirable,
La unidad en el grupo y su fortaleza loable.

Los hermanos de la tierra son artistas por excelencia
Aúllan a las estrellas que transcriben su nobleza,
Ellas conocen de las hazañas de esos lobos poetas
Descifrando los misterios que esconde la naturaleza.

Hipnotizada la noche tiñó en colores al firmamento
Describiéndose en matices el secreto de los guerreros,
Magnífica serenata despertó a la aurora boreal
De un plácido sueño que a la primavera hará recordar.

FOREST DREAM

The forest, dressed in white
A fair carpet covers the fields,
The thin countryside sings a soft melody
The exquisite tune gives to winter a greeting.

Along the way plays a shy hare
Watching the dance of snowflakes,
Near the hour when the trees fall asleep
Guarded by the sky and all the wild princes.

From the twilight a crow from the hills takes flight
Preparing the scenery for a beautiful poem:
The sons of the moon will herald the night
Their deepest verses to forest's heart.

The poems profess their innate virtues
The loyalty or the craftiness, even their spell of monogamy,
The magic in their unique and marvelous romance,
The unit of a group and its commendable power.

The brothers of the earth are artists by excellence
Howl to the stars that transcribe their nobility,
They know about these wolf poets' feats
Unraveling the mysteries nature keeps.

Hypnotized, the night is stained in colors of the firmament
Describing in hues the warriors' secrets,
Magnificent serenade waking the northern lights
From a peaceful dream that will bring the spring to mind.

RYFT SARRI
THE NIGHT PACK

Ryft Sarri has been writing for himself for nigh on ten years now and has only recently started putting those stories out into the public. He writes more than anything else, but in those few moments he is not putting pen to paper, you could find him in front of a computer, playing games and watching terrible horror movies.

Silver moonlight cascaded down over the tree covered hills of Lyricea, and the howls of the wolves that lived there raced the light through the forest. The full moon itself was one night away, signaling the start of a celebration that every living creature in the valley knew and most feared: the Solstice Hunt.

Every year, the pinnacle of winter came and went, and the wolves that ruled the valley organized a great celebration. It brought the valley's strongest pack together in one location for races, fights, and, most importantly, the Hunt itself. Cocky males and competitive females faced off to bring down the biggest game they could find before dawn once the Hunt had started. The glorious winners were rewarded with the best dens near the top of the Gathering Rock, closest to the king.

This year, Calin was going to win.

Calin knew he didn't stand out amongst his pack as far as brute strength went, but he was faster, and, more importantly, smarter than most others. He just *had* to win this year. He'd been stuck in the same den since he was given one after his initiation hunt. It was small and far enough away from the Gathering Rock that he was almost always last to any meeting the king called. No status, no mate. But this year would be different.

Calin woke in the mid-afternoon, restless. He thought it was his nerves that woke him originally, until he heard again the noise that had broken through his sleep-haze. An all too familiar greeting-bark sounded from the entrance to his den. He lifted his head from his paws and stared out at the intruder, silhouetted against the setting sun as it reflected against the snow. "What is so important, Rillis, that you have to wake me before dusk?" Calin rolled onto his side and closed his eyes again.

"I can't sleep! C'mon, let's go for a run or something. You have to be as nervous about the Hunt as I am," Rillis whined, trotting further into the small cave. "You slept plenty, anyway. I could hear you snoring from my den."

Calin snorted and rolled back onto his paws, pushing himself up so he could shake the sleep from his body. A good shake always woke him up well enough. "You've been up all day, haven't you?"

Rillis rolled onto his side and tilted his head to watch the other wolf. "Obviously. C'mon, get your gray butt out of the den and let's go run. It'll be good practice for the race tonight."

Calin yawned wide, then padded forward to bat his friend's russet-furred muzzle with a paw. "Like I need the practice. Everyone is so focused on the Hunt itself that there's gonna be no competition in the race." His tail swayed, and he opened his muzzle to pant, a growling chuckle echoing out. "It's not like you'll beat me."

Rillis sprang to his paws again and made as if to pounce the gray wolf. "Oh really now? Well let's find out just how close it'll be, hmm?"

The two dashed from the mouth of the den, their howling laughs echoing off the cliff wall at their back until the trees of the valley swallowed up the noise. Onto the worn down trails they raced, flashes of gray and russet fur catching the slowly dying light that filtered between the branches. From the moment they entered the woods, the two wolves fell silent, as if their impromptu race was a part of an actual hunt. Even though it was just for fun, Calin still felt his blood pump with the adrenaline that the Hunt would bring. He was ready for it, without a doubt. He just needed another pair of hunters.

They broke through the tree line once again, racing across the snow covered clearing back towards the cliff. Both were panting hard by the time they chased each other onto the Gathering Rock, but it was a good tired they were feeling. There were no other wolves at the Gathering Rock yet either, since twilight had only just begun to tint the duskward sky. The others would be emerging closer to sunset to hear King Barthan call the annual celebration to start. Calin didn't mind getting there early. He wanted to have one of the best spots to watch the king's address when the moon rose.

Calin settled in on the bottom tier of the towering formation, snagging one of the bones left there from a previous kill to gnaw on. "Who do you think will win the females' race this year?" Calin asked once the sun touched the horizon. The light made the snow look as if it were on fire.

Rillis sat himself next to the gray wolf. "You kidding me? Niera, no question. She's leagues ahead of anyone else, except maybe us. Gorgeous, too. Think she'd run with us in the Hunt?"

Just the thought of it made Calin bark a humorless laugh. "Her, run with no-rank trash like us? Maybe if we win it all this year, but not before. No, she's way too high-tier for us. I'd rather not try to make more trouble for myself."

"You generally don't even have to try for trouble, Calin." A third voice called out from above them. Calin's ears snapped backward.

"N-Niera! What are you doing out so early?" Calin tipped his head up to regard the wolfess. She was sleek, with almost silvery tinges to the rusty red fur that covered her frame. "You should still be resting up for the Hunt!"

His words were met with a wagging tail and ears lazily splayed. She hopped down from her higher tier and grabbed a bone from the pile for herself. "How can I be resting when two paws-for-brains are chatting right outside my den?" She didn't sound upset, but her words made Rillis close his muzzle and watch her carefully. "I'm pulling your tail. I was already up. Excited for the races tonight?" She looked between the two males with perked ears.

"You know it! Calin here is gonna win the males' race, without a doubt. I doubt even King Barthan could keep up with him."

Calin flicked his ears. "The king has always been more about power than speed, though. I could never stand up to him in a challenge fight. He's smart, too."

Niera dipped her head in agreement. "He *is* king for a reason, after all. That and it was one of his ancestors who found this valley and started the Solstice traditions. He's got it in his blood."

Calin huffed a breath through his nose and said nothing, turning his attention back to the bone trapped between his fore paws. He didn't have any issues with King Barthan, but he wasn't particularly fond of him either. Of course, as his hunt-brother, Rillis knew this.

"Calin's gonna be the king someday. Isn't that right, buddy?"

Calin froze, then glared at the red wolf with the kind of hate that only best friends feel. "I'm gonna kill you for doing that one of these days."

Rillis ducked his head. "What? You're the one who said it. I didn't even tell her how you said that you think Barthan is too stubborn to seek help from the ravens and the foxes. Oops." He dropped his head lower until he just sunk down onto his belly. "Sorry, Calin."

Calin dropped his head onto the ground beside his paws and sighed. "It would have gotten out eventually. Welp, go ahead, Niera. Feel free to take that to the king. I'm sure it was only a matter of time before I was exiled anyway."

A short bark of laughter met the statement, getting Calin to pick his head up again and look at the wolfess. "Are you kidding me? Barthan is as mud-brained as you two half the time. Besides, why would I ever wanna see you exiled, Calin? I like you." Calin stared at her until she barked another laugh and nosed her bone back into the pile. "Anyway, I'm gonna look for some breakfast. See you two tonight!" She pushed off the rock and trotted off into the trees.

"Hear that?" Rillis whispered. "She likes you! Might have another one for the Hunt after all. She's good, too."

"Yeah, maybe," Calin said, sounding distracted. His gaze was still on Niera as she stalked away.

Rillis snorted and bumped the gray wolf with a paw to bring him back. "You even listening to me? C'mon, we should ask her to run with us. We could totally bring down a bull elk with her along!"

"Keep dreaming. We might get one of the stags, but a bull elk? That's the king's territory there. Only one wolf is allowed to fight a bull for the kill." Calin crosses his paws and noses the bone he was chewing on back onto the pile. "Anyways, want to nab something to eat now, or wait for the speech?"

Rillis pushed up to his paws again and swayed his tail. "Sure, let's see if we can find some hare. I thought I saw a burrow on our run earlier."

"Wolves of the Night Pack!" King Barthan's voice echoed off the cliffs, carrying it to every perked ear of his wolves. Calin finally had a seat on the Gathering Rock itself for an address, and was even more pleased that Rillis, Niera, and her brown-furred hunt-sister Ilar were sitting at his sides.

"My hunters! Tonight is the night of our Solstice Hunt, and the middle mark of our long winter!" A chorus of cheering howls met the king's words, though Calin noticed that none in his little group added to it. Nerves, he thought. "The snow is fresh, and good for tracking. The Goddess' Light shines in the sky for us, blessing our great Hunt! Tonight is a night of triumph and celebration, of bringing together our pack and honing our skills so that we may prosper throughout this next year! Through our competition, we grow our bonds as a pack and learn to trust each other with honor and respect." More howls sounded out as the last of daylight died away. Soft moonlight lit the pack on its own, casting everything in a silvery hue.

Barthan paced to the edge of his highest tier and gazed down over his pack. "This year we are graced by the moon being full for our celebration. Not once during my rule has this been the case, so this year will be a different one than ever before. My hunt-brother has informed me that there has been movement from the Great Elk herd, and they have strayed further into our territory than ever before. Young hunters! Know that I look upon this Hunt with great anticipation, and the highest of hopes for all of you! Let us celebrate, my pack, and feast! Let us find out who will join me on my tier for this year!"

One final howl went up among the wolves gathered. This one, Calin and his companions joined with enthusiasm, eager to prove themselves. Though Niera was already in one of the dens on the Gathering Rock itself, there was always another tier to climb to the King's Peak.

Once the cheer was over and the king had retreated from his peak, his chosen hunt-leaders moved through the pack, assigning groups for the races--the first event of the celebration. Groups for the Hunt itself had to be arranged before the moon's high mark, and the winners would be chosen before first light of the sun. That was the main event after all, so the majority of the special night was dedicated to it.

That being so, the whole pack still loved watching the racers as they tore through the underbrush. But, distracted as they were by the looming hunt, so few ever cared to participate. It left the minor honors so easy for Calin to snatch up, it almost felt like taking a rabbit from a pup.

Calin stood after giving the hulking hunt leader his decision to race and stretched out. "Ready to run, Rillis?"

The ruddy wolf bared his teeth in a playful growl. "Never not. What about you two?" He turned to the pair of wolfesses. "You going to run with us for the Hunt, too?"

Niera spoke first, standing beside Calin and stretching as well. "I don't see why not. You are the only ones to ask me aside from Vreil, and I would rather not see him climb the tiers. You understand." Ilar woofed her agreement.

Calin shuddered at the name, then shook himself to be rid of the feeling. "Don't get me thinking about that oaf. He's been harassing Rillis and I for years now. He thinks that the races are a farce and that the king should exile any wolf that doesn't participate in the Hunt."

Ilar canted her ears back and lowered her head. "He is so brutish. It's no wonder he hasn't found a mate yet. I can't think of any female that actually likes wolves like him."

Calin snorted. "He's just like Barthan half the time--so convinced that we can prosper on strength alone, by ourselves. Meanwhile, the ravens hear the winds whisper from on high and the foxes weave the dreams of both living and dead. So much wisdom is simply ignored in this pack, it sickens me."

"And you would change it, if you were in charge, right?" Niera looks at Calin in askance, though there was a light of mischief in her golden eyes. "Already making plans for your eventual rule?"

Calin lowered his head at her words, but met her gaze all the same. "I wouldn't call them plans. Wishful thinking. It's not like I could beat Barthan by myself."

Rillis stood taller and perked up his ears, trying to bring back the good mood. "Ah, don't let it bother you for now. All we have to worry about tonight is beating Vreil in the Hunt after you two show everyone else up in the races. We can deal with wishful thinking and lofty ambitions later in the year. C'mon, let's get some water before they call the runners to start." He trotted between them, followed closely by the black-furred Ilar.

Calin turned to follow, but Niera stepped in front of him first. "You know that King Barthan is growing old with no heir, yes?" she asked. He did not answer, so she continued. "I hear things, as high up on the tiers as I am. The king doesn't want his line to lead us anymore. He waited this long because he wanted some sort of sign from the Goddess that his rule could be passed to someone else, and here we are with a full moon on the Solstice Hunt. Take that for what you will."

She turned and stretched out her legs, then ran to catch up with her hunt-sister and Rillis.

Does she really want me to take his place, or is she trying to make me look like a fool? Calin thought as he stretched again. He had never tried to out-think a female before, and he found it as infuriating as his sire had said it would be. Without dwelling on the actual words she said, he could just be happy that he finally had a female's attention. Perhaps, this would be a better Solstice than he thought.

He shook his head to clear it, then followed after his hunt group. As his paws crunched through the snow, he had to wag in contentment. The night of the Solstice was said to shape the year that came after it. If that was so, his next year was going to be quite pleasant indeed.

He caught up with his group at the stream and bent his head to lap at the frigid water. "Wow, Calin. Maybe I will beat you in the race, if it takes you that long to get here. Head in the clouds with the birds?" Rillis nudged his friend's shoulder with his nose and chuckled.

Calin glanced at his friend, then lifted one paw and splashed the red wolf. "Better than in the ground with the hares."

"I hear you're joining the real wolves in the Hunt this year, Calin." A booming voice brought Calin's ears up, then made them cant back again when he recognized the speaker. "It's about time. I was getting tired of supporting little would-be exiles as well as actual pack members."

Ilar whipped around and stared at the approaching group of three wolves, all dirty-brown-furred with sharp hazel eyes. Their leader, the biggest of the three, they knew all too well. "That's right, Vreil, we're finally gonna show you and your goons up," Ilar said, her hackles raising up.

Vreil shook his head and glanced at the wolfess. "I have no quarrels with you or Niera. Both of you have actually participated in the Hunts since your initiation. In fact, after I win this year, I'd be pleased if either of you would share my den with me."

Niera echoed Ilar's growl in response. "We wouldn't even dream of it, not in a thousand seasons."

Vreil snorted and flicked his tail as if to swat the words away. "We'll see if you say the same after I crush these would-be exiles. I'll take down a bull elk and challenge the king when I'm done."

Calin lowered his head and ears, fighting the urge to snarl at the bigger wolf. "Not if we bring him down first. You'd only drive this pack apart if you became king."

"If by drive it apart, you mean drive you out of it, then yes, you're right. There's no way I'd keep weaklings like you around to eat our food and force pups on the females." Vreil didn't have the same restraint as Calin, and growled aggressively at the smaller wolves.

Calin stepped forward and curled back his lip to show teeth. "Back off, Vreil. We'll settle this during the Hunt, like we should. Fighting now won't solve anything."

One of Vreil's followers stepped up to meet Calin with the same challenging expression. "I think it'd solve quite a lot. What do you think, Vreil?"

The big wolf snorted again and turned to leave. "Let the little coward be. We won't have to worry about him much longer, anyway. Don't waste the energy." He started to trot away and called back over his shoulder, "You won't have to settle for trash like them for long, Niera!"

Calin watched them go with narrowed eyes and a stilled tail. Rillis moved beside him, then rolled onto his side as if nothing were wrong. "Guess we really do have to take down the bull elk this year. I've heard they can really run."

Niera settled onto her belly and lifted her head up. "Then it should be no problem for us. Nobody can keep up with Calin and I. We'll definitely need a plan to sniff them out and take down the bull, but I think we can do it."

Rillis rubbed his face through the snow and sneezed. "I've got the nose for tracking them down. Think you can find a raven or a fox to tell us the general area of the herd, Calin?"

Calin sat back and lowered his ears. "I can try. I'll see if I can sniff one out during the female's race. Goddess willing, I'll run across one who won't weave riddles around me."

A howl called from near the tree line, signaling the males who wished to race to gather. Calin let out a sigh and pushed to his feet. "C'mon Rillis. Keep an eye out for burrows while you're eating my dust."

They weren't the only ones participating in the races this year, though Calin wasn't terribly worried about the lanky wolves who lined up on either side of him and his hunt-brother. He'd run with every wolf in the pack who would even think of participating, and he could outpace them all.

He turned his head to look up at the sky as the king's hunt leader recited the rules, saying that it was along the deer trail that has been used and worn down over the many years that the Night Pack has lived there. Calin only half listened, trying to pay more attention to the noises on the wind. He could hear the voices of the twittering birds, speaking nonsense about the spirits of the sky. He could hear the breaths of the wolves beside him. He could hear the wind as it blew through the trees before him. But he could not hear a raven, or even a crow, who might be able to provide aid to him in the Hunt. He let out a sigh and shook his head to refocus on the hunt leader.

"Now if there are no questions, let's get this first event underway!" King Barthan's voice overrode his hunt leader's. "Send them off, Nero."

"Yes, my lord. Ready, racers?" The wolves braced themselves, and each grunted an affirmative. Nero sat back and raised his muzzle high. "Get running then! Go, go, go!"

Calin shoved off the ground into a headlong sprint, immediately opening the distance between himself and the next closest wolf. He'd run this very route more than once over the preceding moons, so he only needed to let his body get into the feel of it once more before he could turn his attention to observation.

His eyes roved over the worn path and the underbrush beyond for the signs of a fox den, if indeed there was one in those woods at all. He knew that he had seen a couple of families of them, but it had been many moons since the last time. Trees flashed by him as he ran, body tilting this way and that to follow the trail. Nothing presented itself to him as he ran, though, and by the time he passed the final hunt leader and broke the tree line for the final stretch of the path, he resigned himself to the need for further searching.

Until he saw the snow near the base of the Gathering Rock shift just enough to reveal a tiny patch of black, standing out against the white and brown of the snow and rock. *Worth checking out, at least,* Calin thought.

He noted the location and extended his legs once more, putting on a last burst of speed to blow past the growing clump of spectators right where they had started the race. He panted hard, not so much tired as he was winded. Once the fervor of how quickly he'd finished died down, he padded along the outer edge of the pack, back toward the Gathering Rock.

He avoided the rest of the groups as he walked, focused on where he saw that patch of black. His steps slowed as he approached the towering, tiered rock formation and the black he saw took shape. It was the legs of a red fox kit, and said kit had been wrapped around by a larger arctic vixen. That vixen now stared at him with wickedly intelligent blue eyes.

He checked his normal response and instead dipped his head down, lowering his front half as he would to his king. He let his ears relax, and he closed his eyes before addressing the white vixen. "Greetings, Dreamer. I have been looking for one like you."

Her snow white ears perked up with his words and decorum. "I am aware, Calin of the Night Pack. That is why I have come to you." She covered the little kit with her tail again. "You seek the wisdom of other creatures of earth and sky, as other packs have done in the past. You seek information, as well."

Calin settled onto his belly and lowered his head further. "Yes, Wise One. For the good of this pack and of this valley, I wish to succeed in this year's Solstice hunt. My hunt-mates for tonight believe that our king is looking for an excuse to step down, but he does not have an heir. He wants to lift up a new king from our pack."

The vixen tilted her head and seemed to consider his words. "And you would be this new king? What will make you so different from mighty Barthan, descendant of the Cloud Runner? Even though you seek help from the creatures you share this world with, what guarantee do we have that you would treat us any differently?" Her words were sharp as a thorn bush, and they made Calin's hackles prickle in aggravation.

He knew, though, that getting angry at the vixen would only cause her to run off again, and he could not let that happen. She was more than likely his only chance to put down Vreil. "You have my word, Wise One, and the fact that I come to you asking for your help, not demanding it of you. I seek a peace in this valley, and I will work to keep it that way. Even now, I honor my kills as they deserve and thank them for providing for me." Calin lifted his head to meet the vixen's cold stare. "You weave the dreams of both living and dead. Surely, you know my intentions even better than I do."

She considered these words as well, her expression never changing and her eyes never leaving his. Finally, she bowed her head and spoke again. "I will help you, but I will ask of you a favor in return. I will not speak of this favor now, but once you have risen to your desired position, I will find you again. Do you accept?"

Inwardly, Calin seethed. Foxes, though wise beyond their years and gifted with dreams of both the future and the dead, were known for their treacherous deals. "Never trust a fox in his den" was a saying that his sire taught him early on. He should have known that this one would want something from him in return. He took a moment to calm himself, let his hackles smooth down once more, then answered. "As long as that favor is within reason, I accept."

The vixen let out a soft laugh and curled around her kit further. "Perfect. I am yours to command. What would you have of me, my lord?"

Calin stared across the treetops at the Bear's Teeth Mountains at the far end of the valley. He hadn't been this far away from his den since his sire took him on his first hunt. He shivered as he thought about it, remembering how he had been told to stay away from the elk herds if he could see the bull male at the head. "He's a stupid beast, but he'll kill you sure as he'll look at you. Don't bother with him. That's royal territory."

Well Father, I bet you never thought your pup would try and be the king, Calin thought.

"Calin! You sure this is the right spot?" Rillis trotted up the hill Calin had been standing on. "I thought the herd was supposed to be coming closer. Are you positive Sarya isn't out of her head?"

"This is where she led us. I do not doubt a vixen's wisdom."

The white vixen in question trotted up to Calin's other side, her ever present red-furred kit clinging to her hackles with his teeth. "And neither should you, young Rillis. Follow your hunt-brother's example. Your huntresses will confirm what I have dreamed when they return momentarily."

"Sorry, Mistress Sarya."

She just nodded to the red wolf, and her kit squeaked in agreement. "Better. See, there they are now." She motioned with her nose toward the tree line.

Sure enough, Niera and Ilar came running from the wooded flats, ears up enough for Calin to recognize them as excited. Their tails waved back and forth as they sprinted up to Calin. "We found them!" Ilar called. She sounded out of breath.

As Ilar panted and flopped onto her belly atop the hill, Niera trotted right up beside Calin and lowered her head. "We spotted them, in the meadow just on the other side of the trees. It's a smaller herd than we expected, but the bull is with them."

"Lovely. Now we just have to find a way to separate him from the rest of them. I doubt he'll just trot on over if we ask him nicely." Rillis rolled over onto his side and stared up at his hunt-brother. "I don't suppose our guide has anything to add?"

Sarya fixed Rillis with an icy glare. "If you continue with talk like that, I will be sure you do not find your way back to Skyward Point. Be silent and listen to your would-be king." She turned her eyes to Calin and perked her ears. "I will enlist the assistance of the children of the sky to separate the bull from his herd, but you must draw him further away. Birds can only do so much."

Calin shook his head and stepped toward his hunt-mates. "We can pull him away. Sarya tells me that the elk are as intelligent as us, but that means they are equally suspect to anger as us. If we taunt him away from his herd, we can circle him and take him down. All we have to do is get him to charge."

Sarya cocked her head to the side. "You could challenge him. A challenge will make his blood hot, and he will charge. Once he charges away, you continue to taunt him through the woods. He will follow. Then you can circle him and do what you wolves do." She flicked her tail dismissively. "I'll follow at a distance to observe."

Calin looked over his hunt-mates and flicked his ears. "Then let's get running. The sooner we take that bull down, the better."

The other wolves voiced their agreement, and they took off down the hill. The Hunt awaited.

The woods this far out were sparser than the ones closer to the Gathering Rock, and Calin did not know them near as well. He paid close attention to the scents and surroundings, keeping his nose to the wind for any sign of their prey. Moments before breaking the tree line, he caught the scent of elk and whuffed a command to his hunt-mates. They turned, skirting the open area ahead of them, edging ever closer to the tree line to try and catch sight of their prey.

Niera saw them first: a small herd trotting through the meadow, just as she had seen them not two marks ago. From far off, the howls of the rest of their pack reached them, and it only served to put the elk further on edge. They were wary.

Calin barked another quiet command to bring his party to a halt, then peered through the underbrush at the massive creature that led the herd.

He saw why they were targets reserved for those who would be king. The beast was more than twice the height of a wolf and had antlers that added on another wolf-height atop his head. There was a majesty about the creature that confirmed that this was the bull. That, and there was no other male near as impressive.

The wolves stayed quiet, the only noise being the near silent press of paws on the ground. This was in their blood, and the thrill of the hunt was taking hold of all four. All they had to do was wait for their vixen guide to work her magic.

They did not have to wait long. All of the ears near that snow-covered meadow perked as the chattering of birds grew louder, noise that was out of place in the silvery light of the moon. Crows added their raucous cries to the flock that winged in from over the treetops, and words grew from those few caws that reached Calin's ears. *"Horned One! Great Horned one! We heard, we heard, that your herd is too small! Come with us, Great Horned one, we heard that you're too weak!"*

Calin bared his teeth as he listened to the birds' taunting; he was pleased. Pleased and hungry for the kill. Deeply rooted instincts were turning in his mind and urging him to move forward, to call to his pack to circle the beast and take him down. But there was more to do.

He turned from the scene and bobbed his head in Rillis' direction, getting the red wolf's attention. "We need to get him into the trees. You and Ilar circle around and stay out of sight until I call. Niera and I will get his attention and force him to charge."

Rillis flicked his ears in acknowledgement and took off, Ilar just behind him. They would stay out of sight and downwind from the big elk until he started to move, then cut off his route back to his herd. The birds should keep the rest of the herd distracted.

Calin nudged Niera aside before stalking further through the trees, muzzle open to pant in anticipation. The bull whipped his head around, clearly disoriented by the crows taunting, and bugled a challenge at them. *"Deceitful creatures of the sky! Leave my herd alone, we have no dead for you to scavenge. Be gone with you!"* The words rolled into Calin's ears like the pounding of hooves on earth. The beasts spoke! He knew this, in his mind, but he always had doubts that it was true.

He shook his head. Best not to let stray thoughts distract him. He watched as the bull shook his head as well, trying to clear the birds away from him as he stepped away from his herd to call another challenge at the crows. The words escaped Calin's understanding as he saw an opportunity.

With a low growl to warn Niera, he pushed into a run and broke through the trees, almost immediately catching the bull elk's attention. Calin brought himself up short and called to the beast. "Great Horned One!" he taunted, as the crows had. "Why is your herd so small, Great One? Are you too weak to lead them all anymore? Have you been ousted by some young buck? Or is it that you are too stupid to lead them well, so they all died off?"

Calin could near smell the fury from the bull elk as another bugle rang out. He heard those words far too clearly for his liking, but he held his ground. *"I will not be disrespected like this! Jerl Winterhoof does not back down from a challenge!"*

Calin answered with a howl that his hunt-mates echoed. "Then fight me with the courage of a wolf, Great One!" He braced himself for the charge.

And charge Jerl Winterhoof did. He lowered his head and stampeded straight at Calin. The gray wolf let out another howl, lower in pitch, calling to his hunt-brother. "Come, Rillis! To me!" He turned after, and jumped away from the charging elk, letting the beast's momentum carry him into the trees. He leaped after Jerl then, keeping the elk's side to avoid the stomping and kicking hooves that could break near every bone in his body. A nip at his flanks here, a threatening growl there, and he managed to corral the elk further into the woods, where he and his hunt-mates would have the advantage. He could hear them circling the elk, boxing him in. This was as good as over.

But he still had to kill the magnificent beast. "Keep him from leaving," he commanded the rest of his party. "Your new king needs to prove his worth." He felt the part, staring down the enormous elk. He felt fear, but it coursed through him and enhanced his reactions. He felt the Hunt flow in his veins.

He stepped forward to face against the enraged creature, his head lowered and teeth bared. He stalked between the trees, moving closer to his prey. "Know that in killing you, Jerl Winterhoof, I will bring about a new era for your herd. They will prosper under their new leader, and the wolf pack will guard these lands as they once did, but under my rule." He circled with the elk, watching those widened eyes for any tell. "Your death will be meaningful."

"I will not die to the likes of you, wolf!" The elk charged then, leaping into the motion with a practiced fluidity that nearly caught Calin off-guard. Nearly.

Calin hopped to the side and rocketed forward into a pounce, dragging claws across the beast's flank. A pained bugle rang out through the trees as Jerl whipped around for an even faster charge, followed by a veering to the side that Calin tried to dodge. Razor sharp antler points swept a claw's breadth away from his belly, and he barely managed to land on his paws. He panted with a lowered head and ears, tail hanging limp. He could not underestimate such a creature.

Jerl tried to run while Calin was recovering, but Rillis and Ilar harried him back around toward their leader, sinking claws and teeth into his legs and flanks to get him to stumble and turn. Calin crouched and growled, fully focused on the elk now and ready to prove himself. He braced for another charge, and was not disappointed.

This time, though, he held his ground. When Jerl was but a leap away, he did just that. He jumped forward at just the right angle to throw his weight against one of those massive antler racks. The bull's head turned, and with it went his momentum, pushing his other set of points into the ground. With the full force of his charge behind it, he threw both himself and Calin into the ground. Calin jumped to his paws again and lunged forward at the elk, teeth bared for the kill.

Something stopped him. He pulled up short, claws dug into the shoulder of the downed elk, those wild eyes staring up at him. Jerl knew he was beaten, but he looked like he was waiting. Calin looked past the elk and saw Sarya watching him.

He leaned close to the elk and whispered into his ear. "You fought well, Great One. I will keep my promise to you and your herd."

Jerl's eyes closed and with his last breath, he answered, *"Thank you for a good death, my lord."*

Calin moved his muzzle forward to deliver the final blow as his hunt-mates raised their voices in a victory howl.

"Wolves of the Night Pack! I give you your Solstice Champions!" Calin had never been at the top of the Gathering Rock before. Standing there, just behind King Barthan with Niera, Ilar, and Rillis at his sides, was almost more than he could handle. "Not only were these wolves the only hunters to bring down a kill, but they took down the prey of kings! The biggest bull elk this valley has seen in seasons!"

A chorus of howls echoed off the high cliffs behind them. Calin stepped forward when King Barthan looked back at him and bobbed his head. "Thank you for the honors, my lord. I could not have done it without my hunt-mates."

"As any good wolf recognizes. You will be welcome on my tier for this upcoming season, Calin, along with your hunt-mates." The king turned back to his pack. "My pack! Rejoice and feast on this, our hallowed night! Celebrate until first light of the morning as you see fit!" With that, the king turned and padded away from his perch, indicating that the festivities were to resume. But he wasn't finished with Calin. "Champion, come with me. Hunters, you may go choose your dens before returning to the celebration."

Calin let his ears and tail fall. King Barthan's tone was serious, and the look in those stormy gray eyes was not one that he liked. Nonetheless, he followed his king back into the largest den at their tier. When the king lay down on his belly and snagged a bone, Calin followed suit. "What may I do for you, my lord?"

Barthan chuckled at him. "Relax, my boy. I imagine Niera has been filling your head with high-tier gossip all night. I've talked to her a few more times than I perhaps should have. You, on the other paw, I do not believe I've ever said a word to." He chewed at the end of the leg bone in the pause between his words. "Though that isn't to say I haven't kept an eye on you. Never looking to move up the tiers, never trying to move in from the edge of the pack, only participating in races since your initiation hunt. A strange kind of wolf, one that we haven't had in our pack in many seasons."

Calin's ears went back further. "My lord, I can explain--"

Barthan snorted loudly to interrupt the younger wolf. "Don't bother. My kind are old news, my boy. I know of the Elder Ways, and I know that you sought out help from the vixen Sarya in order to achieve your success. I do not even hold it against you! Sarya is wily, as you would expect." Calin's whiskers twitched, and he turned just his head to see the vixen and her kit trot into the den as if they slept there as well. "She has even told me of your deal with her. Thank the Goddess that we have a wolf like you in our pack."

Calin's ears perked back up again, but he watched the pair cautiously. "You know Sarya, my lord?"

Barthan chuckled again and shook his head. "She found me while I was trying to figure out what to do about my lack of an heir. Old bat has driven me insane with that kit of hers."

"Watch who you're calling an 'old bat' or you might end up one yourself," Sarya snapped, though Calin could hear the warmth in her voice.

"We all get there eventually. And that, my dear boy, is why I am infinitely glad that it is you who won. I had my doubts, but you put them to rest."

"What are you trying to say, my lord?" Calin lowered his head and narrowed his eyes.

"Oh, don't give me that look, pup. And you can just call me Barthan, in here. We'll be on equal footing soon enough." Barthan's eyes shimmered with the same kind of mischief that Calin saw in Sarya's. "You're the perfect candidate for the heir to this pack, and if Sarya is to be believed, you already had your sights set on my position."

Calin's muzzle dried up, and he had to lick his chops to wet it again. "I had ideas on what I would do, if I were to ascend to such a position, but they were just dreams and moon-wishes. I wasn't planning anything, sir!"

Barthan snorted again and nosed his chewing bone back onto the pile. "I am not upset with you, Calin. In fact, if you haven't figured it out yet, I am quite pleased." He sat up and looked down at the gray wolf with a serious expression. "This next season, I will be grooming you to take my place. With Sarya at your side, I expect you to lead our great pack back into the prosperous ways of our Elders. By the next Solstice Hunt, you will be King of the Night Pack."

DAWN SHARMAN
SNOW TIME

Dawn Sharman is a self-taught artist and designer who lives in the UK with her husband Murray, and has many other interests including photography and writing. At the moment she is in the process of writing and working on all the illustrations for a book. Something which she has never attempted before. Of course, one of her main characters is a Wolf. Dawn also gives up some of her time as a volunteer to help out at a charity shop which raises money for the local hospice.

Snow Time. Pastels.

DANA SONNENSCHEIN
ATKA'S VILLANELLE

Dana Sonnenschein makes a monthly trek to the Wolf Conservation Center, where she spends her time photographing and painting the ambassador wolves and catching glimpses of the endangered red wolves and lobos that also make their home there. In fall, winter, and spring, she's a professor of English at Southern Connecticut State University. In summer, she works on poems; her collections include Bear Country, Corvus, Natural Forms, *and* No Angels but These.

I Stand for Wolves

The world is riddled with scent and turns
from mud to seedling, moss, oak leaves, and rime
beneath my paws. I nose each thing and learn

what the day brings—coltsfoot, aster, and fern,
a frog or litter of voles, strangers who climb
in a whirl, riddled with scent and turns

of speech. They howl, and I howl in return.
The red wolves wail and moan; the grays chime in
beneath my pause. I nose each thing and learn

its natural history, the past airborne
in echoes I breathe deep, tracking the rhyme
the world is. Riddled with scent and turns,

I walk fence lines and cross a twilight bourn,
my eye on the horizon, treading time
beneath my paws. I nose each thing and learn

which way the hill wind blows. I yawn and yearn
and shift my stance to face the darkening times.
The world is riddled with scent and turns
beneath my paws. I nose each thing and learn.

GUARDIAN SPIRIT

Arctic wolf in a blizzard
is black eye-rim and lip,

bloodstain where tooth meets bone,
shattered topaz gaze unblinking

as icy crystals come to rest
on the tips of guard hairs,

fur drifted deep over rounded ears,
sides and throat, snowshoe paws,

and inside all that weightlessness
his *gravitas*, his knowing

he was born for this chill
and shiver he stretches to fit.

Blow on your fingers, lean in,
look long into Atka's face

and winter's burden slips
from a pine branch; you feel

what he is not and what
he is: this ghostly creature

stumbled upon your pack once
and took you into his.

ZEPHYR

Not running but resting, headlong in dead leaves,
front paws outstretched, hind legs flung back
as if he's leapt after a herd of whitetails flashing
through the woods. Not resting but running,
his ears flicker, awake in that twilight place
where the raven knocking on this hillside
enters dream, where his shadow catches
the spirit of a deer hit by a car this morning
not far away, and the scent of blood
becomes salty and red in his mouth,
and there is no harm that is not also good.
The wind ruffles his fur, black guard hairs
and gray haloed around his face.
Some angels must have teeth.

TELEVASSI
SHIFT TO SPRING

Televassi is a writer currently living in south-east England, but secretly wishes to move back to the south-west where he studied for a degree in English Literature so he can resume exploring the beaches and woods there. He is fascinated with imagining the world as other animals see it. Televassi writes both poetry and prose, and has a slight obsession with Beowulf, The Elder Edda, Celtic La Tène culture, and Germanic cultures. Considering these interests, it is ironic that his nickname is TV. Yes, as in a television.

You can find Televassi's work in Fragments of Life's Heart, Gods with Fur, Heat 2016, *and* Civilized Beasts 2015. *You can also find him on Twitter regularly talking about writing, history, and rock climbing; or bring him to you by collecting lots of books on the Celts.*

I smell—different,
No longer so cold.
There's something sweet
Now she's finally talking to me;
Songs among frosty hedgerows
And swelling buds.
My wolfishness blooms
From his winter coat:
Yes, still I have fur
Though now not so thick:
She can touch my hide
And see what scars lie hidden.

ALLISON THAI
SOLONGO

A Catholic Vietnamese-American hailing from Houston, Texas, Allison got her first taste of stories from true accounts of how her parents fled from communism as war refugees. Her imagination then grew like a weed from the likes of C.S. Lewis, J.R.R. Tolkien, Ursula Le Guin, and Brian Jacques, while her love of wolves stemmed from Jack London and David Clement-Davies. When not reading and writing, she's studying for medical school, delighting in all things science, and indulging in her guilty pleasure for Japanese cartoons. She has been published in journals and anthologies featuring Asian writers and speculative short fiction.

Man called it Mongolia, the Great Steppe. Wolves called it the Silver Pawstep. Man looked to the eternal blue sky, the sky father Tengrii. Wolves listened to the howling wind, the silent chill clawing at their fur—signs from their god, the Cold Khan. The lifelong struggle for survival hardened man and wolf alike. Plains stretched as endlessly as the sky itself, the sparse grass reaching barely a whisker's length. Competition for game and water was unbelievably fierce. Man and wolf knew it all too well.

Young Solongo felt the pressure bear down on the nape of his neck. As the son of a steppe chieftain, Solongo would certainly be the spotlight of today's hunting rite. The young wolf paced the rocky outcrop with small, nervous steps. He could hardly believe that half a year flew before his eyes. It seemed just days ago when he was a cub, constantly chided by his mother for venturing beyond her protection. Snow drifted down in silence, melting on his nose and making his fur stand on end from the cold. He resisted the urge to nip at them. Those silly attempts of leaping at the sky he could never reach, and chasing his own tail, didn't feel too long ago.

Here he was now, about to join the throng of tribal warriors should he grasp deer flesh in his jaws. And be the first to present it to the elders' council.

The eagle of anxiety swooped inside Solongo's stomach once more. Its wings spread down to his paws. His claws scraped at the snow as he mentally steeled himself. The ceremonial hunt was his golden chance to prove his worth. He would make his father proud.

He would satisfy the Cold Lord as the god issues a favorable breeze and an open, blue grin. Above all, Solongo would instill respect in his peers: fellow cubs around his age. No longer would he be teased for his unusual name. 'The days of being called "Rainbow Cub" are numbered,' he thought to himself. A few moons ago, Solongo had mustered courage and asked his father for the reason behind the name's absurdity.

"A khan's word is law." The chieftain, Tomorbaatar, had replied. "So is his choice for a name."

Solongo had plopped down on his rump, sulking. "I understand, Father. But why?"

The cub's discontent could not be blamed. It is a common trend among wolves of the Steppe to name male cubs after strong features, characteristics or natural qualities. It wasn't uncommon to have names such as Stone, Blood, Flame, Storm or Blizzard attached to "baatar," hero.

"I want to be a baatar, Father. Just like you."

Tomorbaatar had snorted. "Too many baatars roam the steppe. That name has become the definition of mediocrity. No imagination. Life isn't all about the name, you know."

"But the other cubs think so. They always ask why I'm named 'rainbow,' and I can never come up with an answer."

Tomorbaatar eyed Solongo with rare paternal gentleness—rare enough that the expression conflicted with his worn, unflinching muzzle.

"I'll tell you, son, and pray that you will carry this knowledge with pride. Your mother conceived you in the camp of the Northern Lands. When prey ran thin, our clan was forced to move elsewhere. We followed the migration routes of musk deer…all the way to the south, I recall. It was a rough journey on our paws and spirits. At the peak of our weariness, a powerful and terrible storm ravaged the plains. We did not mind the Cold Lord's flood; our thick coats and iron wills are built to endure the torrents."

Tomorbaatar's brow had furrowed until it looked to Solongo that his father's own face resembled a storm. "The Cold Khan's fangs of light…it shattered our ears and shook our paws." He growled. "In all my moons as Khan, I still remember the rattling of my bones from those angry booms."

Solongo shuddered at the mere thought of it. Wolves gave it the name Skyfire; man called it thunder and lightning. Blinding white bolts were a sure sign of godly wrath, the most dreadful and foreboding omen. Older wolves claimed that Skyfire crashed like the rockslides by a thousand fold. If the chieftain admitted his fears, then the elders were hardly exaggerating. Solongo had yet to witness the Skyfire in his young life. And he hoped the day would never come.

Tomorbaatar continued his story: "The Skyfire wasn't our only problem. Your mother had to give birth soon, and we searched desperately for shelter. Fortunately, some scouts had sniffed through the rain and came upon an earthly smell—a freshly dug cave. It had been abandoned, with the stale scent of a human tribe. The stink of their tame dogs still lingered, but we had no choice. We thanked the Cold Khan for that stroke of luck. And so your mother gave you life in the midst of a moonless storm."

Solongo repeated his father's last words as he rolled it in his tongue. "A moonless storm…" It sounded mysterious and dark, almost poetic. "Then how come you didn't name me 'moonless storm,' Father? I would've been fine with that."

Tomorbaatar curled his tail in amusement. "Patience, my little warrior. A cub would do well to hang upon the words of his elder in tolerant silence."

Solongo bowed his head meekly despite his father's gentle yet firm tone. The Khan lifted his gaze to the azure heavens.

"The rain and Skyfire had ceased, but darkness still overshadowed us. It showed no mercy for your brothers and sisters. The Cold Lord snatched up their little souls before they could reach the safety and warmth of your mother. We feared that our entire first litter had perished." A glint betrayed the brooding darkness in the chieftain's eyes. "Then with the parting of clouds, a brilliant light overwhelmed the skies. Never had I witnessed a more moving sign of hope. You, Solongo, had been fighting the cold and darkness at your mother's side. When the time came for us to name you, I proclaimed you the living hope, a rainbow born from shadow."

Tomorbaatar stopped and observed his son. Solongo looked half-convinced, half in awe over the unusual circumstances of his birth. Tomorbaatar gave a toothy grin and nudged the cub affectionately with his muzzle. He gave a deep, gruff chuckle at the look on Solongo's face. "What honorable Khan would make up silly fairy tales for cubs? That is the truth behind your name; wear it proudly."

One of the senior warriors had padded up to the chieftain, ending the intimate conversation between father and son. "My Khan, would you like to join me for a hunt? Our scouts picked up a strong antelope scent to the east."

"Yes, thank you for the offer, Chuluun. I could grab a bite or two over those prancers."

Solongo watched his father rise from his haunches and follow the other warrior. Then, the cub strove to keep up with the pair's strong and quick gait. He stared up imploringly. "May I join you and Chuluun? I promise I won't get in the way. I'll be strong and run and bite as hard as I can."

Tomorbaatar shook his great head. "Not yet, son. Wait until you are properly trained."

Solongo snapped back to the present. Now was the time to show off the effort and skill his father sought from him. The ceremony would commence once the elders were readily assembled.

"The hunting rite's about to start, Rainbow Cub." Odnyam, Solongo's least favorite half-brother, brushed past without a glance back.

Pretending to ignore his prickling fur, Solongo joined the trail of young wolves. They gathered in a huddle before the semi-ring of elders. Despite their small and aged bodies, something about the elders' dignified stances and sagely eyes subdued the young wolves. Next came the warriors, who completed the ring and arranged themselves by seniority. A pair of elders parted to make way for the khan. Backs straightened, ears perked and muzzles faced forward. Solongo held his breath as Tomorbaatar came forward, his silent strength and confidence demanding the attention of every wolf within his radius. Beneath the dark, gray fur laid a body of chiseled rock. The wolf leader's majestic stride only emphasized the vigor of his knotted muscles. His scarred face bore the air of experience, the vibe of self-assured authority, the energy of a wolf in his prime.

Tomorbaatar surveyed the gathering before him. "Family, friends, fellow pack members—we had long awaited this momentous day. Before I proceed to the ceremonial rules, we must be sure that our young ones are well aware of who they hunt for in the first place."

The Khan's eyes rested upon the group who awaited the test of their lives. "Anar, you look particularly excited today. Tell us what you know about our pack."

The light-gray wolf to Solongo's right responded with high-pitched gusto. "We are the Altan Urug—the Golden Kin. Our clan is among the biggest and well-known throughout the Great Steppe. We draw our inspiration from the Cold Lord's golden heart in the sky. Nobility glows from our own hearts, and honor is our top priority over everything else."

The Khan nodded his head in approval. "Excellent. Solongo, what are our most important values?"

Solongo met his father's expectant eyes. "Never give up, never back down, never run away. An Altan Urug wolf must always keep to the promises that escape his teeth. He must always finish what he started. There is no room for cowards and weak hearts within our pack."

Tomorbaatar regarded his son with approval as well. Solongo thought he could see his father's chest swell. Then, the Khan lifted his eyes to address the entire group of young wolves. "Take heed of the answers from two sharp wolves. Commit them to memory, and lead a life of honor until your last breath. Is that understood?"

There was a rippling of fur and soft growls as the wolves nodded solemnly. Tomorbaatar's chest rumbled as he cleared his throat. "Months of training have prepared you for this occasion. Winter is upon us, but do not let that dissuade you. Press on and stay strong. Your first act to honor the clan begins now, and your success heavily depends on the elders' judgment." He looked to the sky. "It is gold-high—you have until gold-down to deliver prey to the elders. May the Cold Lord favor the future warriors among us. Now go!"

Like a flock of eaglets eager to take off on their first flight, the young wolves dispersed. Solongo felt like flying as he sprinted to the vast plains. He ran until he felt that the camp and other wolves were far behind him.

Solongo remembered advice from a senior warrior: 'Prey runs heaviest where wolf scent runs thinnest.' The young wolf craned his neck and drank in the cold, crisp air. He let the scents around him hit the roof of his mouth. All he could smell was his own fur, cold and wet from the snow. Then, he sniffed the ground. He hoped to catch the scent of burrowing rabbits or lemmings. All he got was disappointment.

'Don't give up yet. Keep scouting around for a scent. Stay focused. Be persistent.'

Solongo made a quiet, brisk trot as he surveyed the area. He did so until his neck hurt, and the frustration he had been trying to stave off overwhelmed him. He stopped, lashing his tail in agitation. What was once a vast expansion of opportunity now seemed to him a land of fruitless scarcity.

'How did warriors manage to bring back prey every day—*many* times a day, enough to feed the entire clan?'

Self-doubt crept in and blurred his focus. He resumed trotting again, this time with less enthusiasm and dedication. What if he came back empty-jawed by gold-down? What if he would miss his only chance to claim warriorhood? What if he, the Khan's eldest son, brought shame to his family with his incompetence? Solongo couldn't bear to picture the deep frown etched on his father's muzzle.

Solongo furiously shook his head to dispel the negative thoughts. 'An Altan Urug wolf never backs down…I'll finish what I had started. Thinking like a dying dog won't help me or anyone.'

He pressed forward to explore more of the pack's territory. The sheer vastness of the plains intimidated the young wolf. Until now, the farthest he had ventured were the rocks scattered just beyond the camp's border. None of the training he had completed up to this point could prepare him for the awe and significance that pressed on him.

"Our old dens in the north have nothing on this land of opportunity," Tomorbaatar once said. "The Cold Lord's golden heart gives a rare and strong warmth here. I thank him every day for that blessing. Our little ones can prosper without the bitter cold, and prey is bountiful year round. You may not believe me, little Solongo, when I say that the plains are a sight to behold. Until you enter your warrior passage, until you sink your teeth into fat prey—you have yet to experience the beauty of our lands."

"I believe you now, Father…" Solongo breathed. "I can't imagine how I would fare in the north. The first few minutes in those blizzards would kill me."

But whatever beauty the landscape might have was lost upon him. He would rather rejoice over even a lemming's whisker. Winters here may pale to the ones howling in the north, but the young wolf began to grow numb and tired from trudging through the snow. Solongo's ears perked when he spotted a rocky outcrop, which loomed over his head. The scraggly patches of green made his heart lift. Prey could be hiding behind the sparse foliage. As he approached the nearest bush, Solongo crouched on all fours till his belly fur brushed the snow. Fleshy coils bunched as he tensed his muscles. He set his unblinking eyes and cocked his ears attentively. In just a few minutes, his tendons screamed for relaxation. The young wolf gritted his teeth as his eyes remained unwavering. Still, the bush didn't do so much as twitch.

Solongo slackened his crouch in dismay and bit back a frustrated growl. His eyes darted from tree to tree in search of potential game. None held promise. Solongo even trotted up to kick at a skinny trunk. The sapling gave a rippling tremor as it slapped its branches against the rockside. Solongo shut his eyes as a cloud of ice and sediment rained upon him. He ruffled his powdered fur crossly. 'What I would give for a juicy squirrel or two!'

Solongo attempted to clean himself with rough, brisk licks. But it led to no avail; now he had the dry and gritty texture stuck to his tongue. 'Cold Lord's teeth! Now I need a miracle to save me from this terrible day.'

Then, he snapped still. As still and rigid as a rod. A powerful and savory aroma flooded his nose like a flash flood. It streamed in so thick that Solongo could barely take in the thin air. He feared to even turn his head. His heart nearly stopped as a telltale groan confirmed his suspicions: a wapiti. The undisputed king of the steppe deer, only rivaled to its counterpart in the far west: the elk.

Solongo recognized the rare scent from last summer, on the evening of a bountiful feast among the clan. Even the most ravenous appetites weren't enough to reduce the wapiti to the bone. Tomorbaatar had laid claim to the kill, of course. He had the scars to prove it, which he eagerly elaborated to the little ones. Hooves as great as polished rock, antlers as deadly as man's spears…snippets of the Khan's tale left Solongo nearly breathless.

His legs trembled as the groan sounded much closer. He heard it again, this time directly behind him. Only the rock face stood between the young wolf and his prey—no, his foe. No way would this be an easy hunt. Solongo thought he picked up the sickly sweet tang of blood. But he wasn't taking any chances. Throwing caution to the wind, Solongo brandished his claws and leaped forward with an explosive snarl.

He braced himself for a startled bellow, or a lashing kick to his small snout. But no such thing occurred. Solongo halted in surprise at the unusual sight before him. No doubt the animal was a wapiti. Its antlers seemed to curve toward the sky in bearing arcs, like the fangs of an enraged wolf. The deer towered over Solongo by at least two heads. But what shocked him was not the deer itself, but the state it was in.

The wapiti simply stared back at the wolf as bright blood trickled from its leg wound. Solongo wondered how a mere stick could take such a toll on a majestic creature like the wapiti. He couldn't take his eyes off of the strange, smooth pole that looked like an abnormal growth of the deer's thigh. Solongo leaped in surprise as the animal addressed in low, rumbling cough.

"Never seen a man's weapon, young cub?"

Solongo bristled in defense. "I'm no cub. I'm about to earn my warriorhood."

The wapiti softly barked and tilted his great hood. "So I had reasoned from your bravado earlier. I am well aware of this ritual you wolves cherish so dearly. Longer before you were even born, in fact."

It suddenly occurred to Solongo that the wapiti before him was a wizened elder, with a great number of years upon its graying back and the many tines on its head. Solongo sheepishly dipped his head. Embarrassment prickled his fur. "Sorry for being so rude."

The deer's barking laugh was thick with blood. "A wolf apologizing to his victim for his fighting spirit? That's a first even for me."

Solongo felt hot all over. The seemingly ridiculous situation banished any fear Solongo may have had. Then, the wapiti let out a harsh cough as a spurt of blood blossomed from its mouth. It staggered to its knees and collapsed to one side. Solongo couldn't help himself from the deliciously tempting scent. He crept forward to the fallen deer. A dizzying desire took hold of the young wolf as he involuntarily bared his eager fangs and lolled his tongue. He was close, so close to the pool of blood lapping at his paws, the scrumptious flesh just under that deer's coat. So close to sinking his teeth into it all and feasting guiltlessly. Solongo thought it might as well happen in a flash. That is, until his disillusioned, frenzied eyes met the wapiti's calm and dignified own. Confusion shut down his hunger.

"Aren't you afraid?" Solongo asked. "You, an injured victim, are at my mercy. I'm your worst nightmare."

The wapiti heaved a strained sigh. "I am old and tired. Even if I could be a young deer again, with legs propelled by fright, my injuries wouldn't get me anywhere. Do you see the man's weapon? Man can take a tree branch and mold it into a hurling leg crippler."

Solongo stood still and listened as the old deer went on, "My herd had been ambushed by a pack of young hunting men. I was among the slowest. It was no surprise that even a young man's ill-aimed weapon managed to hit me. My herd fled without looking back, with the men in hot pursuit on their tame horses." It heaved a tired sigh. "They've migrated south, I reckon, to warmer lands where the grass can grow free of ice and snow."

"Your own herd abandoned you?" Solongo asked in disbelief. It seemed strange to him. Wolf tribes occasionally banished those not up to standards. But a clan would never abandon individuals in cowardice.

"You must understand," the wapiti said. "A deer in fright will only think of himself. We make up for this innate weakness with our agility." He indicated his wound ruefully. "But take away even that speed, and we are reduced to nothing. If I were a learning youngster such as yourself, I'd keep all this in mind."

Solongo grew even more bewildered. "You're sharing with me a secret about your kind. You don't seem to be afraid at all about your fate."

"As I have said before, I am old and tired. I've lived long enough, and have been through more flights than you could imagine. There's little I can do now…it's the end for me, and I accept it. At this point, I have nothing to fear."

Solongo admired the wapiti's unusually strong dignity, so much that he felt bad for even thinking of devouring the deer.

"I feel that I don't have much longer," the wapiti rasped. "But perhaps there is something I can still change. Young wolf, are you still listening?"

Solongo nodded. "What do you want?"

"When I die, I'd like you to eat a part of my body and deliver the rest to your pack."

The young wolf bristled with astonished, speechless shock.

"You look famished from your fruitless search for prey," The deer went on. "I could tell from our struggle to restrain the temptation. You could do with some nourishment before your returning journey." The old wapiti gazed at Solongo with a strange light in his dark, liquid eyes. "I sense that you are no ordinary wolf. Am I right?"

"I'm…the son of a Khan." Solongo replied hesitantly.

"Ah, I see. The cub of a wolf leader able to set aside his own desires for others…I admire you. I would rather have my flesh consumed by your pack than be picked at by vultures. You will grow into a wolf of greatness and honor. I look at you and I just *know* it." The old animal laid its great head down and struggled to keep its clouding gaze on Solongo. "It's time...for my spirit to leave this earthly body...so that I can prance across the endless skies like a young stag once more. Farewell...little wolf of honor."

The Great Steppe deer wheezed its last breath, leaving Solongo alone and truly humbled by the vastness of the deer's words.

ANGEL L. THURSTON
WINTRY DREAMS

Angel L. Thurston started writing in the seventh grade, and has created many stories and poems since then. She is a junior at Middle Tennessee State University and studies Accounting. While in college, she tutors Math and English at the residence halls. Along with attending classes and tutoring, she works as a marketer at Thurston Howl Publications. When she's not busy with school or work, she loves to pamper her sweet but evil cat Buttercup.

Riiing. Riiing. Riiing.

Rex lifted his head up as the church bells rang and the snow fell on his paws.

The last time he heard that sound was when he had fallen to his death ten years ago on Christmas Day.

Now, in his dreams, his heart beats again.

SEAN WEAVER
ECHOES

Sean Weaver is a freelance writer originally hailing from Kodiak, AK and grew up in Anchorage until the age of 18 when he joined the USN for six years. After a 20 year career as an Electronics Technician, Sean decided to abandon that dwindling field and make writing, his lifelong hobby, his new focus. Currently, working part-time odd jobs affords him ample time to pursue his writing dreams, specifically poetry.

An avid lover of wolves his entire life, Sean has also lived in California, Illinois and Arizona, but currently calls Southern Oregon his home in the town of Medford. He is married to his wife, Jenny, for 16 years, who works as an Elementary school teacher.

Well into our species' age of reason
The persecution continues.
Our sins muttered briefly by the winds
As the echo of another retort slowly dies out,
The reverberations nestle safely into the trees
As the silence returns
Along with the solitude
Against the white woodland clearing.
Shadows thrown by night's nearing
Perhaps skewing perceptions
Of the rigid branching leaves
Now hanging ever so imperceptibly lower
Since the thunder struck
From deep within the heart of man,
For vengeance has won the day
As the young wolf lay still on the snowy ground,
Dots of red surrounding like winter roses,
Guilty of crimes not his own
But of nature's beauty and agony
To humanity's prejudice and abhorrence
Of an untamed wilderness
Now controlled by a jealous hand.

T. F. WEBB
FINAL BREATH

T.F. Webb lives in the United Kingdom with her menagerie of animals. She has a voracious appetite for reading. She loves to walk and listen to all genres of music. She also likes to explore the dark side of human nature through her writing. She is currently in the process of editing her first self-penned novel.

A crack shot, a lupine yelp.
Blood moon reflected on a snow-white carpet.
Crimson hail forms black red pools
under ice draped trees that pierce the darkness.
A shivered whine in the throes of death
as the lone wolf draws his final breath.

FOREST WELLS
WINTER'S DANCE

Forest Wells was first inspired by the events of 9/11. Though he didn't know anyone involved, the day lit his passion for writing, beginning with poems of emotion, transitioning to works of fiction. Wolves, and really all wild canines, are his second passion, which Forest put into his first published short story "The Line," as well as a longer young adult novel currently seeking publication. When he's not writing, you can find Forest cheering for the San Diego Chargers, the Arizona Coyotes, and either playing League of Legends, or watching the professional matches online. He also spends much of his free time volunteering with a local Girl Scout troop. Forest currently lives in his hometown of Thermal California. For more information about Forest Wells, check out his website at www.forestwells.com.

White and gray,
the darkness and the light,
merge together as I wait.
It has been too long since I stained the snow.
Too long since my fur stopped the cold.
The youngest,
they wait beside me,
eager to learn the dance of death.
They do not understand the need,
for they have only known the chase.
We cannot chase.
Not as we are,
not in drifts so deep.
We must instead be still.
We must allow the dance to come to us.
It is our only chance,
but it is one I have done before,
as have those we wait for.
At last it's time.
The pack,
my family,
they are coming closer.
Their barks echo toward me.
Their scents travel on the wind,
merging with my heart.
Life,
offered and taken with due respect and honor,
they bring my way.
Chomp chomp I go on the snow,
for even my breath could give me away.
I must remain unseen.
I must be ready for the moment.
The young ones,
they do as I do.
They prepare just as the dance comes into view.
We can see it now.
A worthy sacrifice for the future.
Driven forward by the pack.
Today will be a good day.
Today, I will feed my family.

LAYSON WILLIAMS
FIRST CONTACT:
FROM THE FILES OF DEPARTMENT 118

Layson Williams is a 43-year-old writer in West Sacramento, California. He has been happily married to the same woman for 20 years. He appreciates the importance of harmony, tolerance, respect, diversity, wolves, and cheeseburgers, as well as their respective places in the fabric of reality. When not working on his stories or working full-time, Layson enjoys watching movies and Facebooking (but not simultaneously).

Wolf Warriors II *and the now-defunct magazine* Fang, Claw and Steel *have samples of his works. Other short stories, poetry and novel manuscripts are being fine-tuned for publication. Are you interested in learning more about the world in his head? Let him know. He'd appreciate your feedback on any of his creations.*

<u>1</u>

One of the pups nipped at his heel. Ruun stopped in his tracks and pounced backward, high over the young one. It tried unsuccessfully to reach him with its claws, but very nearly caught his loincloth. Ruun landed deep into the snow, digging his muzzle into the cold powder. As the pup approached, Ruun tossed his head in the air and a spray of powder obscured the pup's advance, but did not sway his playful determination. The pup's interest in catching Ruun fell away as the second male pup tackled the first. It gave Ruun a chance to look over and see how Maaren fared.

Maaren nipped the female pup's tail as it tried to get away. The pup darted straight toward Ruun, probably expecting to use him as an obstacle in thwarting Maaren's chase. Ruun saw the ploy early enough to leap out of the way. However, he didn't expect Maaren to divert from the chase and deliberately collide into him. They both tumbled in the snow, yipping with laughter. Ruun raised his head as he righted himself and scanned the surroundings. Off to the right was Garra, the

Alpha mother, chasing the two male pups, tongue lolling between the smile on her lupan lips.

Back in the tribe, none of the Alpha pairs would have joined in play; it was beneath them. But now he was with Maarag's pack. The rigid rules of the tribe had no foothold here. Ruun did not have to prove anything. He felt grateful to Maarag for being accepted into the pack. When Ruun's heart began to intertwine with his daughter Maaren, Maarag did not object, but merely observed. For that, Ruun would always be indebted to his Alpha. And as long as his secret was never exposed, this could be a very happy life.

Coming out of the tree line, a large gray lupan approached. Correm was as physically sound as his loyalty: unshakable, silently fierce. His amber eyes shifted under a mask of dark gray fur, quickly and efficiently assessing all those present. When his eyes locked onto Ruun, Correm redirected his course. Apparently, Garra noticed the action as well. Leaving the pups to antagonize each other, Garra trotted over to Ruun and Maaren's location, getting there the same time Correm arrived.

Ruun stood on all fours and faced Correm. Maaren did the same.

"Maarag has returned from patrols. He is asking for you." Correm pointed his nose behind him and to the left, and then looked back at Ruun. "He waits at the sight stone, near the old den."

Maarag requesting his presence meant he likely had a task for Ruun to perform. It would be another chance for Ruun to prove himself.

Maaren brushed up against Ruun, nudging his jaw with her muzzle. Her beautiful blue eyes gazed into Ruun's dark brown. "Take care, beloved. Nose to the wind."

He licked her cheek once and wrapped his head around her neck, mentally bestowing his tender warmth upon her. Nodding at Garra and Correm, Ruun turned and cantered into the trees.

Sitting on an outcropping of rock curiously devoid of snow, a lupan with light gray fur awaited Ruun's arrival. He sat with his eyes closed, but his ears pivoted with every sound from the forest, and his nose brought in any odor the surroundings offered. Clearly, he was life-linking; identifying the sounds and scents of the Earthlife with their sources. Life-linking was the way all lupans kept in tune with the Earthlife. As he passed by, Ruun happily greeted Agraya, Maaren's older sister, and Shamag, Correm's brother. When Ruun arrived at the foot of the outcropping, he stopped. It was a tail's length higher than his head. He looked at the top, where he originally saw the Alpha sitting, but Maarag was no longer there. Ruun stood on his hind legs to look above the edge of the outcropping, only to find it vacated. Returning all four paws on the ground, Ruun looked to his right. The other lupans nearby had disappeared into the trees. He looked to the left and there Maarag was, standing right next to him, as if he had appeared from thin air. This must be why Garra said she stopped playing hiding games with Maarag while they were courting.

"There is a scent on the eastern border." Maarag looked toward the east, then back at Ruun. "It is not familiar to me. With your experience outside this territory, I thought you might recognize it."

Ruun nodded. "I will investigate it immediately."

"No, do not investigate. Merely observe, remain a shadow on the white. If you identify the scent, we will make further decision when you return."

Ruun understood, and nodded. "May I take Maaren with me?"

Maarag narrowed his amber eyes and smiled. "Not this time. It is easier for a sole lupan to stay hidden. But perhaps she can assist you if we choose to investigate."

Ruun smiled as well. Maarag was flexible, personable to each member of the pack. It was so different from the tribe. He appreciated how Maarag led with the strong, loving firmness of a father's arms. Ruun had a father once; he missed the security such a presence offered.

"I look forward to your return." Maarag inclined his jaw. "Nose to the wind."

A nod accompanied by a yip closed the conversation, and Ruun headed east.

2

The trek was short, not at all difficult. Before Ruun reached the borders of their territory, his nose caught the scent of burning wood. In the current temperatures, along with the recent blanket of white powder, this was not natural. There was another scent, something vaguely familiar, but too deep in his memory to completely recall. It was salty, a kind of meat, a scent that had not met his nose since before...

He remembered its name. Bacon.

Trepidation brought tension to his muscles. Bacon was cooked meat. Only one other being would ever intentionally put flame to meat.

Ruun redoubled his efforts at stealth. He had to be sure. His ears and nose identified an individual presence, alone in the clearing ahead. A nearby trunk among the evergreens was wide enough to hide his form. Ever so quietly, Ruun crawled over to the tree and, with one eye, peered around its trunk into the clearing ahead. There, in bright orange clothing and facing away from him, was the most dangerous creature known in the Earthlife. And where there was one, there would be more.

Cautiously, Ruun turned backed away. As his distance increased, so did his speed. He must warn the pack. He must keep them from this danger. He poured more energy into his sprint. Timbers and shadows blurred into gray lines as he rushed past. He strained with each planting of his paws, forcing his limbs to carry him even faster. At last, he reached the pack's domain, and found them grouped under a cluster of large evergreens, lying on ground devoid of snow.

"*Humans!*" Ruun called out as he approached.

The rest of the pack raised their heads, looking back in his direction. A dozen pairs of ears focused on his arrival.

Ruun came to a sudden halt at one of the evergreens, spraying white powder in front of him. He took a few heavy breaths before continuing. "Humans are on our border! It is only a matter of time before they invade our territory. They will slaughter us all. We must move the pack now!"

Agraya and Shamag looked at each other, alarm growing in their faces. Picking up on their anxiety, the pups lowered their heads and whimpered with unease. Correm instantly stood on all fours, and then quickly turned his head to his left.

Suddenly, Ruun felt a massive blow from his right, dislodging his senses from the rest of the world. Ruun rolled in the snow. When he came to a stop, the world kept spinning. Strong claws raked him onto his back, and then he felt something pressing down on his throat amidst infuriated snarls. Finally, Ruun's disorientation fell away. Standing over him was Maarag, jowls pulled back, baring glistening fangs.

"You *dare* panic my pack!"

Instinctively, Ruun whined and brought a paw up toward Maarag's face, not quite making contact. Maarag stood above him with ears down, raised hackles and jowls. He snarled and lashed his tongue between his fangs, but he removed his paw from Ruun's neck. Ruun pulled his head up and licked Maarag's chin, signifying submission to the Alpha, and whined again.

Maarag's penetrating amber eyes locked together with Ruun's dark brown. Suddenly Maarag stopped snarling. He narrowed his eyes and cocked his head to the left. Maarag retracted his tongue, but still kept his fangs exposed. He took two steps backward, allowing Ruun to rise and right himself. Ruun sat with his tail underneath him and diverted his eyes, hackles raised in fear.

Correm approached, cautiously. "I will guide preparations to move."

Maarag darted a look back at him. "You will not, Correm! There is still food in this area, and two of the passes are open. We will not leave merely because of this."

Correm looked at Ruun, then back at Maarag. "But humans are-"

"-The scent has been on our borders for three days. My patrols show no sign of humans crossing our borders, and they cannot hide their tracks in the white. Whether by intent or by accident, they have not invaded our territory."

"So which is it?" Shamag asked. "Intent or accident?"

Maarag stared at him.

"Maarag will determine that soon." Garra approached and turned toward her mate. "This was meant as a trial for Ruun, was it not?"

Maarag lowered his head in agreement.

Ruun's head sunk below his shoulders. It was a trial he clearly failed.

"Maarag would not put Ruun or our pack in danger. If there was danger, we would have moved the pack days ago. Regardless of Ruun's fear, we are safe."

Maarag looked at his mate admiringly, and then swept a glance across the pack as he continued. "Prepare yourselves for the move west, if you feel you must. But we will not leave until it is necessary."

The other adult pack members gave affirmative yips in response, and dispersed. Ruun kept silent, looking at the white powder surrounding his paws.

"Ruun."

Ruun looked up apprehensively.

"Follow." Maarag walked into the trees.

Ruun looked at Maaren, who only responded with a supportive stare. With his tail still between his legs, Ruun followed as instructed. Uncertain what to expect, he must now face the consequences of his panic. When they were no longer in the vicinity of the pack, Maarag stopped. Ruun stopped next to him. Moments passed silently. Ruun did not know what to do or say, but the silence ate away at him. Against his own judgment he looked at Maarag. Maarag looked upon him with caring, soft amber eyes; there was no trace of the fury inhabiting those eyes only moments before. His voice came across soothing and calm.

"The fear in your actions does not match the fear in your eyes, Ruun. I ask you to explain this to me."

Ruun shrank. If there was a different fear in his eyes, it was the fear of his secret being exposed. If he told his secret to his Alpha, his fate might very well be sealed. But then again, the failure of this trial may already have done that. Choking on his words, head hanging low with ears pulled down, he replied. "If... if I tell my fear, you will make me Omega."

Maarag inclined his head with understanding. All lupans knew there was only one circumstance which unfailingly leads to the clan Omega, lowest of the pack.

"I understand. You can shift form, but you do not want to be Omega. Have you noticed, Ruun, we do not have an Omega in our pack?"

Ruun exhaled, submitting to the outcome. "All the more reason I will fill that role."

Maarag shook his head. "Being able to shift is not good enough reason to betray our Calling."

Ruun looked up. How could his becoming Omega betray the Lupan Calling?

Maarag sat on his haunches and gestured for Ruun to do the same. Ruun complied, his hide loincloth resisting the cold snow almost as well as his fur. Maarag continued.

"What is the Lupan Calling, Ruun?"

Ruun cocked his head. "Our Calling is three-fold. We tend to the Earthlife, we seek the best parts of wolf and human to make our own, and we place the needs of the pack before ourselves."

"Just as we all are taught, yes. Now, focus on seeking the best of wolf and man. Wolf packs always have an Omega, and it works very well, to the benefit of the whole pack. If it works so well for wolves, it must be part of their best, correct?"

Ruun nodded.

"And yet, what happens when you mix Omega with human traits? It attracts the worst in man: oppression, slavery, hatred, even violence. You have seen this happen, yes?"

Ears folded, Ruun nodded.

"Those traits flourish when lupan packs or tribes have Omegas, but they do not manifest in wolf packs. Why?"

Ruun thought for a moment, hoping his conclusion was correct. "Wolves are not part human, like we are, so having an Omega would not attract the human traits."

Maarag nodded. "Very good, Ruun. So, if having an Omega in the pack brings on the worst human traits, even though it is the best of wolf, is it really the best for us?"

Ruun's brow furrowed as he cocked his head. This idea challenged a fundamental teaching, yet the reasoning was simple, logical. It showed a deeper level of thought to the Lupan Calling, focusing not only on the best parts of wolf and man, but how they interacted with each other. "Then why do other lupan packs and tribes still have Omegas?"

This time, Maarag cocked his head. "I cannot say for certain. Perhaps these human traits have already taken root, and after centuries, those roots run deep. However, I choose to not have an Omega in my pack, whether they shift or not. Though it is good for wolves, it is not good for lupans–or humans, for that matter."

The weight of a thousand worries softly evaporated from Ruun's shoulders. Tears tried to fill the void, but Ruun focused and held them back. "I thank you, Maarag. I am thankful to call you Alpha."

Maarag huffed. "You are part of my pack, Ruun; your needs come before mine. Besides, if I made you Omega, then for the same reasons I would also be Omega."

Ruun's eyes widened. "You?"

Maarag respectfully lowered his head, keeping his amber eyes fixed on Ruun.

Incredible; the Alpha of the pack was a shifter himself! No doubt it was a primary reason why Maarag did not support having Omegas. And thankfully not, for the pack would lose his loving guidance, wisdom, and protection simply because he could shift. Indeed, there were great benefits to this new understanding.

"Most of the pack knows about me, but if you wish to keep your secret, I will support you. As for me, I shift to wolf form. I was bitten by one called Rammag when I was Alpha for a wolf pack. Rammag was a beta, and brought me to his pack." Maarag paused. "When I first shifted, they made me Omega. I tried returning to my own pack in wolf form, but they rejected me. I lived in a tribe and even a colony for a time. After I courted Garra, we left to start a pack of our own." He paused. "I never asked about your past, Ruun, but now it seems appropriate. To what form do you shift?"

Ruun shook off his bemusement. "I shift to human."

"Were you born among us, or bitten?"

Long forgotten memories began to surface in a sea of emotion, once placid, now unsettled with swells. "I was nine years old. Other humans taunted me, so I ran into the woods. I fell off a cliff. One called Graan bit me to save me, and then took me to a tribe." Ruun looked off to his left in memory, and his ears slightly folded. "I often thought of my human pack. When I learned I could shift and the tribe made me Omega, I thought about returning to my human family." He looked directly at Maarag. "But I know that would be the Coyote way, so I stayed."

Maarag yipped. "A good decision. Graan did not bring you into his pack?"

Ruun shook his head. "He walked as a 'lone wolf'. He could not tend to me until his pack was formed. But I never saw him again."

"And then you ran away from the tribe, also a 'lone wolf' looking to belong, but refusing to walk the Coyote way."

"Yes."

Maarag nodded again, and took a deep breath. "I am glad you found our pack, Ruun. You strengthen our pack, and you complete Maaren's heart. Just as you thank me, I also thank you."

Grateful appreciation welled in Ruun's eyes; he could not fight it back anymore. He turned away momentarily, but thumped his tail in the snow to show his gratitude.

Maarag paused for a moment, looking at the ground before him, clearly pondering the circumstances. Finally he looked at Ruun. "Regardless of our abilities, we must still find out about these humans. We will investigate together. Follow." Maarag walked toward the eastern border.

Partially disoriented due to these revelations, yet bolstered by his anchored position in the pack, Ruun followed the lead of his Alpha.

<u>3</u>

Finding and following the trail to the Eastern border was easy enough. New snow had not fallen, and the sun filtered through thin, light clouds. The only disturbance in the white was Ruun's frantic tracks from his sprint. As they proceeded, Maarag periodically brushed up against trunks and shrubs to reinforce his presence in their territory. He also investigated scents along the way, ensuring the protection of his pack.

Before the clearing was in sight, Maarag lifted his head and sniffed the air. The scent of bacon was gone, but the air still carried the odor of burning wood. They inched closer. Maarag leaned his head to the right, peering into the clearing. He looked over to Ruun and gestured for him to follow. They both circled the clearing to the left, well within the tree line. The middle of the clearing was populated with tall reeds, obscuring much of the area. They continued to circle until a dark gray tent came into view, and a fire with dancing flames perhaps five steps in front of it. And fifty steps away, strategically placed between the tree line, the tent, and the reeds, was a singular human.

The human sat with his legs crossed in front, still wearing the bright orange clothing. Ruun followed Maarag to the left until they clearly saw the human's face. He was male, with dirty blond hair. He sat with his eyes closed, fingers laced together and resting on his lap. Ruun took a step closer, but then felt a paw restrain him from continuing. Ruun looked over to Maarag.

Maarag darted his eyes in the other direction, deeper into the forest, then turned and slowly walked toward that direction. Without making a sound, Ruun followed.

Twenty steps later, with the human still in view, Maarag stopped. "Look at this human, Ruun. What do you notice?"

Ruun focused on the human. "He is alone, for now. He does not sit at his fire, but in the clearing away from his camp. He wears clothing to help bear the cold. He looks deep in thought."

"Yes, but look closer. And as you do, listen to the Earthlife."

Ruun complied. Off to the right, a bird called out. The human slightly turned toward the sound. Moments later, the human took a breath, clearly trying to determine the aromas in the air, and quite possibly their sources. Maarag quietly took hold of a good sized rock, and threw it at a tree branch off to the left. The branch shook off its blanket of snow, which hissed as it fell like an avalanche toward the tree's base. The human moved his head in the direction of the tree.

Both Ruun and Maarag looked at each other incredulously, eyes wide.

Ruun broke the silence. "Is he... Is he life-linking?"

Maarag nodded. "And we know life-linking serves no purpose for humans as it does for us."

"But then...why?"

Maarag nodded as he looked again at the human. "Another question: how does he even know about life-linking, or how to do it?"

Ruun paused in thought. "Perhaps he is a lupan who can shift to human form."

Maarag looked over to Ruun. "Then why life-link as human instead of lupan? And if he is lupan, why stay in human form at our border but not cross into our territory as a lupan? It is not our way to reject lupan visitors."

Ruun returned the bemused gaze, and then they both looked at the human, trying to assess any answers they could glean from such a distance.

"Strange," Maarag breathed, "but also curious."

"It could be an attempt to trap us."

Maarag nodded. "Humans are cunning in that way, I agree. But would they use one of their own as bait?"

Ruun had no answer. Much of his human memory apparently faded over time. He knew humans tormented each other, and picked on their own weak ones. It was much like having an Omega, in that sense.

Finally, Maarag looked at Ruun. "I see an opportunity to approach this human. He shows knowledge of our kind, and our ways, but he might not know about shifters. After all, we are always the minority, and kept under subjection. If we approach in our other forms, perhaps we can keep the presence of our pack hidden for now."

Ruun understood, but did not agree.

"Your brow is heavy, Ruun. Tell me your mind."

"Humans do not live alone in the forest. If I approach wearing only a lupan loincloth, he will know I am lupan. If it is a trap, we would be caught."

Maarag inclined his head with understanding. "But if I approach him alone in wolf form, without my loincloth, he might be less suspicious."

"I do not say this out of fear, Maarag."

Maarag smiled. "No, you say this out of good thought." He paused. "I will approach in wolf form. But if we want to speak with him, we will need you. Can you remember human speech?"

Ruun thought back to what he could remember of the first nine years of his life, trying to recall some of the human words. "I think so. The sounds of our languages are similar."

"Then we will shift our forms now, but further in the trees."

They both retreated twenty steps. Maarag hesitated, but then modestly removed his loincloth. He exhaled sharply and looked at Ruun. "Do you remember how to make the change?"

With almost a human shrug, Ruun responded. His first shift happened as the result of a bad dream, but the other Omegas in the tribe taught him how to invoke the shift and control it.

"Then let us begin." Maarag faced forward and closed his eyes.

Ruun closed his eyes as well. He listened to the inner workings of his body, his heart pumping. Deeper. The blood travelling through his veins. Deeper. The churning of his morning food. Deeper. His cells maintaining his body. Deeper. There it was: the hum of his vibrating molecules. It needed to be different, a lower tone. The hum of his molecules met the tone Ruun had in mind. Finally his skin began burning with heat, and he opened his eyes.

Ruun watched his front claws fall out and his fingers lengthen. The intense pain as his body twisted shape suddenly fell away, and his dark brown fur coat followed suit. The appendages of his digitigrades became feet and toes. His jaw and muzzle retracted, until only his nose was pronounced from his face. Ruun's skull expanded upward and rounded off, making his shrinking ears feel like they were sliding down the side of his head. His coat of fur exposed hot, reddened skin. With his tail gone and his thighs now as long as his calves, Ruun kneeled in the snow and raised his torso. He was in human form once again, a young African-American, eleven years older than when he first became lupan.

He looked over at Maarag, who had already completed his change into the form of a wolf. The gray color of Maarag's coat did not change, but grew thicker. His amber eyes, however, still held the wisdom and intelligence belonging to the Alpha of their pack.

Maarag looked at their previous vantage point. He jutted his jaw at Ruun.

Surprisingly, Ruun had an instinctive knowledge of Maarag's actions, expressions, and gestures in his wolf form. Maarag wanted Ruun to go back to where they were monitoring the human and watch from there. With understanding, Ruun nodded and stood. The lupan loincloth chafed against his thighs as he stepped forward. Standing fully upright and walking on bare human feet made him even more awkward. The heat from the change continued to diminish and the cold temperatures replaced them, sending a heavy shiver through his body. Ruun would not have much time as a human in these surroundings.

Maarag gave Ruun an expression indicating he would move with haste. He padded toward the clearing.

Rubbing his arms with his hands, Ruun looked on as Maarag approached the life-linking human. A hushed stillness engulfed the area as a gray wolf halted thirty steps in front of the human, sniffing a clump of grass sticking out from the white. Ruun looked at the human who, while his eyes were still closed, smiled. Slowly, his blue eyes opened, and they focused directly on Maarag. And then, he made sounds. Ruun could hear them in the stillness. A flood of memories reactivated, full of words, how to make them and what they meant. He could understand the human.

"Welcome to my camp," the human said.

Raising his head from the grass, Maarag looked at the human and cocked his head to the left, then to the right, then to the left again.

The human raised his arms, using gestures and expressions to compliment his words, similar to the way lupans did. "I am called Gareth. I mean no harm to you or your pack. I am alone and unarmed. I have food."

Maarag looked back toward the area where Ruun waited and watched, then looked at the human again.

The human narrowed his eyes. "Can you understand me?"

Although Ruun understood the human, he was not certain Maarag could comprehend any more than parts of the human speech at best. No doubt the added gestures and expressions boosted any understanding. And there was a strange way the human spoke the words. Another surge of memories pressed in on Ruun's mind. The strange way was...called...accent. Yes; the human had an English accent. Maarag needed to know he could understand the human. He made a short howl followed by one slightly longer, signifying he was present and ready to assist. Ruun was surprised at his human voice; it sounded frail, shallow.

Maarag responded with two yips and a howl, calling Ruun to his side.

This human knew of lupans. If he saw another human responding to this wolf's call, he would determine their truth. But his Alpha was calling him, and Ruun would follow the lead of his Alpha.

As Ruun walked out into the clearing, each step into the frozen white brought increasing pain. Cold, so cold. He stumbled, but caught himself and continued. When the human caught sight of Ruun's freezing form, his eyes widened. The human stood.

Maarag lowered his head, reseated his stance, and growled.

The human raised his hands in a calming fashion, then slowly opened his orange clothing and removed it. He held it open toward Ruun.

Ruun looked at his Alpha, who nodded. He quickened his pace. When Ruun arrived, the human draped the clothing around Ruun's shoulders and gestured to the fire. Maarag slowly walked over to the fire himself and sat, setting the example. Ruun stumbled toward the fire and knelt down next to Maarag. He held his hands out toward the flames, soaking in the heat they offered. Even so, he could not stop his body from shivering.

Between the fire and the tent was a large red box. The human raised his hand as he opened the top. He removed a blanket, slowly approached around the fire and spread it on the snow next to Ruun. He clicked a button on the corner of the blanket, gestured for Ruun to sit on the blanket, and then backed away to the other side of the fire near the opened box. Finally, he squatted and waited for Ruun's response.

Ruun quickly moved sideward onto the blanket. It did not take long before he felt heat radiating from the blanket, thawing out his feet and legs. When he looked at Maarag, Maarag did not return the gaze, but kept his eyes on the human. The human retrieved more items from the box, closed it, and then sat across the fire from them. He donned a covering retrieved from the box, this time black in color. Not surprisingly the human focused his attention on Ruun as he continued.

"Can you understand me?"

Ruun nodded hesitantly.

The human put his hand on his chest. "I am called Gareth." He gestured to Ruun. "Do you have a name?"

Ruun shivered again, pulling the clothing draped over his shoulders closer around his self. He waited for his teeth to shop chattering and then responded. "Ruun."

The human, Gareth, nodded and repeated the name. He looked at the wolf, then back at Ruun. "A human and a wolf, together in the wilderness, calling to each other. I realize you are lupan shifters." Ruun thought so; the human saw through their deception. "Your secrets are safe with me, as my secrets are safe with you. I will not attack you, and I will not try to provoke you."

Ruun paused. Knowing the human speech was different than speaking it. He found the words he wanted. "How you know us?"

Gareth brought forth a gentile smile. "I have met other lupans, in other places. I put the needs of their packs before myself."

Those words—was this human referencing the Lupan Calling? Ruun looked at Maarag, who lowered his head, telling Ruun to continue. Ruun looked back at the human. "Why you here?"

"I want to know your pack. I want your pack to know me. That is why I have been here for three days. I keep my distance until you are confident I mean no harm. I try to life-link to show that I know you exist."

Ruun furrowed his brow, trying to remember. There was a human word which described these actions. "Tame. You tame us."

Gareth increased his smile. "Yes. I wanted to tame you to my presence here. I want you to understand you do not need to fear me."

Ruun narrowed his eyes, remembering how he was treated by his classmates just before he ran away into the forest. "Humans cannot be trusted."

Gareth's smile dimmed in the cold. "Yes. Humans cannot be trusted. But I want to prove that I can be trusted by myself."

Maarag huffed, and Ruun looked over to him. Maarag used lupine expressions to convey a message. Ruun looked back at Gareth. "Maarag says we must discuss this with the pack."

Gareth looked at the wolf. "Your name is Maarag?"

Maarag very slowly nodded, but his amber eyes did not leave Gareth.

"Thank you both for approaching me, Ruun and Maarag. I will stay here for two more days. I hope to earn your trust by then. But if your Alpha pair wants me to leave and not return, I will follow their decision."

Apparently, Gareth was not only aware of the Alpha pair's position, but he seemed to think the two lupans before him were Omegas because they could shift. In any other case he would be right; but this was Maarag's pack, and they did not betray the Lupan Calling simply because they could shift.

Maarag softly growled a message to Ruun.

Ruun looked at Maarag, then at Gareth. "We must return."

Gareth nodded. "I understand. You will shift again?"

Ruun nodded.

Gareth pointed behind him to the red box. "Shifting takes much energy. I have food to help renew your strength." With arms open, Gareth slowly rose, backed away to the box and opened it. As he removed a bundle of meat from the box, the scent of elk permeated the air. He methodically paced around the fire, stopping only a few steps away from Ruun. Placing the bundle on the snow, Gareth moved back and pointed at the bundle. "This is for you."

Ruun sniffed, verifying the scents of elk from the bundle: liver, ribs and most of a hind quarter. Cautiously, Ruun crawled over to the bundle. When he left the blanket, his human feet and legs instantly reminded him about the freezing cold snow. He grabbed the bundle and jumped back to the heat of the blanket, then looked at Maarag. Maarag darted his eyes at the tree line and then ran in that direction. Ruun looked back at Gareth, shook the covering from off his shoulders, and then hastily followed Maarag on unsure legs, leaving Gareth behind.

Maarag awaited Ruun's arrival in the trees. He gave Ruun an expression indicating he would watch and protect Ruun as he shifted. Ruun dropped the bundle into the snow, fell to his hands and knees, and closed his eyes. The cold attacked his skin, and the shivering came back with a vengeance. He opened his eyes. Any chance at focusing melted away instead of the snow.

A warm furred neck braced against his back. Calm concern from his Alpha reinforced Ruun's resolve. He closed his eyes again and turned his attention inward, beyond the cold, beyond the shivering. Heartbeat, blood, electrical impulses, the hum. Make it higher. The hum increased, the heat returned. The pain made a short-lived appearance. Coarse hairs erupted from his pores as aches from writhing muscles and bones radiated throughout his changing form. Moments later, Ruun stood on all fours, back in his lupan form. He showed his gratitude for Maarag's protection by responding in kind.

As Maarag finished, pangs of hunger invaded every fiber of Ruun's being. He looked over to the bundle, lying in the white. Instinctively, Ruun walked to the bundle. When he reached out for it, Maarag's paw reached it first.

"No."

Of course; the Alpha eats first. Ruun fought the hunger raging inside him. He must control his instincts. But to his surprise, Maarag picked up the bundle and looked at Ruun.

"Follow."

Despite his lack of understanding adding to the frustration caused by his hunger, Ruun followed his Alpha. Even so, he needed to eat. Shifting twice had drained his energy, stamina, both mental and physical stability. How could Maarag manage to shift twice and not need food? But then Maarag's growling stomach protested loud enough for Ruun to hear it. His Alpha was suffering the same hunger. So be it; they would suffer together.

Before they reached the pack, Maarag veered left and began heading south. They crossed a small gully and a frozen stream, and then climbed over a hill. Ruun's hunger increased as the light of the day faded. Maarag stopped and scanned their location. Slowly, he continued to the dead trunk of a fallen tree. He sniffed it, placed the bundle from Gareth in the snow, and began to dig at the base. His efforts revealed a hollow with a small cache from a female deer carcass, not cooked but not yet frozen from the temperatures. This was a fresh kill, probably from Shamag or Maarag himself. Maarag pulled out a shoulder and tossed it to Ruun, then retrieved a hind quarter for himself. Once Maarag began to eat, Ruun tore into the shoulder.

Ruun devoured every part of the portion, sucked the marrow from the bones, and finally ate the bones themselves. The relentless taunts of his hunger subsided, and he took a moment to savor the calm coursing through his form. Ruun closed his eyes and listened to any sounds the Earthlife provided, matching them to their source. In winter, in this part of the forest, there was very little noise at all. But the breeze carried the scent of the pack, and the pack members.

Maaren. He missed her. He missed his pack.

Once Ruun felt sufficiently stabilized, he opened his eyes and saw Maarag life-linking as well. His eyes trailed downward to the bundle Gareth gave them. It seemed a mystery why Maarag stopped Ruun from eating it. He looked back at Maarag, who returned his gaze.

"Beware any gift from humans."

Ruun understood. Though the human seemed trustworthy, he had not earned that much trust.

Maarag placed the bundle into the cache, then turned around and kicked dirt and snow over the opening. He began walking toward the location of the pack, and Ruun followed.

4

Correm stood fast in his resolve. "Humans cannot be trusted."

Nine pairs of eyes glowed amidst the firelight. The pups slept nearby, both Garra and Agraya periodically looking their way for assurance. Ruun and Maaren sat next to each other, with Garra on their right. Garra sat next to Maarag, her mate. The circle of lupans around the flames continued with Agraya, Correm, and Shamag. The circle completed with Tuurmen and Gaalam, who had returned from a hunting expedition, bringing back several braces of hares from a nearby warren.

Maarag took in a deep breath. "Who among us has dealt with humans in the past?"

All except Ruun and Correm looked down and to the right; a negative response.

Maarag nodded. "What Ruun or Correm experienced ended poorly. Even so, are those experiences enough to judge this human on our borders?"

Gaalam raised his head. "My knowledge comes from others with experience." He glanced at the other attendees and then back at Maarag. "A human is a human. They all threaten us."

Maaren scoffed. "In that case, a lupan is a lupan, even Coyotes."

Agraya yipped. "We cannot judge the whole by the individual, and we cannot judge the individual by the whole."

Maarag nodded. "You bring the eagle's wisdom, Agraya. This human does not treat us like their hunting parties. He respects what he knows of us, and he wants to earn our trust."

"So he says," Correm objected. "What he does might be different."

Maarag gestured a paw to Correm. "And the wolf's caution appears. Yet what this human has done so far shows respect and compassion, Correm. Tell us: what would you like to see from this human if you are to trust him?"

Correm paused. "Tell him to leave and not come back. If he does so, I will trust him."

Maarag nodded, his eyes glancing at every other pair around the fire.

Others, including Ruun, groaned their disagreement. Correm's caution was getting too close to paranoia.

Maaren offered her opinion. "If our people are flourishing, then humans are as well. At some point we will not be able to avoid them any longer."

"Ah." Maarag inclined his head as other attendees yipped. "There is the meat. Many of our people believe a confrontation with humans is inevitable. Some believe we will be slaughtered by humans. Others think there is a chance to live peacefully, whether segregated or integrated." Maarag brought his paws apart, then brought them together and laced his fingers to further explain his words. "If this happens, no one knows when."

All pairs of eyes exchanged glances, and then Tuurmen spoke. "This could be the beginning."

"And there is the bone. Are we prepared to have contact with this human?"

Ruun cocked his head. He had not considered the significance of meeting this human. Could this be the first time? No; he remembered what Gareth told them. "But the human has knowledge of us, and our ways. He also said he has met other lupans. We are not the first. We are not the beginning."

Shamag narrowed his eyes. "But did he meet lupans, or Coyotes?"

Shamag had a point. Gareth might have gained his knowledge from Coyotes, lupans who reject the Lupan Calling and solely follow their own way. Every lupan who chooses to stay in human form, frequenting human communities, are labeled Coyotes. Gareth might have met those. Still, gaining his knowledge of lupan pack structure, and the Lupan Calling itself, did not likely come from one who walked the Coyote way.

Garra scratched her ear, and then scanned the attendees. "When the whole of lupans and humans finally meet, the circumstances will control the outcome. With this human, we might control the circumstances."

Maarag nodded. "Control, yes. The human said he wanted us to be comfortable with his presence. He wanted to tame us, as if he was in control. This also concerns me."

Almost with reflex, Ruun responded with a huff. "If we want to keep control, perhaps we should be taming him."

Maarag's glowing eyes focused on Ruun. The flickering light, revealed a slight smile on the Alpha's lips. Maarag took a breath. "Before I make my decision, I want to know where each of the pack stands. Do we continue with this human?"

Correm, Gaalam and Shamag looked down and to the right for a negative response. Ruun, Maaren, Garra, Agraya and Tuurmen crossed their paws, looking down and to the left in positive agreement. Five pack members for yes, three for no.

Maarag nodded and then stood. "I will consider this. My decision will come with the morning. Until then, rest." Maarag stood and melted into the darkness beyond the firelight.

Slowly, others either curled up to let the fire help them endure the cold night, or chose to bear it on their own. Ruun and Maaren decided to rely on each other's warmth. Maaren nuzzled up to him once Ruun had settled.

Ruun's night met little sleep due to the musings churning through his mind. Nevertheless, when he heard two yips and a howl from his Alpha, he proceeded with the rest of the pack to Maarag's location, accompanied by fresh falling snow. Maarag was on the outcropping where Ruun met him yesterday, standing on all fours with Garra by his side. Once all were present, Maarag paused. He slowly closed and opened his amber eyes.

"Correm, we will prepare for the move west. Assist those who are not yet ready. Agraya, help Garra prepare the pups. Those who are already prepared will help Maaren gather the food caches–except the fallen tree to the south; leave that cache intact. We will proceed as soon as we are ready." His amber eyes locked on Ruun. "Ruun, come with me."

They walked roughly in the direction of Gareth's camp as the rest of the pack moved to their tasks, no one questioning the Alpha's decision. After fifty steps, Maarag turned to Ruun.

"Return to Gareth."

Ruun lowered his head as his ears folded.

Maarag shook his head. "Patience, Ruun. The answer is not yet. Our pack will return late in the spring. If he also returns, and respects us as he has now, we will consider a closer acquaintance." Maarag raised his head. "The pack is not ready to face humans, so we put the needs of the pack before ourselves. For now, we will attempt to tame Gareth."

Strange; this contradicted the events of last night. "But most of the pack agreed to continue with him."

"I listened to what they said," Maarag narrowed his eyes, "and I also listened to what they did not say. My decision holds." He took a breath and continued. "When you approach Gareth, stay in lupan form. He will understand your lupan speech."

Ruun cocked his head; another odd conclusion. "How do you know this?"

"Gareth understood me in wolf form."

Ruun cocked his head to the other side. How could he possibly know that Gareth understood Maarag while he was in his wolf form? Gareth only spoke to Ruun. But as they conversed, Maarag did watch them intently. Obviously, Maarag saw something Ruun missed.

Maarag twitched his head, telling Ruun to dismiss any worry. "I learned what to look for long ago, just as I learned how to listen. But it is not time for you to learn this. We will tend to the needs of the pack. Gareth must earn our trust with patience."

Ruun bowed his head, questions still nagging his mind. How much of human ways did Maarag know? If Gareth had enough knowledge of lupans to understand a lupan in wolf form, why withhold contact? What was *not* said by the pack to bring Maarag to his decision? The questions would not be answered now. Looking at the strength and stance of his Alpha, Ruun took faith that answers would come forth when the time was right. He would follow his Alpha.

"One thing more." Maarag held up a paw. "This decision comes from the Alpha, but do not tell Gareth I am the Alpha. He already knows I can shift. It is not time to explain our views on the Lupan Calling. Perhaps in the spring."

Ruun inclined his head with understanding, and then cocked his head again. "May I take Maaren this time?"

Maarag smiled. "Since you will stay in lupan form, yes. But this task is yours. Do not stray from it."

Ruun nodded.

Maarag jutted his jaw toward Gareth's direction. "Nose to the wind, Ruun."

5

Gareth's fire still danced. His dark gray tent stood silent, now covered in snow. Ruun and Maaren approached quietly, carefully testing the air to determine if Gareth was present. As they circled to the left, the front of the tent came in view. It stood open with Gareth sitting in the entrance, hugging his knees, sheltered from the falling white. He was once again wearing the orange jacket he placed over Ruun's shoulders the day before. His open eyes watched the light flakes of snow lose their futile battle with the flames.

Caution was still paramount. Ruun wanted to make sure Maaren would follow his lead. Maaren continued by his side but slightly behind, never going ahead of Ruun's shoulders. When Ruun stopped, Maaren did the same. The action was all Ruun needed to see. However, she also kept her head at a lower position than his as they walked.

"I am not the Alpha, Maaren."

"No, but someday you will be my Alpha." She eyed him in that playful way she did. "I'm practicing."

Oh, how he loved her. Ruun licked her chin with tender affection and then raised his head with a smile. "Follow."

Maaren smiled and complied.

They approached from the opposite side of the fire. When both lupans passed the fire on their left and stopped near the red box, now covered in white, Gareth tensed.

"Ruun?" His voice shook with apprehension.

Ruun gave a single, slow nod, just as Maarag often did.

Gareth smiled and relaxed. He sat up on his knees, but did not leave the shelter of his tent. Of course, he would be more susceptible to the falling white than a wolf or lupan. Gareth looked at the other attendee. His smile faded. "I was expecting Maarag to return with Ruun, but you are female. Do you have a name?"

Maaren looked at Ruun, and he nudged his nose with positive encouragement. She looked back at the human. "Maaren."

"Maaren," Gareth repeated, emphasizing his words with gestures. "I welcome you to my camp."

An awkward silence hung in the air, interlocked with the tufts of falling snow. Ruun focused his dark brown eyes on Gareth's blue, the weight of the Alpha's decision on his brow.

Gareth's smile faded. "The Alphas wish me to leave."

Ruun shook his head, snow falling from his coat of fur. "The Alpha says the pack will return in the spring. If you come here again," Ruun gestured his paw to Gareth's tent, "so will we."

Gareth nodded. "I understand. But please tell your Alphas: human numbers are growing. Their territory is expanding." He widened his arms. "If humans make their tracks here, please find me. Other lupans know the name of my pack, and how to find me."

Maaren cocked her head. "Your pack?"

Gareth smiled. "Yes, I belong to a pack." Gareth gestured to his two visitors. "There is a lupan in my pack. And there are others in my pack, others that are not human. My pack is called Department 118."

Department 118. Ruun's memories awoke once more. He lowered his head. "Empire."

Gareth nodded slowly, apparently undeterred by the growl under Ruun's voice. "Yes. The Empire does not know lupans yet, but my pack does. We protect lupans from the Empire."

Ruun narrowed his eyes.

Gareth raised his hands in surrender. "We keep the secrets of lupans from the Empire. We put your packs above ourselves. But someday soon the sun will rise on lupans. The Empire will see you in the light. My pack cannot stop the sun from rising, but we can provide shelter from its heat."

So, now they knew why Gareth appeared to them. He held a warning about the inevitable meeting between humanity and lupanity. Gareth's analogy reminded Ruun of how Maarag conducted the discussion last night. He looked at Maaren. Her expression mirrored Ruun's own feelings. Gareth's message was born of concern, not threat.

Ruun looked back at Gareth, raising his head in the manner of an Alpha. "We will take your message to our pack. We will remember your name, and the name of your pack."

Gareth slowly leaned forward, placing his arms in the snow. He crossed one arm over the other, and then looked down and to the left in lupan acceptance. When he looked up, Ruun nodded at him once more, then turned and left the camp with Maaren beside him.

"This human is...persuasive."

Maarag yipped, agreeing with Garra's sentiment. "He did not pressure you?"

Maaren shook her head. "I never felt threatened. He showed respect."

"As with me." Maarag nodded, but then furrowed his brow. "He said a lupan was in his pack?"

Ruun nodded. "And I do not believe Gareth would be so honorable if the lupan walked the Coyote Way."

Maarag's amber eyes trailed off into the trees. The snowfall continued, covering any and all items in the open, including lupans. Maarag looked back at Garra. "Whether he has earned the trust of the pack or not, I will have questions for him in the spring."

"I might have a few as well," Garra replied, mirroring Maarag's silent awareness.

Ruun took note of the Alpha pair, looking at each other with wisdom and experience. They seemed to have a conversation beyond mere words. Would he and Maaren act the same when it was their turn? It was an enticing prospect. But until it was time for him to lead, Ruun would follow his Alpha pair.

Correm approached Maarag, his dark gray fur frosted with the white. "The pack stands ready. Tuurmen, Shamag and Gaalam will each pull a travois. Agraya leads the pups until Garra joins."

Maarag looked at his mate, Maaren, and Ruun, and finally turned to Correm. "Then we are ready to move southwest. Ruun will scout ahead. Agraya and Garra will take turns blazing the trail and tending the pups. You and I will tend the tail."

The others yipped and padded toward the rest of the pack.

"Ruun."

Ruun stopped and looked at Maarag.

"When you returned from Gareth, I saw the strength of an Alpha within your steps, but tempered by self-control. Your actions show wisdom."

Ruun looked down and to the left, then returned his gaze to his Alpha.

"If the sun of the Empire will soon shine upon us, as Gareth says, then all Alphas will need to show such wisdom. You met this first contact poorly, but you learned, and your wisdom managed the contact into a success."

Though Ruun appreciated the summary, he did not understand. How could this be a success if Gareth was not permitted to meet the pack?

As if he read Ruun's mind, Maarag answered. "Not only did you put the needs of the pack before yourself, but you sought the best of wolf and man, and avoided the worst of both. In so doing, you were tending the Earthlife." Maarag smirked, a twinkle of pride in his eyes. "You upheld our Calling, Ruun. That is your success."

Finally, Ruun understood. The trial did not end with his scouting out the human. It ended with the safety of the pack and the Earthlife, despite any other sacrifice or success. And now Maarag was telling him it must always end that way.

Maarag jutted his jaw to the southwest. "Begin the scout ahead, and keep in contact with Agraya."

Ruun yipped. "May I take Maaren with me?"

Maarag nodded with a smile upon his lupan lips. "Nose to the wind, Ruun."

LIST OF WOLF VETERANS

Here is the list of contributors who have had works accepted in both the first and second volumes of this anthology. We continue to honor our ever-constant Wolf Veterans.

Chris Albert

Shannon Barnsley

Autumn Beverly

Hannah Christopher

Chelsea Dub

Samantha Dutton

A. M. Duvall

Christian Esche

William Huggins

Jane Lee McCracken

Hemal Rana

Dawn Sharman

Dana Sonnenschein

Forest Wells

Layson Williams

35349538R00159

Made in the USA
Middletown, DE
29 September 2016